TARA N. HATHCOCK

Shattered Highways

Some Roads Lead Everywhere

quiet + kin
PUBLISHING

First published by Quiet Kin Publishing, LLC 2019

This novel is entirely a work of fiction. The names, characters and incidents portrayed in it are the work of the author's imagination. Any resemblance to actual persons, living or dead, events or localities is entirely coincidental.

Tara N. Hathcock asserts the moral right to be identified as the author of this work.

Tara N. Hathcock has no responsibility for the persistence or accuracy of URLs for external or third-party Internet Websites referred to in this publication and does not guarantee that any content on such Websites is, or will remain, accurate or appropriate.

Designations used by companies to distinguish their products are often claimed as trademarks. All brand names and product names used in this book and on its cover are trade names, service marks, trademarks and registered trademarks of their respective owners. The publishers and the book are not associated with any product or vendor mentioned in this book. None of the companies referenced within the book have endorsed the book.

Book design by Trey Hathcock

First edition

ISBN (print): 978-1-7342018-3-3
ISBN (digital): 978-1-7342018-1-9

This book was professionally typeset on Reedsy.
Find out more at reedsy.com

This book is lovingly dedicated to the memory of the good pirate Magdalene and the brief, brilliant life that she lived.

"To live in hearts we leave behind is not to die." Thomas Campbell

Contents

Preface

While Quincy O'Connell is a fictional character and not based on any one particular person, I did draw many of her symptoms from my own experiences with migraines. If you suffer from chronic migraine, you understand the intensity of the pain, the inability to sleep no matter how tired you are, and the physical and mental exhaustion that comes from trying to live your life in spite of your circumstances.

Depression is a very real consequence of living with that kind of constant pain and fear and, left unchecked, can easily and too-often lead to suicide. If you or someone you care about suffers from depression and persistent thoughts of suicide, I urge you to reach out for help. To a pastor, a police officer, a trusted friend - just reach out.

https://suicidepreventionlifeline.org/

Acknowledgments

Lest no good deed go unpunished, I'd like to thank everyone who helped make this pipe dream a reality.

To my brother and sister, who read the very first draft of the book. Thank you for volunteering your time and your patience. And thank you for not pointing out that when an older sister asks you to do something, it's no longer considered "volunteering."

To my other brother, who was trapped under my roof while I was in the talking-instead-of-doing phase. Bless your heart for listening.

To my parents, who keep telling me I can do anything I want to do. I guess I must have taken your words to heart.

To my dear friend Joan, who read the final draft without knowing what she was getting herself into.

And finally, to my Savior. We fought and we wrestled but you never let me give up. You give me the courage to try and I will do my best to honor you always.

Your support and your encouragement helped shape this book and this moment. And because I don't say it enough, thank you from the bottom of my heart.

PROLOGUE

The Colonel

One Year Ago

The warehouse was damp and the evening chill had settled over the area hours ago. The day had been warm for this time of year and the change in temperature created a thick fog that crept along the ground and blanketed the area, keeping visibility at a minimum. It was his kind of night, to be sure. When one made a living by keeping to the shadows, dark, dreary, and remote was a fact of life.

But why did it always have to be warehouses, he thought wryly, as his foot landed for the third time in one of the many puddles of dark, dirty water standing about the room. He resisted the temptation to shake the extra water from his pant leg through sheer will power built up over many a late night surveillance. He was the first to arrive and didn't want to take the chance of giving away his position in case someone had eyes on the place, no matter how remote the possibility.

The head of the corporation only rarely called him in for a chat, and never during daylight hours or on company property. His division was one of the agency's most valuable assets but only so long as they stayed off the books. Medical research was a booming business in today's economy and the government had strict protocols and procedures in place to make sure companies maintained the highest level of ethics.

Unfortunately, scientific advancement didn't always thrive on integrity and rarely happened through humanitarian efforts. Which was the sole reason his division existed. He, and others like him, performed tasks that were imperative to the operation of the agency but that no one else could, or would, touch. He had long since become accustomed to dirty hands. He didn't classify himself as a bad man, or even a good one. He preferred to think of himself as a problem solver. A fixer. He did the job he was paid to do - no emotion, no hesitation, no qualms - no matter how unsavory or inconvenient the assignment.

So he understood why he was never invited to the office Christmas party. Why most of the department heads wouldn't know him if they passed him on the street. Knowledge of his division was restricted to the highest levels of administration, and very little contact with anyone of actual authority.

In fact, most of his communication was with the head of the agency's assistant since the man at the top would never risk his own security and reputation to meet with him. His team's only communication came through him. They didn't know who called the shots or paid the bills. It was cleaner that way. If one was exposed, the problem could be eliminated and the hole closed quickly and efficiently with little risk of exposure.

He would kill for a cigarette right now. Something, anything, to pass the time and provide a little warmth. He wasn't as young as he once was.

Damp nights like this had a way of seeping under the skin and prickling at his weaknesses. He was under no illusions about his chosen career. And he had chosen it - no pretenses, eyes wide open and all that.

As former military intelligence, he was used to finding needles in haystacks, plugging holes, etcetera. He was good at his job and he knew it. Which is why the agency had come calling in the first place. They had been following his career for some time, apparently, and decided a man of his abilities and scruples, or lack thereof, would fit well into their organization. They made him an offer that was most generous and he had never looked back.

Except during these late night meetings. They always seemed to feel the need to meet in wet, unpleasant places. Minor annoyances, but annoyances nonetheless. He had gotten to the meet early enough to clear the building and pick an observation point. He liked having his back to a wall and being the first to arrive let him watch for any surprises the other party might be planning. The agency had never tried to screw him over but that didn't mean they wouldn't.

The boss's assistant wasn't exactly stealth. The man, young and nervous, had shown up almost five minutes ago but he'd let him sweat for a while. Wrong-footing your opponent was just part of the process. Any advantage was worth exploiting and he let the kid get good and uncomfortable before stepping from the shadows and clearing his throat.

"What's the word Ronald?" he asked casually.

The man's name wasn't Ronald. He didn't actually know the man's real name. At their first meet, the man had stammered something about being instructed not to give any names and keep things as general as possible. And he could certainly appreciate the wisdom in that.

The less information each person had, the more protection afforded the rest of the circle.

But he wasn't going to spend the length of his employment

without having something to call the guy. Kid looked like a prepster, dressed immaculately without fail. His hair was conservatively cut and he was always impeccably groomed. In fact, if he wasn't mistaken, the kid even enjoyed the services of a good manicurist.

So he decided to call him Ronald. Seemed to fit. Tonight, Ronald was dressed to impress as usual. If Armani had an espionage collection. The black turtleneck under a black sport coat did nothing but scream *clandestine.* He rolled his eyes. Big business power-types were tough in a boardroom but soft outside their own turf. Which was why they needed men like himself, he supposed. Circle of life and all that. At least the outfit let him know that, whatever the reason for the meeting, it was serious.

Ronald had spun to face him at the first sound and took an instinctive step back. At least Ron's instincts were decent. He practically oozed menace and he knew it.

He gave the nervous little man in front of him a moment to collect himself before saying, "You know I don't much like to repeat myself."

Ronald swallowed compulsively and grabbed for a tie that wasn't there. He had noticed Ronald seemed to feel better when he had the tie to worry at. It was one of his many nervous tells and he doubted the man would go with the turtleneck again.

He almost felt sorry for the kid. He was playing way outside his league and they both knew it. He hoped the pay was worth it. But he didn't have the time or the patience to drag this out and Ron knew it. He managed to compose himself enough to extend the portfolio he had been clutching to his chest.

"Our tech team managed to partially recover the research

from Dr. Garrison's protected files. This is all we have from the patient data he was reviewing. It looks like he managed to delete all identifying information on the patients but we have their medical information and most of his case notes. My boss asks that you track down each patient as quickly as possible."

Ronald was always so polite when handing out his boss's orders. But not always thorough. He stared at him, waiting for the rest. When nothing else was forthcoming, he tried, and failed, to not roll his eyes.

"How would your boss like me to proceed?" he asked.

When Ronald floundered, unsure how to respond, he allowed a slight sneer that had the man taking another quick step back.

"Do you want them dead or alive Ron?"

Ronald flinched as if he had taken a shot at him. But he was mildly impressed when Ron managed to reign himself in. It was entirely too late in their acquaintance to fake confidence but he squared his shoulders and stood as straight as he could and good for the kid for trying.

"Alive is the preferred delivery method, of course. We can learn so much more if they're living." He took a moment to steel his facial expression before continuing, but it still looked like he was trying not to be sick. "But we'd rather have a dead specimen than no specimen at all."

He was already flipping through the files in the portfolio but nodded his head once in acknowledgment. "I'll be in touch when I have the first delivery."

He expected Ronald to leave immediately. He usually did. But this time, he hesitated. "My boss asks that you remember to only contact him through the..."

Ron's words faded at the look on his face. Did the boss really think he needed to be reminded of the contact protocol?

"Get out of here Ronald, before I get offended." Ronald backed slowly towards the door, towards his car and the false sense of security it represented, while he turned back to the files. He never left until Ronald was gone.

"Hey Ron," he called, right before the man made it to the door. "You're in the wrong business kid. You know that, right?"

He didn't glance up but heard the shaky sigh, acknowledgement and weariness all rolled into one small sound, and then Ronald was gone.

He didn't bother sparing Ronald another thought. Finally, something concrete to wrap his hands around. He'd been months without a solid project to work on. They'd had him running surveillance on the doctor for a while but that was a soft job and he'd farmed most of it out to one of his newer hires as a way of giving the man some field experience.

Of course, if they'd thought Garrison was going to run, he'd have handled the entire job himself. The fact that Garrison had completely vanished had been an interesting surprise but no matter. He would find Garrison by finding Garrison's pets.

Tracking and detaining these people wouldn't exactly be difficult, considering they were ordinary civilians who weren't hardwired to expect danger in their everyday lives but still, they were living, breathing targets to chase.

The lack of identifying information wouldn't hinder him. He had prey to track. He thrived on having a goal, a target. And now he had five. He tucked the portfolio under his arm and headed back out into the cold, wet night, blending seamlessly into the shadows.

No one ever saw him coming or going and these unfortunate people would be no different.

* * *

Eight Months Ago

In the last four months, the assignment he'd considered a cake walk had turned out to be anything but. Well, maybe that was a bit of an overstatement. He had located, detained, and delivered four of his five targets without difficulty.

He'd run a routine background check on each and hadn't discovered anything to make him wary or cautious. No law enforcement or military personnel in the bunch, no one that would try and play the hero.

He'd decided on the soccer mom in Poughkeepsie first. He made visual confirmation during her weekly yoga class, watched her for a week (a bit of overkill but he wasn't in a hurry), and made the grab during a Saturday soccer game. The day was bright and sunny and Amy Madison had separated herself from the pack to run to the family minivan for juice boxes and fruit snacks, a mistake she'd never get the chance to repeat.

The nightly news reported the disappearance and featured the crying five-year old left behind most prominently.

After the first grab, he'd been assured that his read on the situation was accurate and there would be no surprises in this group. He'd settled for the construction worker in Brooklyn next. Mostly it was a tactical decision. Brooklyn was the closest target to Poughkeepsie; the rest of the targets were spread around the country. And this guy was likely to be his biggest challenge. He was a former college football player and at 36, as foreman on a construction crew, likely to still be in pretty decent shape.

So he went with a lighter touch on this one. He'd observed for a couple of days but it didn't take long to figure out the bar across the street from the guy's third floor walk-up was a routine stop after work. So he'd gone in and bought the guy a drink, slipping a little something in to help him relax. Two hours later and he had the guy down, out, and on his way to the agency's black site. And then things started to get tricky.

His third target had seemed completely routine as well. College kid, early 20s, took classes at the local junior college and worked as a waitress at a truck stop on the outskirts of Boise during the night. An easy enough target.

He had taken a seat in a corner booth, facing the door and windows, and ordered coffee, black. And then he'd settled in to wait. His intel had found Gracie Elliot worked every Monday and Wednesday evening, and every weekend. A college kid with a work ethic. An oddly pleasant anomaly.

He had pulled her records from the college, which came with a photograph, so he knew what he was looking for. Average height, thin, but he hadn't expected her to look so small when she came in. Lack of emotion was par for the course with this job but still...he felt like he was snatching a kid off the street.

Her long blonde hair was pulled up in a sloppy tangle at the back of her head and she wore very little makeup. Add that to the oversized Joey's Diner t-shirt and scruffy jeans and she looked much younger than she should have.

He watched Gracie as she floated around her section of tables, topping off coffee and filling orders for some of the regulars without even asking.

His own waitress refilled his cup, again, and asked if there was anything else he wanted. He ordered a slice of pecan, his favorite, so he wouldn't attract too much attention just sitting in the booth. When the waitress, Gwen, dropped it off, he thanked her. He took his eyes off the target for exactly 20 seconds, no more, no less. And when he'd looked back, she'd been gone. Not just out of the room, gone. Or even gone home, gone. After waiting another 30 minutes, thinking she might have gone on break but without a reasonable excuse to ask, he'd paid his bill and left the diner.

He knew exactly where she lived, having driven the low-income neighborhood earlier, and parked three doors down, as far from the nearest street light as possible. But it was too late. The door to her apartment opened easily under his hand and when he stepped inside, he found something entirely unexpected. Nothing. There was nothing. Nothing except used, worn furniture. No clothes. No books. Nothing personal at all. Only a shabbily furnished apartment that looked immediately available for occupancy.

Gracie Elliot had completely and effectively disappeared.

* * *

Six Months Ago

He had tried to take losing her in stride. After all, it did happen on occasion. There was no such thing as a perfect record. But it ate at him. Why did she run? Even if she'd caught him watching her in the diner, she was, after all, a college-aged waitress.

She must be used to being looked at by now. And if she'd felt threatened, the normal response would have been to call the police. Or alert the regulars - they clearly adored her. They were big, burly trucker-types, one and all. They would have taken care of him.

Or attempted to, at any rate. But why run? And not just run, but completely scrub her life in Boise. She'd been able to walk away from her apartment, her job, and her classes with nothing more than a 30-minute lead. That did not mesh with the the nobody college kid identity. He knew what it looked like, but he just couldn't square the research he'd done with the reality of the situation.

The next target was a 65-year old retiree in Boca, Florida. He decided to go for the win and passed the task of tracking Gracie Elliot off to one of his most experienced analysts.

Brenda Caulfield in Oregon rounded out the list of names and by the time he'd contained and delivered the last two, his analyst had gotten a hit. There was a girl in Chicago who loosely matched Gracie Elliot's description. Average height, slightly overweight, attended similar classes at the local college and worked as a bartender at an older dive during the evenings and nights.

Sure, there were lots of girls who fit that particular profile but there was something very familiar about Kara Scott. She only took one class, as an audit, and worked in an out-of-the-way place close to both campus and her apartment. If felt right. So to Chicago he'd gone. Not even a glimpse of her this time. He'd staked out her apartment, waiting for a visual confirmation in the privacy of his rented vehicle, before moving in for the grab. He had a handy drug that worked quickly to create a more pliant target, capable of nothing but absolute compliance, one of his favorite weapons of choice. But she never appeared.

The notes he'd received and studied indicated she left work at exactly 11:45 every evening and went straight home, putting her in his field of view by 11:55 at the latest. By 1:30, he knew he'd been had. Which told him exactly what he'd needed to know.

Kara Scott was Gracie Elliott.

1

Chapter 1

"**S**leep, those little slices of death – how I loathe them." *Edgar Allan Poe*

The girl cannot sleep. She tries, she always tries, but she rarely succeeds. I watch. I wait. I do not sleep. I am not made to sleep. I am made to survive. And at last, the girl accepts the battle for what it is – lost.

She will continue to try, night after night, to fight the battle, knowing it's lost before it begins. But she tries, all the same.

And still, I watch. I wait.

* * *

Quincy

Quincy's eyes were closed more out of principle than any real hope for sleep. She had been wide awake ever since she'd shut off the lights and crawled into bed over four hours ago. She still had a couple hours until her alarm went off, but what was the point? And what was the point of setting an alarm when her brain kept her wide awake every night? It was frustrating. And it was getting old. Nighttime, or, as she'd come to think of it, the Place Where Time Goes to Die, always went one of two ways - a few hours of broken sleep, punctuated by waking way too early, which she had learned to be grateful for, or not falling asleep at all. More often than not, she was spending her entire night staring at her bedroom walls. When she did happen to fall asleep, it came and went much too quickly. There was no gradual dropping off or fading away. The phrase *lulled to sleep* meant nothing to her. And awareness didn't slowly creep back in, gently prodding her with a yawn here and a stretch there before allowing her to curl back down into her quilts to savor the lazy return of thought. Her brain was a switch flipped, shutting her down and bringing her back online instantly. There was no warm up, no yawning and stretching, burrowing back under her covers for an extra few minutes. No sir. Wide awake and ready to go. Which wouldn't be so bad if the rest of her was on the same page. But the rest of her was in no way, shape, or form ready to go at two in the morning. Or three. Or even five.

She sighed, resigned to the fact she wasn't getting any sleep this night and rolled onto her right side, facing the bedroom door. The paint on the wall near the lower corner of the door was peeling in the shape of Texas. Quincy had been staring at the same spot for months now so she felt qualified to judge. The rest of the walls in her beat-up, low-rent apartment were peeling too but this one spot had found its way into her heart. It was the exact spot her eyes seemed to find, night after night, as her brain refused to shut down. Insomnia kept her awake for hours every night, staring blankly at the Lone Star State as it spread slowly up the wall, her mind blurring a hundred different directions at a thousand miles per hour.

Logically, Quincy knew if she would just pick up a book or turn the television on, there was a chance she might still get some rest. Those were the only things that could ever touch her frantic mind, not exactly slowing the roll that kept her constantly alert but exhausted but focusing it. Tonight, though, she just couldn't do it. The thought of pushing back the covers, rolling out of bed, and digging through her backpack to find what she needed seemed like so much work at the moment. Instead, she continued to lie in the dark, staring at the wall and letting her thoughts race by.

Thanks to her cheap apartment, she was currently blowing through all of the completely random and useless information her mind held on Texas, that great state known for both their cowboys and their salsa. It really was random, all this useless knowledge. The Dallas/Fort Worth airport had the largest parking lot in the world. Austin was home to the largest urban bat colony in North America. Both true. Both totally useless. She had made the mistake of reading a book once named *Remembering the Alamo – Historical Trivia for the Lonestar State* and had regretted it ever since. She loved reading and did so tirelessly, mostly because it was one of the few things that brought her peace. She could spend hours with a book, forgetting all the noise and confusion in her own head. Content didn't matter much to her. She loved good fiction but she had read everything from a biography of Martin Luther to a book on explosive ordnance. She read whatever was convenient and readily available at the time. If it had words, she could use it. Whatever it took to convince her brain to be quiet for a few minutes here and there. Although admittedly, she had rather enjoyed *Explosive Ordinance and Its Disposal.* It had made for dry yet intense reading.

Her alarm went off three hours later, jolting her out of her thoughts. Finally. She rolled out of bed and sat for a minute, mentally reviewing her day. A minute might have been overshooting it. Since every day was about the same as the next, she didn't have much to review. A quick glance at her phone showed a clear sky and no wind so she dug into the drawer beside her bed and pulled out the first clothes she touched. She tried to keep a t-shirt and tights on top so she didn't waste time digging for gear. Her shoes were lined up beside the bed, ready to slip on at a moment's notice. In less than five minutes, she was dressed, hair tied into a loose knot, ready to go. The goal each day was to be out the door in less than 10 and she had perfected the routine. Because one never knew when one might need to leave. Quickly. And she liked to be ready for anything. Plus, she audited a class at the nearby university every morning at eight, which gave her exactly one hour to get her run in and one hour to clean up and get to school.

She stepped out the door of her small apartment and glanced around, taking note of the small, cramped parking lot and the nearby vehicles. Martin's black suburban was in its usual parking spot next to Shelly's white sedan. Quincy had made a point of memorizing all the vehicles that frequented her building so she would be able to spot anything that didn't belong. It was a move that had saved her life more than once.

Nothing seemed out of place. She took a deep breath of the early morning air and blew it back out slowly as she started to jog, breathing even more deeply to make sure her lungs were awake and ready to go. There had been a crispness to the air over the last week or two that the locals said meant fall was coming. She had never spent a fall in the midwest and was rather looking forward to seeing what all the fuss was about. The reading she had done on the area cited the changing of the leaves and praised the bright foliage the area was known for. Local magazines described bold reds, oranges, and yellows, a somewhat difficult picture to imagine in her head. Last week's copy of the university newspaper included a schedule of activities and events for the coming season, including haunted houses, hay mazes, and something called a "Pumpkin Patch". The paper hadn't given a description of what exactly this pumpkin patch was or what happened there, but she intended to find out.

She slid her earphones into place and hit play, picking the lesson back up where she'd left it after yesterday's run. Running was another one of those rare activities that soothed her frantic mind and she took advantage. She was already fluent in Spanish and was working on French and Latin - French, because it could be useful and Latin, because it never would be.

The loop she typically made while running was simple enough but she had to push herself to finish in her allotted hour. Her apartment complex was older and sat on the outskirts of town, only a mile south of the university, which was why so many students used it as off-campus housing. Half a mile past the school, the road turned and wound around a historic downtown, most of which was still original buildings and masonry. The neighborhood was built around an old-fashioned square with a gazebo in the center and several small parks surrounding it. One of the parks featured a botanical garden with benches surrounded by hummingbirds, butterflies, and honey bees. Another had walkways and paths that wound around a water garden and the third featured playground equipment and sandboxes for the local children and their parents to enjoy.

The entire square was beautiful and even at this early hour, Quincy could smell the honeysuckle and cherry blossoms that framed the gazebo. The square was ringed by original buildings, the beautiful architecture a throwback to simpler times, meticulously maintained throughout their lifetimes by the local families and businesses who owned them. Most of the buildings housed small, family-owned shops and eateries and were popular with the college and professional crowds alike.

Quincy jogged passed Sit a Spell, a coffee shop owned and operated by a retired couple from Massachusetts. The front door was propped open and the mingled scents of fresh grind and cinnamon rushed out to greet her. She waved at Mr. Boatright, who was outside setting up a couple of small tables and chairs on the patio, and he waved back. A small bookstore named PaddyO's shared a wall with Sit a Spell. Quincy's favorite spot in the entire town, it was a cozy, scattered place with an eclectic feel. Classic book covers were framed and mounted on the walls and books were stacked about the rooms to serve as makeshift tables. Thick homemade quilts were laid out around the floor, in the corners and under the book stacks, in case anyone felt like getting a little more comfortable. Rarely were there more than three or four people in the store at one time, and Quincy was their most loyal patron. She liked to pick a book at random and curl up in the farthest corner with whatever drink Mrs. Boatright had decided she needed to try that day and read for hours. Mr. and Mrs. Sanders, who owned the store, did a very profitable business online, buying and trading rare and antique book volumes. They claimed PaddyO's was necessary to the business and served as their unofficial headquarters but Quincy suspected they kept it more for sentimental purposes than practical ones. But whatever the reason, she was grateful. Surrounded by books and silence, she had found a great deal of peace on the floor of that little store.

It was too early for the old-time ice cream fountain and soda shop to be open for business but the bakery lights were on and she could already smell the fresh bread sitting on the windowsill rising. Not only did they sell breads by the loaf but they made fantastic sandwiches. A small Italian place sat on the next street and a nearby chocolate shop that invited shoppers to wander in and out created a homey, small-town feel to the area. Interspersed throughout the eateries were random businesses. An attorney had recently moved in above the Boatrights' coffee shop and a local art studio adjoined the Italian restaurant, displaying paintings and photographs from local artists and students, creating a shared space and a cozy atmosphere for date night, or so she had heard. There was a small daycare adjacent to the bakery that had a fenced-in playground that gave the children space and freedom to roam, and a yoga studio sat on the far side of the street. All in all, downtown was the kind of idyllic setting one might expect to see in a '50s television show, not a moderately-sized college town on the verge of a population boom. As Quincy lapped the square and veered onto a road on the opposite side, she couldn't help but wonder if it was for real. She had been here long enough to feel the lull of peace and pseudo-safety the hometown atmosphere provided and it would be so easy to give in completely. But she knew that kind of safety was nothing but a pipe dream, at least for her. But as she left downtown behind, she couldn't help but hope that she could fit in some place just like this. Maybe. Some day. Just not today.

Quincy took the road that cut towards a more heavily-populated, modern section of town, leaving the quaint family atmosphere of downtown behind. This was her least favorite section to run and she would never want to run it during commuter hours but at six o'clock in the morning, traffic was still relatively light and she felt comfortable as long as she stuck to the sidewalk. Business 14 took her up and around a newer industrial park before crossing over a creek that wound its way back towards the downtown botanical garden. But instead of following the road and going back through downtown, Quincy went off-road. There was less artificial lighting out this way, which made the sunrise even more spectacular this morning.

On mornings like these, when the sky was clear and the moon was full, she could see what felt like millions of stars. As she ran, she looked at the sky ahead of her and sighed. Her headphones provided steady background noise and she breathed deeply, inhaling the scent of freshly cut hay and clover. Much like downtown, this section of her run provided a backdrop that was soothing and oddly reminiscent of something she might read in a book. It seemed so safe, which was probably why it didn't seem real. But she allowed herself to enjoy it for a few minutes each day as she passed through before forcing herself back to reality when the farm road she was currently on eventually met up with the outer road where her apartment complex sat. All together, it was a seven-mile loop and as she finished her run this morning, her breathing was calm and steady. The cool temperatures made for a much more pleasant run than she'd had earlier in August and even parts of September. With October only a few days away, she knew the heat of summer was officially behind her and she hoped the nice weather would hold for awhile before the cold set in.

After walking a quick couple laps around the building to cool down, Quincy headed back inside and grabbed a bottle of water and checked her time. 6:48. She frowned. Off-pace by three minutes. It was still fine. It only took her 15 minutes to walk to campus so she had enough time to shower, dress, and grab a granola bar on her way back out, but still. She'd do better tomorrow.

As she stood under the steady stream of hot water, she mentally played through the notes she had read over last night. She had a test today in her electrical engineering class but she wasn't concerned. The campus library where she worked had been slow last night and she'd done a quick review before heading home for the night, though it hadn't really been necessary. Just like it wasn't necessary now. She had excellent retention skills and knew the material by heart. She had always been pretty good at absorbing new information the first time she read or heard it, which meant she spent very little time outside of class studying. She was also a fast reader, so she usually got through the week's reading material the first day it was assigned, which left most of her week free to explore the random and ever-changing selection at PaddyO's. Working at the library was really more of a hobby than actual work for her. It was on-campus, which meant it was close enough to both her home and her class to walk and it afforded her free access to as many books as she wanted. Since she didn't have a car and no spare money to spend actually buying the books at PaddyO's, there really wasn't anything better likely to come along.

The shower was quick, just like it always was. There were days, Quincy thought, that she'd give almost anything to let herself relax. Just stand under the steady stream, water so hot it turned her pink, and let the heat and steam erase everything from her head. But that was a luxury she didn't know if she could afford and she wouldn't allow herself to chance it. Not after last time. She picked up her backpack, rifling through it to make sure she had what she needed for class and work later that afternoon, and anything essential she would need if she was forced to skip town with no notice. The check was merely perfunctory. She always carried the necessities. But she did grab the book she'd been reading before her ill-fated attempt to sleep and slid it in with her other supplies, just in case she had free time after the test. Her one and half hour class started at eight o'clock and she reported to her shift at the library at 10, which usually allowed just enough time for a pit stop at the coffee stand on the corner on her way to work, but if she finished her test early, she would be able to sit on one of the benches in the quad and read while she enjoyed her drink. She slid her sunglasses on and headed out the door, the early morning chill already giving way to a mild, sunny day. Quincy popped her earphones back in and shoved the sleeves of her plaid shirt up past her elbows. It wasn't quite warm enough to go without sleeves but it would be soon, especially with no cloud cover.

Traffic was light on this side of campus but she waved at several other residents of her apartment complex as they drove by. When she'd first moved in, several of her neighbors had stopped to ask if she wanted a ride and always seemed confused, almost offended, when she turned them down. They couldn't figure out why she'd want to walk, especially lugging a backpack that looked like it could be used as a weapon of mass destruction if the situation called for it. The campus shuttle made the short trip out to their apartments and a couple that were further down so even if she didn't want to accept a ride with her neighbors, she had options. But that was okay. Why would anyone want to drive when they lived close enough to walk? Especially on nice days. Between all the running and walking she did, she knew the neighbors thought she was kind of strange. But the truth was, walking and running helped her stay calm and put the brakes on the constant whirlwind in her head. Plus, buying a car wasn't really an option for her. For anyone looking, large purchases provided a solid link that could be traced back to the buyer and she wasn't about to willingly leave that kind of trail. Renting an apartment was easier, especially if you could find one that accepted cash and asked no questions. Smaller, older places tended to look less closely than the big chain complexes did. But a car was a liability and if, or when, she needed to walk away, she wanted to leave as little evidence behind as possible.

Quincy slid into her seat in the back of the classroom with a little less than five minutes to spare. It was a full class and occupied a large lecture hall in the engineering building on the far side of campus. Most of the seats were usually full but there were always a couple around her left open. Since she was just auditing the class, she didn't feel obligated to participate in class discussion and the few times her classmates had attempted to start a conversation, she had kept her answers short, seeing no reason to encourage familiarity. The less people noticed or remembered her, the safer she was. She could hear nervous whispers around the auditorium and forced herself to feel a touch of nerves, too. Maybe she shouldn't have been so cavalier about studying. If everyone else was worried about the test, maybe it was going to be harder than she thought? But no. The professor started passing out the test at 8:00 on the dot and she glanced briefly over the pages. All the questions seemed straightforward and reflected both the reading material and the lectures - which she knew by heart. She turned back to the first page and settled in.

Chapter 2

Quincy

The coffee kiosk was practically deserted when Quincy ordered a hot chocolate with a shot of caramel. She had been one of the first to finish the test and when she'd handed it to Professor Michaels, he'd glanced at her name and then quietly asked if she wouldn't mind to drop by his office sometime in the next few days. He would like to speak to her privately during office hours if he could. He didn't say what they needed to discuss that would require so much privacy, but it weighed on her. Quincy thanked the barista when she handed her the drink then turned and slowly made her way toward the quad. Professor Michaels's request had caught her off-guard. Since she was an auditor and not on his official roster, she hadn't had any real contact with him other than handing in tests and homework assignments and getting her grades, but that mostly happened through email and the campus intranet. So why he wanted a private chat was anyone's guess but she really doubted it was anything good. In her experience, being noticed never ended well.

She found the bench she was looking for and tossed her bag on one end before settling onto the other. She pulled her legs up in front of her and let her feet rest on the very edge of the seat while she blew on her hot chocolate and took a long, slow sip. Glancing around the quad, she noticed a few others between classes or just killing time. She had seen the skater kid around a few times before. Today he was sprawled across the top of the brick railing dividing the walkway from the grass with his earbuds in and his board propped up beside him. He had his eyes closed and whatever he was listening to must have had some serious beat because his feet were tapping erratically and his hands were drumming along enthusiastically. There was a couple on a blanket in the grass a few yards away. The girl looked young, 18 maybe, and she had her boyfriend's jacket pulled tight around her to block the light breeze. She was leaning against him with her head on his shoulder and both were laughing at something playing on his phone. They looked happy and carefree and Quincy glanced away before they noticed her watching.

She sighed. The thing about Professor Michaels was, he was the kind of teacher that made his students a priority and they knew it. He welcomed one and all, no matter the problem, no matter the time. Ironically, he was a quiet man who loved to talk. If the thing he was talking about was mechanical engineering. How anyone could feel so strongly about math and mechanics, she wasn't sure. But he had a passion that came through in his lectures and, despite the subject, his students were hooked from open to close. So, from a distance, Professor Michaels was great. Quincy thoroughly enjoyed the class. She made excellent grades, but she was just one name in a sea of names. And she wasn't on his official roster, which should have meant he wasn't paying her any attention. College professors were busy enough – why was he noticing nobodies?

Quincy knew it was a mistake to put the professor off. She would fixate on the request, running possible scenarios through her head until she could concentrate on nothing else. It was her m.o., as it were. But she needed time to process. To decide what she was going to do. The last time someone had paid her extra attention, she'd had to blow town fast, no-showing at her bar tending gig, which had bummed her out because the owner, Gus, might have been a gruff old guy but she had a sweet spot for him and him for her and it had felt like a betrayal. So before she showed up at Professor Michaels's door, she needed to run through her options. There weren't many. Three, to be exact. The first was simple – she could disappear right now. She'd done it before and she'd no doubt have to do it again eventually. She had always known this place, this beautiful, quiet little town where she could breath, at least a little, wasn't forever. It was just another stop over. Like Boise. Like Chicago.

Option two was a little riskier. She could show up at Michaels's office early, staking it out before anyone else got there. See if he was alone or had company. Maybe try to spot anyone that might be out-of-place lurking about. She'd done that before too. Then, if it seemed safe, she could go to the meeting as requested and gather as much information as she could from the professor. See if he kept things academic. She was pretty sure she'd know if he was working on someone else's dime. And then, after the meeting, she could still disappear. It was safer to stay away from campus if someone was looking for her but it was also smart to gather as much intel as she could before leaving. Escape and evade was a game that relied on brains as much as on skill or luck.

And then there was the third option. She could stay. No deliberation, no paranoia. Just stay. She could go to the meeting like a normal student would, check her issues at the door, and hear what the man had to say. Then, if she was really lucky, she would be free to grab lunch on her way to her shift at the library. But who was she kidding? If she was lucky, she wouldn't have had to disappear twice already. She wouldn't have to become someone new for each new city she landed in. She would have a car, or at least a bike. She would have a checking account instead of carrying all her cash so she could bolt at a moment's notice. But she wasn't lucky. She hadn't been lucky in a long, long time. There was no sense grieving over what she didn't have. Sheraton was a nice little town, sure. She loved her perfectly circular running loop. She loved the flowers and the birds and the butterflies and the children that practically lived in the downtown parks like tiny little garden gnomes. And she loved the old buildings and quaint atmosphere that surrounded them. She loved Sit-A-Spell and PaddyO's. Each taken individually, they weren't really anything special. She had seen places like them in other small towns. But mash them together, wrap them in a neat little bow, and you have something extraordinary. And she didn't want to lose that. Not just yet.

A shout shook her out of her thoughts. Right in front her, a game of Frisbee was going on in the middle of the quad. Very aggressive Frisbee. Frisbee as a contact sport. Football Frisbee, maybe? She had never seen anything quite like it. A group of guys, upperclassmen by the look of it, were diving and running and throwing and generally having a jolly good time. She watched as one guy, a tall, gangly redhead, flipped the frisbee to a buddy, a large, broad-shouldered athletic type, who jumped the sidewalk and dodged one of the oak trees scattered around the lawn before slamming into a guy who was apparently on the opposite team. Both guys went down in a tangle of arms and legs and lay on the ground, laughing and shoving each other until the rest of the group helped haul them to their feet.

The frisbee had landed a couple yards from her and when the big guy spotted it, he came jogging over to grab it. As he came nearer, she could see he wasn't a kid like the rest of them. He was older than the other guys, early to mid-30's maybe. He was wearing a set of dog tags. No, two sets of dog tags. So, military. There were numbers on the tags. 3725625897 and 6752459581. She wondered which was his and who the other set belonged to. Someone he had lost, probably. He bent down to grab the frisbee and when he straightened, he glanced up at her. He smiled and she noticed his eyes were a deep, dark blue, which embarrassed her because she wasn't the type to notice a guy's eyes. Usually. But he did have nice eyes. And a really nice smile. She broke her own rule without even thinking, giving him a small smile back as she lifted her cup for another drink. He grinned and turned back to rejoin the game. She sat for a few more minutes, enjoying the weather and the entertainment, and completely forgetting her concerns over Professor Michaels and their upcoming meeting.

3

Chapter 3

Quincy

Okay, maybe a few extra minutes was a minor understatement. She sat drinking her coffee and watching the game, completely zoned out, until it started to break up and she realized she only had five minutes until the start of her shift. Classes had already let out and the sidewalks were full of people rushing from building to building. It was normally a leisurely 15 minute walk across campus to the library so she was going to have to hurry. But since she was always 15 minutes early to work anyway, she already felt late. She grabbed her bag and swung it across her shoulders, hustling down the sidewalk as fast as she could without making a scene. Out of the corner of her eye, she could see the big blonde guy from the frisbee game watching her speed walk away but she didn't have time to worry about that now. Peggy, the afternoon manager, was a real hard case when it came to their hours and she loved nothing more than busting late arrivals. As Quincy was always early, Peggy had never had the particular pleasure of Quincy's humiliation and would no doubt have the staff lounge staked out to bust her when she walked in.

When Quincy got to the building that housed the library, she pulled open the heavy wooden doors and rushed inside, bypassing the main library entrance for the smaller side door that led directly to the staff area. She was hoping she could grab her name tag out of her locker and sneak out to the reference desk before anyone noticed she wasn't there. But when she pushed the door open, the nightmare became the reality. Peggy really was in the lounge, sitting at the beat-up, stained little table where most of the staff took their breaks, going over what appeared to be staff schedules for next week. Quincy gritted her teeth and prepared to make her apologies but she needn't have worried. Peggy never even lifted her head as the door slammed shut and Quincy walked around the table to her locker. Weird. She opened the locker door, letting it bang against the other lockers. Still nothing. Her lanyard was hanging on a hook in her locker so she grabbed it and pulled it on over her t-shirt. Okay. Now it was a point of pride. Could work schedules really be so fascinating or was she just that invisible? She wandered over to the ice machine, grabbed a styrofoam cup from the cabinet, and filled it up, making as much noise as possible. Finally, she cleared her throat.

"Hey Peggy," she started. "Did I miss any announcements or anything when shift started?"

Peggy finally looked up, a bit startled. "Oh, Quincy, I'm sorry. I didn't see you there." Clearly. "Did you need something?"

"Nope," Quincy said after a beat. She held up the cup. "Just came in for some water."

"Oh, well, alright. But you'd better get back to the desk in case someone needs help."

And just like that, Quincy was dismissed. Okay, so only crazy people actually wanted to get busted by their boss but seriously, had no one noticed that she hadn't shown up for work? That was...depressing. She knew it shouldn't have been. It was ludicrous to feel that way since she went out of her way to engender that exact sentiment. She should be thrilled it was working so well. But seeing proof of the attitude she had worked so hard to earn just made her feel empty. Unsettled, somehow. She wandered through the main floor of the library, past the unused history books and the dusty political collection, to the wide spiral staircase that led up to her department. It was a pity, really, how often books went unused these days. Technology had made them all but obsolete, which almost depressed her as much as her own invisibility. She felt a sort of kinship with the outdated, heavy volumes. Her and the books, she thought wryly. Both had their uses, but neither were actually useful.

The second floor housed multiple departments, including circulation, career resources, and reference, which was her area. She waved to Hattie, who was helping a student at one of the computers in career resources. Hattie gave a little nod and rolled her eyes at the kid beside her, who seemed to be having a miniature panic attack as he pounded on the keyboard. Quincy grinned. Most visitors to career resources were seniors who had put off thinking about future employment until the last minute. Four years of freedom and all-nighters and suddenly they realize they're about to be kicked out into the real world. Not enough parties in the world to make those student loans disappear.

She took a quick lap through the reference department, making sure aisles were clear and the shelves were orderly. While Hattie had to deal with anxiety-ridden seniors, Quincy's busy season came mostly around midterms and finals. Reference was a good place to study in peace-the shelves of giant, musty, leather-bound books dampened sound and lent an air of awe to the place. There were resource computers at the end of each row of books that students could use to access a large variety of online databases; since most research and study resources could be found online these days, the resource books suffered the same fate as the history and political science books – mostly unused but still shelved for historical reasons and the odd journal article that couldn't be found electronically.

There were large square tables and individual desks scattered around the massive bookcases, giving students the ability to take advantage of the quiet and also provide them easy access to the books and reference computers. During the middle and end-of-semester rushes, it wasn't unusual for every available seat to be full but now it was practically deserted. There were a couple of regulars but everything seemed quiet. Exactly how Quincy liked it.

She circled back around, tossed her bag on the floor behind the giant desk, and dropped into her chair. She logged into her work station and checked her assigned tasks for the afternoon. She automatically crossed the first item off her list. She spent a good portion of her shift roaming the aisles, straightening and re-shelving books that had been used and left on tables or on the cart in front of the desk so she never worried too much about that one. But a new shipment of up-to-date World

Encyclopedias had come in overnight so she would need to deal with those. While she was a little surprised printed copies were still being produced, she didn't complain because it was an easy task. Mundane and repetitive, but she rather enjoyed the monotony and rhythm of it. She would log each book into the catalog system and print out bookends for them before pulling the old copies off the shelf and putting the new ones in their place. It would take a couple of hours but again, it wasn't busy and it gave her something to focus on. Plus, she needed to flip through each volume to check for obvious signs of damage before shelving and would probably pick up on a couple of new topics she could explore later. Yes, she could just as easily log into the databases the library allowed her to access but if the last 20 minutes had taught her anything, it was that she had a soft spot for hard copies. They were tangible, something she could feel and smell and hold. They soothed her. And they were so rarely unavailable.

The only other task on her To Do list was account checking. Once a year, each department was required to go through student and educator accounts for overdue materials and unpaid fees. One of the other Reference employees had already gone through the accounts and created a list of missing books. Quincy just needed to physically confirm each book was, in fact, MIA and hadn't been misfiled or returned and mistakenly left on the user account. This was the job she dreaded most. Not that she minded looking through books, but trying to find books that could be anywhere, but probably weren't, was a headache she didn't need. She almost always had one of her own – she didn't need the extra help.

4

Chapter 4

Quincy

As easy and relaxing as her job usually was, 10-hour shifts could really drag along on slow days. By 4:00 she had her list of chores done and her mind was starting to spin again. It had been blessedly still while she was cataloging the new books and making a pass through the user accounts but now that she was finished, she could feel the rumble, like a tornado forming. Or rather, reforming. Looking for something, anything, to do, she was seriously debating pulling out the ancient vacuum sweeper that resided in the maintenance closet and making a run over the floor. It's not like it needed it all that badly but desperate times and all that. The carpet was old and a good vacuum might help perk it up a bit. There wasn't a single person on her floor so the noise wouldn't be a bother and if she caved to her more compulsive desires, she could be extra thorough and move all the chairs out of the way. That would take quite a bit of extra time, considering just how many tables and chairs there were scattered throughout the aisles. Yes, she thought with grim satisfaction. That's exactly what she would do.

Twenty minutes later, she was finished with an extremely thorough cleaning of the carpet, which really looked no better, and back in the exact same spot she'd started. That hadn't taken nearly as long as she'd thought, nor had it done as much to quiet the crazy as she'd hoped, which was now starting to spin towards manic. She reached under the counter of her desk and pulled out the book she'd finished last night. *Emergency Field Medicine for Combat Situations* wasn't a book the typical reader might enjoy but she'd flown through it in less than a week. It had covered everything from how to plug sucking chest wounds to performing an emergency tracheotomy in the field. She'd found it fascinating. But she knew if she was going to get a couple hours of sleep tonight, she'd better find something else before she went home. She usually waited a little longer to wander over to the subject department but since there was no one here anyway, she figured there was no reason not to stretch her legs.

She had been staring at the same page for roughly eight minutes. Again. She had picked up two different books on her walkabout through the library, a classic novel and a how-to guide for criminology majors on the vast and varied techniques employed in criminal interrogation. She had read *Persuasion* several times before. She had read all of Jane Austen's novels, of course, but *Persuasion*, although considered one of Austen's lesser works, was her favorite and never failed to pull her in. There was just something about poor Anne Elliot. Ignored and overlooked in her own home. Treated like an inconvenience at the best of times, an unwanted burden at the worst. It wasn't like Quincy could relate to that specifically - she didn't exactly have a home or a family to treat her ill. But she certainly understood how it felt to be invisible and, in that way, Anne was a comrade-in-arms.

But regardless, old faithful had let her down and she'd moved on to *Interrogation Techniques: A Psychological Study.* But even the methodical rhythm of overly-dry reading material wasn't cutting it. Very rarely did opening a book not take up her entire focus but all she could think about today was, ironically, the frisbee game on the quad. Or, more precisely, the man playing the frisbee game with a bunch of boys on the quad. She had been worried she'd obsess over Professor Michaels's unexpected request but it just seemed so bizarre the more she thought about it. Not the professor. The guy on the quad.

He had to have been in his 30s. That was old, even by grad student standards. He could've been a professor, she supposed. But did professors spend off-hours playing Ultimate Frisbee with their students? Maybe. It did seem like that would be an activity frowned upon by the school. She had read a couple of law books a year or two back that discussed liability issues in different settings and she was positive the school wouldn't want to take the fall for an employee causing bodily harm to a student.

Maybe he was a brother or cousin of one of the kids? A possibility. There had been a couple of boys that looked similar enough to be family. Not that a resemblance was necessary. Sharing a genetic pool didn't always mean sharing physical traits. And there hadn't been a single kid there that had the same build. He had been tall, several inches over six feet if she were guessing. And he was built strong, but not in that bodybuilding-meathead kind of way. He was lanky but solid, like he spent a lot of his free time playing basketball or soccer or, well, Ultimate Frisbee. So maybe it did kind of make sense. And then there was the hair. Brother needed a haircut, to be sure. Didn't all those curls get in the way as he was jumping over benches and diving around overgrown schoolboys? It was completely ridiculous. At the very least, he should try running a comb through it now and again. It had a windblown, rakish look that would've been perfectly at home on the beach. Maybe barefoot. And carrying a surfboard. The blue eyes sure didn't do anything to take away from the surfer dude look, either. So then, he was an athlete of some kind. Not for the school - not at his age. Coach maybe? And why on Earth was she thinking so hard about this guy? She was on a college campus. Hot guys were everywhere. Was "hot" a bit of an overstatement? She mulled it over. No, it really wasn't.

She sighed and slammed the book shut in frustration. Why couldn't she stop? Why couldn't she just stop thinking? Not just about this guy, when she had more important things to be over-analyzing, like her test grade and imminent meeting with Professor Michaels. Why did she have so much trouble shutting her brain off at all? Was this normal? She had never heard anyone else mention it in passing. No, "How was your night?" "Oh, you know, another night staring at the ceiling, pondering the cyclic nature of physics and how random it really seems, in the grand scheme of things, for Einstein to have discovered relativity." She felt like she was on the merry-go-round she'd seen jogging past the playground on the square, spinning around and around and around, kicking up rocks and tossing people around like an afterthought. Stupid brain...

The hand on her shoulder startled her out of her own head

and back to the present. She reacted instinctively, dropping her book and pushing away from the unexpected touch, coming out of her chair prepared to run or fight, whichever option was smartest. Brandon from the Circulation desk was staring at her in shock, seemingly unsure of how to proceed in the presence of the queen of overreaction. Quincy made a concerted effort to slow her breathing, knowing from experience that once she got her heart rate back down, her fight or flight reflex would relax and she could try to act normal. She closed her eyes, took one more deep breath in and out, then opened her eyes.

"I'm so sorry. I must've been totally spacing to jump like that." She attempted to laugh it off and aimed an only slightly strained smile in Brandon's direction. "So what's up?" To his credit, he seemed to shake off the shock fairly quickly.

"I didn't mean to scare you. I just wanted to say hi," he said awkwardly. He glanced away and cleared his throat before meeting her eyes again. "You looked a little distracted."

Quincy stared. Brandon was a newish hire and a bit of a mystery. He had started a couple weeks ago but, unlike a lot of the newbies, he didn't seem to be trying to fit in or make friends. He was always on the outskirts of the crowd, watching, listening, but never really joining in. She had heard a few of the others talking about him, referring to him as The Creeper, and a lurker, but she had never really gotten that impression from the guy. Sure, he didn't seem interested in making friends. And, okay, maybe sometimes he was kind of abrupt when dealing with people. But it seemed more subconscious than deliberate. Like he was severely lacking in social skills but didn't know how to fix it. He seemed, well, a bit like her actually. Always watching and waiting, weighing people's actions and words for underlying meaning, ready to react if her spidey sense tingled, conspiracies around every corner, and so on. If her co-workers were gossiping about Brandon, heaven only knew what they were saying about her. Which was why she was confused. She hadn't seen him ever wander the library, on a break or otherwise. And she had never noticed him start a conversation with anyone. The fact that he had just done both was a little disconcerting.

"Oh. Um. Yeah, just lost in thought, I guess." She smiled at him, attempting some warmth this time. "I hope Peggy didn't notice."

"Nah," he said. "Peggy had a meeting in the admin building. She said she'd be gone for a couple hours at least." He stuck his hands in his pockets and dropped his eyes. "So, uh, what time are you off? I was thinking of hitting the taco truck down on the south quad for dinner. Want to join?"

He was shuffling his feet and still not looking at her. Quincy's heart rate spiked for the second time in less than five minutes. No matter how hard she tried to keep people at bay, now and again some stalwart soul would brave the battlements and attempt to breach her walls. She had learned early on that it was better to shut it down, hard if she had to, before it really even got started.

"You know, I think I'll just head home. I have some things I need to take care of tonight. But enjoy."

He finally looked up. "What kind of things?" he asked.

Well, that was annoying. Poor social skills aside, you don't call people on that excuse. Everyone knew that. It was just rude. And now she had to think up something on the fly because really, what was she going to say? That she was planning to head home and plot another escape route out of town that she could access in a speedy and efficient fashion should the need ever arise? Or that she was going to research towns in the northwest so she would have a couple of predetermined destinations in mind? That wasn't going to work. So instead, she went with old faithful – the fake boyfriend, every single girl's best defensive weapon.

"He's in the military so we don't get to see each other very often. That's why we plan these little Skype dates. And I would never miss one. But I'll tell him you said hello."

She tacked on the end for extra insurance. Very few men wanted to run the risk of offending a military guy by making a move on his girl. And it must've hit its mark because Brandon went from normal to pale to tomato red in the time it took her to finish talking.

"I didn't know. Sorry." He started backing away, like he was sorry he had ever come over in the first place. "Have a good time, or night, or, uh, talk. Have a good talk."

He turned tail and fled back to Circulations. Quincy stared after him, kind of unsure where that had even come from. Brandon had never paid her any more attention than he did anyone else and even though she'd blown him off, that reaction seemed a little...off.

"Man, O'Connell," said Clara, who happened to be casually strolling past, no doubt having seen Brandon make his move and hoping to get a good show. "You lay the beat down hard girl." She gave a smirk, condescension and snark all rolled into one tidy package. "Boyfriend? Sure." And she was gone, probably to share the inside scoop with the rest of her posse.

5

Chapter 5

"'Many are the strange chances of the world,' said Mithrandir, 'and help oft shall come from the hands of the weak when the wise falter'." J.R.R. Tolkien

The girl does not believe in chance. It has been her experience that chance is never chance. But she's not wrong.

It never really is, is it?

* * *

Quincy

The seconds slowly but inevitably ticked away until it was finally 8:00. The day had stayed pretty quiet, her only real challenge involving helping an overwhelmed freshman who was well into panic mode and quickly progressing toward full breakdown find one more reference from an online healthcare database. And then getting her some serious caffeine to stave off the adrenaline crash sure to follow. But otherwise, her duties had remained light and the afternoon and evening had crawled by.

She shut down her computer and rolled the chair back under the desk, pausing to swing her bag up onto her shoulders, and made a final walk-through of the floor, checking to make sure there weren't any stragglers she had missed and straightening the few newspapers and books that were out of place on the aisle display. As she walked down the stairs, she could see the others doing final checks of their areas, too, herding slow-moving students and difficult-to-remove faculty out of their sections so they could close down and head out.

Quincy was lucky that the Reference department seldom had visitors that needed to be chased off. Yes, occasionally it was a popular place to study, but that was usually restricted to high-anxiety points in the semester. The other departments had cozier settings that invited students to sprawl out and stay for awhile. Which was great, until the library closed. Chasing students, who tended to stay up until the early hours of the morning, out of their nests when their night was just getting started could be a daunting challenge. As she walked through Literature, she nodded at Clara and Mitchell, who both smirked as she went by, and gave a little wave to Brandon, just to keep it from being weird. He was currently being held prisoner by a professor who appeared to be lecturing him on the various aspects of customer service and describing, in great detail, how the Circulation department was lacking in each and every one. Sounded like the poor guy wasn't going to be grabbing that dinner any time soon. She ducked her head and smiled, relieved to not have to walk out with him.

The sky was dark and clear, with a not-quite-full moon hanging low overhead. She hadn't wanted to have dinner with Brandon but she'd been thinking about tacos ever since he'd mentioned them. And a coke. Nothing beat Mexican food and a good, strong coke. The southwest quad had an assortment of food trucks that stayed open late to accommodate student hours so she headed that way. It really did look like he was going to be stuck with the professor for a while, so she was probably safe to swing by the truck and then head home. She could watch a couple of sitcom reruns as she ate and then settle down with *Interrogation Techniques* and pray for a few solid hours of sleep.

There were only a few people hanging around the food pavilion when she got there and a blessedly short line in front of the taco truck. She put in her order, relieved to see there were still a couple of tacos wrapped and ready to go. Sometimes, after a long night, supplies ran pretty low and you got what you got.

"Got here just in time kid," Taco Guy said. "I'm down to my last two and about to hang it up for the night." He dumped the tacos into a to-go bag with some salsa and napkins and pushed it and her drink across the plywood that doubled as his counter. "It's on the house." Quincy had already pulled a $5 out of her bag but the guy shook his head. "Last tacos of the night are always cold. Trust me, you're doing me a favor." Then he smiled. "Have a good night kid."

"Thanks," she shot at his retreating back. She avoided having dinner with Brandon and still got her meal for free?

She was coming up aces tonight. She turned to go, making a mental note to come back sometime this week and leave a big tip, when a voice spoke up right beside her. She jerked, startled to hear someone so close. Inside the circle of food trucks were several benches and picnic tables so people could sit and eat. Since it was night, very few of them were occupied. Only one, in fact. A guy sat on a table to her right, eating a taco. Not his first, judging by the wrappers crumpled up beside him.

"Wish I had been a few minutes later. I had to pay for all mine."

It was dark but the food pavilion had lights scattered around to make it more livable. The guy sat on the top of the table, one leg propped up on the bench, the other stretched out towards the ground, turned to watch the late nighters come and go. He took another bite and grinned.

"One of the kids on my team today told me the tacos here were the best. He wasn't wrong."

She wouldn't have thought he'd recognize her. Not after just one glance, hours ago. She recognized him, of course. She had spent the last several hours obsessing over him, after all. If the long, lanky legs hadn't given him away, all that blonde messy hair would have.

"In my experience, kids usually know where the best food is." she said.

She noted his use of the word *kids*. She had been right. He was older. But as he sat there, crunching on his tacos like he didn't have a care in the world, he seemed younger somehow. She glanced around. It really was dark outside their little circle of lights. There was no one else around except for the Taco King and the rest of the food truck royalty and they were all shutting down for the night.

"Got one of each there, do you?" she asked mildly, motioning toward the pile of used wrappers beside him.

"If you're going to figure out which is the best, you've got to try them all," he said in a matter-of-fact way. He pushed the trash to the side and waved her over. "Come on. Sit down and eat your two tiny tacos. I won't bite."

Oh, that smile. A smile that said he was cute and he knew it. A smile that was no doubt used to getting its own way. A smile that was nothing but trouble. And yet, she found herself moving towards him. She didn't want to give him total satisfaction, though, so she walked around the table and took a seat on the opposite side, forcing him to turn if he wanted to talk to her. He grinned, got up, and plopped down on the bench facing her.

"So, which one?" she asked, taking a bite of one of her own tacos.

He frowned. "Which one what?"

"Which one is the best?"

He laughed. He really did have a nice laugh. "Definitely the southwest chili." He gave a little fake cough. "It has just a bit of a kick."

She shook her head, said, "Tried it. Not that impressed," and shoved the rest of her girly American taco, minus the beans, lettuce, and sour cream, into her mouth before she got up. "Good talk. See you around."

She turned away, ready to make for home. This whole day had been surreal. First, a professor in a class she was only auditing asks for a private meeting. Then she sees this guy in the quad and, what's more, actually notices him, no small thing for her. Then Brandon, who never talks to anyone, asks her out. And now, quad guy is sitting on a bench, eating tacos, and wanting to chat? Just...surreal.

"Now hold on." Quad guy didn't get up, but had turned to watch her leave. "You still have a whole other taco to eat. No sense running off before you're done. What's the rush?"

"The rush is, it's after dark and some guy I don't know wants to sit and chat. It's a page straight out of Smart Girl 101. Just, no." Quincy should have felt empowered by her bold exit. She'd meant to impress upon him her street savvy and powers of self-preservation. If only she hadn't flipped her hair over her shoulder as she said it. Which was weird because when was the last time she'd flipped her hair for anyone? Had she ever? Did that negate the power of the last word, she wondered?

Behind her, she heard him laugh and realized yes, it apparently did. She sighed. So much for one-upmanship.

"Hey, *some guy*'s name is Logan. And we're surrounded by food truck dudes who would put me down if I made an ungentlemanly move. I think you're safe."

She kept walking.

"Aren't you even going to tell me your name?" he called after her.

Quincy lifted her hand in a dismissive wave without turning back, hoping it was enough to salvage what small amount of dignity she could.

6

Chapter 6

The Colonel

The phone rang at 6:37, interrupting his dinner. He was at his favorite restaurant, the same one he visited every Monday. A small mom and pop place, it boasted a narrow menu of homemade recipes and the best desserts in the Northeast. Mondays were the meatloaf special and he never missed it. He glanced and the caller i.d., annoyed at having been disturbed.

"What?" he growled.

He was a man of habit and everyone who worked for him knew it. They also knew how he felt about having his dinner interrupted for nothing. So this had better not be nothing. Although, this particular caller had not set the bar high in the past so his expectation was low.

The man on the other end got right to the point. "I think I found her."

He clearly thought this was important enough to break protocol but it was nothing new to the Colonel. Every few weeks, someone on the hunt thought they caught a scent. It usually amounted to nothing more than a woman, right age, right build, wrong place and time. After months of false starts, he most definitely wasn't in the mood for more leads that led nowhere.

"You either found her or you didn't. Which is it?"

He forked another slice of his meatloaf and sopped up some of the juice and breadcrumbs before putting it in his mouth, savoring it as it went down. He had never met anyone who could make meatloaf that tasted just like his mother's, but this was close. The owner came over to refill his glass but the Colonel suddenly motioned him away. He sat up straighter, fully tuning in to what the man was saying.

"Have you established a pattern?"

Apparently, he had. The Colonel sat and listened as the man outlined several characteristics that he had linked to the girl over the last few years. Why bother tracking physical characteristics when those are easy enough to change? An interesting approach, the Colonel admitted to himself as the man continued. She didn't seem to gravitate toward similar surroundings twice. Towns, cities - she'd been linked to both. But what the towns she had been seen in previously did have in common were colleges that accepted audit students on a class-by-class basis. And those weren't as common as, say, hair color and height.

"And you think you've got a hit?" the Colonel asked when the man finished.

It was obvious the man thought he'd found her but the Colonel still had his doubts. "No," he interrupted, shutting him down. "I want hard proof. We need to limit collateral damage. If you act rashly and create a mess, the company will not be pleased."

He thought for a moment. Did he trust the man to pursue this lead on his own? Hardly. But it was only reconnaissance. As long as he didn't try to make contact or get too close, the girl should never know he was there.

"Observe. Watch what she does, see if she displays any symptoms that might give her away. But do not engage."

When the man didn't answer, the Colonel persisted. "Do you understand your orders soldier?"

His voice was quiet, mild even. But there was no mistaking the steel that ran through it. This order was not to be disregarded. Yes, the man finally answered. He understood.

The Colonel smiled, picking his fork back up. "Well then, keep me informed. We'll move as soon as we have a positive i.d. Losing her again isn't an option."

Before he hung up the phone, he paused. He did believe in credit where credit was due, after all.

"Auberdeen? Well done."

7

Chapter 7

"We're all islands shouting lies to each other across seas of misunderstanding." Rudyard Kipling

The girl exists in isolation, as much as one can. Her world is limited to that which will help her survive.

People will not help her with this. Friends will not help her. People will hurt her. Friends will be hurt. And so she lies.

In this, we are agreed.

* * *

Quincy

Quincy lay awake again, staring up at her ceiling and thinking. She had decided to go to Professor Michaels's open office hours before work but that slightly risky decision wasn't what was on her mind. Not at all. After she had collapsed into bed, she had spent a few minutes determining the best course of action, for now, was to approach him first thing in the morning when there would be, hopefully, fewer people around, making it easier to spot anyone out-of-place. Well, maybe not *the best* course of action, but that's what she was going to do. He had asked her to come within a few days but he hadn't nailed down a specific time, which didn't make sense if he was looking to lay a trap. And if she went first thing tomorrow, she wouldn't have to sit and worry for the next three days. So yes, she would go and see how things played out. Option three was the riskiest, and the stupidest, but she was tired of running all the time. The professor seemed on the level and she was willing to chance it, within reason.

Once she had decided, it was amazing how fast her mind switched gears. Amazing, yes, but also incredibly irritating that some random guy could completely take over her thoughts. Granted, it wasn't unusual for something random and unimportant to take over the tornado that was her brain. The great state of Texas, the mystifying phenomena that was the hot dog, and the complete dichotomy of the phrase *Baker's Dozen* were all topics she had agonized over at some point or another. She supposed, since she had literally spent hours over-analyzing these most minuscule of details, spending her insomnia on a boy might actually be considered normal. But seriously, why use the term *dozen* if you don't mean twelve?

Despite these more pressing concerns, she had spent the night replaying her run ins with Logan over and over, looking at the few facts she knew and trying to piece them together to make sense. It was so not like her to notice a boy. Or to overreact when he noticed her. She had never seen him before. Worst case scenario, he was a plant sent to get close to her. She was invisible to most people, having perfected the technique after so many years. She was older than most of her classmates and frankly, next to the perky, size 0 coeds roaming campus, flaunting what God and daddy's credit card gave them, she didn't merit a second glance.

But maybe that's why he'd noticed her. She was, admittedly, closer to his age. And he hadn't just noticed her; he'd *seen* her. Well enough to recognize her hours later, in the dark. Quincy sighed and closed her eyes. This guy, Logan, he'd said his name was, had nice eyes. And a nice smile. He seemed friendly enough and he was right, it wouldn't have made sense if he was planning to mess with her to stake her out at the food truck pavilion. Those grizzled old cooks would have had him by the throat in a heartbeat if he'd tried something. She pictured it in her mind, a bunch of middle aged, grease-stained, hard living trucker types dog piling the giant blonde surfer for stepping out of line.

The thought made her smile. They were like her boss back in Boise, at the truck stop. Grumpy but protective, and loath to admit it. She had to admit, it was kind of nice to be noticed by a guy who looked like Logan. He must get attention everywhere he goes. It was kind of odd, she thought suddenly, to have 2 different men show interest in the same day. Three, if she counted Professor Michaels. A snap in her intentionally wrought dry spell? Or something more serious? She frowned. She should probably give that a little more thought. Of all her random wonderings tonight, that was probably the only one with actual merit. But the thread of her thoughts was becoming inexplicably frayed, weaving together and splitting

41

apart amongst the sheer improbability of those wretched hot dogs. She decided not to fight it. She had already decided on a course of action for Professor Michaels. The question of whether Logan and Brandon's attention was sincere or manufactured would hold for another day. Instead, she let the thread drift; floating her harried thoughts out to sea, she slid off into a shallow sleep, grateful for whatever she could get.

Quincy's class started at 8:00 so she was used to being on campus early. She preferred it that way. Everything was quiet. The few people who were there at that time of day were there for a reason and went about it without a fuss. Maybe because it was too early for 20-years olds to make a fuss, she didn't know. But the campus had a slow, sleepy feel to it in the morning that Quincy loved. It was kind of eye-opening to see what it looked like even earlier. College kids weren't a big fan of 8:00 a.m. classes sure, but 7:00? The place was like a ghost town. There were a couple of people scattered here and there, haphazardly dressed and barely awake. Even the guy manning the coffee kiosk was moving slow, something Quincy found mildly ironic. He had taken a painfully long time handing her cup over. Something about grinders that needed to wake up. Or warming up his steamer. She wasn't positive and she didn't think he was either. As he was struggling with her order, Quincy noticed a girl rushing towards Bennett Hall. She was a mess, hair tugged into a messy knot, shoes untied. Obviously running late, the girl shot a quick look toward the coffee kiosk before yanking the door to the lecture hall open and darting through. A painful sacrifice for a few scant minutes of extra sleep. Quincy couldn't understand it. Of course, Quincy couldn't sleep either, so maybe her judgement wasn't the one to trust.

Edgar Hall was a magnificent old building that housed all of the classes in the engineering programs. It was also home to faculty offices, and Professor Michaels, as the young kid on the block, had been pushed as far south as he could get, sandwiched between two larger corner offices that hogged all the window space. Quincy settled onto a bench near the middle of the building so she could see both entrances. Since there were two, she could only guess which one he would come in but the spot was about equidistant to both doors and enough out of the way that, hopefully, he wouldn't spot her right off. She had grabbed the only cap she had, an old, ratty thing that had been with her longer than she could remember, and hoped that, since he'd only put the name to her face once, it, combined with all the others coming and going, would be enough camouflage to hide her in plain sight.

She had brought a book of course. Staking out a possible threat's office seemed like a suitable moment to continue working through *Interrogation Techniques.* But she kept one eye on the cluster of offices, looking closely at each person that wandered down the hall. Quincy truly expected to spot someone lurking about who appeared to be up to no good, but after an hour, she was almost disappointed to acknowledge that it seemed like a perfectly legitimate meeting with a college professor. Professor Michaels had shown up at 8:15, his sweater-over-untucked t-shirt and Converse sneakers combo boldly screaming *young idealistic do-gooder.* Several students had come and gone during the hour since he'd opened his office, and each meeting had been an open-door, agreeable affair. One thing she had noticed during their classes was that his students all seemed to like him. They paid attention in class, asked questions, and responded when he did the asking. It was possible the kids in Mechanical Engineering all had a legitimate, unquenchable interest in the subject but it seemed more likely that Professor Michaels was just that compelling of a teacher. Which was why Quincy found herself, albeit reluctantly, tapping on Michaels's open door.

He looked up at the sound and broke into a smile when he saw her.

"I honestly didn't know if you'd stop by," he said by way of explanation. "Since you're not on the official roster, you aren't obligated to participate in any class activities, including office hours. But I'm really glad you did."

He gestured to the chair situated to the left of his desk and she took it without a word, relieved her back wouldn't be to the open doorway. As she sank into the chair and dropped her backpack to the floor at her feet, Michaels sat back in his own chair and turned so he was facing her. He seemed to be sizing her up so she took the opportunity to do the same, although by this point she knew she would come to the same conclusion. This was just a teacher, a young one, who loved his subject and was on the lookout for others who might share his passion. She didn't know if that made her feel better or worse.

"So," he finally said, "You're wondering why I asked you to drop in?"

He was obviously looking to make this a conversation and, though he seemed safe, she wasn't entirely sure she wanted to get that friendly with him. So she just shrugged, leaving his verbal invitation open. But the awkward silence didn't seem to phase him because he picked that ball up and rolled with it.

"To be honest, I don't get that many auditors in my classes. Mechanical engineering is a pretty dedicated sphere and most people who audit are looking for entertainment or experience in subjects they already dabble in." He shrugged good-naturedly. "And most of the auditors I do get don't pull the grades you do."

He dropped the easy-going smile, leaning forward so that his forearms rested on the desk in front of him, and looked her square in the eye.

"Would it surprise you to know that you carry the top grade in the class? In all my classes, actually. By a significant margin?"

For someone who got caught off-guard so rarely, it seemed to be happening with alarming frequency lately. But Quincy honestly didn't know what to say. No, she didn't know she had the top grade in class. Did it surprise her? Not really. She usually got good grades and mechanical engineering wasn't any different than any other subject. But what did surprise her was Professor Michaels's attention. In her experience, professors didn't really care who made what grade. As long as there weren't too many failing, it wasn't worth thinking about. But this young, enthusiastic teacher did, apparently, care, and she was terribly afraid that was going to be a problem for her.

He was still focused on her, waiting for an answer. She shrugged again, using self-deprecation as a shield.

"I have a head for numbers so this class seemed like a good fit. It's really not a big deal." Michaels shook his head.

"No, it really is." He leaned back in his chair and watched her for a few seconds, not saying anything. Which was not what she wanted. She didn't need him interested in her or her situation.

"I add so many extra credit assignments to my classes every semester because this is a very difficult subject and even my most dedicated students need help keeping their grades up. No one has ever passed this class with 100%." He grinned and swiveled his chair side to side, clearly burning off a little spare energy. "And you're passing it with 110%."

He glanced down, adjusted his notes. "Strike that. 111%. You haven't missed a single point, extra or otherwise, all semester."

His eyes were still boring into her, giving her the distinct impression that he knew she was uncomfortable but wasn't willing to let her off the hook. "So you tell me, just how far would you like a 'head for numbers' to take you?"

Quincy was confused by the question. It was more likely for a student to cheat than to have a perfect semester but that thought didn't seem to have entered his mind. Of course, as an auditor, she had nothing to gain by cheating. Her grades weren't being recorded. She wasn't benefiting from a scholarship or competing for an internship. But still, most other teachers would have at least considered it. And most students would have been defensive, denying the accusation before it could be made. But Michaels was still idealistically wide-eyed and optimistic. And coming from this earnest young professor, with his puppy dog eyes and can-do attitude, she took it for what it was - kindness. He was simply interested in helping her. Which would be a refreshing change if it weren't so dangerous. And the next words out of Professor Michaels's mouth only confirmed what she already knew. He wanted *more* for her.

"I think you should enroll officially in the class. You've already paid the auditing fee. It wouldn't take much more to backdate your enrollment and make your grades official. With your scores, I can talk to the Dean and see about getting you scholarship money so you can continue with an actual course of study. You can pursue an education, formally."

He was warming to his topic now.

"Think of the research you could explore for your thesis. And eventually your dissertation. This is such a broad subject that you could literally move any direction you want with it."

He finally took a breath and looked at her, waiting for the obvious reaction to such an offer. And why would he expect any different? What poor college student, struggling to survive on a minimum wage job, wouldn't jump at the chance to be able to afford real classes, with the real diploma that comes with them? She could have an actual career, a well-paying one at that, and her life could change completely.

Of course, with real classes and a real diploma comes real records and real documentation and the very real threat that'd she'd be found. So her diploma would probably have to be awarded posthumously and her well-paying job would go to the number two student in her graduating class. And poor Professor Michaels, with his pure heart and obvious innocence, would give a moving tribute at her funeral, proclaiming that at least she died well-educated. Of course, that's assuming her body was ever found. Which seemed doubtful, considering she was running from shadowy secret agent types who wanted her for who knows what reasons. They just didn't strike her as the type to leave pesky little things like bodies lying around.

"Quincy?"

She looked up. Professor Michaels had come around the desk and was perching on the corner, looking down at her with concern. The man had a serious case of bleeding heart and if she wasn't careful, it would be fatal for both of them.

"Sorry. I zoned out for a minute." She summoned up her sunniest smile and prepared to backpedal.

"I really appreciate you taking the time to talk to me. I really didn't know I was doing that well in class. I know it's kind of strange but I like to take tough classes. I usually only take one at a time because they're so hard. That's probably why I'm doing so well. I don't have any other classes to split my focus."

He didn't say anything, waiting for her to continue. Awkward. She cleared her throat and went on.

"I can't say I'm actually all that interested in mechanical engineering. It's not even a hobby. I looked through the course catalog to see what classes were available for audit and this looked like the hardest one. I'm really not interested in making a career of it."

She shot a glance at her watch. 9:20. She still had 40 minutes before she had to be at the library. But he didn't know that. She stood and looped the strap of her backpack over her shoulder.

"I need to head out, work and all. But thanks again for taking the time. I'll see you in class tomorrow."

She wasn't sure why she said that. Going back to class now, with him so interested, would be a mistake. It would be smarter to just pack it up and leave. Still, it seemed the polite thing to say.

She turned to go but he stopped her with a light hand on her shoulder. She instinctively stiffened but kept from jerking away. She did her best to look natural as she turned back to him and he dropped his hand.

"Look, I know it can be really hard. I don't know what your individual situation is but I want you to know that I'd like to help if I can."

He smiled kindly. *Trust me*, that smile said. *Please.*

"If you change your mind, or need to talk about anything, please know I'm here and I'll listen."

He smiled again and backed up a few steps, sinking back down onto the edge of his desk, effectively dismissing her.

"I just hate to see good go to waste. And you are something good."

8

Chapter 8

Quincy

Quincy felt unexpectedly sad as she left Professor Michaels's office. She pushed out of Edgar Hall and took a deep breath of the crisp fall air, trying to shake the feeling. For anyone else, that would have been a dream offer. A whole new life, offered up on a silver platter. Someone who believed in her, who thought she was special and was willing to step out on a limb for her.

But Quincy wasn't anyone else. And as much as she wished she could take the professor up on either of his offers, she couldn't. It was too risky. She couldn't risk staying in one place long enough to finish a degree. She couldn't risk putting down roots, creating a life tied to any one place. She couldn't risk laying that kind of trail. She couldn't risk letting someone in like that. She would love to turn around, go back into his office, and pour it all out. Tell him how someone was trying to kill her. How she didn't know who or why. How they had been trying for years but she had managed to stay one step ahead of them by nothing more than sheer, dumb luck.

She'd get it all out - how tired she was of being on guard all the time, how she couldn't shut her mind off. How she just wanted to sleep, really sleep, for once in her life. Then she'd sink back into one of his ridiculously overstuffed chairs and wait for him to make it better. To take it all away. Which he wouldn't, because really, who could listen to that and *not* believe that crazy had come out to play? No, Professor Michaels's look of understanding and encouragement would shift, ever so subtly, to worry, maybe a little fear, and then pity. Pity for the sad girl who seemed so bright but obviously had some major issues in her life. Pity that this was beyond him, that he wouldn't be able to help her like he so obviously wanted to. Quincy sighed. Life was what it was. You played the hand you were dealt. And right now, she decided life was going to deal her a coffee. A big one. With caramel. And the full fat milk.

Campus was more alert at 9:00 than at 8:00. People coming and going, in less of a rush than before but still harried. Or maybe that was just the style of the day. It would certainly be easier, Quincy mused, and faster too, if she ditched her hair brush. And the act of putting on pants. Pajama bottoms seemed to be acceptable college fashion she noted, watching a pair of fuzzy flannels sashay past her with a grin.

"Back again?" the kid manning the cart asked.

Quincy sighed. "It's been that kind of morning."

"I should make it a big one then?" the kid asked.

"Grande mocha latte with a shot of caramel and extra whip".

"Skim like last time?"

"Absolutely not," Quincy answered. "Sugar and fat, as

much as you can pack in there."

"It really has been a day," he said. "Hey, we got a new snickerdoodle flavor in. Crazy good if you're interested. And I can still put a shot of caramel in for you."

"Why not?" Quincy said. If cool coffee cart kid said it was good, it was probably a safe bet. He should know.

"Make it two," a voice behind her said. She turned as a giant hand dropped a $20 on the counter. The man attached to it leaned casually against the cart and smiled down at her. "If it isn't the girl with no name. What are the odds?"

That was an excellent question. Because meeting Blondie for the third time in twenty-four hours seemed pretty long. Logan, she reminded herself. He'd said his name was Logan.

"We'll take those to go," he told the kid and accepted both drinks. "Keep the change."

"Thanks man," the kid said, obviously not used to such stellar treatment.

"That's basically a 50% tip," she pointed out, trailing after Logan as he started down the walk. Maybe he was an idiot and she just hadn't picked up on it yet. That would actually make her feel a little better.

"That kid works eight hours a day for people who barely look at him." Logan said as he handed her coffee over. "He deserves a little something extra now and again."

So, not an idiot, or at least not yet. Just kind.

"You coming or going?" Logan asked.

"A little of both," Quincy said. When Logan looked at her, she debated briefly and then decided, why not. "I just left a meeting with my professor and I have a little time to kill before work."

"Care to walk?" he asked. Before Quincy could blow him off,

which he clearly saw coming a mile away, he went on. "It's broad daylight, in the middle of a campus full of students and staff, on a walkway in full view of anyone who cares to see. There's no stranger danger here."

So they walked. It was a beautiful day, sunny and cool, a light breeze making the coffee even more welcome. Quincy sipped at hers, acutely aware of the very large man walking beside her. He was quiet, which seemed incongruent with his behavior the last time she'd seen him. She took a drink, sneaking a glance from the corner of her eye. He didn't seem to be in any particular hurry, blowing on his coffee before taking a drink and just generally enjoying the day. But old habits die hard and she couldn't quite keep the suspicion out of her voice.

"So. Just happened to be in the neighborhood, did you?" she asked, physically unable to let the silence linger.

"You're kind of paranoid, you know that?" he remarked mildly, taking another slow drink of his coffee. "And this is bad," he said, dumping the entire cup in a trash can as they wandered past. "It's so sweet. How can you drink that?"

She glanced down at her own cup. "I didn't really notice," she said. "Huh. It kind of is, isn't it?"

Logan smiled. "And yes, I did."

"Did what?" Quincy asked, annoyed by the thought that she'd wasted good money on that coffee.

"I did just happen to be in the neighborhood."

It was Logan's money though, so maybe it wasn't such a tragic loss.

"Most of my classes are in the afternoon but I'm always up early. Sometimes I run, sometimes I just come here and wander around. See what kind of trouble I can get into."

"Like Frisbee on the quad?" she asked. He grinned. It was that same, reckless grin from last night. The one that said he was going to wrap her around his finger and he knew it.

"Exactly like Frisbee on the quad. You can usually find some kind of game going on."

"I'm sure," she said. "Frisbee's not usually a contact sport though."

"No, but it's definitely more fun when it is."

"Boys," she said, rolling her eyes. But she couldn't help smiling as she took another sip of her terrible coffee. Trouble or not, his smile was infectious.

"Where are we walking to?" he asked. She hesitated again. This was usually where she'd shut him down, politely or not, and walk away. Although really, who was she kidding? She was already way beyond that point. She'd blown past it last night, in fact, when she'd chatted with him over tacos. That stupid smile was just so disarming. It was hard to walk away from.

"I work at the library on campus," she finally said, momentarily forgetting her rule about not giving out useful information. Or just outright ignoring it. "I had a meeting with my professor and I got finished a little early. I like to walk so I figured I might as well kill the time."

"Then I guess it's lucky I happened by," he said.

"How so?" she asked.

"Well, spending my morning roughhousing with a bunch of overgrown boys is fine. But I don't get the chance to walk a beautiful woman to work every day."

"Hmm. Charm," she said wryly. "That does nothing for me."

"Hey, I'll have you know I've had average to medium

success with my charm."

"Well, everyone gets lucky now and again I guess," she said lightly.

He laughed, clearly pleased with the back and forth. "You've got spirit," he said. "I'll give you that. But the real question is," and he paused, for nothing more than dramatic effect if she had to guess, "Do you have a name?"

"I do," Quincy said. "But I only give it out to my friends."

"I bought you coffee," he pointed out when no name was forthcoming.

"So?"

"You accepted. A gift given and a gift received. That constitutes a binding accord. It's contract law."

"I don't know," she said. "I've read several law books in my time and I'm pretty sure coffee exchange isn't binding in a court of law."

"You've read law books?" he asked skeptically. "Plural? Why?"

"Because they were there," she answered. "They make for excellent reading when you can't sleep."

"I suppose that's true," he allowed. They were both quiet for a moment. "You must have a lot of trouble sleeping to get through more than one," he said.

Quincy shrugged. "I guess." That wasn't that weird, right? Lots of people had trouble sleeping. Didn't they? "Who doesn't have trouble sleeping now and again?" she asked, a little defensively.

"Now and again, huh?" he asked, glancing at her sideways. "Yeah, a little insomnia is normal. But I'm not sure two or three law books worth would be considered normal. Or healthy."

"Then I guess I won't mention the medical and forensic books," she said, only half joking.

He looked at her askance, seemingly torn between amusement and concern. She needed to refocus this conversation, fast.

"I like to read and I work in a library. I read more Jane Austen than world encyclopedias but if it's handy, yeah, I read it. I'm not snobby about my literature."

"Oh, pointed and barbed. I like it," he said, accepting the redirect with more grace than she expected. "I'll have you know, I've read my fair share of Jane Austen."

"Really?" she asked, more than a little skeptical.

"Well, okay, I've watched a couple of movies. But I've read Mary Shelley. And I love a good western."

"Frankenstein and cowboys." She pretended to think it over. "I'll accept it."

"Does that mean we're friends yet?" he asked hopefully.

"Nope." She took another sip of the coffee, deciding she could tolerate it. She was more interested in the caffeine than the taste anyway. "But you moved a little closer."

"Tough crowd," he said, looking more gleeful about it than he really had a right. "But I like a challenge".

Oh yeah. Trouble with a capital T. Maybe she should just tell him her name, save herself what she suspected would be more trouble than it was worth.

"So. Roughhousing with a bunch of kids?" she asked.

"Overgrown kids," he corrected. "And yes. I believe our game of Frisbee yesterday counts as *roughhousing.*"

"Do you just roam about campus, looking for new friends?" she asked brightly. "Because suddenly, I'm sounding like the normal one."

Logan laughed. "I'm taking a couple of courses this semester and when I have breaks, I try to find something fun to do. I live a couple miles away but it seems like such a waste to go home, especially when it's nice outside. And even though I'm 10 years older than some of them, I like to think I give them a pretty good run for their money."

Quincy thought back to the game she'd seen yesterday. "I'd say that's fair," she admitted. "What kind of classes are you taking?"

She regretted it the minute she asked. It was a classic mistake. She didn't care what classes he was taking. Or she shouldn't, anyway. It was one thing for him to pester her with questions and endless chatter. It was a whole other matter for her to question him. The more interest she showed, the more he was going to read into it. He already wouldn't go away. She didn't want to give him any encouragement.

"I'm retired Army," he said and she flashed back to the dog tags she'd seen around his neck yesterday. "I always considered myself career military, so now I'm at a bit of a loss." He paused, running his hand through all that beautiful hair. "I have to find something new. Something that matters."

She didn't respond. There was pain in his voice. A story to be told. But she couldn't let him tell it. Nothing personal. Nothing shared. Nothing she couldn't walk away from without looking back. Thankfully, he moved away from it on his own. Maybe he wasn't so willing to jump right in either.

"So I'm taking an anthropology class, a mechanics class, and an English class." He grinned down at her, shaking off his momentary lapse. "Variety is good for the soul."

She couldn't help but smile back. "It's been said."

She stopped at the foot of the stairs leading up to the library and he followed suit.

"This is my stop," she said, surprised by how reluctant she was to go in. It had been almost nice having someone to walk with. Conversation. Coffee. With someone who could have been a friend in another life.

"Here," she said, handing him her empty coffee cup.

"Really?" he called as she jogged up the steps. "That's all I get?" He said it like a challenge.

Quincy pulled the door open and turned, shooting him her own version of his megawatt grin. "That's all."

If it was a challenge he wanted, then a challenge he would get.

Chapter 9

Logan

Logan lost the smile the minute Quincy was out of sight. He reached into his back pocket and pulled out his phone.

"Well?" the voice on the other end asked as soon as the call connected.

"I'm sure."

Silence. "Well," the other man said again. "We knew we were close. What's your assessment?"

Logan stuck his free hand into his pocket, making sure to keep a casual posture. He had been watching Quincy for awhile and he couldn't afford to attract any unwanted attention. The last thing he needed was for her to get spooked and take off again. He didn't think she was close with anyone on campus but he didn't want to draw the eye of anyone who might be watching out for her.

"I think she has no idea. About any of it. She can't sleep and she's reading electrical engineering books. She won't tell me her name and she displays obvious signs of paranoia and suspicion. She clearly knows she's in danger but I don't think she has any idea what it means."

"Interesting. Most patients in her condition have either been heavily medicated for depression by this point or have already ended things. She must be beyond exhausted."

"Well, she definitely looks it and she's always out on her run by 5 every morning. If I had to guess, I'd say she's sleeping less than three hours a night. No one can survive like that indefinitely."

"No, certainly not. We've seen the fallout firsthand. If we're right, her condition may be all that's keeping her alive. But at what cost? We've both seen where this leads."

Logan sighed. "You're right. But what am I supposed to do? We've never gotten this close before and I'm afraid if I push too hard, she'll disappear. She's done it before."

"Keep doing what you think is best. We've tried it my way, with no luck. Maybe we'll have more with yours."

"Thank you. She's not going to make it easy, but I'll get there. I just need a little more time."

"Do you think we have it?" the other man asked and Logan considered.

"She may be exhausted and paranoid but she doesn't seem desperate. Not in the typical sense, anyway. She's going to her class and working everyday, running every morning. Suicidal people don't do things like that."

"The running is undoubtedly a coping mechanism. You're right though. She doesn't seem like she's on the edge yet. But if that changes and you need to step in quickly, be careful. You can't let her see you coming."

Logan hung up the phone and shoved it back into his pocket.

He'd tried to sound confident but it wasn't so easy. He took this assignment seriously. His boss was putting a lot of trust in him. Quincy was the first target he'd managed to get close to. If he messed up, there would be a heavy price to pay.

Quincy. He rolled the name around in his head. He hadn't been sure about her at first. There was really nothing about her that stood out or set her apart. On the surface, anyway. But they hadn't had any other leads and he figured, until they did, he might as well be thorough. He'd kept his distance at first, reading over the paperwork he'd managed to scam from the admissions office. Observing from a distance had managed to pique his curiosity but it hadn't yielded the concrete results his boss had wanted so he'd decided to take a chance and go against his orders. He had thought, if he could create an opportunity for her to see him instead of the other way around, she might chalk it up to coincidence and not bolt the second she was out of eyesight.

The risk had paid off. In the last twenty-four hours, he'd been able to observe some of her symptoms up close. Exhaustion, trouble sleeping, massive caffeine consumption. Taken by themselves, or even together, they weren't that alarming. They were on a college campus, after all. What student didn't run on coffee and fumes? But it didn't explain the severe, almost pathological exhaustion that seemed to surround her like a cloud. Not that she acted tired. It was the little things - the dark circles under her eyes that never seemed to fade, the paleness of her complexion, the constant vigilance to her surroundings, the giant wall she built around herself to keep everyone else out. But spending just a few minutes with her had confirmed his theory. This wasn't his first rodeo after all. The question was, what was he going to do about it?

10

Chapter 10

Quincy

Quincy rubbed at her forehead, annoyed. She'd noticed the headache around 2:00 and wasn't sure whether to feel grateful it wasn't one of her brain splitters or irritated it was there at all. She leaned her elbows on the desk and cradled her head between her hands. The headaches came without warning and existed as two varieties - Painful but Livable and Exploding Aneurysm. The first was far more common, thankfully. They came and went every few days or weeks and they could last for hours. But they were usually treatable with caffeine and heavy-duty ibuprofen. Annoying, yes. Painful? Like stabbing yourself in the head with a screwdriver. But ultimately, life went on. She could function with those headaches; as well as she ever did anyway. But the Dear God, Why? headaches were a whole other story. They were still like stabbing yourself with a screwdriver but this time, the screwdriver was an ice pick and it was being shoved behind your right eye so deep it might as well be making scrambled eggs out of your brain. Sometimes, in rare moments of lucidity, that's exactly what she pictured - a big, ice pick-wielding lumberjack digging whatever was the cause of these wretched attacks out of her brain with no thought to what was left behind.

The pain was bad. And if it was only pain, she could deal. But it wasn't just pain. It was total incapacitation. She couldn't function, because she couldn't see and she couldn't breathe and she couldn't walk. She was completely and entirely vulnerable. During one of these headaches, if whoever was looking for her found her, she would be completely helpless.

The migraines, for lack of a better word, always snuck up on her. Much like her daily headaches, there was never any warning, which meant she had no time to prepare. Maybe if she had a couple of seconds to brace herself, they wouldn't be so bad. Or maybe that would be worse, she didn't know. They didn't usually last as long as her other headaches, only a few minutes. Maybe an hour, tops. Time didn't seemed to really matter in the moment, though. In fact, when they hit, time became irrelevant. It was nothing but waves of agony, crashing over each other again and again in a cycle that seemed utterly endless. She couldn't move. She couldn't speak. She certainly couldn't form a coherent thought.

She had been at the bar in Chicago once when one hit. She'd been carrying a drink to one of her regulars and when she'd doubled up and collapsed, he had been more worried than angry. She had managed to rasp out "No ambulance" before she shut down and George had scooped her up like the fireman he was and carried her back into her boss's office. Even though she'd told them not to, they had been on the verge of calling for help when she came out of it. She was incoherent, they told her. Not even sure she was conscious. She managed to make her excuses, *Just a migraine* and *My doctors know all about it.* but she must have truly traumatized them both because her boss had insisted on driving her home, which she had allowed despite her usual objections only because she was physically incapable of getting there herself.

These attacks always left her exhausted and worn out, unable to really function even after the pain was gone. And not just physically. Mentally, her brain felt like it had been hammered into nothing. Which was a blessing, really. The moments following a migraine were the only times her mind was ever completely silent. In fact, those were the only times she slept, really and truly slept. Deeply. For hours at a time. So there was a silver lining in the end. But Quincy wasn't entirely convinced the sleep was worth the price she had to pay for it.

Quincy sighed and lifted her face, propping her chin on her fist, and glanced around her floor. Another slow night. At least this headache was only the painful variety. She'd already taken a handful of ibuprofen an hour or so ago. Maybe she'd wander down to the break room and get a refill of the very bad but free coffee someone, probably Brandon, had made. Brandon. She sighed again. That had morphed from an awkward dinner invitation the night before into uncomfortably intense attention from a distance, which seemed worse somehow. His chair had been turned towards her section since he'd come in and even though he couldn't see over the balcony from where he sat, it still gave her an odd feeling to know he was down there, staring in her direction. Which she had caught him doing the last time she'd wandered downstairs. He didn't try to speak to her but his eyes followed her as she made a circuit of the floor. So maybe she wouldn't go get a coffee right now.

"Excuse me miss," said a voice behind her. A deep voice. A mocking voice. "I'm looking for a book on British female literary references from the 1800s. Maybe you could help?"

Quincy turned to find Logan not three feet away, smiling that smile and looking extremely pleased with himself.

"Certainly. You can find it on the other side of that balcony," she said, nodding towards the second story railing. "Why don't you take a flying leap."

That was maybe a little harsher than the situation called for but she could blame it on the headache. Logan laughed, though, so clearly he hadn't minded.

"That seems a little harsher than the situation calls for, don't you think?" he asked.

Or maybe he had. She quirked an eyebrow at him, not amused that he was quoting her own internal dialogue back at her. She could think it. He could not.

"Or maybe not. Hey," he put out a hand, suddenly a little hesitant, "is this weird? I didn't mean to freak you out. I actually do need that book and I have no idea where to find it."

"What do you need with a book on 19th century British authors?" she asked skeptically, not ready to let him off the hook yet.

"Female British authors," he corrected. "And I'm taking a class."

"You're taking a class on female British authors?" She looked at him, waiting for him to crack a smile or let her in on the joke, but he didn't flinch.

"I didn't know anything about them," he said by way of

explanation. "So I thought I'd learn."

She felt herself soften minutely.

"A career military man finds himself unexpectedly out of the Army with no backup plan. I took a gamble."

The ice cracked.

"Well, I do love a gambler," she said. Before he could take that comment and run with it, she stepped around the desk. "Come on," she said, before the words that would ruin the moment could escape his mouth. "This way."

Quincy headed towards the back of the floor, winding her way between rows of encyclopedias and atlases to the lesser-used resources. To be honest, this was her favorite place in the library. She had discovered some amazing writers back in these dusty, lonely aisles. She had read Austen of course, and the Bronte sisters. But there were so many more. Charlotte Lennox, Mary Wollstonecraft, Mary Shelley, George Eliot. Eliot being a woman had been a shock sure, but far be it from her to judge anyone for using an alias.

"So, other than Shelley and *Frankenstein*, who's your favorite so far?" she asked.

"What?" Logan said, sounding distracted. Quincy glanced back and saw him looking over the side of the balcony. "Who's that?" he asked, motioning over the rail.

She didn't even need to look. "That would be Brandon" she said, embarrassed.

"Does he always watch you like that?" Logan asked, sounding genuinely concerned.

"He's new" she said. How that excused it, she didn't know. "He doesn't have many friends yet"

"And creeping you out is supposed to help him with that?"

"He's not creeping me out," Quincy argued, trying to

ignore the fact he actually was. "He's just kind of awkward," she said, trying to play it off. "He doesn't really know how to talk to people."

"Yeah, but he's staring at you specifically."

Quincy turned the last corner without bothering to reply, leaving Brandon and his watching eyes behind. "Down this way," she said. "All the British literary references you could want."

She turned and found Logan right behind her. "He asked you out, didn't he?" he said, looking torn between amuse-ment and concern. "And you turned him down."

"Well, he wouldn't be the only one I've shot down recently, would he." Quincy reached up, and up and up, and planted her hands on his chest, giving him a shove back. He moved and she reached around him. "Here. Enjoy," she said, smacking him in the chest with the thick book she'd grabbed off the shelf.

Logan looked down. "*19th Century English Novels*?" he said. "This isn't exactly what I need. I need one about the ladies."

Quincy smiled as she walked away. "Then I guess you'd better start reading."

11

Chapter 11

Q uincy

Quincy marched herself to the maintenance closet and grabbed the vacuum. She'd just taken care of this yesterday, quite thoroughly in fact, but it was a good way to burn some energy. Maybe if she looked busy, Logan would leave and Brandon would just plain leave her alone. What was it with these guys? She could go months without anyone so much as saying hi to her but in the course of two days, she'd managed to pick up not just one, but two guys she couldn't seem to shake. Ridiculous. What were the odds?

She stopped in the middle of a rather aggressive attack on the area rug in the middle of the room. It sat in the middle of the coziest chairs, the ones that tried to invite students to settle in with little success. But she had to admit, who really wanted to hang out in the middle of old, dusty books? The people who appreciated those kinds of things were few and far between these days. And just what *were* the odds? Probably not all that great. Brandon had been with the library for what, a couple of months now? And Logan had just popped up yesterday. For all she knew, he might not even be a student. She had no proof. It was possible they were working together, watching her, clocking her schedules and routines. Working for *him*. The man she'd seen in Boise, and then again in Chicago. Maybe he realized he'd been made so he'd sent in a couple of ringers who knew how to blend. But if that was the case, she thought wryly, they weren't doing a great job. Brandon was too intense and uncomfortable to blend easily with other people and Logan? Well, Logan didn't exactly blend either.

Quincy blew out the breath she'd been holding. She was being overly paranoid. She'd seen the same guy twice before, which made her think he was inclined to follow her himself, not send two overgrown teenagers to do it. She'd been running and looking over her shoulder for so long now that it was hard to know what was normal. Maybe boy drama was just something that happened to everyone once in awhile. Maybe attention wasn't always a bad thing. Professor Michaels seemed on the level so maybe Logan and Brandon were too. Clearly they weren't working together. Logan seemed genuinely concerned with Brandon's attention towards her and it would have been hard not to notice Brandon's ever-darkening expression at seeing Logan trail after her like an overeager puppy. She needed to relax, not worry so much. She was going to set off another headache if she wasn't careful.

Actually, now that she thought about it, her headache seemed to be gone. That was something, she guessed. Maybe the stress of Brandon's disappointment and Logan's effervescence had been exactly what she needed to get her mind off of it. Weirder things had happened, after all. Quincy looked down. This poor rug. Even her overzealous enthusiasm with the vacuum wasn't going to save it. She might as well throw in the towel. She shoved the ancient sweeper back to the closet. It had to be at least 20 years old. Did they even make this model anymore? The wide mouth of the sweeper caught the frame of the door as she tried to wrestle it inside and she stumbled at the sudden stop. It had to weigh at least 50 lbs. Could the library seriously not find an extra $60 in the budget for a new one?

As she headed back towards her desk, she vaguely wondered if an unexpected and sudden accidental trip down the stairs would take care of it or if that would just anger it more. She was so lost in the thought of unintentionally unleashing the anger of an ancient inanimate object that she didn't realized Logan was still there until it was too late to disappear again. He had pulled a stool from one of the computers up to the front of her desk and was propped up reading his book. On 19th century British novels. She found she couldn't even feel any anger. Did the man really never give up? She was exhausted by the sheer weight of his undaunted spirit. What must that feel like? She couldn't even imagine.

Quincy walked around to her side of the desk and hauled herself up into her chair. "See those tables and chairs over there?" she asked him.

"Hmm?" he asked, pretending to be absorbed in his book.

"Or even that couch in the middle of the room. That nice, big, comfy couch? The one that's empty? That might be a good place for you to read. Actually," she said, while being soundly ignored by the man across from her, "now that I think about it, I believe that's actually what those chairs are for." She looked at him pointedly. "Students. Studying."

Without looking up, Logan reached across the desk and pressed his hand over her mouth. She froze at the unexpected contact, tensing under his hand.

"Shh," he whispered. "I'm trying to read."

He pulled his hand back before she had a chance to react, and then glanced up and gave her a wink before turning back to his book. Leaving Quincy with nothing to do but pick up her own book, not entirely sure when the power had shifted back into his hands.

"Quincy?"

She glanced up at the voice, startled to realize Brandon had managed to walk up on her, again, without sound. Logan glanced up, gave Brandon a nod, and turned back towards his own studying, which had grown from a single book into a book, a notepad complete with pen and highlighters, and three encyclopedias. All sprawled across her desk.

"Hey Brandon," she said, giving him a small smile. "What's up?"

"We ordered pizza for dinner," he said after a beat of hesitation. "We have a bunch left over and Clara thought you might want some."

Clara? Unlikely. Unless she spit on it first. If he'd said Hattie had offered to share, Quincy might have bought it. Hattie was friendly, if in a polite, distant way, smiling and offering up a wave as Quincy wandered by her department. But not Clara.

"Um, no thanks," she said. "Pizza's not really my thing," she added, hoping not to sound ungrateful.

Brandon stepped back, glancing at Logan and then back at her, like he was trying not to get caught staring. "Okay," he managed to get out. "No problem. Just thought I would ask."

"Thanks anyway," Quincy said. "That was really nice of

you." And then she waited. But he didn't leave and he didn't speak again. "Well. See you later," she prompted. Brandon turned red at her words.

"Yeah. Sure," he managed, then turned and walked away without a backward glance.

"Smooth," Logan said from his seat slumped on the stool.

"You're supposed to be studying," she said, looking over to see him watching with that same slightly amused, slightly concerned look on his face.

"Yeah, well, it's hard to look away from a train wreck when it happens right in front of you," he drawled, causing an unusual reaction in Quincy. She blushed. She knew she was awkward, thank you very much. She didn't need him pointing it out.

"So my people skills are a little rusty," she defended. "Not everyone can be the cool guy on campus."

"If you're referring to me, then thank you. Saying it myself sounds like bragging." He grinned and she rolled her eyes. "And I was talking about *Brandon* over there. He's not so good with the ladies."

"Oh," Quincy said, a little off balance. She hadn't considered that maybe she wasn't the weird one. "Thanks. I think."

"Don't thank me," he said. "I wouldn't have minded some of that pizza."

"What are you reading?", Logan asked a few minutes later. "It looks way worse than mine and that's saying something."

Quincy looked down in confusion. "*Nautical Mile*. It's about boats."

"Right, yeah, I can see that," he said dryly. "What I'm wondering is, why are you reading it?"

"Why not?", Quincy asked, still confused. "It's better than

73

Emergency Field Medicine for Combat Situations." She paused. "Right?"

"Huh," Logan managed. He seemed to think it over. "I'm not sure. Is it?"

"I thought guys liked boats," Quincy said as she slammed the book shut. "I'm learning about sailing knots and nautical miles and rigging. It's practical."

"You live in Arkansas," he said. "A landlocked state in the middle of the country."

"So?"

"So? So sailing is about the last skill you need to learn."

"One never knows what might come in handy," she sniffed, tucking the book back into her bag. "But fine. If it bothers you so much, I'll read something else. "Hey," she said, pulling *Pride and Prejudice* out of her backpack. "Maybe this is something you'll appreciate."

Logan grimaced. "I'm sure Jane Austen was fine. In fact, about an hour ago I learned she's 'one of the foremost pioneers in romanticism in the 19th century." He tapped the book he was reading with the end of his pen. "But I think I'll stick with my Tom Clancys and my Robert Ludlums."

Quincy shook her head. "That's a shame. I'm sure your little research project will confirm it, but Jane Austen was brilliant."

"What was so brilliant about her?" Logan asked, turning to look at her. "No, really. Defend the statement," he challenged.

"Fine," Quincy answered. "She was funny."

Logan waited, obviously expecting to hear more. "And?" he finally asked.

"And, in an era of Victorian stoicism and dry prose, sarcasm

74

tends to stand out. Especially," she added, "for a woman."

"Ah ha!" Logan exclaimed. "I knew it. You only admire her because she's a woman."

"Not true," Quincy protested. "There were plenty of female writers who only wrote dime novels and fluff pieces. They dumbed it down because that was what was expected. But Austen was smart. And she wasn't afraid to be smart in a culture dominated by men."

Logan smiled.

"What?" she asked.

"I don't doubt you. I just wanted to hear you fight for it. You really like her, huh?"

"I do." Quincy thought about it. "And it isn't just because she's smart and cutting. She writes real people. Even written two hundred years ago, her characters still make perfect sense."

"Well then," he said, "you'd better get to it." He sighed. "And I'd better keep going. If I stop, I may never start again. Hey," he said, "I don't suppose…"

"No," Quincy said, cutting him off. "I'm not going to make you a cheat sheet of the authors you're supposed to be studying."

"I wasn't going to ask that," he said, indignant. "And also, you already know them all, so why not just…"

"Not going to happen," she said grabbing his chin and turning his face back towards his book.

"Fine." He sighed again. "I guess I'll just muddle through."

They sat quietly for a few more minutes, Quincy reading and Logan pretending to read, before she broke the silence this time.

"You're not going to say anything?" she asked.

75

"About what?" he asked, looking up at her.

"I know you heard Brandon say it. My name," she prompted when he still appeared clueless.

"Oh. That." He turned back towards his book, picking up his pen to scribble something completely illegible in his notebook. "Doesn't count if someone else tells me."

Quincy smiled and went back to her book, glancing at the man next to her now and again, thinking she might not mind so much if he decided to stick around for a little while.

12

Chapter 12

Quincy

Quincy wasn't quite ready to go back to her apartment when she got off work so she decided to walk the long way home through downtown. Logan had, surprisingly, not volunteered or insisted on walking with her. She almost felt like they had reached some sort of understanding tonight. He was so pushy and she'd figured, once Brandon said her name, he would become even more impossible. But in a shocking turn of events, he had instead been...gracious. He hadn't rubbed it in her face or been smug, both things he had proven himself more than capable of being. Instead, he had backed off. By not using her name, he was allowing her to set the terms of their friendship. It seemed completely out of character, based on the few interactions they'd had so far. But the disparity made him interesting.

Against her better judgement, she was intrigued. He honestly didn't seem to want anything from her besides friendship. He could be playing her, of course. Maybe he had already known her name and was trying to ingratiate himself after his original approach failed. Who was she kidding? If it had failed completely, he wouldn't still be hanging around. He would have made a move already. And besides, there were easier ways to get close to someone than investing four hours in a ten pound book about Victorian women who liked to write.

Someone called her name and Quincy glanced up. "Hi Mr. Boatright," she answered with a smile.

It was a nice evening, cool and clear, and the locals were out en masse. Mr. Boatright had stepped out onto the sidewalk in front of Sit-A-Spell, broom in hand, and noticed her walking by.

"Quincy, my girl. Come on over here. I need your opinion on something."

Quincy jogged across the square, not minding the pit stop, and followed Mr. Boatright into the store. "Hi Mrs. Boatright," she called.

"Hi sweetheart," answered the woman wiping down the bar. Stout and matronly, Mrs. Boatright served as an impressive foil to her always affable husband, who seemed to take life as it came. Quincy had never seen them not bickering. She had, however, seen the loving glances Mrs. Boatright aimed at her husband when she thought no one was looking and the way Mr. Boatright couldn't seem to keep from touching her every time she came near.

They're not fooling anyone, Quincy thought with a smile.

Mrs. Boatright tossed her rag down and rolled her eyes. "Did Mackey drag you in here to prove him right? Because it's going to backfire."

Quincy grinned. "He just said he needed an opinion."

"I've already given him his opinion but he's too stubborn to hear it," she answered, shooting a mock glare at her husband.

"Well, I'm glad to be of service," Quincy assured her. "Especially if it involves drinking coffee."

"You drink too much of it," Mrs. Boatright scolded. "It's not good for you."

"Interesting opinion, coming from a coffee shop owner," Mr. Boatright observed wryly. "Here," he said, sitting a mug down in front of here. "Tell us what you think."

"What is it?" Quincy asked, leaning down and breathing deep. It smelled amazing.

"That," Mrs. Boatright said, "is our new fall coffee flavor. Mackey doesn't like it."

"It's fluffy coffee. We don't sell fluffy coffee!" Mr. Boatright insisted.

"It's pumpkin cider. Pumpkin cider is not fluffy. It's seasonal. People go crazy for pumpkin-flavored anything this time of year." Mrs. Boatright rolled her eyes again and then smiled brightly at Quincy. "Go ahead dear. Give it a try."

Quincy wasn't really sure how she felt about pumpkin-flavored coffee but she took a tentative sip. "Huh." And then she took another one. "Is there apple in this, too?"

Mrs. Boatright beamed. "I brewed it with apple cider and added a splash of pumpkin creamer. What do you think?"

Quincy looked at Mr. Boatright apologetically. "Sorry Mr. Boatright. But this is amazing." She looked back at the woman trying oh-so-conspicuously not to gloat. "Inspired. Life-changing, even. Definitely a winner."

Mrs. Boatright laughed outright. "For that, you get a cup to go - on the house."

Mr. Boatright sighed. "Well, I suppose if you want to cater to yuppies and hipsters, it is your business too," he said.

"Yuppies and hipsters need coffee just like everyone else," Mrs. Boatright answered, turning back to Quincy. "Now, dear. Tell us how you've been. Anything new to report?"

Quincy took another sip of her coffee, thinking of how to answer. Her usual reaction was to deflect. Give a vague answer and change the subject. But nothing out of the ordinary had happened lately so maybe she could tell the truth this one time and get away with it. Even though she tried not to, she actually cared what these two people thought. And it was nice to have them care about her. So she threw caution to the wind and took the plunge.

"My engineering class is going pretty well. Professor Michaels has taken an interest in me. Says I should be enrolled as a student instead of auditing for no credit."

"Well, he's right," said Mrs. Boatright fiercely. "I never could understand what a smart young thing like you is doing working in a library for minimum wage."

Quincy opened her mouth but Mrs. Boatright wasn't done.

"You read all the time. And not just the squishy stuff like I do. Hard stuff, like doctoring books and law books. It can't be that hard to get a scholarship if you're hurting for money. In fact," she pointed at her husband, "Mackey, go get the checkbook. We're going to pay for this class."

Quincy couldn't help but grin as Mr. Boatright shoved himself up out of his chair, no questions asked.

"Really, it's okay. That's so nice of you," she said, as Mrs. Boatright tried to interrupt, "but it isn't the money. I don't really know what I want to do and until I do, I'm okay with trying out different things. Plus," she smiled gently at Mrs. Boatright to soothe any indignation, "the library is the perfect job. It's close to work and I get to spend most of my day reading. What's not to love?"

"Well," Mrs. Boatright said with a sigh, "I still don't understand it." She pointed her finger right in Quincy's face. "But the offer still stands."

"Yes ma'am. I appreciate it."

They sat in silence for a few more minutes, the women sipping their pumpkin cider coffees and Mr. Boatright drinking a straight black, before what looked to be a late-night study group came in.

"I'd better get going," Quincy said. She stood.

"Make sure you come by tomorrow. We've got a tent set up to sell our new fluffy coffee down by the corn maze. We'll save you a cup."

Quincy looked at Mr. Boatright. "What's a corn maze?"

Mrs. Boatright put a large to-go cup in her hand. "Sweetheart, don't tell me you haven't noticed all the hubbub out on the street tonight?" Quincy just shook her head. "Child, I just don't know about you sometimes. This weekend is our fall festival."

"It's historic you know," Mr. Boatright chimed in.

"Yes, yes," Mrs. Boatright huffed, annoyed at being interrupted. "We have apple bobbing and pumpkin carving and all sorts of games set up around the square and a hayride that takes you out to the corn maze. We always have lots of people."

"It's really great for the local businesses," Mr. Boatright had the nerve to add. "We all get in on the festivities."

"The best part is," Mrs. Boatright said, ignoring her husband's obvious delight in ruffling her feathers, "the streets are blocked off to traffic. If you want to come, you have to park and walk in. The kids have a great time running and playing."

"The petting zoo is always a big hit."

Mrs. Boatright gave her husband a wry smile. "That's always been your favorite."

He leaned across the counter and gave his wife a kiss on the cheek. "Second only to you." Quincy shook her head. "Okay you two. I get the picture." She turned and headed toward the door. "Thanks for the coffee. Maybe I'll see you tomorrow."

Quincy took a sip of her coffee as she pulled the door open and stepped out into the night air. It was a clear, brisk night and the locals really were out in full force, setting up tents and decorating the square with hay bales and pumpkins. She frowned. She had to have been very distracted to not notice. She was slipping. She tipped her head up to look at the stars, letting her irritation go and savoring the moment. The Boatrights' always had a way of making her feel at home, almost like a part of their family. They talked to her like she was important, let her know she mattered. Kind of like Gus and the girls back at the diner in Boise. Just one more reason she was finding it harder and harder to think about leaving, and one more reason why she should. She took another drink of her coffee, shaking off her suddenly pensive mood, and turned to go, slamming face-first into a wall. A moving wall of flesh and cotton. And coffee.

"I'm so sorry," Quincy gasped, wiping awkwardly at the soaked shirt in front of her.

"My fault," the wall said. "I shouldn't have snuck up on you." Quincy finally looked up, recognizing the voice with some trepidation.

"I didn't know you lived out this way," she said.

"I don't," Brandon answered. "But I know you like to walk

this way so I thought I'd take a chance." He paused. "Looks like it paid off."

"Ah," Quincy replied, not really sure what else to say. Maybe Logan was right. This was getting kind of creepy. "Well. I was just heading home actually."

Brandon cut her off. "I was going to offer to buy you a coffee but it looks like someone beat me to it." He nodded towards her cup.

"If you're looking for coffee, you've come to the right place," she said, gesturing behind her towards Sit-A-Spell. "They should be open for another hour or so. Order their fall special," she said, lifting her cup. "You won't regret it."

"Good to know. Listen." Quincy tensed, already knowing where this was going. "Are you going to be at this fall block party they're having tomorrow? I thought, if you were, you might like some company."

"That's such a nice offer," she said, reaching out and squeezing his arm so he'd know she was sincere. Sincerely trying to put an end to his awkward, stilted attempts to ask her out. "But I actually have plans to meet someone here."

"Someone I know?," he asked with suspicion.

She fought the urge to roll her eyes. Seriously, what was with this guy and his complete inability to let things go? And not in a somewhat charming way like Logan. Speaking of Logan ...

"I don't know," she answered casually. "He goes to school at the university, so maybe you've seen him around. He's tall." She stopped for a minute to size Brandon up. "A couple inches taller than you, I'd say." Brandon frowned. "Um, blonde hair. Loud and annoying." How else could she describe Logan? She didn't think Brandon would be interested in hearing about his beautiful eyes and infectious smile.

The idea to use Logan had been a spur-of-the-moment yet brilliant decision. A desperate attempt to ward Brandon off yes, but effective just the same. One of the dearest lessons she had learned was that the most believable lies were based in truth. And if there had been anyone she might go with, it would be Logan. Mostly because she didn't have anyone else, but still.

"Oh. Him. The guy hanging out at the library tonight." The way he said it made it sound like Logan was the gum Brandon had stepped in and couldn't scrape off his shoe. Come to think of it, that had kind of been her experience with him too.

"That's the one," she said. "So, anyway, I guess I'll head out."

"Want me to walk you home?," he asked, in one last shot at the title.

"Oh, wow." Absolutely not. "So nice of you to offer." So concerning of you to offer. "But that's okay. I don't want to stand in the way of your coffee." Brandon started to respond, probably to shoot down her excuse.

"Good night," she said brightly and turned on her heel, speed walking away as quickly as she could go without running. That guy was really starting to creep her out. She couldn't put her finger on why, other than the pushy invitations, but he did. And now, thanks to him, she was going to have to track Logan down, convince him to go to the festival with her, and then convince him it was his idea. Fantastic.

Chapter 13

Quincy

Quincy groaned, reluctant to get up, miserable. The night had been a long one, even by her standards. After tossing and turning for the better part of the night, she'd finally hauled herself upright and grabbed a book off the nightstand, flipping on the lamp as she went. But she hadn't been in the mood to read. She hadn't been in the mood to do anything except sleep. Even with her usual broken and erratic sleep habits, she could usually piece together an hour here, thirty minutes there. But tonight, she just couldn't calm down.

Maybe it had been the coffee. It didn't usually bother her but maybe Mrs. Boatright put something extra in her 'special' coffee. Something to give it more of a kick. Whatever the reason, sleep just hadn't come. Even reading hadn't slowed her mind enough to let her rest, which was unusual. Quincy had been on the verge of going for a 1 a.m. run, almost desperate. She was so, so tired. Tired enough to want to stay where she was, hoping against hope she'd eventual nod off. But miserable and uncomfortable enough to force herself out of bed anyway. Despite herself, Quincy had been looking forward to the festival. She had never been somewhere long enough or been comfortable enough to go to a town event before. That little voice in the back of her head kept nagging her, telling her she was going to be sorry for getting so cozy, sorry she was leaving herself vulnerable. But she buried it beneath the raucous stream of background noise in her brain. One day. She could give herself one day. One day to not think about safety. One day to take life at face value. One day to just assume she'd survive and actually enjoy herself. One day to pretend she could have an actual friend.

Surely he would be there, she thought, trudging towards the bathroom. Logan hadn't mentioned the festival during any of his inane and unending yammering yesterday but he seemed to be everywhere she was lately so she was just taking it on faith he'd pop up. Quincy turned the water on hot, letting the heat fill the tiny room while she brushed her teeth. She wiped the steam off the mirror and winced. She looked like death. Or something really, really close to death. She always had shadows under her eyes. It was a fact of life she had learned to accept but now, the shadows had deepened to a dusky purple and the skin around them looked waxy and pale, making the darkness stand out even more. Her eyes were red-rimmed and her whole face had a chalky, dull look. She leaned over to spit the toothpaste in the sink and grimaced as she came back up. If she went out looking like this, she was going to scare people.

She turned away from the horror and stepped into the shower, sighing as the hot water hit her tired, aching body.

That was the stuff, she thought, closing her eyes and letting it run over her head and down her face. She usually hated water around her eyes but right now, she just didn't care. Maybe it could work a miracle and erase the wretched night she had just spent with nothing but Mr. Darcy and her own mind for company. Not that Mr. Darcy was bad company. Well, he was. At least at the beginning of the book. But he was still usually enough to chase the noise away. If not completely, then enough to let her drift off for a little while.

But last night had been bad. Quincy sank to the bottom of the bathtub, leaving the shower on full-blast, huddling under the heavy stream with her head resting on her knees. Sleep. She just wanted to sleep. Even now, relaxed and surrounded by steam and the sound of falling water, she couldn't let go. Her eyes wanted to close but the banging and pounding in her head wouldn't relent. She thought fleetingly of the sleeping pills she had tried once or twice. The normal dosage hadn't touched her but she had kept them anyway. She bet if she took every pill in that bottle, she would finally sleep. And sleep and sleep. She probably wouldn't wake up. Would that be better, she wondered for a moment. The thought was...appealing. Those pills would probably make everything very, very quiet. So quiet, in fact, that she would never have to wake up again. It was a nice thought, actually. She just wanted to sleep. And if that was the only way to do it –

Quincy jolted as the water suddenly turned cold, jerking her head up and out of whatever place she had just gone. She pulled herself up and shut the water off, shivering as her body adjusted to the shock of the sudden change. She must have been in the shower for a long time to lose the hot water like that. Longer than she thought. Had she managed to nod off for a few minutes? She grimaced, thinking of the path she had been spiraling down. Not that she would ever do something like that, taking enough pills to make sure she slept permanently, but she would do well to not dwell on it too closely. As tired as she was, it was a more attractive choice than she'd like. But still, she would never. Certainly not. Would she? The thought was troubling so she did what she usually did so well - she diverted. She had enough thoughts bouncing around in her head, it wasn't difficult to pick another one at random.

She toweled off and wrapped up in the battered, threadbare fleece robe she'd picked up at a yard sale for 25 cents a few weeks ago and padded barefoot into the kitchen to start the coffee maker. She might have blamed the coffee for keeping her awake all night but she certainly wasn't going to skip it. She'd decided during her night from Hades to skip her run altogether in honor of the one day of freedom she'd granted herself out of spite and indulged in the shower that obviously couldn't work miracles instead. She wasn't as young as she once was and the long, sleepless night had taken a bigger toll than all the hot water in the world would be able to fix. She poured the coffee and took a long, measured drink.

What she wouldn't give for one uninterrupted night of sleep. No pills or migraines required. Maybe instead of the shadows under her eyes growing, they would shrink. Or disappear altogether. Maybe the paranoia that plagued her every waking minute would disappear too. Maybe she'd stop seeing assassins around every corner and could let herself make a friend. Maybe that friend could be a giant blonde teddy bear of a guy who'd be up for a spur-of-the-moment walk around a downtown fall festival.

She stood in her tiny kitchenette, leaning back against the outdated counter and sipping her coffee, taking her time and letting the shower and the coffee work whatever magic they could, when she realized It was darker than usual for, she shot a glance at the clock on the coffee maker, almost 9:00 in the morning. Quincy pushed off the counter and wandered over to the sliding glass door, looking out over her balcony towards downtown. It wasn't raining but it sure didn't look like what she would consider festival weather. Granted, she had never been to a fall festival but still, shouldn't it be sunny? If felt like it should be sunny. Instead, it was overcast and dim, without a hint of break in the clouds.

She stood there with her coffee, debating whether to go. She could use the weather as an excuse; Mr. and Mrs. Boatright would certainly understand and it would mean not having to deal with either of the men in her life. It would be easy. She could stay in her sweatpants and flip on the television for a movie marathon. Or keep working her way back through *Pride and Prejudice.* She could even curl back into bed and...what? Not sleep. And if she couldn't sleep, what was the point? Really, what was the point of any of it? She couldn't sleep, she couldn't make friends, she was utterly exhausted. Life was little more than a habit some days, barely worth living. Maybe it would be better if she just...no.

She shut the thought down. She had told Mr. and Mrs. Boatright she might come. If nothing else, she would see it through for them. She turned and set her half-empty mug on the banister and walked back into her room. Five minutes later, she slipped out the door, hair up and running shoes on. It had been a mistake to skip her run, she'd decided. So she'd just run to the festival - two birds, one stone. Her feet found their steady rhythm as she headed out on her normal loop, allowing the familiar cadence to slow the pounding of her head and her heart, washing away all thoughts save for two - finding Logan and having one single, solitary day of normality.

By the time she reached downtown, Quincy was feeling a little more human. The run hadn't completely cleared her mind but it had helped her tuck the noise back into a corner of her mind, safely away so she could at least function. And while she was still exhausted, she didn't feel desperate enough to wish her life away. Since she was only running the few miles to downtown and not her whole loop, she'd left her ear buds at home and had been able to hear the festival from a mile away.

She dropped out of her jog to a walk when it came into view. She wasn't sure what she had expected but this was, well, *more*. The entire historical downtown area had been blocked off from traffic like Mr. Boatright said and booths and tents had sprung up all over. The botanical garden had been transformed into a giant, open-air greenhouse and dozens of people were milling through the flowers and plants on display. The playground had an assortment of bounce houses and sprinklers set up for the kids, with a park attendant keeping watch so little ones couldn't accidentally slip away while their parents relaxed a few feet away. There was Mr. Boatright's petting zoo off to the side, complete with an area for pony rides.

Quincy smiled as she walked, taking her time and looking at all there was to see. Like Mr. Boatright said, all the local businesses were set up outside their shops in booths or at tables, selling drinks and snacks for quarters. Mr. and Mrs.

Sanders had a big tent set up in front of PaddyO's with bean bag chairs and blankets spread out in the shade and there were several people taking advantage, perusing the piles of books spread out like coffee tables between the seats. Mrs. Sanders waved as Quincy walked by and she smiled, waving back. She felt like she had stepped out of real life and into an old-fashioned episode of *Andy Griffith*. It was the perfect little town.

"Quincy!" Mr. Boatright hollered, and she jogged across the gazebo to find him and Mrs. Boatright surrounded by a small crowd.

"Here you are dear," Mrs. Boatright said, handing something iced to a worn father of three, before turning to Quincy.

"You made it," she said, beaming. "What do you think?" she asked, turning and looking out over the crowd. "Do we know how to throw a festival or what?"

Quincy grinned. "I had no idea it would be this big," she said. "This is amazing."

A block down from the Boatrights' tent, there was a group of tables set up with what looked like a pumpkin carving contest in progress. To her right, a line of people stretched out in front of a giant tank of water, waiting for their turn at a chance to dunk the town mayor as he called out good natured taunts to anyone who missed.

"It's really amazing," she said again. "But I'm sorry the weather isn't better. It's so cloudy," she said, glancing up to where the clouds were still hiding the sun.

"Actually," Mrs. Boatright said, "that's a blessing. It can get so hot some years when the sun is out. There's usually a much bigger crowd at Martin and Lou's book tent. Helps us when it's cooler too. Coffee just sounds better when it's not blazing hot outside."

Quincy supposed that was true, although it wouldn't deter her.

"And speaking of." Mrs. Boatright turned and opened a cooler she had set up under the table. "I iced yours this morning. Figured you might run out here and would need something for a cool down." Quincy accepted the large cup gratefully.

"You look tired dear," Mrs. Boatright said kindly. She put a hand on Quincy's back, patting it maternally. "I hope you don't mind my saying, but you look tired a lot. Is everything okay?"

Quincy sipped her coffee, trying not to let Mrs. Boatright see how on-the-mark she was. "Just a long night," she finally said. "I didn't get much sleep. But the run helped." She held up her cup. "And this is the icing on the cake."

"And that's all it is?" Mrs. Boatright asked, still looking concerned. "Because if it's something else, you know me and the mister would be glad to help. Would insist on it, actually."

Quincy forced a smile, blinking back the tears that seemed to come out of nowhere. She had never had anyone act like they cared about her the way these people did. It was both wonderful and terrible. She had no doubt that Mr. and Mrs. Boatright would do whatever they could to help and, in that moment, she wanted so very, very badly to let them. She had a momentary regret that she had shoved her sunglasses on when she left her apartment despite the cloudy weather. If Mrs. Boatright had seen the tears, it might have been all the excuse Quincy would have needed to let it all out. As it was, the giant aviators did their job and kept even the most kindly of concern away.

"That's all it is. I'm going to try to turn in early tonight. Maybe I can get caught up."

"Well," Mrs. Boatright said, still not looking completely convinced. "I'd better get back to it. I need to brew another batch of the pumpkin fluff the mister detests so much." Mrs. Boatright beamed. "It's selling like crazy."

She gestured out towards the crowds. "You get out there and see what you can see. And then go home and take a nap," she scolded, shaking her finger in Quincy's face. "I don't like wan and worn. It's not a good look for you."

As she scuttled off, Mr. Boatright appeared at Quincy's side. "She's taken quite a shine to you," he drawled lazily. "She worries." He shot her a side glance. "We both do."

Again, the sunglasses were her saving grace.

"I know," Quincy said. "I'll try to drop by more, let her know I'm okay. Let you both know," she added. "See you around Mr. Boatright."

She was a few feet away when she heard Mr. Boatright call after her. "That man you bumped into last night outside the store. Brendan, was it?"

"Brandon," she corrected.

"Yes, Brandon. That was it. Is he a friend of yours?" he asked.

"We work together at the library," she said. "He's new." She frowned. "Why do you ask?"

"Well," he said, hesitating. "I can't put my finger on it, but that boy bothers me. He came in after you left, asking questions. Seemed nice enough," Mr. Boatright said, trailing off. "But still, he just rubbed me the wrong way."

Brandon seemed to have that effect on people, she thought. "He's just awkward," Quincy said, trying to reassure Mr.

Boatright. "I'm sure he doesn't mean anything by it."

"You're probably right," he said, "but still, never hurts to be careful these days."

"No sir, it sure doesn't," she answered. "Thanks for the heads up."

He finally smiled and waved her away. "You have fun now, you hear?" he said. "And come back when you're ready for a refill." He turned back to the booth and Quincy stepped down off the curb and headed into the fray.

There was so much to see and do packed around the square that Quincy didn't really know where to start. But the longer she looked, the more she realized there was a method to the madness. The games and petting zoo were set up in the center of the square, ringed by food and drink tents - everything from grilled burgers, soft pretzels, and pizza by the slice to slushes, snow cones, and cotton candy. And surrounding all of that were the vendors selling handmade goods, all manner of woodworking, jewelry, and clothing.

She took another drink of coffee and decided to just start from the outside and work her way in. It wasn't like she was in a hurry. She might as well enjoy the day. Stick with her determination to have an ordinary day. The sun was finally starting to peek through the clouds and she was more glad than ever she had her sunglasses. She waved at Mr. and Mrs. Sanders again, stacking some of the books scattered between the bean bags and quilts under their tent as she stepped off the sidewalk towards the first group of booths.

She took her time wandering around the crafts, admiring the different odds and ends, watching as others haggled with the owners, looking for a better price on this necklace or that scrolled leather purse. Frankly, she thought anyone with the ability to carve such beautiful swirls and flowers on a piece of leather or etch designs into a piece of glass should be able to set the price at whatever they wanted. But this seemed to be something the buyers and sellers were comfortable with, so what did she know.

A couple of the buyers noticed her looking and tried to wave her in closer but she smiled and shook her head. She was just looking. It didn't make any sense to buy something that's she'd either have to pack around with her or abandon at a moment's notice. She already had enough stuff she was going to have to walk away from. No use adding more. As she wandered, the different scents of food cooking on the grills mingled in the air and she knew it wouldn't be long before she'd be ready to start sampling. She might not be interested in buying the homemade goods scattered around but she was going to enjoy the food.

"Hey Quincy!" someone yelled and she turned to see Caroline from the bakery waving her over. "I didn't think we'd see you today," she said. "Don't you only hold vampire hours?"

Quincy paused, not sure how to respond.

"You know." Caroline said. "We only see you jog through early in the morning and walk home at night. In the dark. Vampire hours."

"Oh," Quincy said. Vampire hours. Super. "Well, you know. Got to get the exercise in where I can."

"I definitely wouldn't be getting up so early if I didn't have to," Caroline said obliviously. "I don't know how you do it. Here," she said suddenly, grabbing a spoon and sticking it in the jar she was holding. "Give this a try."

She shoved a heaping spoonful of red stuff at Quincy, who

took it out of self-preservation but didn't know exactly what to do with it. "What is it?" she finally asked, holding it up to smell it. It looked...wet. And red.

"Jam," Caroline said slowly, clearly having an internal debate about Quincy's intellectual prowess, or lack thereof. "Strawberry," she added, as though that might help. "It's super good. We make it from scratch."

It didn't really look like any jam Quincy had ever seen but it did smell good, so why not? She popped the spoon in her mouth, afraid further hesitation might invoke further wrath. And was shocked.

"Oh wow. Caroline, this is amazing!"

And it was. It didn't taste like the strawberry-flavored stuff she'd bought at the store. Quincy could taste the real strawberries and something else, something she couldn't quite put her finger on.

"What is that?" she asked Caroline. "It's almost...minty, maybe?"

Caroline beamed. "We added some fresh mint leaves while we were boiling the strawberries. And we don't use any of the preservatives and fillers big companies use." She shrugged. "It's a little runny but totally worth it."

"For sure." Quincy agreed. "I wasn't planning to buy anything today but give me a jar of that." Jam was an acceptable purchase, she decided. She'd eat it for breakfast a couple of times and be good to go. Besides, it was too good not to take home for later. She gave Caroline her money and tucked the jar into her backpack, $5 well-spent.

"Bye Quincy," Caroline waved and Quincy stepped back off the curb, deciding she'd take a look at the games before grabbing some lunch.

The games had a fair mix of children and adults lined up to take part and it was fun watching what everyone was doing. There was a booth where kids were tossing rings at a pyramid of 2-liter soda bottles, trying to land a ring around the top of one of the bottles to win their prize. Quincy grinned as a tiny girl who couldn't have been much older than five lumbered past her, trying and failing to carry her soda bottle back to where her mother lounged with a toddler, sweaty and red in the face, sprawled across her lap, sound asleep.

Behind the ring toss, a group of people were walking in a circle in time to a fiddle being played with pizzazz by an elderly gentleman who looked to be roughly 105 years old. He was wearing a pair of worn overalls, one strap flung haphazardly off his shoulder, working the bow over the strings with hands that looked gnarled and twisted from either years of heavy labor or arthritis. Most likely both. But it didn't seem to hamper him in the least. The bow flew and both the people playing the game and those watching from the sidelines were clapping their own hands in time with the music. All the setting lacked, she decided, was an old guy playing a jug.

Quincy stood and watched the way the fingers of the man's left hand played over the strings, pushing at one here, letting go of one there. There was a rhythm to it, a kind of symmetry that absorbed her. The man's right hand slid the bow back and forth across the strings, almost too quickly for Quincy to keep up with. The movements of his fingers were subtle, set apart only by the tiny differences in angles and the sounds they produced. She stood watching those minuscule movements in a daze, every sound except the notes of the fiddle dying away until even the noise in her head was blissfully silent.

She stood that way, absorbed with the man's hands, listening to the music while the breeze played across her hair, until the music stopped abruptly, jarring her out of her reverie. The players froze and Quincy realized they each stood on a paper number staked to the ground. The old fiddle player dropped one of his gnarled hands into an upside-down hat propped up beside him and called out "Four!" A cheer went up as the sweet little lady standing on the number four stepped out of line and walked to a row of tables stacked with cakes that Quincy hadn't even noticed. A woman was standing behind them and handed the winner a cake that was sitting in the spot marked with a paper four just like the circle on the ground.

"You act like you've never seen a cake walk before," a voice beside her piped up.

Quincy jumped, startled at the sudden intrusion. But only for a moment. "I haven't," she said wryly, not bothering to glance over to where Logan had suddenly materialized out of the crowd. "And I'm not entirely sure what the point is."

"The point," Logan said succinctly, "is to win cake."

"Ah," Quincy said. "Yes. That does explain it."

"Come on," he said suddenly, grabbing her hand. "They're getting ready to start back up." He dragged her over to the circle and dropped two tickets into a hat held out to the walkers by a little girl and stepped onto the paper number nine at his feet.

"Come on," he said again, giving her a little tug. She stepped up onto number ten.

"What are we supposed to do with a cake?" she asked. "Do you have a car? Because I walked here."

"You really overthink things, you know?" he said lazily.

Quincy was gearing up to respond, to defend herself. Of

course she overthought things. Life wasn't easy when an unknown entity was following you around for unknown yet assuredly despicable reasons. But she didn't have the chance because just then, the music started back up. Logan nudged her in the back and she started walking.

"The trick," he said from behind her, "is to keep one foot on a number at all times." Quincy glanced down at her feet to make sure she was following along. "That way, once the music stops, you don't have to scramble to find one."

They kept moving at a snail's pace around the circle, Quincy being careful to not overrun the man in front of her. A couple of kids, siblings by the look of them, broke away from the quilt their parents had laid out on the grass for lunch and were darting in and out of their circle, chasing each other and laughing like only children could. The brother finally caught up to the sister and grabbed her from behind, tripping her and sending them both rolling. The laughter hit a new level and the people walking to the music couldn't help but smile too. Childhood was so simple, Quincy thought. Nothing but sunshine and laughter. Or at least it should be. She missed that.

The music stopped as abruptly as it did before and the line halted. The old fiddle player reached into his hat again and this time produced the number twelve. Quincy closed her eyes and shook her head.

"Now I'm going to show you what we do with a cake if we win," Logan said, jumping out of line to claim his prize.

14

Chapter 14

Quincy

It didn't surprise her at all that Logan had won. Of course he had. She followed him to the cake table and watched him accept some sort of pie from the woman presiding over the table, his smile and wink enough to make her blush. He had a way with people, she'd give him that.

"Come on." he said, turning Quincy towards a tree set a little way from the main festivities. "I've got a blanket in my pack. We can spread it out in the shade and take care of this," he said, holding up his pie.

"Take care of it?" Quincy said skeptically. "Like, the whole thing?"

"Please," he said dismissively. "Like you can't eat half a pie."

He transferred the pie to one hand and used his other to grab hers, pulling her towards the tree. "Here," he handed her the pie and pulled his backpack off. Before he tossed it on the ground, he reached inside and pulled out a thick flannel blanket that he spread on the ground around the tree's trunk. Then he toed his shoes off and sprawled down in the shade.

"This will work. Come on," he said, reaching for the pie, "you know you want to." She really kind of did.

"Fine," she said flopping down on the other side of the blanket. She dropped her backpack and kicked off her own shoes. "What kind of pie is it?" She scooted closer, watching as Logan unwrapped the pie. He handed her a fork.

"Gooseberry," he said with delight. "I haven't had gooseberry in years!" As amazed as he'd been that she'd never seen a cake walk, she wasn't about to admit she'd never heard of a gooseberry.

"Here," he said, setting the pie down on the blanket between them. "Dig in."

He did, with gusto, so she followed suit. She wasn't sure what a gooseberry was or why they were green but with Logan inhaling it like a starving man, she supposed it couldn't be that bad. She took a small bite and smiled. Not bad at all. They sat in silence for a couple of minutes, enjoying the pie and letting the festival wrap around them.

"I suppose," she said after awhile, "that if we're going to roam the festival together, and if I'm going to eat your pie, then maybe you should call me Quincy."

Logan nodded gravely, keeping his eyes fixed on the pie. "Does this mean we're finally friends?" he asked, scooping up another forkful.

"Well," she said, considering. "Despite my excellent wards and security measures, you did manage to claw your way in so," she paused and he finally looked up, "I suppose it does."

"Never doubted it for a minute," he said, smiling at her. "And it's 'cobbler'."

She shook her head. She had so much trouble keeping up with this guy. "What?"

"It's cobbler. You keep saying pie, but this is a cobbler. As you friend, I feel a sincere obligation to educate you."

"What's the difference?" she asked. Pie, cobbler, whatever. It was good either way.

"A pie," he said haughtily, "has a bottom crust."

He speared another piece of the pie, or cobbler, with his fork and held it up so she could see.

"Note the distinct lack of bottom crust. Clearly this is cobbler. Plus," he said, shoving the fork in his mouth, "look at this crumb topping. This is the most amazing thing ever."

She did have to admit, she'd never had anything with a top crust like this. It was crumbled and golden brown, which she would normally have frowned upon, but the juices from the pie/cobbler thing had soaked into the crust and softened the bottom layer, leaving it gooey and delicious.

"It's called streusel," he said helpfully. "In case you didn't know that either."

"Well, whatever it's called," she said, tossing her fork down, "I can't eat anymore."

"Oh, come on," he retorted. "We're just getting started."

"Not if we're going to hit up that pretzel stand over there," Quincy said, pointing in the general direction of the food tents.

"You know what? You're right." Logan tossed his fork down too and dusted off his hands. There was still almost half a pie left and Quincy felt justified in her smugness.

"How are you going to walk around with a half a pie, or cobbler, or whatever, for the rest of the day?"

He scoffed. "Like that's a problem." He held the pie up over his head. "Free cobbler," he bellowed. "Come and get it!"

"Logan!" Quincy exclaimed, aghast. "We ate out of that container. You can't just give it away!" But apparently you could.

"Is that gooseberry baby?" a sweet lady with a soft drawl asked.

"Yes ma'am," he answered. "Homemade, straight from the cakewalk. We ate all we could and decided to pass it on."

"Well bless your hearts," she beamed. "Gooseberry's my favorite. Thank you baby," she said again, in the way that only southern women could get away with. "You've made my day."

She turned away. "Clara Belle!" she yelled. "Look what I got for us!"

She disappeared into the crowd and Logan turned back towards Quincy. "See. No need for thinking." He jumped to his feet. "Come on."

Clearly, Quincy thought, climbing reluctantly back to her feet. She still couldn't believe someone had taken a half-eaten pie from them. Was that sweet little lady and Clara Belle really going to eat something strangers had just been eating? She glanced over to where they'd fanned themselves out under a big shady tree. Apparently so.

"Things are just different this far south." Logan remarked. Her thoughts must have been written all over her face because he grinned. "They're a trusting lot. Especially the older generation."

"I suppose," she said. "You'd have to be to eat after complete strangers."

"Well, worry about it later," he said. "Let's go get some pizza."

Quincy trailed Logan through the food vendors, watching in wonder as he bought them massive slices of pizza, a couple of soft pretzels, a giant plate of nachos, and then two ice cream cones.

"Here," he said, handing one over. She almost groaned.

"Where are you putting it all?" she asked in amazement.

"I'm not exactly outpacing you. You've eaten everything I have," he bluntly pointed out.

"Yeah, well, I wish I wouldn't have. I'm stuffed."

"You've got enough room in you for one little ice cream cone," he challenged, taking a big bite off the top of his.

She sighed and gave her own a good lick. "I suppose," she said doubtfully.

"You're not a calorie counter, are you?" he asked disdainfully. "Food should be enjoyed, not measured."

"Easy for you to say," she snapped. "Guys never seem to worry. It takes actual effort to stay in shape you know."

He shot her an appraising look. "You're a runner, aren't you?" he asked. "I'm army. I know a runner when I see one."

"So?" she asked.

"So you have to worry about it a lot less than other people. Which means no complaining."

He did have a point, she conceded silently. It didn't change the fact that she had spent the entire afternoon eating and was so full she could barely breathe, but somehow she still found room for the cone.

They walked as they licked, stopping to watch the pony rides for a few minutes. With Logan momentarily preoccupied with something besides talking her ear off and stuffing her full of junk food, Quincy took a moment to look around. The squares were still packed with people, although the families with younger children were scarcer than before. She glanced at her watch, surprised. It was later in the afternoon than she'd thought. It wouldn't be much longer before the sun began to set. They had passed Caroline and her bread and jam again an hour or two ago and she'd mentioned there were going to be fireworks once it was dark. Quincy hadn't intended to stay this long, let alone stick around until dark, but she didn't want to go. Her one day of normalcy was wrapping up too quickly and she hated to see it end.

Logan nudged her. "Hey, there are some chairs open in the shade over there," he said, pointing towards the south end of the fair. "Want to snag them?"

Quincy nodded gratefully, ready to get out of the sun. It certainly wasn't as hot as it would have been the month before, but without the cloud cover, the sun was surprisingly strong. She let Logan plow a path through the masses and they both collapsed down into the chairs right with relief.

"Well," he asked. "What now?"

"What now?" she repeated. "Can't we just, I don't know, *sit* for a few minutes? Preferably in silence," she added meaningfully.

He laughed. "If you're trying to tell me I talk too much, don't bother. Meaner folk than you have tried and failed."

She couldn't help the small smile and he smiled back, reaching up and tapping her nose with a finger. "The sun really brought those freckles out."

She pushed his hand away. "Is it bad?" she asked, almost afraid to know the answer. She had kept her freckles covered as Kara Scott and Grace Elliott, just like she'd changed her hair and eye color, height and weight. But she'd gotten tired of the charades and had decided to forego the disguises as Quincy. It was still a different look, after all, than she'd ever gone with and no one had to know which was her actual appearance. But maybe she should have covered the freckles up after all.

"Nope," he answered, poking at her face one more time. "They're cute."

"Stop it," she said, swatting at his hand again. But it was only a halfhearted swatting. This was her day to be normal. Maybe it was okay to get a compliment. The fiddle player was still at it but the cakewalk had folded for the day. The table that had been loaded with different cakes, pies and/or cobblers, and cookies had been cleared off and the paper numbers pulled up off the pavement. Now that the game was over, he had settled into softer tunes, slower, lulling Quincy into a daze. Her lack of sleep from the night before had been held at bay by the constant walking and sugar Logan was pushing on her but now that she was still, the music filled the corners of her mind, overwhelming the static and the noise she'd shoved off to the side just like before. She let it roll over her, closing her eyes and drifting along with the music. She wasn't sure how much time had passed but suddenly, she felt an absence beside her and knew Logan had moved away. She opened her eyes and saw the fiddle player had stopped for a break and Logan had moved over to talk quietly to him. When he saw her eyes open, he waved her over and she reluctantly pushed up to her feet.

"What are you doing?" she asked, curious.

"Mr. Edgar here was just showing me his fiddle. He made it himself."

Mr. Edgar, whether that was his real name or something Logan had made up on the spot, ran his hands along the neck. "Carved the body out of an old maple in my backyard what got struck by lightning," he said. "Weren't easy, and it took a couple of tries, but I got her eventually."

"Wow," Quincy said. "That's...amazing." And it was. It was hard to believe this old farmer had made such a beautiful piece out of nothing.

"Can I hold it?" Logan asked suddenly.

"Logan!" Quincy scolded. "You can't hold someone's hand-made fiddle. You could break it."

Logan looked almost hurt by that. "I'm not going to break it," he said as Mr. Edgar held it out willingly. He took it, holding it softly by the bow and the body.

"Here," he said after a minute, pushing it suddenly into her hands. She took it out of reflex, not really sure what to do with it.

"Like this," Mr. Edgar said, helping her curve her left hand around the neck the way she'd seen him do. He picked up the bow and pushed it into her right hand. "Go ahead Little Missy," he said. "Give her a pull and see what happens."

"I know what's going to happen," she muttered darkly. "Horror. Terror. Nothing even resembling music."

But no one seemed to be paying them any attention and Mr. Edgar didn't seem terrified that she was about to desecrate his beautiful fiddle. Logan grinned at her.

"Come on Quince," he said. "What's the worst that could happen?"

Now there was a happy thought. But she shoved it aside. Day of normalcy. Day of normalcy. Sure, she decided. Why not. As she adjusted the hand holding the neck of the fiddle slightly, letting her fingers slide along the strings a little more, she felt the noise in her mind finally die. Completely. Totally. She felt her focus narrow sharply and then blast outward, both taking in and shutting out everything else around her. Her eyes swept the crowds without really seeing as her right hand brought the bow up towards the fiddle. The sight of Mr. and Mrs. Boatright pointing at her was there and gone. Caroline, still at her booth, tucked into a cozy chair behind a table, taking a long drink of something cold and dark. Brandon, standing off to the side of the main action, watching her with a speculative look in his eyes. The screams and yells of excited children, racing to escape both their parents and sleep for as long as they could. She played. She didn't know how long she played or what she played, but when she stopped, there was total silence. And then applause. Loud, exuberant applause that woke her slowly from the haze she had fallen into.

"You should have said something, Little Missy," said Mr. Edgar, taking the fiddle back and giving her an approving nod. "You play better than me."

"What?" She was confused. She couldn't play the fiddle. Playing an instrument took years of work and it's not like it's the kind of skill one could forget having. But she had played it. She didn't really remember it, but there it was. She turned towards Logan, who was watching her with an almost sad look on his face.

"What's wrong?" she asked, jarred more by the look on his face than by the revelation of her stunning hidden talents.

"Nothing," he said after a long moment. He forcibly shook the mood off, trying to smile, but she could tell it was an effort. "Nothing at all. I just didn't know you played."

"Well, is that really a surprise?" she asked, trying to ignore that it was a surprise to her too. "You've only known me for a couple of days."

"True, true," he admitted. "Still, that's the kind of thing you brag about. You know, *Hi, I'm Quincy and I could be a concert violinist.* Something like that."

"Ah," she said, allowing him to fall back into their familiar pattern of banter. "I'll keep that in mind for next time." She gave him a smile, coaxing a small but sincere one from him in return.

"Come on," he said. "Let's go get something for dinner and settle in for the fireworks."

"Dinner?" she asked. "You can't be serious?" Was he? She was pretty sure he was.

"What? We haven't hit the taco stand yet," he said. "It's our thing."

15

Chapter 15

Q**uincy**

It hit without warning, the pain slamming into the base of her skull and jolting her out of a shaky, shallow sleep. It was razor sharp and hot, searing itself behind her eyes and stealing her ability to think of anything beyond the pain. Her breath came in gasps as her fingers dug into the sheets beside her face. She curled her body as tightly as she could, knowing it wouldn't help - it never did - but it was instinctive and the only thing she could do. Quincy didn't know what caused these attacks but they came on hard and they came on fast. She much preferred the attacks that hit her when she was awake. She usually had a few, very few, seconds before the pain hit when she could feel it building. It wasn't enough time to do anything but brace herself, but at least she could do that. When she was asleep, she had nothing. The attacks were always immediate and the shock of being jolted awake left her confused and even more disoriented.

Quincy did her best to breath through the pain but it wasn't easy. She shoved the heels of her hands into her eyes, trying to grind the pain away. A sudden, sharp spike left her gasping, the agony leaking out in short, pitiful bursts of air. Tears made their way silently down her cheeks, squeezing out around her clenched eyelids. There was nothing in that moment, these moments, but pain. She was completely vulnerable - that was the only coherent thought she could form. She was vulnerable and if they found her now, she would be helpless. It was a terrible feeling, that helplessness. She wasn't a helpless person. She made sure of that. She planned. She plotted. She lived in a constant state of preparedness. Like a doomsday hoarder, she was constantly alert and vigilant. But this, she couldn't control. She didn't know what caused these attacks and she couldn't treat them. They came when they came and they left her paralyzed and, later, exhausted.

The waves of pain stretched on and on and Quincy wasn't sure how much time had passed when her body finally started to relax. That was usually the first indication the pain was subsiding, and the rest quickly followed. Her thoughts started to clear, the roar that had sent spikes of pain through her head settling back to its usual angry buzz, and then quieting completely. If there was a plus to these attacks, it was the momentary silence that followed them. She was soaked in sweat but couldn't muster the energy to roll herself out of bed. A hot shower would probably help. She could rinse off and let the heat and the steam soak into her tight, trembling muscles and soothe the soreness in her neck, not to mention chase the aching cold from her bones. But the silence and absence of pain was pulling at her, lulling her back towards sleep. She was weak and exhausted and completely unable to fight it. Why not sleep when she could? Post-migraine sleep was the best sleep she ever got. When she woke up in the morning, she would no doubt be sore and weak but for right now, she could appreciate the reprieve. Her last thought before being pulled completely under was that she'd better enjoy it while she could.

16

Chapter 16

"*Murderers are not monsters, they're men. And that's the most frightening things about them.*" *Alice Sebold*

The shadows haunt. The dark hides our secrets. The girl feels safe here, in the dark. She believes it helps her, it hides her. It does not. It only hides the monsters in the shadows.

She knows this. *We* know this. But still she trusts.

* * *

Quincy

Sunday morning came late by Quincy's standards. She had managed to fall asleep almost immediately after the migraine disappeared and didn't wake up until 6:00, which left her feeling almost decadent as she yawned and stretched her arms and legs. There was a bit of chill in the apartment because she hadn't turned on the heat the night before but the weather forecast was calling for a bright, clear day with a slight breeze which should warm things up nicely. Her eyes and neck ached from the migraine last night and already she could feel the familiar throbbing in her head, the flow of thoughts threatening to avalanche, her body aching to hit the pavement and clear it all away but it was so nice not to move and she didn't think she had the reserves to push herself to run. She knew she should after only getting in a partial run yesterday but these headaches always left her feeling so wrung out. Running would only make it worse.

So instead, she started running through her agenda for the day. She had nothing pressing, which was standard for her, but since it was Sunday she also had no school and no work, which was less standard. Weekends always seemed to loom before her, an endless expanse of countless hours to fill and very little with which to do so.

The festival yesterday had helped pass the time, what now? She had neglected her security protocols recently and her one day of normalcy hadn't helped. She should probably use today to catch up. She wished she could blame her lapse in judgement on Logan, but if she were being honest, she knew she had started to let things slide weeks ago. It had been months since she'd last spotted a tail and, true or not, she was starting to feel safe. But it wasn't real. It was just a false sense of security and she knew it. She wasn't usually so quick to jump into a friendship, or whatever was going on with Logan, and she knew she needed to put a stop to it. Or at least take a step back to recover her equilibrium. He might be interesting and he might be a breath of fresh air in her otherwise mundane, routine existence, but he was also a safety risk and she couldn't allow that. Today would be the first step back in the right direction.

Every time she moved to a new place and established a new identity, she learned the town and mapped out numerous escape plans that could be enacted on a moment's notice. Her primary escape plan, if and when she needed it, was the train station on the outskirts of town. In today's climate, trains were one of the last options most people considered, which made them one of her first.

It had been awhile since she ran through the logistics of this particular plan and she didn't like being out-of-date. She liked to practice her escapes to get her timing down and keep on top of any possible hang ups that could get in the way, construction and detours being two of the biggest issues, and it had been too long since she'd checked either of those. The train station was exactly 10 miles from her apartment, which was runnable if the need arose, but it was quicker and more efficient to take a bus from a stop near the college.

She finally rolled herself out of bed and headed to the kitchen to jump start her coffee pot. She had finally finished *Pride and Prejudice* last night so while the coffee perked, she sat at her small kitchen counter with her newest book - *War and Peace* was her light reading at the moment. She had read it before, of course, but it never hurt to brush up on the classics. She would have to stop by PaddyO's on her way back, maybe kill a couple of hours curled up under one of their book piles with an atlas and scout another emergency location. Then she'd grab an ice cream from the soda fountain and walk back to the apartment. That sounded like a pretty good day.

Her walk to the bus stop took 20 minutes since it was just outside the far end of campus and when she got to the stop, she double checked the bus times to make sure her last check-in was still accurate. Then she settled onto the seat and waited exactly eight minutes for the number five bus to pull up. As she dropped into a seat near the back and closest to the emergency exit, she frowned. 28 minutes to catch the bus was a long time to wait when she needed out *now*.

She might need to consider changing her primary escape route. Maybe option four, buying a bike, would be better? Although there were numerous issues with that, too. One of which was having the bike with her when she needed it. She could ride it to school and work but if she were spotted at either of those places, she might not have the time or ability to go out the entrance she was parked by. She supposed she could buy several bikes and park them at convenient locations, like school, the library, and on one of the squares downtown? She really didn't want to spend enough money to do something that would, with 100% certainty, result in multiple losses when she had to leave. Bikes weren't cheap and they didn't come in a bubble – you needed helmets and chains and locks to go with them. And reflectors, in case one was needed after sundown. Plus, the chance of theft when you left a bike parked in the same place was high. She definitely couldn't afford to depend on a bike that wasn't there when she needed it.

The bus pulled into the train station and she sighed, knowing she had been spinning again. It happened so easily. She shot a glance at her watch to confirm the time – five minutes. The dependability of this route made her feel a little easier about how long it took. Total time of 33 minutes from the moment she left the apartment to the train station. Could the time really be improved significantly with a bicycle? Maybe she could borrow one from a neighbor and test it. But then she would have to talk to a neighbor. And borrowing something made a larger impression in someone's mind than a quick "hello" on your way past. She shook her head and attempted to focus. She would worry about that later. Right now, she needed to focus on the plan in front of her.

She took her time as she got off the bus, checking as nonchalantly as possible for security cameras and vantage points that could be used against her. The bus stopped at a turnstile approximately 12 feet from the train depot door, a big glass number that opened and closed on motion sensors. Glass was less than ideal when it came to cover but it was thick, bullet-resistant if she were guessing, so that was something. There was a security camera above the doors pointing out toward the drop-off zone that would get anyone entering from that point. There was also another camera right inside the doors that caught the main thoroughfare of the station, all the major traffic points, and one located outside of the main exit, scanning people going. The three cameras covered the vast majority of the station but they did have one big weakness – they were stationary. The main ingress and egress points were covered but someone aware of the cameras' positions could move through the station using the blind spots created by their lack of movement. It wasn't a lot of space but Quincy had visited the station several times and had developed a pattern that should keep her off the cameras most of the time, and when it didn't, she was able to at least keep her face hidden.

She walked this pattern now, making sure no new security

measures had been added. It took her exactly three minutes to maneuver through the station, avoiding the cameras, and reach the ticket counter. So, 36 minutes. Of course, no matter how many times she practiced, there were too many variables to pin down an exact time. If she performed perfectly, her time was still dependent on what time of day she needed to catch the bus, how crowded it was, how many stops it needed to make on the way to the train station, how many people were milling around, and how many people were in front of her at the ticket counter. Her best guess was she could have her ticket in hand somewhere between 30 and 45 minutes. She preferred an exact timetable but there wasn't much else she could do to narrow it down. She knew the plan, knew the route, and knew the variables. It was as solid as it was going to get.

She strolled up to the departure board and checked all of the current destinations. Her primary plan was to buy a ticket on the first train out of town, regardless of destination, using her current name. There were usually trains coming and going every five minutes or so, which meant the train would ideally leave before her assailants had a chance to catch up with her. The first thing they would do would be to check the ticket counters to confirm her destination. Once they had that, they would be off in pursuit, leaving her free to buy another ticket under a different alias to anywhere else. It was a solid plan, she knew. Not foolproof maybe, but solid. The timing was close and the destinations hadn't changed. Cameras were in the same positions as last time and the foot traffic was still heavy enough to provide some camouflage if needed. All things considered, Quincy felt pretty safe. She wasn't going to need to change her primary escape plan after all. She would still spend some time running through her other options, just to make sure they were still valid too, but she didn't feel the urgency to brush up on them that she'd felt about her train plan.

Without any real plans for the rest of the day, she decided she might as well sit for a few minutes, maybe do some people watching. Mr. and Mrs. Boatright loved weird stories and a train station seemed like the perfect place to find them.

She settled back on one of the benches outside the range of the cameras and looked around. Nothing particularly interesting caught her eye. There was an older lady on the bench directly across from her. She had a bag of yarn sitting on the seat next to her and was knitting what looked to be a large scarf. Or maybe a blanket. Either way, it looked like she had been there awhile. There was a young couple arguing with a ticket agent at the west counter. Quincy couldn't hear what was going on but the couple seemed very upset. The man had his hand flat on the counter in front of him but was obviously working to keep it from clinching into a fist. He was big and burly, with dark hair and a beard that covered the entire lower half of his face. He towered over the petite red-headed woman with him, who tugged on his elbow, trying to pull him away from the counter. Her eyes were red and teary, and her half-hearted efforts weren't even making a dent in his tantrum. As for the ticket agent, she wasn't even blinking an eye. Despite the man's significant height advantage, she was clearly unimpressed. Just another angry traveler, taking out his frustrations on someone who had no control over the situation. She looked like she'd heard it a million times before.

Quincy continued to watch and marvel at the ticket agent's

ability to remain utterly unflappable in the face of pointless rage until something strange happened. In the middle of the man's renewed diatribe, Quincy saw the ticket agent's eyes shift to the left, furrow in confusion, and then her entire demeanor changed. Where she looked almost bored before, now she looked horrified. Quincy glanced reflexively over her shoulder, trying to find what had caused the sudden, extreme change. Her eyes locked with the glazed gaze of a woman standing behind her and she jerked away in shock.

17

Chapter 17

Quincy

Blood. So much blood. It covered the walls. It covered the floor. And it covered the woman staggering from the north rest area hallway. She was grasping at her neck, which seemed to be where the blood was coming from. She had caught the attention of almost everyone in the depot now, having made it almost to the north ticket counter before collapsing against a wall. Her mouth was open but she wasn't making a sound, other than the wet, gurgling noises of someone who wasn't long for this world. No one had moved toward her, all too stunned and too afraid to do more than stare frozen in shock.

The woman was pretty, if you could get past the blood smeared over her face and in her hair. She was wearing a trendy, inexpensive suit, probably from one of the department stores in the commercial district that catered to business women on a budget. Quincy knew these observations were random and completely inappropriate given the circumstances. But worries over random observations had been pushed to the very back of her mind by the ever-present buzzing in her head, once shoved and locked in a back corner of her mind, now flooding over the walls she had put up to keep it back, blocking out the noise of the station and the screams that were coming from some of the other passengers.

Quincy started to move towards the woman without conscious thought. She felt like she was moving through a fog. Or maybe a dream, because she was suddenly in front of the woman, kneeling in one of the puddles of blood that were forming around the woman, leaking out from between her clasped fingers. The scene had a very surreal feel to it, kind of soft and misty around the edges, like the world was out of focus just outside the line of her periphery. Quincy wasn't sure why, but she found herself reaching forward, tugging the woman's hands from around her neck. *Lacerated carotid*, she thought to herself.

To the still stunned crowd around her, she said, "I need something to hold pressure."

When no one immediately moved, she looked up. "A towel, shirt, blanket, something - anything!" she snapped.

Her tone of voice must have finally broken through because the angry guy from the counter stepped forward, whipped his hoodie over his head, and handed it over without a word. He knelt hesitantly near her, ready to help if she needed anything else. *Not so angry now*, Quincy thought distantly. She spared a quick glance at his face, which was white as a sheet, and decided to cut him some slack. He was the only person in the entire station who had made any sort of move to help, so maybe he wasn't as bad as he'd seemed from a distance.

Quincy glanced back down at the girl. Up close, she looked

much younger than Quincy had originally thought. Twenty-four, maybe twenty-five. And then Quincy panicked. What was she doing? This little girl was bleeding to death under her hands. What did she know about treating gaping wounds and blood loss? It was so, so bad. Even without medical knowledge, everyone knew a torn carotid artery was bad. Like, fatally bad. And here she was, getting ready to push down on the poor girl's neck. She blamed the foggy dream state that had washed over her when she saw the blood. It wasn't the first time the misty, surreal aura had prompted her to act without any real thought and do something she had no idea how to do. Even yesterday, she thought, with the fiddle. All it led to was trouble. And she didn't need any more trouble. But she couldn't worry about trouble right then. She couldn't worry about anything that wasn't right in front of her.

"Don't worry," she told the girl, and attempted a smile. "I need to push down on your neck to help stop the bleeding. It will probably hurt but I need you to hang on, okay?"

The girl's eyes had been half-closed until Quincy had spoken but she'd looked up at the sound of her voice and locked onto Quincy. Quincy folded the hoodie as tight as she could and then pressed it against the wound, lightly at first but gradually building pressure until her whole weight was pressing down. The girl flinched but otherwise didn't react. She kept her eyes on Quincy, though, never looking away. Quincy felt like she was a lifeline. That as long as the girl was looking at her, she was still there. So Quincy looked back. She looked back and didn't blink.

She looked back until something warm and wet broke across her hands and when she finally looked away, she wished she hadn't. The bleeding might have been slowed by the pressure bandage but not stopped. It had soaked through the shirt and was spilling out from under her hands. When Quincy looked back at the girl, her eyes had shut and Quincy felt it like a punch to the gut. She had looked away. She had broken the lifeline. Quincy could hear sirens in the distance. Help was coming but it was too far away. Much too far away. And now this little girl was dying under her hands. No. No, she wasn't going to die. That wasn't going to happen. Because Quincy knew what to do. She hadn't even noticed the fog creeping back in but she didn't fight it or even question it this time.

She peeled the soaked shirt away from the girl's neck and used it to wipe as much blood from the wound as possible. It wasn't very effective, saturated as it already was, and as she looked up to ask for something else to use, the jerk who wasn't actually a jerk was already reaching out with another shirt, this one a white, thin cotton, pulled from the bag laying open at his feet, odds and ins and a toothbrush scattered around on the floor around it. She didn't have time to thank him but snatched it gratefully from his hands and sopped around the wound and, for the first time, saw the cut. It was a long, jagged tear that ran from the girl's jaw to her collarbone. The edges of her skin were flayed open and pulsed as each beat of her heart pushed the wound open a little more.

People are weird, Quincy thought blandly. Five minutes ago, no one could seem to look away from the train wreck of the dying girl on the floor, pushing in close enough to see it all play out. But getting a glimpse of the actual cause of death itself? When Quincy had cleaned the wound enough to be able to see it, she heard one of the women standing over them gag and the crowd seemed to move a couple steps away, like they were suddenly afraid of contamination. Or being asked to help. Her big, blustery helper had swayed a bit but was stalwart enough to stand his ground. Quincy actually wouldn't have blamed him for moving away, especially when she used the thumb and finger of one hand to spread the gash open even more and reach in with the other to apply pressure directly to the artery itself. That was the last straw for someone, judging by the sound of vomit splattering across the floor behind her.

Where was that ambulance? Her hands were only a poor, temporary fix. The medics would be able to use hemostats to clamp the artery so they could get the girl to the hospital. Without taking her eyes off her hands, she addressed the guy still kneeling anxiously beside her.

"Could you wipe the blood away from my hands? I need to make sure I haven't missed anything".

A second later, shaking hands reached around her and blotted the blood away from the makeshift surgical site. *How many t-shirts does he have in there*, she wondered vaguely as she watched the black cotton soak the blood up like a sponge. She watched as the white emblem on the front slowly became red and when he pulled back, only a little blood seeped from the wound. She looked up at the guy. He had helped save this girl's life. If she survived. She might. But she might not. Quincy didn't know. And the guy helping didn't know either. But as he stared back at her, eyes watery and scared, she smiled, hoping he understood. And hoping everyone else around them did too. He was still too pale for his complexion but he shot a weak grin back.

"Do you think she - ," but he was cut off abruptly as the main doors to the station crashed open and two paramedics charged through the crowd of onlookers, followed closely by two police officers who immediately began establishing a perimeter around the injured girl.

One of the paramedics, an older guy with a shock of salt-and-pepper hair and a thick beard, dropped down opposite Quincy and assessed the situation as his partner, a young guy with red hair who looked like he might be on his first run, started digging in his kit. The older guy, *John* according to his name tag, didn't hesitate.

"Get started on vitals," he directed. "Get me a pulse rate and blood pressure. It'll be low, but that's normal after so much blood loss. I'll get as many lines in as I can so we can push fluid on her fast, try to get her pressure back up to a decent level."

Quincy watched the kid, or *Mike* according to his name tag, calming slightly as his more-experienced partner took control with ease, seeming unruffled as he leaned casually over the girl and examined Quincy's makeshift patch job.

"Nice work kid," he said, referring to her now. "Not just anyone would have known to clamp the artery, let alone know how". He looked like he wanted to ask more, but after a slight hesitation, he looked back down. "Mike, hand me the hemostats."

John took the proffered clamps. "How're we doing on vitals?" he asked, going to work as Mike rattled them off.

"BP is really low, 70/40. Pulse is 130."

"Right you are," said John. "Go ahead and start working on lines while I get this artery clamped off nice and tight and then we can get some fluid going. I'd like to see that BP come up a bit before we transport."

Then John looked back up at her. "Okay kid, I want you to keep the laceration open but when I say so, move your right

126

hand off the artery so I can clamp it off, okay?"

Quincy nodded, just noticing the cramps running through both of her hands, ready to let go. "Okay then. On three."

When John hit three, Quincy pushed the cut open as wide as she could with her left hand and pulled her right all the way out, giving John as much space as possible. The black t-shirt was suddenly back in front of her, the hands a little steadier this time, mopping at the fresh flow of blood so John could have a clear view.

"Got it," he said. He pulled a package of gauze from his kit and packed it in around the wound to stabilize it, then turned and started setting up an i.v. Mike already had two lines in place and was working on getting the fluid running.

Finding herself suddenly free, Quincy slid away from the scene, putting as much distance between herself and the drama as possible. Now that her part was done, reality was setting in. She hadn't only been part of the show, she had had a starring role. Survival wasn't being front and center of the spectacle, it was turning your back and walking away from it. And she hadn't done that. All eyes were still on the paramedics, working purposefully on their patient. She managed to slip to the back of the crowd without being noticed, where she stood rubbing at her stiff hands. She was exhausted but she couldn't rest yet. She had to get out of here fast. Hopefully everyone in the station had been too focused on the gory sight in front of them to remember the face of the girl with her hands inside the victim. She quietly backed up to the restroom directly behind her and then stepped inside. She needed to clean up and get as much of the blood off as she could.

It took some scrubbing but eventually most of the blood

came off her hands. It was still caked under her nails but luckily she had a sweatshirt in her backpack that would cover her ruined shirt and that she could tuck her hands inside. A pair of "in case of emergency" glasses and a ball cap over her braided hair and she looked like a new person.

She left the bathroom as the ambulance was pulling away, lights on and sirens blaring. Which meant the patient was still alive, still had a chance to pull through. But no one was leaving. Instead, the police were lining everyone up to take statements. A major crime had been committed, that much was obvious. There was no way that kind of injury was accidental. Quincy knew that trying to leave would only attract more attention so she swallowed her nerves and allowed herself to be corralled with the other onlookers, even though it went against every survival instinct she had.

But just because the police had questions, it didn't mean she would be seen. She peeked up from under her hat when the policeman got to her but he barely even looked at her. When he started throwing out the same standard questions he was asking everyone – What did you see? Where were you when you first noticed the victim? Had you been anywhere near the north restrooms or exits? – Quincy answered the questions patiently, tearfully, trying to fit in with the other witnesses. It looked like the woman came from the north hallway. She was sitting on a bench near the west ticket counter when she first noticed her. No, she had never gone near the north exits. Was she going to be okay? She managed to burst into tears at one point and the harried police officer, looking extremely uncomfortable with her hysterics, patted her awkwardly on the back, thanked her for her statement, and sent her on her way. One thing she had learned in her years of running and hiding was that tears almost always worked. She kept her face down, hidden in a tissue, and almost smiled as she walked slowly and unsuspiciously towards the door. No one had asked about the woman who had stepped in to help. And no one seemed to recognize her as she walked away. So maybe she was in the clear after all.

18

Chapter 18

The Colonel

The call came just as he finished packing. He'd been expecting it for a couple of days, really, and was annoyed it had taken so long.

"Well?" he asked curtly. He didn't appreciate having to wait.

"I have confirmation," his associate said without hesitation.

"Finally," the Colonel snapped. "It certainly took long enough."

His associate did hesitate then. "I'm sorry sir," the tinny voice sounded over the line. "I didn't want to make any mistakes."

"And what did you confirm, exactly?" he asked.

He listened quietly over the line, taking in the report. "I concur," he finally said. Silence stretched between them as he considered what the next move should be.

There were two options - only two. But which was the better

course?

"What are my orders sir?" his associate finally asked, either unwilling or unable to let the silence linger any longer. He took in a breath and exhaled slowly.

"Terminate," he finally said. "Quickly. Quietly."

That really was the smart option. Better to bring in a dead specimen than allow her to rabbit again. Each time she disappeared, she got better at staying gone and he didn't want to risk losing her again. The situation might be different if he were there in person instead of this mewling nitwit that was fast coming to the end of his usefulness. Better to trust him with an assassination than a kidnapping. Kidnapping victims could talk. The dead tell no tales.

"And if you can't do that…"

"I understand sir," his subordinate rasped out. "Consider it done."

The Colonel ended the call, no more pacified than when he'd answered. He glanced down at his open suitcase, waffling for the briefest of moments, before slamming it closed and swinging it off the bed. His car would be here shortly anyway. He might as well continue with his plans. If all went well, his subordinate would never even know he'd been there. And if it didn't, well, at least he was that much closer to the fire.

19

Chapter 19

"To die, to sleep...'tis a consummation devoutly to be wish'd. To die, to sleep. To sleep, perchance to dream. Ay, there's the rub. For in that sleep of death what dreams may come when we have shuffled off this mortal coil." William Shakespeare

The question is not easily answered.

Death...death could be silent. Death could be peaceful. Death could be better. Death could also be angry. Death could be nothing but noise and pain and terror. Death could be more of the same.

Death could be better. But it could also be worse.

* * *

Quincy

Or maybe not, Quincy thought the next day. She had barely made it home from the train station the day before when another massive migraine blew in from out of nowhere and left her stranded in the middle of her small living room floor. She spent the rest of the day and the night there, actually, just barely managing to drag herself up in time to shower and make it to class on-time. She couldn't remember ever having two migraines in the span of as many days and this one had been so much worse than even the usual torture. It was lucky she'd made it home when she did. *It usually is,* she reminded herself. But this one, it had been bad. And it had lasted so much longer than the others. It hadn't just felt long; when Quincy had cracked her swollen, bleary eyes open at the sound of her alarm this morning, the pain was still present. It was manageable now, but still, it was there. She'd tried to sit up and the nausea that had been roiling just below the surface surged, forcing her back to the floor. Her neck and shoulders felt like they'd been battered by a baseball bat and her legs felt so weak and exhausted that she wasn't sure if walking was even an option, let alone running.

As she lay there, swallowed in misery, she couldn't help but wonder why. These moments seemed to be happening more and more frequently lately and they were taking a toll. How long before reading and running gave way as her stop-gap for dealing with the noise and the exhaustion and the pain? How would she even function?

Her head was blissfully silent at the moment, the noise muted while her brain recovered from this latest attack. But it would be back. And then the cycle would begin again - noise, exhaustion, pain, and, finally, sleep. Not enough sleep of course. Just enough to get her back up on her feet so she could do it all over again.

Quincy felt her eyes, swollen, red, and bleary, tear up at the weight of that thought. She reached up and wiped at the wetness, surprised and a little afraid of it. The last time she'd cried had been....she couldn't remember, actually. She wasn't a crier, not by any means, but she should be able to remember crying at least once in her life, right? But it just wasn't there. Which made the tears come in earnest. What was wrong with her?

She threw her arms across her face, grinding the palms of her hands into her eyes with fury. It was all pointless, wasn't it? This struggle. The exhaustion. The pain. That noise that she couldn't escape. Was any of it worthwhile? Wouldn't it be better to just close her eyes and then, nothing? Surely death was quiet. Surely she would be able to rest. She would never have to know why she didn't remember the last time she'd had a good cry. Or how she could play a musical instrument she'd never picked up with ease. Or how she'd performed surgery in the middle of a rundown, dingy train station. She wouldn't have to know any of those things. She wouldn't be dogged by questions and doubts. No more keeping people at a distance and lying to those who snuck in close enough to see. It would just be silent. Wouldn't it?

That last question drew Quincy up short. Maybe death would be better. But maybe it wouldn't. She couldn't know that. No one could. Despite the hell her life had become, it was a hell she knew. It was familiar, comforting in a way that was difficult to explain, even to herself. She began to calm, the tears slowing, as the old, familiar buzzing began to make itself known. Quincy squeezed her eyes shut and wiped the tears away, steeling herself to do what she had to do. And what she had to do right then was haul herself up off the floor, shower, and go to class. There was really no reason she couldn't skip a day. She wasn't even officially on the roster. But she had never missed before and any break from the routine made you stand out, even to people who had never noticed you before. And Professor Michaels had definitely noticed her. Besides, falling back into her pattern would only serve to settle her nerves sooner.

All of which was explanation enough for why the excited chatter of the other students caught her off-guard when she tossed herself down into her usual seat in the lecture hall.

"I heard it was a bloodbath," one student said behind her, causing Quincy to snap to attention in the middle of digging her textbook out of her bag.

"It was," her friend replied. "I saw pictures of it posted online. There was blood everywhere."

"I wonder what happened? Do the police know anything?" the first girl asked her friend.

"No," the girl answered. "The news just said a girl was attacked and they were *investigating*."

"So weird."

"No doubt."

Yeah. No doubt, Quincy thought wryly. Instead of sounding horrified by such a violent attack on someone in their own town, the two girls sounded excited. Curious. Almost in wonder. *Sensationalism at its finest*, Quincy thought again, shaking her head. Professor Michaels came in and she was hoping that would be the end of it. But instead of getting into his lecture, he broached the subject himself.

135

"Has everyone heard about the attack that happened at the Moberly train station yesterday afternoon?" he asked, immediately capturing the attention of every student in the room, Quincy included.

And then he proceeded to give a startlingly accurate description of exactly what had happened yesterday, down to the Good Samaritan who stepped in to stop the bleeding. Quincy tensed at that, but she needn't have worried.

"The victim was lucky. There was someone with enough medical knowledge to step in and stop the bleeding. Probably a doctor or a paramedic - someone who knows how to take care of arterial bleeding. Not an easy task."

Quincy breathed a silent sigh of relief. If there had been a description or any curiosity at all about the person who stuck her hand in the dying girl's neck, it would have come up in this bizarre PSA of a lecture.

"But this kind of tragedy is shocking here in our own backyard," Professor Michaels continued. "It's not something we're faced with often, but that doesn't mean we shouldn't be prepared in case we are. So I'd like to skip today's scheduled sleep fest," he said with a smile for his audience, "and talk about how you can protect yourselves in cases of unexpected violence."

What then proceeded was a lengthy and surprisingly detailed discourse on how people with no self-defense training could avoid danger and fend off attackers. The same passion Professor Michaels demonstrated in his lectures on mechanics and physics shown through just as clearly here and Quincy had to smile. He was a kind man, this young professor. A champion of the poor, the marginalized, and the unarmed and unprotected. His students loved him for it. Quincy glanced around the room, taking in the rapt expressions and the near-total attention riveted on their professor. She hoped it helped, this impromptu self-defense course. After what she'd seen yesterday, and the trouble that seemed to follow her around like the mosquitoes in Sheraton followed her during her a run, it wouldn't hurt her to pay attention too, and she turned her attention back to the front.

It turns out, it wasn't just the students in Quincy's class talking about the attack. The break room in the library was alive with gossip. The girl had survived. The girl had died. Her attacker had been shot dead in a hostage situation twelve hours north. The attacker was in the wind. No one mentioned the girl with the blood on her hands, who had somehow managed to stop the bleeding long enough for the paramedics to get there. And for that, Quincy was grateful. But she was also miserable. Her headache was all but gone, but it had left behind something like a hangover. Her eyes were still swollen and red and she could barely move her neck.

All she wanted to do was lay down somewhere. She had a sneaking suspicion, though, that sleep wasn't going to come. Not after almost twelve hours yesterday. Her shift at the library was unending, made worse by Brandon's inexplicable, uncomfortable presence. She had spotted him on her floor no less than three times before he finally made his way over to her.

"I guess you heard," he started suddenly.

When Quincy merely looked at him, too drained to pretend he was welcome, he shuffled his feet.

"The attack at the train station," he pressed. "I guess you heard."

"Uh huh," she managed.

Silence, and this time, she didn't try to break it or let him off the hook.

"Oh. Good," he said, unsure of where to go when she didn't provide any direction.

"You should be careful you know," he said suddenly. "It's not always safe out there."

Quincy quirked an eye. *Really?*, she wanted to say. But she kept quiet. She just wasn't in the mood to pander to him today.

"Okay," he said slowly, maybe realizing how that last line had sounded, and backed away. "I just wanted to make sure you knew. So, I guess I'll see you later."

Like, in five minutes, watching you from behind a planter, she thought to herself. The girls downstairs were right. He was a creep. But she didn't have it in her to give him any more thought tonight. She made it through the rest of her shift on autopilot and when it was time to leave, gave in to the impulse to board the bus instead of walking. There was no way she'd make it all the way home tonight. But that was okay. She'd been down this road enough to know the lethargy would pass. She might not be able to sleep tonight, but her body would at least rest, and that would have to be enough for now.

20

Chapter 20

Quincy

The week passed much like it always did. She went about her daily routine like always, running, work, school. But things seemed even more quiet than usual, if that were possible. Logan had been making himself scarce for some reason. She'd been so miserable right after the train station that she hadn't noticed right away. But after a couple of days, she couldn't help but notice, and it annoyed her. She'd caught a brief glimpse of him in the campus quad on Wednesday. His back had been to her and he'd been talking agitatedly into the phone, all rigid and stiff-backed. He seemed disturbed by whatever was being said on the other end and as curious as that made her, considering she'd never seen Logan in less than a stellar mood, she'd had to get to work and hadn't had time to chat.

Thankfully, the gossip around school and work about the attack had died down a little but she was still having trouble letting it go. She had lain awake all night, again, replaying the scene in the train station over and over. What had happened. What could have happened. What should have happened. And the big question – how did it happen? How could something like that happen, in public, in broad daylight?

The girl hadn't been conscious when the paramedics rolled her out, and certainly hadn't been in any condition to talk when Quincy had been trying to staunch the flow of blood. But it seemed very unlikely that she could have been attacked and not seen who had done it. It was too intimate a wound. And it was certainly a *who*, not a *what*. One did not simply step out of a public restroom and into something sharp enough to severe an artery. It was possible she had rushed out of the bathroom without looking and bumped into someone carrying something very sharp. If it had been an accident, that person would have been horrified, called for help.

But there had been no warning, no call for help. The woman had been utterly alone. Which made Quincy believe the woman had been purposely attacked. But again, in public, in broad daylight? It wasn't the best choice for a murder, obviously, so why? In the rush of trying to blend in and get out of there as quickly as possible, Quincy hadn't even glanced towards the west hallway where the woman had staggered from.

Now that she'd had time to actually think, she wished she would have tried to see the scene, or at least eavesdropped on the cops containing it to see what they were thinking. Was there any physical evidence left behind? The cameras would have caught whoever attacked the woman so....wait. That wasn't right. Quincy knew the position of every security camera in that building. She knew exactly how much space each covered, where they overlapped and where they didn't.

The hallway coming from the west restrooms was located in one of the areas Quincy planned to use if she needed an unobserved way out of the building. It was a blind spot.

A cold feeling crept over her, settling deep into her chest at that thought. Could someone else have staked out the cameras? Chosen that exact spot to act? It was the oldest section of the depot, making it the least populated, and it was without security coverage. It suddenly made perfect sense why someone would act right there. But again, why? This was as middle-America as you could get. Yes, the business district was in the middle of a boom but the majority of the population was made up of college kids, young families, and retirees.

There were no Wall Street heavy hitters here. No politicians trying to change the world or financiers trying to change their bottom lines. And the well-to-do local business owners were mostly composed of the Medicare crowd, trying to supplement social security with a second career. Sure, there were always crimes of passion - domestic disputes, arguments over the distribution of pharmaceuticals, and finals-induced rage, but to plan an attack, with the kind of dedication and precision this suggested, would imply a high-value target, and there just wasn't anyone in town with that kind of clout. Quincy didn't know the woman attacked but she could speculate. Based on her clothing, she worked in the business district but probably not high up. She was still fairly young so possibly an intern or an entry-level associate. Someone who ran errands and took care of paperwork. Not someone wealthy or with valuable insider information. Just a perfectly normal, ordinary girl.

It occurred to Quincy that the oddity in the equation wasn't the girl, or even the placement of the attack. It was herself. Was it a coincidence that a girl was attacked in the train depot while Quincy was there, using the same camera angles and positioning Quincy herself planned to use in an emergency?

Tightness sparked in her chest. The previous two attacks against her hadn't been physical - she hadn't given them time to be. Maybe whoever was after her had found her and mistaken the other girl for her? They did have similar hair color and length. But she had changed her basic appearance after each attack so the odds were good they didn't know exactly what she looked like.

So maybe it was a warning, an attempt to spook her into reacting. Into running. They knew where she was but didn't know exactly what to look for. So they shock her. Running might attract attention, give her away. But how would they know she was in the train depot at that very moment? They might have figured out how she was planning to get out of town but they couldn't know that she ran the route from time to time, and that she would be there that morning. It felt selfish to turn this poor girl's tragedy into an attack on herself but none of it made any sense. Hence the earlier-than-normal-for-a-Saturday run. She had to blow all of the clutter out of her head or she would never be able to rest. So she slipped on her shoes, pulled her hair back, slid her earphones in, and headed out the door.

Half of her problem was that she wasn't sure if this was related to her or not. It didn't seem to be, not really. There were better ways, easier, less messy ways, of drawing her out if her shadow man had found her. But she couldn't be sure it wasn't him either. Which meant she should leave. Always better to be cautious when one's life was on the line.

Which led straight to the other half of her problem – she really didn't want to leave. She'd never stayed anywhere long enough to grow attached before. She probably should have left a long time ago but it had been so quiet, with no signs of danger, and she kind of liked not pulling up stakes every two months. It was...relaxing. She liked her class and her professor. She liked her job. They worked together so perfectly, the routine was flawless.

She knew good and well that she'd likely never find anything like it again. She liked her jogging route. She liked downtown, with its squares and local businesses and residences all mixed in together. And, as much as she hated to admit it, even to herself, she liked Logan. She had gotten used to seeing him pop up randomly throughout her week. Whether it was at the library or on the quad or on her morning jog, it was nice seeing a friendly face. It was nice actually having a friend. She had never let herself have one before. And she liked it. She didn't want to give any of those things up. Which was why she had never let herself have any of them before. There was only so close she could let anyone get to her, for their own safety if not for hers, and she would eventually leave, most likely without so much as a "see you later". Forming attachments just made it harder.

The sun was just breaking over the horizon as she started on her 3rd lap and she paused. It really was beautiful here. There were mountains, or rather hills, in the distance and the sun lingered over them, burning through the mist and breaking across the trees in shards of light that reflected off the small pond to her left. The fall colors were now on full display, and the sunlight set the bright reds on fire. There was a slight breeze that added a chill to the air but it felt more refreshing than cold on her face and neck as she ran. She had never lived by the ocean or mountains or deserts. She had lived near a lake in Boise, which was nice. But she had a hard time believing anywhere could be as beautiful and peaceful as here.

In that moment, she was certain that was the real reason she didn't want to leave. It was so peaceful. And she felt safe, which had been a fleeting feeling for so long. It absolutely wasn't because of Logan. Sure, he was maybe a small part, but only a very small part, and it was only because she had realized it was nice to have a friend. That was all it was. And besides, it wasn't just him, necessarily. Carla from Career Resources seemed nice enough the few times they had talked and of course she had Mr. and Mrs. Boatright, who asked about her day and worried over her when she didn't eat enough. So Logan was just a part of the mix. A small part. Barely considerable.

Her pause to admire the sunrise had let her body catch up with her brain. Apparently she had run harder and longer than she thought because she was suddenly exhausted. Sweat had soaked the collar of her shirt and worked its way down her back and the muscles in her calves were burning. But it had worked – she wasn't thinking about The Incident or what it meant. True, instead she was thinking about why she didn't want to leave her current safety net because of The Incident, but whatever. She'd take the win.

Chapter 21

Q**uincy**

A shadow fell across Quincy's face, momentarily blocking the sun, and she looked up. She had decided after her run that she didn't feel like going back inside and wallowing the same problems around and around, driving herself crazy. So she'd bounced up her apartment stairs, grabbed a blanket and a book, and headed back out. The square was still practically deserted when she got back so she'd tossed the quilt under a tree in the botanical garden and plopped down to read. She wasn't sure when the sun had shifted so far in the sky but she must've been here much longer than it felt. She was mildly annoyed when she saw Logan grinning down at her, jumbo coffee cup in hand. Sure, she had decided she liked having a quasi-friend. He was nice enough to hang around with, and helped pass the time, but she was in the middle of a good book so she really didn't need any help with passing time at this exact moment.

"Did you need something?" she asked. She pushed an air

of aggravation into her tone. He didn't look even slightly repentant, which annoyed her even more.

"Nope. Saw you sitting over here and thought you looked a little bored. I figured I'd say hi and break up the monotony." He gave her one of his made-for-the-movies smiles before plopping down onto the blanket beside her. "You're welcome."

"I'm not sitting, I'm reclining," she said, motioning towards the quilt she was sprawled out on like he was some kind of idiot, "And I'm not bored. I'm reading." She made sure her tone of voice was clear on her opinion of someone who could mistake the two and then she smiled sweetly. "So you can take your monster coffee, your rock star smile, your overly-helpful attitude, and go pester someone else."

She rolled over onto her stomach and raised her book pointedly, which had exactly zero effect. The aforementioned giant cup of coffee was suddenly in her face, blocking her view of her entire book, which presented a problem. The coffee was a peace offering. If she took it, she was inviting him to stay. On principle alone, she should refuse it. No one should be allowed to get their way by being pushy and presumptive, simply because they knew how to offer bribes. And what kind of person forced their company onto someone else, someone who clearly wasn't interested in it, and thought that coffee could make it all better? The man was arrogant, obviously having been led to believe that his looks and his charm would get him whatever he wanted. But Quincy wasn't just anyone. She was immune to his tricks and it would be her pleasure to knock him down off that high horse he was sitting on. The cup started a slow retreat from her line of sight and she instinctively snatched it. And then sighed. Maybe she'd knock him off his high horse a little later.

She rolled over onto her back and sat up, crossing her legs and eyeing him warily as she took a sip. She wasn't sure how he knew, exactly, how she took her coffee, but she wasn't entirely surprised either.

"So what, you were just out strolling the gardens with an extra cup of coffee, spotted me, and thought 'Ah ha! An unsuspecting victim'?"

She almost asked where he'd been all week but then thought better of it. He already had a high enough opinion of himself. She didn't want to give him any funny ideas about her caring whether she saw him or not. Hands now free, he was leaning back on his elbows, eyes closed, face tipped up towards the sun. With his overgrown curly blonde hair and natural tan, he looked like he could be on a beach right now. Or should be. He kept his eyes closed but smiled at the sarcasm.

"Nah. But I did see you and think 'Man, she looks like she could use a coffee'. And since I could too, it seemed like it was meant to be. But hey," he leaned forward and wiped the palms of his hands on his shorts where dirt and grass had stuck, "since you're obviously not that interested in your book anymore, and the day is so nice, let's go for a walk." He jumped up and reached a hand back down to her, which she ignored.

"I have a quilt and books and, you know, stuff. Not exactly conducive to a long walk." She wasn't quite sure why she was being so feisty today. Maybe she was just finally feeling better.

"And you have a backpack, which all of your 'stuff' fits into. So shove it all in and let's go."

This time, he leaned down and grabbed her hand, pulling

147

just hard enough to get her moving. "I'll even be a gentleman and carry it."

It really was too nice of a day not to enjoy a walk through the parks. They wound down through the botanical gardens, not really saying much. Quincy had thought the silence might become awkward or uncomfortable but it was surprisingly peaceful. She didn't feel the need to fill the space and clearly, Logan didn't either.

She snuck a quick glance, just to see where his attention was, and found it clearly not on her. In fact, he looked like he was pretty far away. She nudged his shoulder with her own and stepped out of the way of a jogger, into a natural alcove formed by the landscape. The first time she had gone jogging through downtown, the cherry trees had caught her attention and they were still her favorite part of town. Interesting fact - not that many varieties of cherry trees bloomed in the fall. Which just made them feel even more special.

It was quiet inside the alcove, secluded. It made her feel like she was standing in a chapel. All she could hear was the sound of the breeze rustling through the branches and the drying blooms drifting to the ground. She could hear a couple of birds chirping back and forth, although they wouldn't be there much longer as the colder weather started to set in.

Logan had stepped into the alcove with her but he still seemed lost in thought.

"I found this place by accident," she said offhandedly. "I was running and didn't see the limb on the path. It was this huge, mangled piece of tree, I don't know how I didn't see it, and I about broke my leg when I came down on it. My ankle rolled and so did I, right into this little hole in the trees."

She grinned, thinking about what she must have looked

like. At least there hadn't been any witnesses.

"I just lay here for awhile because I didn't know if my ankle would hold me and looked around. It was night and the stars were out and it was almost like looking straight up a telescope, they were so bright."

She realized Logan was finally looking at her, all intense and focused, and she shrugged nervously. "Moral of the story? Don't run if you can't see. You might have to walk five miles home on a bum ankle."

That got a knowing smile out of him. "I've limped plenty of miles on a busted ankle myself, so I can sympathize."

He slung an easy arm around her shoulders and steered them out of the alcove and back down the trail.

"You don't really sound like you're from here," Logan started, apparently shaking off his uncustomary intensity. "You lack that certain...twang...that the locals have. But I can't quite pin down the accent. Where's home for you?"

That small, nagging voice in her head that she'd managed to convince Logan was no threat started whispering. *This is why we don't have friends*, she reminded herself wryly. Luckily, Quincy was quite comfortable redirecting conversation that tried to breech her walls.

"Oh, a little bit of everywhere, really. What about you? You seem like a west coast kind of guy."

Logan laughed. "You're not the first person to think so. I grew up along the coast in Oregon, actually. So west coast, but a little more north than most people usually think."

"Surfer?" she asked, suddenly dying to know if she was right. "Please tell me you surf."

This time he looked a little sheepish. "I do. Love it, actually. But I haven't had a chance to do much surfing in years. The service took too much time and I was rarely in an area where surfing was available. Fishing, yes. But surfing, not so much."

So she'd been right about the surfing and she'd been right about the soldier bit. He'd mentioned it before in passing but never really followed up. He definitely had the build for it but something else didn't quite fit.

"I can't imagine that hair is regulation."

He laughed. "You're right about that."

He reached up and ran a hand through all that curly hair. "First thing I did when I mustered out was stop cutting it. You don't know pain until the top of your head is blistered from digging trenches in the middle of an African summer."

She couldn't help but laugh at the visual. "No. I suspect that is a very special kind of pain."

He poked her in the side. "You're too pale and skinny to be much use in the military, so I know you've never served. So what does life have in store for you Miss Quincy?"

She shrugged. "I don't really know what I want to do. I like to read, so the library is a perfect fit for work. And auditing classes lets me experiment until I do know."

"I don't know exactly what I want to do either, but that doesn't mean I'm going to take electrical engineering – for fun."

"I don't know," she said, considering. "There's something about the math that relaxes me. It's got a certain rhythm to it. It gives my brain something to focus on, which shuts it up for a little while."

Well that sounded weird. Which was why she usually tried not to say things like that. Why she cared if Logan thought she was weird, she wasn't sure, but she didn't want that to be what he remembered about today.

"I mean, I just have trouble shutting my brain down sometimes. You know what I mean? Sometimes it just spins in circles and I need something else to focus on. Engineering helps with that." Oh yeah. Much better.

Logan didn't reply, not at first. She replayed what she had just said and decided it didn't sound too crazy. Didn't everyone have trouble getting their minds to be quiet sometimes? Anyway, he could think what he liked. It wasn't like they were really friends. And she would be leaving at some point anyway, so it shouldn't matter.

"How old are you?"

The question came out of nowhere and caught her off-guard. She felt the pressure in her head jump and she shoved it back into place. That was a random leap with no possibility of a reply. She didn't give that kind of information away. The less people knew, the better. She had survived thus far by keeping people at arm's length and things like birthdays, hometowns, and family stayed hidden. She didn't realize how long she had been silent until Logan bumped her lightly with his arm.

"It's not that tough of a question," he said quietly. "I'm not trying to pry. But from the way you talk, I think you must be older than you look."

She took a breath and tried to recover her equilibrium. "You do know that's not the kind of question you ask a girl, right?" She tried for a joke. "A lady never reveals a weakness."

Logan rolled his eyes. "I hardly think your age could be considered a weakness. You look younger than most of the co-eds around here but you're taking graduate-level courses. So either you're super smart and skipped more than one grade or you just look much, much younger than you are."

"You can attempt to turn the question into a compliment if you want, but I'm not breaking," she insisted.

"I'm 35," he said. "See. It's not so hard. I'm a 35-year old retired army lieutenant taking undergrad classes because I have no idea what I want to be if I'm not a soldier. But that's okay." He stretched his arms up and over his head and then rubbed at the back of his shoulder. "I can still keep up with 21-year olds on the Ultimate Frisbee field, although I'm pretty sure the aches are a little worse now than they were 15 years ago. And as much as you run, I would think you're in better shape than almost anyone on this campus. So age doesn't really mean anything."

"Then why do you want to know so bad?" she shot back, and he huffed in annoyance.

"Why are you so paranoid? It's really irritating. Give me something here. Your age, your hometown, whatever birthday you used on your college forms. Something."

She looked up at him. And up and up, until she could see all 6'4" of him. Seriously, the man was huge. And he wasn't letting this go. She latched on to the last thing he had said.

"Fine. September 18." If he wanted a date so bad, he could have that one. Like he said, the random date she had used to get into her classes would work just fine. It was false, after all, so it couldn't hurt her.

He breathed a huge sigh, closed his eyes, and lifted his arms back up above his head. "Finally!" he yelled, loudly enough that the young couple pushing their baby in a stroller looked over at them. Overly theatrical, this one. She shook her head and started walking again, him matching her pace seconds later. He opened his mouth, presumably to ask another irritatingly personal question, but she cut him off at the pass.

"So, why aren't you a soldier anymore?" She caught him off-guard and she savored the moment, enjoying the fact that he seemed lost for words. "I mean, if you don't know what you want to be other than a soldier, why aren't you still one?"

"That's kind of a hard question to answer. One I don't really like to talk about much," he finally said, and she almost felt bad, watching as his eyes drifted down and his entire body seemed to coil in on itself. But considering how much he had pushed her, not quite enough to let it drop.

"Gee, I hope that wasn't too personal. I would never want to make you *uncomfortable*." She smiled sweetly, letting the sarcasm hang thick in the air between them. The silence held a beat longer before he finally relaxed enough to shrug a shoulder.

"You do have a point," he admitted. He looked down at her and gave a little half smile. "I got hurt. A buddy got killed. The army gave me my walking papers. And now I have to find a new way to protect people."

Well. Now she really did feel bad. They kept walking and this time, Quincy let the silence linger. It really was a nice day, and Logan was nice company when he wasn't pushing for details she didn't feel like giving. There wasn't a cloud in the sky and the sun was bright and warm. She rolled her head to the side, letting the light breeze rustle her hair.

"Frustra Deum naturamque non cooperantur," she said absently, finally content for the first time since yesterday morning. Maybe this was exactly what she needed. An afternoon spent reading had gone a long way towards calming her down but it hadn't relaxed her exactly. But in this small garden, surrounded by trees and flowers and hidden from the rest of the world, she finally felt safe. And then Logan had to go and ruin it.

"What was that?" he asked curiously.

"Oh, sorry," she said, a little embarrassed. "I didn't mean to say that so loud."

"But it was another language, right? What was it? I didn't recognize it. Which is saying something, considering my deployment record."

It probably wasn't a big deal to give him this one. Lots of people were bilingual. "It's Latin. I said 'God and nature do not work together in vain'. It seems appropriate today, yeah?"

"Pretty." He was quiet for a moment. "I didn't know you could speak Latin. Are you fluent or do you just have quotes for special occasions?"

She considered. "You know, I don't really know. I've read a couple of Latin language books and it just kind of stuck, I guess. But I don't get to use it very often, what with its status as a dead language and all."

Logan seemed to find this hard to believe. "You read a couple of books and it 'just kind of stuck'? That's...different."

"Not really," she said, scrambling to dig her way back out. Why did she keep saying stuff like that to him? "I have a photographic memory. It's why I do so well in weird classes like electrical engineering. Once I read it, it's there. It's pretty handy, actually."

"Sure, sure. I can see that," he answered, but he seemed to have settled back into his earlier thoughtfulness. Here, but not here. She let it go, let him have his moment, just grateful that he wasn't asking any more questions.

The sun was starting to set by the time they made it back to the square proper. She decided to call it a day and turned to thank him for the walk and make her excuses but he beat her to it.

"Thanks for letting me hijack your day. I've still got some homework to get done before the weekend runs out but maybe I'll see you around?"

She shook off the abrupt dismissal as best she could. "Oh, sure. I enjoyed it." She held up the empty coffee cup she'd been carrying around. "And thanks for the coffee. I guess my weaknesses are pretty well-known."

Awkward. She gave a little wave, which felt lame the second she did it, and turned in the direction of her apartment, berating herself for letting him get in under her guard. So what if he had somewhere else he'd rather be? And why did she care if he thought her wave was lame?

"Hey," he yelled at her back.

"Yeah?" She spun around too quickly and almost tripped over her own feet.

"How would you say 'See you tomorrow' in Latin?" He had that stupid grin on his face again, albeit it slightly strained, the one that said he could convince a girl to do whatever he wanted and he knew it.

"Cras autem videbo vos." Yup, he definitely knew it.

"Well alright then. 'Cras autem videbo vos'".

She rolled her eyes. "That was terrible," she said, but then she hesitated. "What's tomorrow?"

"Lunch at Delmar's. Noon." He stuck his hands in his pockets, turned, and sauntered away. Whistling. She sighed. So much trouble.

Chapter 22

L ogan

The whistling stopped as soon as he was sure he was out of Quincy's line of sight. He kept walking as nonchalantly as possible as he slipped the phone out of his pocket and dialed.

"I'm moving on her tomorrow," he said by way of introduction.

"Why? What happened?"

"I asked too many questions and she got cagey. We can't risk her running again."

"What's your plan?"

Logan rolled it around in his head, looking for holes. "We're having lunch tomorrow. I'll offer to walk her home after and make sure we end up somewhere...private."

"Well," his boss said after a moment. "It's not great."

"No," Logan agreed. "It's not great. But it's all I've got. She's too alert and paranoid to attempt anything else and I don't think we can afford to keep waiting."

"You're right," the other man agreed. "Losing her again isn't an option. Do what you have to. But Lieutenant?"

"Yeah?" Logan asked.

"Call me as soon as it's done. I want to be in the loop at all times,"

"Yes sir," Logan said, then ended the call.

This was going much too fast, he knew. In this kind of sting, you needed more time to win over the target. He needed Quincy to trust him and it was pretty clear, even if she wanted to, she wasn't there yet. The birthday she'd given him had clearly been a lie, which was fine. But the fact that she balked at even that was telling. Between his getting close and asking questions and what she had done at the train station, she was on the verge of bolting and he couldn't allow that.

Frankly, it would be best to take her tonight. But she wouldn't go quietly and it would be harder to sneak a fighting woman out in the dead of night, when every little noise would be heard, than in the middle of the day with the busy sounds of a bustling weekend filling everyone's ears. Tomorrow would have to do, even if he didn't like it. And if he were being honest with himself, he really didn't. Quincy was.....he searched for the right word. Not nice, certainly. She was too acerbic and cynical for that. But fun, maybe. She didn't let him get away with the flirting and the good-natured pushiness he usually used to such striking effect.

It wasn't often he found a girl who could hold her own. Which was what made this all such a shame. At least tomorrow it would be over. Hopefully the guilt would disappear, too.

23

Chapter 23

Q^{uincy}

Delmar's was a small bistro on the outskirts of the commercial metro area that Quincy had heard of but never visited. As the hostess led her to a small table on the back patio, she wished she had countered Logan's offer with a different restaurant. This wasn't fancy, exactly, but it was certainly nicer than she was used to.

She tried to smooth as many wrinkles out of her plaid button-up as she could when the hostess turned to pull out her chair, but quickly gave it up as a lost cause when she just made it worse. She sat and the hostess set a small menu down in front of her before excusing herself to see to the couple who had walked in behind Quincy. Before she left, she assured Quincy she would bring her guest out as soon as he arrived. Quincy told her he was big and annoying and she couldn't miss him.

It really was nice here, though, Quincy thought as she looked around. The bistro looked out over a commercial district full of small shops and boutiques. It had an almost bohemian look - trendy and free-spirited, all rolled into one. Quincy pulled out the book Logan had given her last week at the library as she looked around. It was a nice day, though a little cooler than the last few. Mr. Boatright had told her this was the true start of fall and every day would be a little cooler than the one before from here on out. She didn't look forward to winter and the cold and snow the locals warned her was coming. It meant she would have to start taking the bus more often, and she hated taking the bus.

A small frown tugged at the corners of her mouth. The bus was so confining. She always felt trapped whenever she had to ride it. To her, the bus was a bad omen. It meant she had been found. It meant she was running. But today, she wasn't running. She was having lunch with a giant gorilla of a man who was growing on her a little more every day. And she was early enough to enjoy the quiet and the ambiance before he showed up and shattered it.

She dropped her backpack onto the ground beside her and propped her feet up in Logan's chair, turning her attention to the book. Why Logan had thought she'd enjoy a book on small engine repair, she had no idea. He'd made himself scarce all week, only dropping into the library for a few minutes Tuesday evening. He had seemed antsy, she'd thought, constantly moving. He'd made himself comfortable at her desk like he'd been in the habit of doing since they met, but then he was up and prowling around the aisles.

It had been very distracting, this constant nervous energy he'd been giving off. She finally asked him what his problem was and he'd mumbled something about putting off a paper on the most boring subject she'd ever heard of before shuffling off again. He'd come back from what was apparently a mission to find a source on British poets of the 17th century and dropped the book onto her lap.

"I saw it and thought of you", he'd said with a grin, trying to force a levity that wasn't there. She had meant to ask how his ramble around the 17th century had brought him to a book on modern-day auto mechanics but a student had popped up out of nowhere at that exact moment, needing help citing a reference. By the time she'd gotten free, Logan had disappeared. There was a hastily-scrawled note propped next to her computer saying he had to run and she hadn't seen him again until he showed up in the park yesterday.

It all seemed out-of-character from what she'd seen of him so far. She'd been so busy dealing with the fallout from the attack and strung out from the headache that followed that she hadn't paid as much attention as she should have. She wondered now, as she waded through terribly dry pages describing the various ways to start an engine, whether something was truly wrong. She didn't know anything about his family. Maybe someone was sick?

A shadow fell over her and she looked up. "Well, speak of the devil," she said as Logan graciously scooped her legs out of his seat and plopped down.

"What?"

"Nothing," she said with a smile, tucking the book back in her bag.

"Been here awhile?" he asked, taking a drink of the water a waitress had brought over earlier.

She looked him over, searching for signs of the quiet, pensive Logan from earlier in the week but none appeared. By all accounts, he seemed like the Logan she'd spent most of Saturday with. A little more subdued maybe, but that could be explained by practically anything.

"Not really," she finally said. "I just always come prepared."

"I can see that. How's it coming?" he asked, nodding towards her bag. "I can't believe you're actually reading that, by the way."

"You're the one who gave it to me," she protested.

"It was a test," he said casually, picking up the menu and looking it over. "One I'm not sure you passed."

Don't take the bait, don't take the bait.

"What kind of test?"

Nice. Way to stay strong.

"A test of your feelings for me, of course. You must like me quite a bit," he said, casually pursuing his menu, "to read a book about car batteries."

"I take classes on electrical engineering for fun," she answered coolly. "I wouldn't read too much into it." She was oddly relieved to see him trying to hide a smile behind his menu. She hadn't realized just how much his weird behavior had been bothering her.

Their waitress showed back up and Quincy ordered a coffee to go with her chicken salad sandwich. Logan ordered the house special without bothering to ask what it was and shot the waitress a smile that made her blush and fumble the water pitcher. He laughed and helped her clean up the spill, pretending not to notice the effect he had on her.

No, Quincy thought, *he wasn't pretending.* He really didn't know. He was such a charmer that Quincy sometimes forgot he really was just a nice guy in the shape of a player.

The waitress bumbled away and Logan glanced over at her,

catching her in a smile. "Don't read too much into it," he mocked with a smirk. "Sure."

24

Chapter 24

Logan

"Don't read too much into it," he repeated, smiling. "Sure."

Quincy let him have that one and his smile slipped just a little. Yes, she liked him. Enough to let him hang around. Enough to spend her weekends with him and go out for lunch with him. Enough to let him close enough to act. He felt like a heel. By all accounts, Quincy didn't have friends. Ever. The fact that she'd let him in enough to be one was both a testament to his undercover skills and a condemnation of his motives.

He felt bad. Really, really bad. He'd used his people skills and his covert military training to get close to people before, but never in such a personal way. He had been afraid that if he used his usual ins, getting a job in an adjacent area, taking the same classes, or renting an apartment in the same complex, she'd get suspicious. She was the type who watched for that kind of thing. She would definitely notice if he started shadowing her.

But if he made contact *on purpose*? If he was open about it, if he acted like he'd noticed her and wanted to get to know her? He'd had a feeling she wouldn't know how to deal with someone who stuck with it when she tried to brush him off. Most people tended to give up right away. So he'd played the persistent puppy who refused to be kicked away. And it had worked. A little too well. When he broke her trust, she was never going to trust anyone again.

It's for the best, he told himself, glancing back down at his menu. She shouldn't trust anyone. Not if his boss was right. And he was right. Logan had no doubt about that. Not anymore. Not after last Sunday. Not after the train station.

Quincy was sipping on her water and looking out over the shopping district spread out before them, almost entranced, and he couldn't help but think about her staring around the train station in much the same way, only then she had been pale and covered in blood. He had watched her then, too. He had watched the glazed look in her eyes, the slight tremble of her hands after the paramedics had taken over.

He had watched as her mind snapped back and her survival instincts took over, watched her fade slowly back towards the restrooms and disappear inside, only to reemerge 10 minutes later in an oversized hoodie, glasses, and baseball cap hiding her hair. Her hands had been shoved deep enough into the pockets of her sweatshirt that no one would be able to see the blood that had to still be packed under her fingernails. Cool as a cucumber, she was. It took a professional to cry so convincingly for the police and then walk away without looking back. He could do it, of course, but he was a professional liar.

Quincy, on the other hand, had been amazing. She had

stepped forward towards the wounded girl and taken command, assessing the injury and treating it. He had watched her perform surgery in the middle of a dingy, half-empty train station with nothing but her hands and a couple of t-shirts. If that hadn't convinced him his boss was right, nothing would. And now here they were.

He sighed and Quincy looked up suddenly, catching him watching her. He knew he should look away, but he just couldn't. He knew his plan depended on getting her away from the crowds, secluded and isolated, and she wouldn't go willingly if she started suspecting something was up. But he just couldn't do it. She wasn't going to forgive him for this. The thought kept circling around and around in his mind. She deserved so much better, and she wasn't going to forgive him. Look away, he told himself frantically. You're blowing it.

Quincy watched him curiously, letting the tension and the silence stretch. He was sweating. Maybe he should rethink the plan. Maybe he should give her more credit. She was smart, after all. Brilliant, quite possibly. *But she's not going to forgive me*, that voice in his head kept whispering.

"Why are you looking at me like that?" she finally asked.

Time was up.

25

Chapter 25

"**B**ut you can't make people listen. They have to come round in their own time, wondering what happened and why the world blew up around them. It can't last."
Ray Bradbury

No one is ever what they seem. Not me. Not her.

Not him.

* * *

Quincy

"Why are you looking at me like that?"

There was a slight pause and then Logan blinked, like the question had surprised him. He cleared his throat.

"Like what?" he asked.

"Like I'm a puzzle you can't quite figure out. Like maybe you think there's something wrong with me," Quincy said, a little self-consciously. She was used to people giving her strange looks, because, well, obviously she was a little strange. But rarely did anyone give her more than that single passing glance. One quick look, one *wonder what's wrong with her*, and they had moved on. But Logan, for the short time she had known him, had stuck like no one else had. He stuck, despite her abruptness. He stuck, no matter how disinterested she seemed. And it wasn't because he was enamored with her. She knew that. Maybe he liked her, but he didn't *like* her. How could he? He didn't know her. It had to be something else. She had caught him in several moments like this, where he was looking at her and seeing something, or someone, completely different, and she was tired of wondering why.

"You're a puzzle," he answered finally.

He relaxed, like he'd finally come to some kind of decision, and leaned back in his chair, stretching his long legs out in front of him and crossing his arms over his chest. He looked completely at ease. Totally at odds with the conversation they were having and the look in his eyes, which was anything but casual.

"You're friendly but you don't want to be friends. You're smart, but you don't want anyone to know it. You're beautiful but you do everything you can to hide it. You try to fade into the background. I'm just trying to figure out why."

Quincy stared, a little shocked, although she doubted it showed on her face. No one had ever called her on her stuff before. Yes, she kept people at a distance. Yes, she tried to be as unmemorable as possible. If you made an impression, you were easier to find. And having friends, having people you cared about, just left you vulnerable. But she couldn't say any of that to Logan. Because if she told Logan that much, he would want to know more. He would want to know all of it.

She may not know much about him, but she did know he was curious. Or nosy. She preferred to think of him as nosy. Insatiably so. She had watched him during his study sessions in the library. Whatever subject he was researching, he pursued it with a single-minded focus that she found both impressive and intimidating. He had doggedly pursued a friendship with her without hesitation, despite her stonewall responses. And he had an endless supply of questions. Knowing the answer wasn't good enough. He needed to know the whys and the hows. He needed to know the inner workings of a thing in order to understand it. An admirable trait to be sure, but one that was dangerous for her.

Maybe it was his military background but she felt like she was on display, and he was systematically picking apart all of her carefully built walls and masks. And how was she supposed to protect herself without her defenses? She needed to put a stop to it, and fast. She took a deep breath and let it out slowly. She should have shut him down when he first started coming around but she hadn't. When it was obvious her usual tricks weren't working, she should have been more abrupt. Or she should have just left. But she didn't. She had let him keep trying and now she rather enjoyed his company, which made it more difficult to hurt him. But her safety, and most likely his, was at stake and she had to cut her losses.

"Have you ever thought maybe it's you? Maybe I'm not the problem here," she said speculatively. "Maybe it isn't that I avoid friendships and try to go unnoticed in general. Maybe I just do it with you, and you can't take a hint when it's subtly given."

"I might think that," he replied lazily, "if there was even one other person in your life. Correct me if I'm wrong, but you don't have family. And you sure don't have any friends. So no, it's not me."

Quincy opened her mouth to argue but then shut it. What could she say to that? It was completely true. Did she tell him it was because she didn't want any friends? That not everyone had a family to rely on? What answer would satisfy his urge to know and get him to leave? He sat there, nonchalantly appraising her reactions, and she found herself frozen, unsure how to proceed.

The stalemate could have lasted minutes or hours and she wouldn't have known the difference. She just sat there, staring at him, until he finally broke the standoff.

"What are you running from?" he asked quietly.

She froze instantly at the gently whispered words. Why would he ask that? He couldn't know, not really. Could he? Quincy sat in silence, which Logan took as permission to continue.

"You know things you shouldn't know. Like how to pick up a violin and give a flawless performance. Generally speaking, only surgeons know how to clamp off hemorrhaging arteries. And I don't know exactly what kind of person is fluent in Latin, but I'm pretty sure it isn't a library resource assistant who audits classes at small town universities."

It hit her like a ton of bricks, enough to shake her out of her stupor. Universities. Plural. He knew. She didn't know exactly what he knew, but he knew enough. She shoved her chair back and bolted to her feet, heart pounding, adrenaline flowing. She felt the noose tightening around her neck and

169

she couldn't draw a full breath.

"How do you know those things?" She felt cold, rigid. "You couldn't possibly. I don't...I keep it...have you been following me?" she demanded.

And then the full meaning of his words slammed into her, hard. He had been at the train depot when she'd stopped the girl from bleeding to death. He had to have been, to know it was her.

The blood drained from her face and she whispered, "You're one of them, aren't you?"

And then a new thought occurred to her, even more horrifying than the last. "Did you...did you hurt that girl, just to get to me?"

The stress in her voice must have reached him because Logan stood as well, but he looked confused, maybe even a little hurt.

"Hurt her? Why would you think that?"

She almost believed him, with his sad puppy dog eyes and his hands held out to his sides, seemingly at a loss. "I would never do anything like that Quincy. You know that. And am I one of who? Who are you running from?" he asked again.

He took a step in her direction and reached out, like he was going to take her arm, but she jerked back violently. He sounded so sincere, so genuinely concerned. But she couldn't believe him. She couldn't afford to. She steeled herself.

"This is why I've had a reprieve, isn't it? Instead of an outright attack, they embed someone to watch me. To get close to me."

The nausea was rolling through her at the thought of being watched by the very people she was running from and she gave a sharp glance around, looking for his backup to move in for the take down.

But it was still just Logan, standing in front of her and reaching out.

"I don't know who is trying to hurt you, but Quincy, it isn't me. I came to help you."

He finally broke, agitation leaking out through his words. "Yes, okay. You're right, I have been watching you. I wasn't sure I was on the right track at first, but I've been looking for you, and others like you, for a long time. Please, let me help you. You'll be safe with me."

His eyes were so earnest that she wanted, desperately, to believe him. She looked at the hand he held out, and for just a moment, considered taking it. If he was telling the truth, she could be safe. She wouldn't have to constantly look over her shoulder, waiting to be found. She could let him take care of her. If he was telling the truth. If he wasn't, she would die. Or at the very least disappear. And no matter how much she wanted answers herself, her survival instinct was too strong to give up without a fight. She met his eyes and saw that he already knew her decision. She backed away.

"Don't follow me. It's the middle of the day. If I see anyone coming after me, I'll make a scene and you can explain to the police why you've been 'watching me'. But I'm fairly sure whoever you work for doesn't want that kind of attention."

Logan opened his mouth to speak but she cut him off.

"I don't know who you are, and I don't know what you want with me. But if you're going to come at me, then just come at me. Don't pretend to care."

She reached down blindly for her backpack, grateful she never went anywhere without it, then spun and walked away as quickly as she could.

She was thankful for the aviators she had slipped on before leaving her apartment earlier. To her embarrassment, the tears had started before she'd even turned away from Logan. She reached up to brush one from her cheek. She couldn't believe she'd allowed herself to fall for the act. How had she not seen it? She thought back over all the run ins and surprise meetings, all the times Logan had popped up unexpectedly. She knew she should have seen it earlier but she'd been so content here. And Logan was so sincere. Or had seemed sincere, anyway. She had bought into the act, hook, line and sinker, because she'd wanted to believe him.

She'd wanted to believe that she could have a friend. That she could belong somewhere for more than a few months. She had been so desperate to believe she was safe that she'd allowed herself some unguarded moments and now she would have to pay for them.

She took a deep breath and blew it out slowly. Now was not the time for pity. She squared her shoulders and took stock of the situation. She was walking further into the commercial district, which meant contingency plan two. Since she had her emergency cash stash on her at all times, she would walk to the bus station and use it to pay for a ticket to whatever location was available on the 3rd ride out. Then she would duck into the restroom and swap out her button up for the bulky pullover she kept in her bag for just such occasions. Then she'd tuck her hair up into her old ball cap and wait it out. Once she was several hours away, she'd decide on a new location and head that way.

She felt marginally better knowing she had prepared for this situation. And unexpectedly relieved she wasn't being forced to use the train station to make her exit. The memory of blood and Logan's role in it was still too fresh. Maybe it was an unexpected mercy, she thought, that Logan knew about the train station. It's where he would expect her to go. And while they were watching the trains, she'd slip onto her bus and be hours away before they got wise.

She rolled her head around, trying to release the tension in her neck and see if she could spot any tails yet. The wind gusted and she ducked her head to tuck a wayward strand of hair behind her ear a split second before the glass storefront to her right shattered.

26

Chapter 26

Quincy

She heard the report of the rifle at the same time she was thrown bodily to the ground. She didn't have time to sort out what had happened before Logan was rolling off of her. He shoved to his feet, grabbed her under her arms, and dragged her around the corner of the closest building. Once they reached the relative cover of the brick building, he grabbed her hand and yanked her to her feet, pulling her deeper into the alley.

"We have to move," he said, apparently thinking that explained everything.

"Someone just took a shot at me," she said dazedly, more to herself than to him. "With a rifle. In broad daylight."

"Which is why we need to be moving," Logan responded. "Obviously he doesn't mind making a scene."

Did he sound exasperated? With her? He glanced back in annoyance and tugged her along. Oh, she didn't think so. Quincy pulled her hand out of his grasp with great dignity. Or

174

tried to, at least. He had a surprisingly tight grip. She set her feet and he finally jerked to a semi-stop.

"Who took a shot at me? Why does it feel like you're trying to help me? Shouldn't you have been trying to push me in front of the bullet, not away from it? Your bosses are going to be so mad. Demotion, for sure."

She was babbling and she knew it. Someone had tried to kill her. She was understandably shaken but, regardless of what had happened between them three minutes ago and the assumptions she'd made, he was trying to help her. And she just couldn't understand why.

"Who *are* you?"

He gave her an incredulous look, one that irritated her even more, but he must've realized she was serious, because he finally stopped trying to move and rolled his eyes.

"My name is Logan Davies, like I said. What I didn't say was that I work for a doctor who specializes in neurobiologic pathology. We try to find and help people like you but we aren't the only ones looking."

He paused to glance around the alley. Quincy could hear police sirens coming on fast and there were cries and screams coming from the direction of the shooting. Logan put his arm around her shoulders and started steering them towards the other end of the alley. Since he was talking, she let him lead.

"There are organizations that are interested in people like you. Organizations much less friendly than Dr. Garrison. My guess is, whoever just shot at you, and whoever you've been running from, work for one of those agencies. And if they just attempted a hit in the middle of a busy, populated area, during the day no less, their interest has shifted from *procurement* to *elimination*. Which is why we need to move. Now."

Apparently, that's all Logan was prepared to say on the subject at the moment. Quincy was by no means satisfied, but she also realized there were priorities and at the moment, background information wasn't one of them.

"So what's the plan?" she asked. "If you don't happen to have a getaway car stashed handily nearby, we might be in some trouble." She caught the barest hint of a smile.

"No convenient getaway car, but it won't be the first time I've been in a pinch and had to...borrow."

Borrow. Great. "Swell. Grand Theft Auto isn't really my thing, but sure. Whatever."

It was kind of a catty thing to say but at the moment, she didn't really care. She had woken up this morning, none the wiser that her life was about to explode. But then it did. Much more literally than she preferred. So really, a little snark was to be expected.

"What are we looking for, exactly?" Quincy asked.

Logan had pulled her along the back alleys and side streets of the commercial district until it merged with downtown, the trendy store fronts giving way to the family-owned businesses she was more familiar with. Now, he was strolling casually through the back parking lot of the north business front like he was at a used car dealership.

"Do you know what the most common car on the road in America is right now?" he asked offhandedly.

"Depends on who you ask and what part of the country. Be more specific," she shot back.

He shook his head. "Okay. What do you know about, for example, the Ford Focus?"

"The Focus was rated #10 on the compact car index by the U.S. News and World Report. It's both cost and fuel efficient, which makes it popular with middle class families. It has less interior space than other compacts and is too lightweight to hold out against hardcore collisions, which I assume is why it's only 10th on the list."

It poured out before she could stop it. She hadn't even thought before she replied. Logan just looked at her.

"What?" she asked, running her hand through her hair nervously. Was that not common knowledge?

Logan started to say something but his eyes shifted over her shoulder and he brushed past her. She turned to see what had caught his attention and saw him heading toward a little silver Camry.

"I thought you wanted a Focus," she said, jogging along behind him.

"I do. And there's a black one three spots down that's calling my name. But I want these license plates to go with it."

He pulled a knife out of a sheath hidden at his back and started turning the screws holding the front plate in place. "Go check to see if it's unlocked and work on getting it started while I take care of this."

Quincy was skeptical. "It probably is unlocked. This is small town America, after all. And it's parked on a private lot, no less. But it's not likely the keys are helpfully hidden in the glove box or under the floor mat. It may be small town America but it isn't Mayberry."

Logan had moved to the back of the Camry but paused to look up at her. He tipped his hat up and grinned at her, which was totally inappropriate, given the circumstances.

"You read the book, right?"

"What book?"

"The one I gave you last week. On small engines."

"Yeah, so?" Where was he going with this?

"So not having the keys shouldn't be a big deal for you."

"You think I know how to hot wire a car?" She laughed. Another totally inappropriate reaction.

"That's exactly what I think," he said. "I think you read that book and now you can hot wire a car." He turned his back to her, dropping down in front of the little Camry. "So get to it already."

She gritted her teeth. This wasn't *Rain Man*. What an idiot. An idiot who might, maybe, have a point.

"Fine, I'll try. But don't get your hopes up." She turned and stomped toward the Focus. "I'm not going to promise I can do it. I'm not Sherlock."

She heard a laugh but didn't bother responding. She had never hot wired anything in her life but sure, why not give it a shot? It was a totally realistic request and not at all out of place in real life. Her mind skipped back to the festival and the violin, and she shifted uneasily. Okay, so maybe she'd done some weird things in the past. If she could clamp off an arterial bleed, how much harder could it be to attach car wires?

But just the fact that she had played the violin, that she had stopped the bleeding, that she could speak fluent Latin, and French and Farsi and Chinese and Spanish, after listening to a couple of audio lessons, seemed wrong somehow. Normal girls...normal people...weren't able to do stuff like that. She faltered, momentarily flashing back to the train station, blood gushing from the gash in the girl's neck, a torn artery clamped between her fingers, before shaking herself free of the memory. Normal people definitely didn't do things like that. But it didn't matter right now. It didn't matter if she was normal or not.

What did matter was getting away from the unknown man trying to put a bullet through her head. Priorities.

She pulled the car door open, which was unlocked like she'd thought, and dropped into the driver's seat. For the sake of thoroughness, she gave a cursory glance through the glove box and all of the other places keys could be hidden, like the sun visors and under the seats, but no dice. She did find the car's registration, though. It belonged to Patricia Simmons, one of the owners of the ice cream parlor. Quincy closed her eyes. The car sat in the private parking lot behind several of the downtown businesses she knew by heart.

Of course she would know whose car she was stealing. The guilt was instantaneous. Patty was a single mom with 2 kids, both in school. How was she supposed to pick her kids up if her car was gone? Quincy slammed the glove box shut and started to climb out of the car, but her hand froze on the door handle. The gunman had only been a street away. If he didn't run after the first failed attempt, and the odds were 50/50 on whether he would or not, he could be here in just a couple of minutes. They didn't have time to grab another car.

She hoped one day she'd have the chance to apologize to Patty for what was about to happen. To tell her it was a matter of life and death. From what she knew of the kindly woman, Quincy thought she might understand and even be glad she took her car, if it was to save a life. That Patty would know Quincy would never do something like this if it wasn't. Then she reached under the wheel and popped the console open, exposing the ignition mechanism.

As she stared at the exposed tangle, feeling overwhelmed

by the mass of wires and fuses, the buzzing that usually filled her head in moments of stress seemed to move from the back of her skull, where she routinely pushed it, filling her ears until it blocked out everything else around her. Her mind seemed to slow, and then sharpened, like it was locking onto a target. And then her body responded, her hands reaching for different wires and striking them together. It took exactly twice for the engine to catch and she automatically wrapped the two ends together, keeping them in contact. She sat back up and jumped when she noticed Logan standing over her.

"For the record," he said, "your intimate knowledge of compact car statistics and the ability to hot wire said car on the fly are examples of why you're on some shadow agency's hit list. Now move over. I'm driving."

She slid into the passenger seat without bothering to respond. Not that she could have anyway.

27

Chapter 27

Auberdeen

The air whistled between his teeth as he blew out his breath in one big rush. Dumb luck, that's all it was. A gust of wind blew a strand of hair into her face, she leaned forward to brush it away, and his bullet missed her by millimeters. That was all that stood between her and a quick, painless death - a sudden gust of wind. There was irony in there somewhere but he didn't have time to find it.

He leaned away from the window and had his rifle stripped down in a matter of seconds. In the mass hysteria the gun shot and shattered window had produced, a man had knocked the target down and she had vanished into the crowd. He wasn't going to get a second shot.

Not now, at least. The restaurants and local businesses had emptied in response to the shot, sending seemingly every person in the vicinity running through the street. Chaos reigned. The opportunity was lost. He carefully placed the pieces of his rifle into its case and then shoved it deep into his duffel bag, slung it over his shoulder, and walked out of the room.

He'd found the empty apartment several weeks ago in anticipation of the current op. He'd been tailing the target for almost three months, watching where she went, and when, and figuring out her patterns. He had staked out multiple nests based on her movements so he would have options when the orders came in.

He was on the street in front of the apartment in a matter of seconds and turned west. She would certainly run now. That was part of the very vague profile he'd been able to build from the file he'd received from the Colonel. One of the few things that tied Quincy O'Connell to Gracie Elliott and Kara Scott was her penchant for disappearing. He'd honestly been expecting it for awhile now. He had forced her into enough situations to put her on alert and she'd finally flinched after the girl at the train station. But a direct attack? There was no question. She was gone.

When he'd first attempted to cross her name off the list of potential targets, he hadn't been too impressed. She was just like every other girl he'd seen that fit the profile. But once he started tracking her, started watching her movements, he'd noticed a very distinctive pattern to her actions. A very routine, methodical precision in her movements. Which told him he was on the right track.

When the Colonel had given him the assignment of tracking down Gracie Elliott, alias Kara Scott, he had read the file and assumed it would be an easy op. He was fairly new to the organization so he didn't blame the Colonel for not trusting him with anything difficult just yet. But still, he would have liked something that required a little more skill. But both

Gracie Elliott and Kara Scott had been surprisingly difficult to trace. Neither had left any bread crumbs to follow. The profile he'd developed was too general, vague in a way that left the search parameters too wide. But as the names started to pour in, he'd started eliminating them one by one.

It had taken dozens of trips to rule out dozens of girls before he'd finally struck gold and even then, he hadn't been sure. Quincy O'Connell had fit the physical description in only the broadest sense. She was in the right age range, which was still too wide to be much help.

She was the right height. She was attending a local college as an auditor and working in close proximity to both the school and her apartment. Those were the only things either of the aliases had in common. That, and the ability to disappear on a moment's notice.

Gracie Elliott was a thin, bubbly blonde with deep dimples and blue eyes who worked at a diner slinging hash to over-worked, underpaid truckers a half-mile from her off-campus housing unit while Kara Scott had been a slightly overweight, bookish-looking girl with thick glasses and mousy brown hair serving drinks to overworked, overpaid corporate slaves in an out-of-the-way dive a quarter-mile from the cheap studio apartment she was renting by the month.

Quincy O'Connell was none of those things. Her hair was so dark it almost looked black, until the light hit it just right. Then it became a deep auburn, tinted red in the sun. Her eyes though, were her defining feature. Like Kara Scott, Quincy O'Connell sometimes wore glasses. Unlike Kara Scott's, however, they did nothing to pull attention away from her eyes. He was sure that was the point of wearing them, to add to the disguise, but glasses weren't going to hide those eyes. Large, almond-shaped, and shockingly green, they were probably the most memorable eyes he had ever seen.

Which was a pity, since the Colonel had issued the kill order. But still, the job was the job and he had never been one to get overly sentimental about the requirements.

He reached his vehicle and tossed his duffle into the back seat. It was a nondescript Honda, one of a million just like it circulating on the roads. When he'd called the rental company, he'd specifically requested something plain and obscure. The better to blend into his surroundings. They hadn't even batted an eye and when he'd strolled up to the kiosk at the airport, they'd had the keys ready.

He slid into the front seat and turned the car on, tuning the radio to a local news station. He wasn't worried about the cops but it would be helpful to avoid them if possible. He pulled his phone from his pocket, debating whether to update the Colonel. Probably should, since his botched attempt to eliminate the target had resulted in mass chaos on the streets of Sheridan. The Colonel would be furious, no doubt. The man's number one rule was to stay off the radar. No muss, no fuss, no undue attention. But he didn't want to call and report bad news without good news to soften the blow.

And he had no doubt he would find her again. He had planned for this circumstance, after all. No, he'd call the Colonel once the job was done.

28

Chapter 28

"'My mind,' he said, 'rebels at stagnation. Give me problems, give me work...and I am in my own proper atmosphere...for I am the only one in the world.'" Arthur Conan Doyle

While the mind works, it is calm. Quiet. At peace. But peace never lasts for long.

The girl is beginning to see now. Finally. She is beginning to see me the way I see her. She doesn't understand yet.

But she will.

* * *

Quincy

The car was silent as Logan maneuvered through traffic. It

was late Friday afternoon and rush hour was just starting. They had hit the highway with no problems but made considerably less progress than Logan wanted once they settled in with all the commuters and people heading out of the city for the weekend.

"This is actually good," Logan said about an hour into their drive. "The more vehicles on the road, the harder we'll be to spot. The car's probably been reported as stolen by now but I doubt the swapped license plates have been noticed. That buys us time."

Logan glanced over when Quincy didn't bother responding. She had been completely silent since they'd been on the road. Silent, actually, since she'd managed to hot wire a car like it was an ordinary thing. Like it was something she did all the time. The predominant thought running through her mind was, *this isn't normal.* Normal people don't know how to do things they've never done before. Normal people don't have snipers shooting at them with high-powered rifles. Normal people don't have mysterious men popping up in their lives and pretending to be friends in order to get close to them. No, these things were not normal at all.

She had been staring out the window since they'd hit the highway, trying to convince her mind to slow back down. After the weird zone out when she'd hot wired the car, her brain seemed to be in overdrive, even for her.

She hadn't been able to relax and could feel a headache coming on. She sighed, knowing she couldn't ignore the situation, and Logan, forever. Leaning her head back on the headrest, she turned away from the window and found Logan watching her. She had absolutely no intention of talking about herself or answering any more of his questions until he answered a couple of hers. She opened her mouth to ask him to explain exactly who he was and why he had been following her, but he beat her to the punch.

"I thought you said you weren't Sherlock," he said mildly, with no small hint of amusement evident in his eyes.

Not exactly the opening she'd been expecting. "Excuse me?" she asked, not really sure where he was going.

He grinned, then turned his attention back to the road. "When I told you to get the car started, you said you weren't Sherlock. But you pulled it off, which means you had the info stashed somewhere." He was quiet for a minute before adding, "I always thought it would be cool to have a mind palace."

Well, this was a weirder start to the conversation than she thought there would be. "What's a mind palace?"

"Oh, come on. From *Sherlock Holmes*? Where he stores all of the crazy information floating through his head." He was looking at her expectantly, like he couldn't believe she didn't get it.

"Girl, his mind palace!" He shook his head in disbelief. "You read literally all of the time. How can you not know this?"

"Do you mean his brain attic?" she asked. "You don't really strike me as much of a Conan Doyle fan and I know you're not a reader. How do you even know that reference?"

He grinned again, never taking his eyes off the road. She was really starting to hate that smug smile. "I'm not," he confirmed good-naturedly. "But I love the show. The Brits really do it right, you know?"

He glanced in the rear view mirror, adjusting it to better reflect the light. "And on the show, he has a mind palace.

Which sounds so much cooler than a *brain attic.*"

"There's a show?" she asked, but then shook her head. "You know what? We're getting off-topic. You need to start explaining exactly what's happening." She held her hands up and motioned out the window. "And it might be nice to know where we're going," she added pointedly.

Logan didn't speak for a minute, the muscles in his jaw and neck tightening subconsciously. He checked the mirrors again, then glanced at her briefly before turning back to the road.

"I'm really not good at this part," he said. "I do the heavy lifting but Dr. Garrison usually does the talking. You're right though. You do deserve to know what's going on and where we're going. And it's not like we don't have the time."

He reached over and found a ball game on the radio, turning it on low for background noise.

"When we first met, I told you I was in the military and that I'd lost someone. That's all true, but it isn't the whole story." He paused to adjust the rear view mirror for the third time, his stress evident in the repetition.

"We were army rangers, working black ops in the middle east. The last mission we went on was messed up from the start." Logan's voice faltered momentarily and there was a look in his eyes that Quincy couldn't quite interpret. But he managed to shake it off and it disappeared before she could place it. "We both sustained some pretty heavy damage. We were medevaced to Germany and both of us went straight into surgery. We had been right next to each other when the explosive detonated."

He shook his head. "What are the odds one guy winds up with busted ribs and a collapsed lung while the other one gets brain damage." He shrugged. "Even after all this time, it doesn't seem fair somehow, you know?"

It wasn't a question that really seemed like it needed an answer so when he sank into his own thoughts again, Quincy let him be. She wanted to believe she wasn't pushing him because anyone could see the memory was difficult. But in all honesty, she knew she didn't quite have that much compassion. There was something about the story that made her uncomfortable. Itchy somehow, like something was scratching inside her head, trying to get out. She saw an exit ramp coming up and decided it would be a good diversion for both of them.

"Let's pull off and find a gas station or something. I'm thirsty." She glanced over when he didn't respond and realized he wasn't listening.

"Hey," she said again, this time shoving against his shoulder.

"What?" he snapped, a little more harshly than the situation really required, but she decided to give him a pass this time.

"I said, pull off here. I need a break and something to drink. And you need a walk. I'm not riding with a cranky army ranger all the way to wherever it is we're going."

"You know," he said, pulling off onto the ramp, "you're a whole lot bossier than I'd expect someone on a hit list to be. Technically, I did save your life. Would it kill you to throw a *thank you* out there?"

He pulled into the nearest convenience store and she gave him a sugary smile. "I'll buy you something caffeinated and we'll call it even."

29

Chapter 29

Logan

They didn't really need gas but Logan didn't want to stop again until they'd cleared the Arkansas/Texas border so he pulled up to the pump closest to the exit. He reached for his wallet, shuffling through several cards until he came to the prepaid credit card he'd charged for just such an occasion. Quincy was already out and rounding the car, heading for the store, when he held it out to her.

"I have cash," she said, turning to head inside.

He grabbed her wrist and spun her back towards him, sliding the card into her hand. "I'm going to fill up while we're here. Put it all on the card. It's untraceable and it will cover everything we need."

He released her and she rolled her eyes as she turned to head inside. He knew he shouldn't but he couldn't help himself.

"Largest coffee you can find. Black. And grab some snacks, too, while you're in there," he called to her retreating back. "Beef jerky would be good!"

She didn't even bother turning around. One thing he had noticed in their short acquaintance was she did not like being told what to do and, for some reason, he just couldn't help but push that button. There hadn't been a lot of opportunity to have fun in his life lately and aggravating her had been a bright spot and temperamental as she was, she never failed to disappoint. He should probably stop before he permanently alienated her. *Too late*, he thought. *The lies have already taken care of that.*

He leaned back against the side of the car, watching the numbers on the gas pump spin. Logan had decided while boosting the car to take a very roundabout route to the clinic in Colorado. They were currently heading for Texas, on a straight shot to the Mexican border. Once there, they would ditch the car and grab something else, pulling the plate switch again, this time with plates he intended to pick up after dark tonight. By the time they needed to use the new plates, they should be several states away and out of reach of a local police alert. He would feel safer once they were headed north. Whoever was hunting Quincy should be looking south to catch them as they presumably tried to cross over into Mexico while they would actually be on their way north. It was a good plan, one that had worked for him in the past.

The pump shut off and he recapped the tank, then settled back against the car to wait for Quincy. She wasn't long. She shoved the door open and bounced back out of the store, carrying a sack full of food, a couple bottles of water, and two extremely large cups of coffee. He smiled as she crossed the parking lot towards him. Temperamental or not, a pretty girl was a pretty girl. He decided he'd enjoy it while he could.

30

Chapter 30

Q uincy

Logan was leaning against the driver's side door watching the store when Quincy came out. His ball cap was pulled low and his sunglasses covered his eyes but she could feel him watching her. She wasn't sure how she felt about being the subject of an army ranger's complete focus, although the word *uncomfortable* came to mind. His arms were crossed, causing the material of his t-shirt to stretch across his very well-defined chest and when he spotted the monster coffee cup in her left hand, he smiled.

It was the smile that did it. That stupid, smug, megawatt smile. Her right foot caught a divot in the pavement and she gave a little stutter step, almost falling before she caught herself. She was so glad, at that exact moment, for the protection her sunglasses provided. She really didn't want him to know she was looking at him when she stumbled. The man's head would swell to inhuman proportions. But really, who looked that good after being shot at, stealing a car, and reminiscing about war injuries and death? She ran her hand through her hair self-consciously. She certainly didn't.

She crossed the parking lot and he pushed off the side of the car, trailing her to the passenger door. Not sure what he was doing, she turned to look at him, thinking maybe he just wanted his coffee really, really badly. But as she turned, he was suddenly in her space, looming over her, and she instantly jerked back, forcing space between them and sloshing the coffee onto her hands and his shirt.

"What are you doing?" she asked, ready to use the scalding coffee as a weapon if necessary. It would certainly be more useful than the bag of jerky and Skittles she had in her other hand. Her burnt hands felt like they were on fire so she could only imagine what a face full of it would do to a man.

Logan raised an eyebrow and looked at her with ...was that pity or disappointment? He gestured down towards the door of the car, which he was gripping with his right hand.

"Being the gentleman my father taught me to be," he replied. "I'm sorry," he said sympathetically. "I should have warned you before I made a move. You're handling everything so well, I forget you were almost on the receiving end of a bullet this afternoon. That would make anyone jumpy." He carefully took one of the cups from her with his free hand and motioned her inside.

"Do I need to get some ice for your hand?" he asked.

"What? Oh, no. It's fine," she answered. Embarrassed, she had pushed the pain aside in the wake of her adrenaline spike and now she was too ashamed to admit it. She ducked her head and climbed into the car. Logan looked at her for a second, then shut the door gently before circling around and climbing back inside. They both stayed quiet as he maneuvered onto the highway and Quincy tried to convince her body to relax.

When Logan had leaned towards her, her mind, so habitually tuned towards playing escape and evade, had interpreted the action as a threat and she'd responded on instinct alone. As her mind replayed the scene, she caught the flash of hurt in his eyes when he realized her reaction was in response to him but he'd backed off instantly, giving her space to come down from her massive overreaction. And it was an overreaction.

Back at the cafe this afternoon, she may have thought Logan had been sent to hurt her, but his actions since then had proven that assumption wrong. He had saved her from a sniper. He had stolen a car to get her away from danger. He'd walked away from whatever life he'd had at the university, and, although she now knew that life had been staged, it was still a sacrifice. And he was driving her who-knew-where, all to protect her. He didn't deserve her suspicion, he deserved her trust. Pity she didn't know how to give it.

They were both silent as the car turned back onto the interstate, the only sounds inside the car coming from the ball game still playing quietly on the radio. Quincy had leaned her head back against the seat and closed her eyes as soon as she was buckled in, trying to create enough distance to calm down.

She was still amped up from the adrenaline spike and she knew she needed to explain. He deserved that much. She had been running and hiding for a long time now. Forever it seemed. And her basic instincts had shifted to self-preservation. It was how she reacted to anything unexpected. She wanted to tell him how much she appreciated what he had done for her today, saving her life and all. She wanted to tell him she trusted him. The problem was, she still didn't. Not completely.

She couldn't remember the last time she'd trusted anyone. Just because he'd protected her from the shooter didn't mean he didn't want something in return. The fact remained that he'd lied to her. He'd come to town specifically to find her and get close. He'd inserted himself into her life, but for what purpose? He had said he worked for some doctor, and that they both wanted to help *people like her*. What did that mean?

Quincy absently reached down into the bag of gas station snacks and grabbed one of the water bottles she'd picked up. Sitting back in her seat, she pressed it against her hand and wrist where the coffee had spilled. As the questions built rapid-fire in her mind, she could feel Logan beside her, calmly sipping his coffee. It was enough of a distraction for her mind to latch onto. She had had what amounted to a small panic attack and yet, there he sat, not a care in the world. Someone takes a shot at him, no big deal. Hot wire and steal a car? Sure. Why not? Relative stranger attempts to throw hot coffee in his face? Business as usual.

There was nothing in her repertoire to explain Logan Davies and his strange sense of equilibrium, which nothing seemed to shake. Super soldier that he was, she had no doubt he could feel her scrutiny, yet he didn't question her. He didn't seem anxious to break the silence. That was nice. But she was jittery and she needed an outlet. Since he was the only one available, she shifted in her seat to face him.

"So, medevaced to Germany?"

Logan didn't seem thrown by the sudden return to their previous topic. "Right. Picking the story back up. I don't actually remember the IED that caused our injuries so I'll just start with me waking up in a hospital, alone."

31

Chapter 31

L ogan

"So, medevaced to Germany?" Quincy prompted.

Logan was thrown by the sudden return to their previous topic. He'd been thinking about her reaction at the gas station, allowing the memory of the painful events that had set him on this path to fade to the back of his mind, and her reminder jarred him out of the present and back in time.

"Right, picking the story back up. I don't actually remember the IED that caused our injuries so I'll just start with me waking up in the hospital, alone," he said. No one was following them and Quincy seemed stable enough at the moment, so he allowed his mind to wander back again. Back to the moment that changed his entire life.

Logan came awake instantly and froze, not sure what had set off his mental trip wire. He tried to concentrate on his surroundings but the pain in his chest made it difficult. He pushed it aside like he'd been trained to do and focused. He could hear what sounded like wheels squeaking by and muted conversation in the distance and, closer, steady beeping and the soft whoosh of flowing air. The tickle in his nose clued him in to the source of the air - he had always hated the feel of oxygen tubing snaking around his head and neck, tying him down. So, hospital then.

Logan's left arm wouldn't move so he gingerly lifted his right to grab the tubing around his ears. There was a sharp, burning pain in his chest and back that flared to life with every breath but despite the heaviness, he could function without the oxygen.

The iv taped into the bend of his right elbow would have to stay for now considering his one-arm status. Speaking of, he glanced down at his left arm and found it strapped to his chest. He wondered vaguely what the damage was. This wasn't the first time he'd woken up in the hospital and it likely wouldn't be the last so he wasn't too concerned. There should be a call button around somewhere but his eyes were heavy and it suddenly didn't seem very important anymore. Besides, Jones would keep watch while Logan was down.....

Jones. Logan's eyes shot open and he bolted upright in the bed. Or he tried to, anyway. The burning pain he'd relegated to the back of his mind tore through his chest and back at the sudden movement and he fell back to the bed, gasping for breath.

Where was Jones? Whenever one of them was down, the other was always there. When one woke up in the hospital, the other would be sacked out in the chair right beside him. Logan had woken up in multiple hospitals and med bays over the years, but he had never woken up without Jones right beside him.

He glanced around for the call button again but it was nowhere in sight. He growled low in his throat, frustration mounting, but decided the call button was irrelevant. He was army, he was hurt, and he wasn't sure where his partner was. He was getting out of *this bed.*

His heart monitor had started alarming the minute he realized Jones was missing, announcing his body's response to panic and pain for the whole world to hear, but still no one came. What kind of low-brow place was this? Logan grit his teeth and, breathing as slowly and shallowly as possible, swung his legs off the side of the bed, pulling on the rail with his good arm to protect his chest as much as possible.

He felt a painful tug against his injured side but ignored it. His head swam once he was upright and he threw out his good arm and made a wild grab for the iv pole. His hand connected and he used it to steady himself. He took a moment to close his eyes and get his bearings before he tried to make it the rest of the way up. He knew from past experience that the dizziness would pass and it wouldn't do Jones any good if he made it to his feet only to pass out again.

He straightened up after a couple of slow breaths and pushed off the bed, making sure his legs were going to hold him. Despite feeling like rubber, he didn't think his legs had taken any damage. And really, even though the rest of him felt like it had been through a trash compactor, if he were guessing, he'd say some broken ribs and a concussion were his biggest problems. He could work with that.

He'd pulled the heart monitor wires off his chest and had almost made the door when it flew open, a tiny, wizened little woman narrowly avoided clipping him as she blasted into the room.

Finally, he thought. Did someone have to die around here to get some attention? But before he had the chance to open his mouth, the small nurse with a grip like iron had a hold on his good arm and was manhandling him back towards the bed.

"Lieutenant Davies, you scared us to death out there. You don't

just disconnect your heart monitor!"

Logan tried to shake her off but she was surprisingly strong for such a small woman. She shook his arm, harshly, he thought, for someone who had just woken up with unknown, possibly debilitating injuries. She glared at him.

"And you pulled out your chest tube!"

Logan glanced down and noticed the blood staining the left side of his gown. He had felt the pull and noticed the wetness against his side, but in the distant way he sometimes had when he was on a mission and had no time to worry about minor details.

"Oh. Um. Sorry, I guess. But I think it's okay."

"You do, do you?" she retorted. "Doctor Morrison had to wire your ribs back together after he dug the splinters out of your lung. In fact, you're lucky you still have your lung. If it hasn't healed enough to hold together, it could collapse and you could very well die. Die! Do you hear me soldier?"

Logan couldn't help the grin. The tiny little woman reminded him of his grandma. Stern and entirely more dramatic than the situation called for.

"Yes ma'am, I hear you," he said. "But I think my lung's going to hold. I'm breathing okay, just a little sore."

"I see. Dr. Davies, is it? I didn't realize," she said caustically. "Now, if you don't mind, Doctor, sit back down and let me listen."

She physically sat him on the bed and whipped out her stethoscope. The metal was frigid against his chest and he couldn't help but flinch a little. He was sure she'd planted it against his chest harder than the situation required.

"You're not really a "blow on the end, warm it up" kind of nurse, are you?" he asked dryly.

"Shut it, you," Nurse Ratchet snapped back.

She listened for a few more seconds before straightening up

and slinging the stethoscope back around her neck. Logan ducked as the end cleared his head space.

"You sound clear. For now. But I'm reporting this incident to Doctor Morrison. I'm sure he'll have words for his non-compliant patient."

She turned to leave but snapped back around. "I'm Shirley and I will be your nurse for the foreseeable future. Your partner, a Lieutenant Levi Jones, is in surgery. His condition was updated an hour ago to stable and he should be out within the hour."

Her eyes seemed to soften minutely as she looked at him. "I'll make sure his doctor stops to see you as soon as he's finished." She opened the door and tossed back, "And your call button is on the bed rail. Use it next time." Then she was gone, leaving a speechless Logan in her wake.

Time seemed to crawl as Logan waited for the doctor. Nurse Shirley hadn't given him any information other than Jones was in surgery and stable. In Logan's experience, 'stable' just meant 'not dying in the next five minutes'.

It left a lot of room for speculation, and Logan didn't have anything else to speculate about. Jones could have a spinal injury and be paralyzed. Or maybe he was bleeding internally. They could be repairing a lacerated liver or spleen. Or it could be worse. If Jonesy lost a kidney, it was an automatic medical discharge.

So many variables and Logan had nothing but time to dwell on them. He took a deep, calming breath but flinched when pain tore through his left side. When he'd pulled the chest tube out in his determination to find answers, nurse Shirley had been worried his lung would collapse again and it would need to be reinserted. But so far it was holding its own, if not a bit uncomfortably. And while his head pounded and ached in tandem, it was livable.

He had been pleasantly surprised to find his arm intact. It had been strapped to his chest to immobilize and protect his broken ribs but was, in fact, perfectly fine. He always hated arm injuries because they made him feel disadvantaged in a way other injuries never had.

Being an arm down made him feel partly blind, like he was leaving his flank unprotected. Jonesy would always laugh when Logan said that.

'Man, you don't need both arms to protect your flank. That's what you got me for, fool.' But Jones wasn't here this time, which meant Logan needed both arms. His partner was down – it was his turn to be the eyes.

Another glance at the clock told him it had been 58 minutes since the last time he'd checked, which was 13 minutes longer than Nurse Shirley said Jonesy's surgery should last. Logan reached for the remote with his free arm and turned the t.v. on. He flipped through the channels, stopped momentarily on a rerun of M.A.S.H, but shut it back down after a few minutes.

T.V. never really got it right. He thought about buzzing Shirley again but decided not to poke the bear. The last time he rang, she had stormed in with a cup of ice chips and practically thrown a magazine at him. Then she slammed her hands on the bed rails on either side of him and leaned over until they were eye-to-eye.

"If you push that button one more time, and I get up and walk in this room, and you aren't actively bleeding or dying, you will be when I leave."

Now, Logan had been reamed out and intimidated by the toughest officers and drill sergeants the army could churn out. But Nurse Shirley was in a class all her own. And Logan believed every word. She had remained frozen above him, staring him down and waiting.

Logan had swallowed and then, like the good soldier he was,

nodded his head.

"Yes ma'am."

The door finally, finally, swung open and Logan jerked his head up off the bed to see a tall man in blue surgical scrubs and cap follow Nurse Shirley into the room.

"Shirley, I see you're taking great care of our young lieutenant." The man grinned at Logan. "How's he doing?"

"Despite pulling his chest tube out ten minutes after he regained consciousness, he's doing just fine."

Nurse Shirley's disapproving look contrasted ironically with her surprisingly gentle arrangement of the blankets covering his legs.

"I'm sure you won't give Commander Marlowe any trouble at all, will you Lt. Davies?" She casually slid a syringe from the pocket of her jacket and held it up to the light, flicking it until all the air bubbles dissipated. "I would hate to have to come back into this room."

"Unless I was actively bleeding or dying. Yes ma'am, I remember," Logan agreed wholeheartedly. Nurse Shirley gave him a grandmotherly smile and left him to consider what other methods of persuasion she had tucked away on her person.

Logan turned back to the commander. "Do you think she keeps that needle in there just for shock value?" he asked.

The commander laughed. "I've learned that Shirley never makes a promise she isn't willing to keep. But a better nurse you will not find."

The man tucked the chart he held under his left arm and extended a hand. "I'm Commander Marlowe. I'm the surgeon who took care of Lt. Jones. Shirley tells me you might like an update?"

Logan exhaled a breath he didn't know he was holding. "So he made it through surgery then?" Logan asked, although at this point it was just a formality. Something about the Cdr.'s casual posture told Logan his partner was still breathing.

Cdr. Marlowe pulled a chair over beside Logan's bed and sat. "He did, but first thing's first."

He flipped open one of the files he was holding and glanced through it. "Lt. Logan Davies. Moderate concussion, left pneumothorax. Chest tube was inserted in-country but Shirley tells me you've already remedied that." The commander paused and glanced up at Logan with a wry smile. "Care to defend your actions Lieutenant?"

Logan rolled his shoulders, trying to loosen the tightness in his head and neck that was aggravating his headache. Or concussion, apparently.

"I'm fine. Talk to me about Jones. How did - ," Cdr. Marlowe cut in, his easy-going attitude suddenly replaced by a no-nonsense commanding officer.

"We will talk about Lt. Jones once we've discussed your condition soldier. You're right - you are fine. Or you will be, soon enough. But Lt. Jones's condition is going to take some time to wade through so I need you to focus for five minutes."

The commander took a breath and seemed to consider for a moment. "He's alive. And I believe, with time, he will recover. Now, back to that missing chest tube."

Logan understood the chain of command. He was a good soldier, and had been one for many years. But he wasn't quite ready to give up on his friend. "Sir, if I may, my injuries will heal. I just need to know if my partner's will, too."

"I understand," said Cdr. Marlowe, and Logan thought he actually did. He looked sympathetic. He even looked sympathetic as he pushed the chair back, stood, and said, "I'll go get your *attending physician. I'll let him discuss your condition with you and we can talk about Lt. Jones after."*

"Wait. What?" Logan was confused. "I thought...you're not my doctor?"

Was his concussion worse than he thought? He did seem to be having trouble following the commander's quick changes in personality. Or maybe it was changes in subject he was having trouble tracking "If you're not my doctor, why do you want to talk about me?"

"Kid, I'm a neurosurgeon. One of the chief neurosurgeons at this facility, in fact. I have zero interest in your case." Cdr. Marlowe tipped his head in thought. "Scratch that. Your concussion gives me maybe a five percent interest in your case. Enough for me to listen to an intern or a medical student break it down. Not enough to actually treat it myself."

He shook his head, like he was shaking off a bum detail from a tyrant drill sergeant that he really didn't want. "As one of the chief neurosurgeons, I do, however, have a vested interest in your partner's case." The commander let out a deep breath, which sounded more like a weary sigh to Logan. "I also know what it's like, in-country. I know the dependence partners put on each other. I know it's the only way we make it out alive most of the time. Which is why I thought I'd do you a solid, look you over myself. I have no real interest in your broken ribs. Pretty much none in your chest tube, or lack thereof. And as long as you keep breathing, I couldn't care less that you pulled it out yourself."

Logan thought it rather ironic that the commander would adjust the oxygen levels flowing through his nasal cannula while claiming not to care about his non-patient's breathing.

"However, I can't guarantee your cardiothoracic surgeon will feel the same. Dr. Morrison isn't military but he imitates a fine

drill sergeant." Marlowe gave that a minute to sink in. "So pick your poison soldier. It's me or him."

Logan was nothing if not pragmatic. He'd been raised by a mother whose wandering, freewheeling lifestyle had insured he'd either be flaky himself or develop practicality as a superpower. So he was willing to accept a generous offer when it was presented. He gave a nod and the commanding officer standing in front of him became an unusually affable chief neurosurgeon once more.

"Okay then," he said. "I believe we were talking about that chest tube. Or lack thereof, am I right?"

He put the charts he carried down on the small table beside the bed and motioned Logan forward. "Let's go ahead and take a look so we can say we did."

Logan shifted so the commander could pull his gown away from his left side and flinched when he started tugging at the bandages nurse Shirley had so lovingly and painfully placed over the wound.

"Looks like you pulled it out cleanly, all things considered. I don't see any obvious signs of bleeding or oozing around the incision site."

The commander taped the gauze back in place and let Logan's gown fall back over his side. "I'm going to take a quick listen. Go ahead and lean forward."

Logan used his good arm to pull himself away from the back of the bed and took in a couple of breaths while Marlowe moved his stethoscope around his chest and back. It was painful, trying to breathe so deeply, and Logan had to fight the urge to cough, but he managed to hold it back. When Marlowe seemed satisfied with what he heard, he straightened and helped Logan lean back. There was a pillow sitting in one of the spare chairs by the window and the commander walked around the bed and grabbed it.

"Coughing is actually good in this situation. You need to cough to keep the fluid from settling into your lungs because it can build up and cause infection faster than you'd think. But it'll hurt for a while. When you feel it coming, squeeze a pillow to your chest as tight as you can and hold it there through the cough."

He demonstrated on the pillow in his arms and then tossed it to Logan. "The pillow will help brace your ribs and give you support. It'll still hurt but it shouldn't feel like your chest is coming apart."

Logan caught the pillow with his right arm and sat it beside him on the bed. "I thought you said you were a neurosurgeon."

The commander smiled. "Oh, you know. I pick up stuff here and there. I have a lot of little tricks. If you ever need to reduce a shoulder dislocation on your own, give me a call. I'll walk you right through it."

"Questions about your own injuries/prognosis/rehab before we move on?"

Logan just quirked an eyebrow, as if to ask 'Seriously?'

Cdr. Marlowe grinned. "I figured but I had to ask."

He settled back into his previous chair by the side of the bed and dropped Logan's chart onto the floor at his feet, then leaned over and grabbed the other chart. The much thicker chart. Jonesy's chart.

"The news isn't all bad, but it isn't entirely great either. I think it will make more sense if we start at the very beginning. How much do you remember about the IED explosion?"

Logan closed his eyes and tried to picture what had happened. It had come back in bits and pieces after he had woken up. "I remember we were on foot, passing through a small town that was little more than a patch of dirt."

Logan remembered everything that happened before the explosion very well. The almost-suffocating dryness of the air as he tried to suck in breaths. The dust that had settled into every available outlet on his face – his eyes, inside his nose, between his teeth.

The fact that he wasn't sweating nearly enough in the debilitating heat. And the town itself, perfectly silent and still. Looking back, that should have been their first clue that something was wrong. Towns like that were never still. Whether it was children roaming the alleyways, stray dogs and cats fighting over scraps of trash, or women sneaking from one doorway to another, trying to remain unseen, there was always movement. These towns might be quiet, but they were never still.

Their convoy had been rolling through the town, on a humanitarian mission of all things. There had been reports in the area of disease-riddled civilian populations that needed food, water, and basic medical supplies. They had been driving a 15-mile stretch, distributing what aid they could. A couple guys had hopped out of the transport vehicles, opting for the dry, arid heat outside the Humvee rather than the thick, stifling heat inside it, Logan and Jonesy among them.

Logan could remember the guys joking and laughing. It felt good to be caregivers for once instead of shock troops and they had been enjoying the reprieve. Logan could remember how Clipper started singing some song about blue skies and beautiful women he claimed to have picked up down in New Orleans.

He remembered McDaniels tossing clods of the dry, packed dirt that littered the countryside at him and Mitch howling like a dying coyote. He could remember looking back at Jonesy, who was grinning like he'd never seen anything funnier.

Which was ridiculous, because McDaniels and Mitch weren't that funny. He could remember opening his mouth to say something to him but he couldn't remember what because there was a sound, a loud, ripping sound, like metal on metal. And there was a flash of white and red and black. And there was a rush of burning heat. And then there was the hospital and the pain and the panic of not knowing where his partner was.

There was Nurse Ratchet and Cdr. Marlowe. And, finally, there was Jonesy. Lying in a bed, breathing through a tube. Jonesy, disoriented and dazed, not able to hear or see where he was.

And then, finally, Jonesy, who could hear too much.

32

Chapter 32

L ogan

Logan sighed and pulled himself back to the present. He couldn't allow himself to get lost in the past. This was about Quincy, not Jones. Logan couldn't protect Jones anymore but Quincy? She was still here. And with a shooter gunning for her, he couldn't afford to lose what little trust she had in him.

He was painfully aware, even if she wasn't, just how close she'd come to dying. He'd followed her, of course, intending to try to calm her down when the shot had been taken. It had been dead on and nothing but dumb luck had prevented it from hitting its mark. Whoever the shooter was, he was a professional and the odds of him missing a second time were non-existent.

Logan had already managed to spook Quincy at the cafe. He knew it had been risky to reach out to her. He had observed her enough to know she kept people at arm's length deliberately and that any obvious push to invade her privacy would be met with instant resistance. But he had spent time with her.

First, to assess her as a potential target. Later, to build trust once he realized she was. Maybe it was flattery, but he thought she even kind of enjoyed his company. He definitely enjoyed hers. Probably more than he should, considering she was the mission.

He had been sent to observe her, and later, to bring her in when they realized they were right about her and he was soldier enough to know that emotions complicated matters, always. But she seemed so alone and so sad. And so utterly unaware of what was happening.

Logan had to agree with Garrison – she clearly had no idea. If he was going to be able to help her, if they were going to be able to help her, he had to do this right.

"The doctors had all but written Jones off by that point. These were all military doctors and nurses you understand, and every one of them had spent years treating combat injuries. To them, it was just one more case of PTSD. Granted, it was a severe case and the symptoms were unusual, but still. You've seen one, you've seen a dozen."

It still burned, all these years later, that no one had believed Jones or tried to look deeper.

"I don't blame them. I think combat medics must be a little traumatized themselves, seeing what they see and doing what they do. But even when you know you sound crazy, when you know you don't make any sense, you still just want someone to believe you, you know?" he asked, glancing over at her.

Her eyes were locked on his face, absorbing his words. He couldn't tell what she was thinking, though she was clearly thinking something.

"Yes," she finally said. "I really do." He thought that might be the most honest thing she had ever admitted to him.

"So anyway, with specialist after specialist giving us the same diagnosis, Jones started spiraling. He became angry and withdrawn. Even I couldn't pull him out of it. At that point, I was researching neurological injuries day and night, looking for anything that could help. I became something of an amateur expert," he said with a laugh. "I can tell you almost anything you want to know about traumatic brain injuries and treatment options. I also know the names of all the heavy hitters in the field," he said, thinking of the list of names he'd compiled.

A list of the most renowned, well-known medical professionals even remotely related to the field of neurology. How he'd contacted each and every one of those experts and then crossed their names off the list one-by-one. Until he came to Dr. Garrison.

"He blew in like a whirlwind. From the get-go, he gave us his full attention. He caused a huge stir, ordering new scans, and scans they hadn't thought to do, and more blood work.

He even put together his own tests to prove that Jones wasn't just imagining the noise. I think the only reason the hospital allowed him access was because they were so tired of having to deal with us themselves. He took complete control of Jones's care and I was just so grateful to have someone that actually believed us."

"So, he proved Jones really was hearing more than he should be able to? That it wasn't a psychosomatic symptom of his brain trauma?" Quincy asked? "How did that even work?"

"It was pretty simple, really. We put Jones in a room in an empty wing of the hospital. Dr. Garrison had this tiny frequency emitter that gave off a low frequency when activated. His phone was attached to the device so he could see when the frequency was on. I moved at predetermined intervals and activated the device."

Logan shook his head, because it was still hard to believe. "I was the one pushing the button and I could barely hear it. But Jones could hear the frequency, with perfect timing, at over 2,000 feet."

33

Chapter 33

Q**uincy**

Quincy stared at Logan. He was joking. Or lying. He had to be. Logan paused, giving her time to wrap her mind around what he'd just said. He obviously wasn't joking though, and nothing in his body language or tone of voice suggested he was lying.

It should have been impossible to hear so clearly from so far away. But Logan was serious. He wasn't playing with her and he wasn't exaggerating. He was completely and entirely sincere. He wanted her to understand exactly what his partner went through. It was very important to him that she believe him. But honestly, it made her uncomfortable.

The headache that had started earlier in the day had arrived in full force and the buzzing that usually accompanied her headaches was starting to drown out the conversation. As Logan told his story, she had felt the pressure start to build, making her feel squeezed tight, like there was a band around her chest, or her head, and she couldn't get a full breath. The whole story of Logan and his partner. The way she was being stalked. The words *people like you.*

The whole situation was jarring but it felt familiar somehow. Like maybe this story had as much to do with her as it did Logan and Jones. Which didn't make any sense. She didn't know Jones. She didn't have super hearing. She didn't have a brain injury or PTSD or whatever this was that Logan was describing. She had headaches, sure. And she didn't sleep.

Maybe she sometimes had trouble concentrating because of all the information spinning through her head and she had a habit of doing things she didn't know she could do. But some people just reacted well under pressure. Lots of people had trouble shutting their thoughts off at night. And who didn't have a migraine now and again?

Speaking of, she suddenly became aware of the pain in blinding fashion. She had gotten so caught up in her own thoughts that she'd pushed the headache off to the side. But it flared suddenly, catching her off-guard. She sucked in a breath and pushed her body flat against the seat, trying to absorb some of the pain. Logan looked over, concerned.

"What's up?"

She couldn't respond, too wrapped up in fighting back the waves of pain rolling through her head. She had had some bad ones before but this...She tried to focus on her breathing. Breathe in slow, count to three, breathe out slower, count to six. She could hear Logan in the distance, saying her name, but it was vague and far away. She needed out of this car. Now.

"Pull over."

She managed to turn her head and blinked, trying in vain to get her eyes to stay open. "I need to get out of this car."

Logan, to his credit, didn't argue or even question. He glanced in the rear view mirror, put on the hazard lights, and pulled slowly onto the shoulder. The second the car was stopped, Quincy threw the door open and leaned out, putting her head between her knees. She felt the opposite door open and Logan was suddenly in front of her, crouched down so he could try to see her face. But it was all very far away.

All she could think about was the pain in her head, blocking everything else out. She wished she could throw up. Maybe that would help. Or pass out. That would definitely help. At least the sun had already set, leaving the sky light enough to still see but not bright enough to make things worse.

If she could just sit here for a few minutes and breathe, and try not to think about what was happening around her, maybe she could get the pain under control.

Logan's voice reached her from far away. He sounded almost frantic and she thought maybe he wasn't talking to her anymore. It didn't sound like her name he was calling. She felt him reach up and touch her neck. She tried in vain to shy away, the unexpected touch almost searing against her skin. But when his cool, gentle fingers pressed up underneath her jaw, she recognized distantly the search for a pulse point and she stilled.

He said something, hesitated, and then murmured something else and then she realized – he was talking on the phone. He must've been really worried to call someone. Phone signals could be traced.

She slid one of her hands away from her face and squeezed the hand pressed to her neck, just enough to hopefully reassure him that she was really okay, she just needed a few minutes. He must've gotten the message because his fingers left her neck and wrapped around her forearm, reassuringly solid and warm. He said something else into the phone, probably telling whoever was on the other end that she had finally responded.

She could feel her breath beginning to slow and the band around her chest easing. The buzzing had cleared enough for her to make out words now instead of just sounds, although they still sounded like they were coming to her from underwater.

"I think she's starting to come around," Logan said.

A pause, and then the hand slid lower around her wrist. "Pulse is back down too. She's around 120. Still high, but more like she just ran a mile and less like she's stroking out."

He was silent. Then, "Yeah, she's starting to respond. Is there something I could be doing to help?"

Quincy managed to crack her eyes open and look down at him from between her fingers. Logan looked frustrated.

"Well, what do you think set it off?" He didn't seem pleased with the answer. "If I don't know what I did, how can I keep from doing it again?"

He sighed. "I know. But you're the expert. I'm no good at explaining medical stuff. Plus, no one's ever gone catatonic on me before."

Another pause, and this time he seemed to be considering what the person on the other end of the line was saying. "No, I don't think we were followed. It would've been another hour at least before the car was reported and even longer before the plates were noticed. Actually, we may still be clean with the plates. As long as there are license plates, no one ever actually looks at what's on them. And then once we hit I-40, we could've been heading in any direction."

Logan finally stood and paced away, facing the forested land on the opposite side of the road and ran a hand through that unruly hair.

"I'd rather put another couple of hours between us and Sheraton but if you think we need to stop, I think we're probably safe enough."

He waited for the response, glancing back in Quincy's direction before looking away again. "Doc, they put a kill order out on her. They took a shot, in the middle of the day, in public. They aren't going to be afraid to make a scene this time."

34

Chapter 34

Logan

From his post by the window, Logan had a clear view of the entire parking lot of the Super 8 he'd found just off the interstate, plus a visual on the front office. The place was pretty low brow but it sat off the road enough to be inconvenient for most passersby to get to and cheap enough to make the cigarette smell negligible.

He had been hoping to drive through the night, putting as much distance between them and whoever was gunning for Quincy as possible, as quickly as possible, but that hadn't been an option. Logan glanced over at Quincy, who was dozing restlessly on the bed farthest from the door.

When they had pulled into the little motel in Pittsburgh, Texas, she had insisted on getting out of the car and into the room on her own but Logan had had his doubts. She was as snippy as usual but her sarcasm had less bite to it than normal and she was pale, alarmingly so. Nevertheless, he'd given her space, grabbing her backpack out of the backseat and shoving the water and leftover snacks she'd picked up at the convenience store inside.

Then he'd slung it over his shoulder and stayed a few steps behind her - far enough she couldn't accuse him of hovering but close enough to grab her if her knees buckled.

She was going to have to explain whatever that was in the car. And soon. She didn't seem overly concerned, which actually concerned him quite a bit. They had just been talking. He had laid Jones's symptoms out there for her and she was asking questions. Skeptically of course, but still, she hadn't seemed completely disbelieving.

He turned back towards the window, scanning the parking lot and connecting exits again. He had told her about the attack and Jones and Dr. Garrison, but none of that should have set off any of her internal alarms. There wasn't anything that she should have been able to relate back to her own situation, especially considering she didn't seem to know she even had a situation to relate to. He had decided to wait before pushing that envelope at her.

So he couldn't think of anything that would have caused that kind of sudden, severe migraine. That kind of anxious panic attack. That kind of anxious, panicky, PTSD-driven migraine. He sighed. He had seen enough traumatized veterans, himself included, have similar reactions that he couldn't really deny it.

He had been hoping that her condition was the result of some kind of brain malformation or hormone deficiency, no matter how much Dr. Garrison shot those theories down. He had been hoping she had managed to avoid the terror and devastation that he'd seen this kind of brain injury cause in others.

That it caused in Jones. But it seemed like she was just as damaged as the others.

Logan shifted in the chair, which was much too small to comfortably accommodate his 6'4" frame. It wasn't just too small, it was also too hard. He highly suspected a deviant had nailed a piece of plywood underneath the seat to keep it from dropping out. He highly suspected this because, in a moment of pure desperation and exhaustion, he'd flipped the chair over to find out just why, exactly, this was the most uncomfortable chair on the face of the earth.

And who but a deviant would visit such an atrocity upon an unsuspecting chair and its equally unsuspecting occupant? But it was the only chair in the room, so here he sat.

He'd pulled said chair into the corner of the room, across from his bed, at an angle that let him see the entire parking area and the main lobby without letting anyone see him. The lights in the room were out but the thin curtains didn't do much to block the light from the parking lot, casting the room into shadow but not allowing for complete darkness.

So Logan could see Quincy tossing and turning, fidgeting in her sleep. Actually, he wasn't sure he would call it sleep. It was more of a broken, restless doze, interrupted every half hour or so by a short burst of sudden wakefulness. She thought he didn't know when she was awake and he'd decided to let her keep that illusion.

She had so little control over her life right now, any he could give her could only help. He hoped this restless, broken sleep was just a by-product of the day but he was afraid it might actually be her norm. He hadn't known her that long of course, but there were things she'd said, and not said, that made him wonder.

Comments about long nights. Her mainlining of anything coffee or caffeine-related. The dark circles that marred an otherwise flawless complexion. And the sheer volume of reading material she consumed. There surely weren't enough hours in the day to get through as much as she did. She had to be supplementing somewhere.

Headlights flashed through the darkness and he snapped back to attention, cracking his neck side-to-side and shaking his arms out. He was no stranger to sleepless nights himself but his hours of endless patrol in deserts far, far away were long past and it wasn't like he was getting any younger.

A newer model Toyota pulled into a parking space 6 doors down from their room. The front door of the rented Prius opened and a middle-aged woman in a rumpled business suit stepped out and walked tiredly to the room adjacent.

Logan watched until he saw the glow of light filter through her curtains and onto the cracked concrete outside before he relaxed back into the chair.

To keep himself alert and his mind off the monstrosity that was this chair, he mentally reviewed the plan for the next morning. Ideally, he'd like to be on the road before daylight. Maybe 6:00, 6:30 at the latest. They had driven about four hours today. Well, yesterday, technically. That wasn't nearly enough distance to make him feel safe but it couldn't be helped. Pittsburgh, Texas was barely a blip on the map, which did make him feel marginally better.

There were only a couple of other vehicles in the lot and while Quincy was in the shower, Logan had slipped out to the Jeep Cherokee parked on the opposite side of the motel and swapped out the plates. Luckily, the Jeep had Arkansas plates too, so the odds of the owner noticing were next to none. He would still feel better once they ditched the car but that could wait a few more hours.

The sound of tires crunching on gravel caught his attention and his eyes shifted to the driveway of the motel. He watched as a dark, four-door sedan, unknown make and model, pulled in without headlights and parked in one of the spaces reserved for customers checking in and out. Logan eased to his feet and slid closer to the window. Without touching the curtain, he peered out into the darkness, squinting his eyes to try to see better.

The car sat idle for a few minutes, no movement inside or out, before the door opened and a tall, thin man climbed out. He closed the door quietly and circled the car, taking in his surroundings before moving into the shadows closer to the motel. But Logan could tell he was still there.

The wind was nothing but a light breeze, barely enough to move the branches of the pathetically scrawny trees lining the drive. And still Logan waited, with the feeling the man was waiting too, watching for something - a rustle of a curtain, a light in a window, anything to give away what he was looking for.

Logan was intensely glad he had moved the car to the back side of the motel. It would be more difficult to get to but it was out of line of sight of the road and from the front parking lot. The street lights cast just enough glow for Logan to see when the man finally moved. If he hadn't been looking for it, he wouldn't have seen it. The man was tall, 6'2", and he had a slight, willowy build.

Not someone Logan would call an athlete, but you didn't have to be a weightlifter to be dangerous. Logan watched as the man moved along the line of cars parked on the far side of the lot, facing the highway. He looked to be inspecting each one individually.

Logan had seen enough. He backed slowly away from the window. He hated to lose visual on the man but they needed to move.

"Quincy," he whispered.

"What is it?" she asked instantly, more alert than he had expected.

"There's someone out in the parking lot, checking vehicles. We need to go."

Logan moved silently back towards the window and peered out, making sure to stay at an angle that would keep anyone watching outside from seeing him, careful not to move the curtains. Quincy swung her legs over the side of the bed and rolled out, landing in a crouch before standing up.

When she moved away from the bed, he could see she had somehow managed to pull her tennis shoes on and get them tied in those few seconds when she had been down. Her bag was in her hand and she was at his shoulder in a matter of seconds. *Practice makes perfect,* he thought idly.

"What makes you think it's our guy?" she asked quietly. "Could just be someone who had a few too many at the bar and can't remember where he is."

He shot her a look. "While the thought of a drunk man driving around with their headlights off after dark is a cheery thought, there aren't many people who know how to move without being seen."

He nodded towards the man, who seemed to have given up on the cars and was heading back towards the front of the motel. "Who keeps to the shadows while inspecting every car in a random motel parking lot without setting off any alarms or attracting any attention. Sure. It could be anyone."

She huffed. "Fine. But your sarcasm is noted and not appreciated."

Logan watched the man lean down into his car and grab something from the inside. Documentation probably, a badge or something convincing to show the desk clerk to insure his cooperation. He squinted out into the night. He had been hoping the dome light in the car would come on when the man opened the door so he could put a face to the guy but no luck.

Whoever this man was, he was a professional. Amateurs often missed the little things, like disabling interior car lights. Experts did not.

"Grab my bag. As soon as he goes inside, we're out of here."

Quincy didn't respond. The man had pulled open the front door and disappeared inside, most likely to have a chat with the night manager about who might have checked in over the last few hours. Logan didn't want to be here when the manager gave up their room number.

"Come on," he said, opening the door and stepping back to let Quincy step through first. When she didn't move, he glanced over. She looked...strange.

"What's wrong?" he asked. Now would not be a great time for a repeat performance from before. They didn't have time for pain or panic at the moment.

She hesitated another second, then shook her head. "It's nothing." she said resolutely. "Let's go."

35

Chapter 35

Q**uincy**

The motel was dark and quiet and for the first time in twelve hours, Quincy could think. This was bad. No, that wasn't quite right. She had been through *bad* before. There had been that first time in Boise, when she had spotted the man watching her from a booth inside the truck stop diner.

She had liked being Grace Elliott. The college was nice and the work was easy. She was the youngest of the waitresses by far, which made her a shoe-in as the group darling. The other waitresses, all grandmotherly types, took her under their wing and the truckers treated her like a princess. They tipped well and kept some of the more handsy, unwelcome attention at bay.

Burning her life there had been regrettable but not all that difficult. Kara Scott hadn't been quite as great, but it was the best she could do on short notice. The bar hadn't been as friendly as the truck stop and while the regulars there certainly paid attention to her, it wasn't in the nice, respectful way she'd come to appreciate.

Her old pal George, who ran a route from Nebraska to Michigan, would have made sure the drunk bankers and lawyers who frequented this particular bar kept their comments, and their hands, to themselves.

She sighed quietly from her position, curled onto her right side on the bed. She missed George. And safety. Or at least the false perception of safety. She rolled onto her other side, facing the door and Logan.

Logan.

He had certainly kept her safe today. First from the assassin stalking her in Podunk, USA, and then from the agonizing migraine and its wretched after-effects. She watched him as he sat in a tiny chair in the corner, eyes locked on the slit between the curtain and the window, watching for any sign they had been followed.

She felt kind of bad. He would have obviously preferred to keep going but she knew from painful experience that these headaches were best handled with sleep. And a distinct lack of motion. One of the bright spots to these sudden attacks, actually, was her ability to sleep soundly for at least a couple of hours at a time. So she had appreciated Logan's willingness to pull over. It looked like a low-rent, pay-by-the-hour kind of place, but still, it was something.

Not that she was getting any sleep now. There was simply too much on her mind. She could tell Logan was worried about her. After the pain had subsided, she had slumped back into her seat but been unable to pick her legs up to pull them back into the car. The sudden force of the attacks always left her exhausted and barely able to function.

Logan had swung her legs back up and in, leaned over and buckled her seat belt, and then sank back onto his heels and watched her for a minute. She could feel his concern like a physical thing, warm and secure and incredibly suffocating. She knew she was going to have to explain what happened, at least as well as she could. He deserved that much. But what was there to explain? She really didn't understand them herself.

Sometimes she got headaches. They were usually unexpected and always intense. The only common denominator she could find between them was stress, but stress didn't always set them off. She was always completely drained after, like a battery that had lost its charge but the sleep she got afterwards mostly got her charge back up.

She had been awake for several hours now but she had kept as still and quiet as she could. She didn't really feel like talking and that wouldn't help her think anyway. There had been something weird about this particular headache, but she couldn't put her finger on exactly what. Yes, today could certainly be called stressful, after finding out Logan wasn't who he said he was, being shot at, stealing a car, and going on the lam with a virtual stranger. Adrenaline had been spiking off and on all day.

There had been sweating and nerves and anxiety. But if that was going to set off a headache, wouldn't it have happened much sooner? Her headache after the train station had hit almost the second she made it back to her apartment, which was the same time she had started to believe she might be safe. So, rush of fear dissipates, adrenaline fades, and her body retaliates with pain. But then, why wouldn't this one have hit once they were on the road, conceivably safe for the moment?

The only thing that had been happening when the pain hit today was Logan telling his story. Or rather, telling Jones's story. But she remembered, with suffocating clarity, the feeling of panic as she listened. The feeling that he was too close, *it* was too close. The feeling that Jones's story would be the end of her.

Or maybe the beginning. Which was a weird response to have to a story about someone she didn't know. That was when the buzzing and pain had forced its way forward. But why should she feel that way? She wasn't Jones. She wasn't military. Her brain was perfectly fine - no blunt force trauma in recent memory. No genetic deformities or mental issues of any kind. Unless you count a photographic memory and insomnia on the list of medical defects, she was perfectly healthy.

Her hearing was only so-so, which eliminated that possible link. She wished she could say Jones's super hearing was the weirdest thing about this whole mess, she really did. What did it say about the situation that it wasn't?

Logan shifted minutely in his chair and drew her attention. He'd been doing that for the last four hours - shifting, stretching, slouching - anything to ease the misery caused by shoving his long, long body into a teeny, tiny chair. But this was different. The slight restlessness, the drumming of his fingers, even the slow tilting of his head back and forth, all stopped instantly. He leaned towards the window, hugging the wall to stay out of sight.

"Quincy," she heard him whisper.

"What is it?" she asked, although she figured she already knew.

"There's someone out in the parking lot, checking vehicles. We need to go."

Yep. That sounded about right. Logan moved back towards the window, trying to keep whoever he was watching in sight. He was in full-on soldier mode, so she figured time was of the essence.

Luckily, this was basically how she'd started her day for years. She swung her legs over the side of the bed and rolled out, landing in a crouch beside her shoes, which were lined up and ready to slip on at a moment's notice. As she stood, she scooped up her backpack and dropped it onto her shoulders, grabbing Logan's as well. They had kept everything packed so very little effort was needed to leave.

"What makes you think it's our guy?" she asked quietly. "Could just be someone who had a few too many at the bar and can't remember where he is."

Not that she doubted him. But she did want to know how he knew. Might come in handy for when she was on her own again. The look he turned on her was part condescension, part exasperation.

"While the thought of a drunk man driving around with their headlights off after dark is a cheery thought, there aren't many people who know how to move without being seen."

His eyes moved back towards the window and she followed suit. "Who keeps to the shadows while inspecting every car in a random motel parking lot without setting off any alarms or attracting any attention. Sure. It could be anyone."

Okay, so maybe he had a point. But the attitude? Man needed a nap.

"Fine. But your sarcasm is noted and not appreciated."

This time, he just rolled his eyes but kept watching the

man, who appeared to be done lurking and was moving purposefully towards the motel lobby.

"Grab my bag. As soon as he goes inside, we're out of here."

Quincy already had his bag, and her bag, and anything else he might think she didn't know to grab, and was about to tell him that when she froze. The man had just pulled open the front door and disappeared into the lobby. But as he was going through the door, he turned back towards them and, just for a moment, the lights from inside the motel had caught his profile.

She might have only so-so hearing but her vision was fantastic. Which meant that one split second had been enough for her to see exactly who was following them. And for her to recognize him. Logan was already holding the door open, waiting for her to step through.

"Come on," he said, When she didn't move, he glanced over, concerned.

"What's wrong?" he asked, clearly worried she was in the middle of another pseudo aneurysm.

She hesitated another second, then shook her head. She would deal with it later. They didn't have time now. "It's nothing," she said. "Let's go."

36

Chapter 36

Logan

Logan didn't relax until they were on the interstate, mixing with the early morning commuters. He glanced in his rear view mirror as he changed lanes, making sure he didn't have a tail. He had been going over and over it in his mind. How did this guy track them? What did he miss? Sure, it had been a rush job but he didn't see any obvious holes that could have led this guy right to them.

Quincy reached out and adjusted the radio and he made a mental note. Apparently she didn't care for talk radio. She finally settled on a station playing 70s rock and sank back into her seat, leaning her head against the window and closing her eyes. She had been quiet since the motel and he couldn't figure out why.

She wasn't exactly verbose at the best of times but this wasn't just quiet. It was disquiet. Something was bothering her. Something other than the obvious. He supposed he could be respectful of her feelings and give her some time to think through whatever it was. But why start now?

"Start talking sister."

She glanced over and her expression could only be described as unimpressed.

"Excuse me?"

He was sure that expression, coupled with the raised eyebrow and the tone of voice, had backed many a man off in her time but Logan was made of tougher stuff than most.

"You heard me. It's zero dark thirty, I haven't slept for almost 24 hours, and we're stuck back in this tiny car for hours. You can pick the topic but you've got to give me something."

He stretched his left leg out as far as he could, which wasn't far at all, and groaned. "We need to steal a bigger car." He thought Quincy almost smiled at that.

"Just how many cars are we planning to steal?" she asked.

"As many as it takes to get to Dr. Garrison."

Now he had her full attention. "Dr. Garrison, the doctor who took care of Jones, Dr. Garrison? What does he have to do with any of this?" she asked.

"You haven't guessed yet?" he asked. Quincy had gotten that weird, random headache and he hadn't had a chance to really get into everything yet. "I know I didn't get a chance to finish the story but this shouldn't be too hard to figure out"

"Dr. Garrison is the guy you're working for," she guessed.

"Tell you what. You tell me what that headache was all about or what happened at the motel to shut you down, your choice, and I'll finish telling you my story."

She was quiet for a long minute, staring blindly ahead, fingers picking absently at a frayed spot in the knee of her jeans, before nodding her head almost resignedly.

"How about you pull over and let me drive for awhile and I'll tell you both." Logan almost didn't believe his luck. He must have looked skeptical because she smiled.

"Like you said, you haven't slept for almost 24 hours. I got a couple of hours at the motel, which is more than I usually get. I'm good to go and you could stand to close your eyes for a little while. Or at least relax a little."

He had to acknowledge the wisdom of the suggestion. He was tired. And sore. And it did seem like they had slipped away from their stalker, at least for the moment. It would probably be the only chance he would get for awhile.

"Okay. Fair enough." Logan signaled and moved over to take the next exit, which had a rest stop where they could pull over and swap seats. "We'll pull in up here and get gas, maybe a coffee for you and a soda for me, and you can take the next few hours. But I'm holding you to your end of the deal."

"Aye aye Captain."

37

Chapter 37

"**A**ll the world is made of faith, and trust, and pixie dust." *J.M. Barrie*

It doesn't come easy. Why should it? It couldn't be held or seen. It couldn't be touched. It was intangible, it was oblique. Rarely given. Rarely earned.

Trust only becomes real when it is tested.

* * *

Quincy

The car was quiet back out on the road. While Logan was filling up, she had run into the gas station and grabbed the largest cup of coffee she could find. She had a feeling she was going to need it. She also bought a couple of bottled sodas and waters, along with packs of beef jerky and a box of donuts.

Logan didn't seem to be in the mood to stop for breakfast and that should tide them over for awhile. Quincy really wasn't looking forward to the conversation to come. She didn't talk about herself as a rule. Certainly not about anything real.

Telling Logan about her life, the years spent running and hiding when she didn't even know why, did not sound like great road trip conversation. But she had agreed to trust him and she really did mean it. She didn't have much of a choice for one. And after putting himself between her and a bullet, stealing cars, and abandoning the life he had set up, even if it was just a ruse to get close to her, to drive her around the country to some unknown destination he hoped would keep her safe, he deserved her trust.

So now, here they sat. In silence. Waiting for the sun to come up and rush hour traffic to provide better cover. Clearly, Logan had decided to wait her out. He had said he would hold her to her promise so she supposed she'd better just rip the bandage off.

"I don't know why I get the headaches. They've been happening for years now." She couldn't remember when they'd first started, or even when she'd first noticed them, but it seemed like it had been forever. "I think my brain maybe works a little different than most brains."

How best to describe it? "I never seem to rest." Accurate, if a little underwhelming.

"I have this, like, constant scramble of random thoughts and information in my head that seem to play 24 hours a day, like an overnight f.m. radio station. No commercials, no dead air time. Just a steady, unbroken stream of information playing on a loop. Which is separate, of course, from the never-ending noise running non-stop in the background." It was exhausting just trying to describe how it felt. "This sort of buzzing sound that I'm able to push to the back of my mind more often than not."

She made a conscious effort to relax her grip on the steering wheel. Saying all of this out loud felt so wrong. It made her sound crazy. But Logan had asked to hear it so she pushed on.

"But sometimes, all of a sudden, the buzzing gets so loud that it starts to drown out everything else around it."

Quincy thought back to the attack in the car yesterday evening. Logan had been talking and she had been doing nothing more than listening, trying to understand what he was telling her, and then she couldn't hear him, or the car, or even the ball game playing in the background anymore. The buzzing in her ears had thundered over everything around her in an instant before she realized what was happening.

She glanced over at Logan to see if he was with her so far. Surprisingly, he seemed unfazed.

"Jones had a lot of headaches after the accident. Really bad ones. The doctors said it was a normal side effect of TBI."

"That's true," she agreed. "Traumatic brain injuries are very common, especially in war vets."

"For awhile, we didn't even notice his hearing sensitivity because we just wrote it off as a symptom of his migraines."

"Okay, well, that's what happened yesterday. I've had them before. I'll have them again. But I am sorry I scared you. And I'm sorry I slowed us up. He would never have caught up with us if you hadn't had to stop for me."

Logan had been looking out the front glass, periodically checking the side and rear view mirrors, presumably for a tail and to graciously allow her to tell her story without feeling overly scrutinized. But at this, he looked over and she felt the full weight of his stare. She let it go for several minutes, hoping he'd share what was on his mind. And then she let it go, annoyed and determined to outlast him. Which she did. For approximately two more minutes.

"What?" she snapped in frustration.

"You recognized him, didn't you?" he asked gently.

This was such a wholly unexpected question, in such a wholly unexpected tone of voice, that she froze for a second. And then she growled in aggravation.

"Of course I recognized him!" she snapped in exasperation. "And of course you would notice." She jerked her right hand off the wheel and flung it in Logan's direction. "How do you do that? How do you see everything? Literally everything!"

He started to say something but she cut him off. "That doesn't require an answer. Yes, okay. I recognized him. I can't believe you didn't, actually." She hadn't thought about it before now, but Logan knew him, too. "It was Brandon."

Saying it out loud sobered her up fast. "It was Brandon," she said again, letting the shock bleed through.

"Brandon?" Logan looked confused. "Brandon from the library, Brandon?"

She nodded. He sat there for a minute, absorbing the news, and then sighed heavily. "That actually fits. Newish hire, started approximately three months after you, avoids most people like the plague but tries to get close to you. Hey," he said, pulling her eyes away from the road. "I'm sorry."

She started to ask for what, but he didn't give her a chance.

"I should have run a closer check on the people who worked with you in the library. If I would have taken the time to look,

I would have seen the threat and never let him get so close."

He seemed so sincere. So disappointed in himself. It was sweet.

"First of all, the fact that you feel like you should have vetted all the people in my tiny little world is creepy. I'm pretty sure that qualifies you as more of a stalker than Brandon. Secondly, who did you 'vet'? I'm pretty sure Mr. and Mrs. Boatright don't exactly stand out as the deadly type."

She took a breath. "And thirdly," and at this, she shoved her finger hard into his arm, just to make sure he knew she was serious. "I don't need you to protect me. You might be a super soldier but I have been keeping myself alive, and off the radar of whoever this is, my whole life. I'll manage, because I always have."

He was silent, to her supreme satisfaction. Feeling proud of her ability to firmly put presumptive men in their place, Quincy turned her attention back to the road. She was strong. She was capable.

And he kept completely undermining her by saying things like, "I know you can take care of yourself. I know you can keep yourself alive. All I'm saying is, you don't have to anymore."

And then leaning his head back and dropping off to sleep. Always with the last word, this one.

38

Chapter 38

L ogan

Logan's eyes opened slowly, blinking in the morning light, confused.

"Puede usted por favor repita que lentamente?" There was a pause, then, "Can you repeat that slowly?"

"No, gracias. La soda está bien." Another pause. "No thank you. Soda is fine."

He cracked his eyes open and turned to look at Quincy.

"Are you teaching yourself Spanish?" he asked.

She shrugged. " Por qué no? Tuve tiempo."

He mulled that over.

"I guess so," he shrugged his shoulders. "But most girls who *had the time* would have flipped on the radio. Or plugged in a playlist. Maybe something upbeat to help keep them awake. They wouldn't be listening to Spanish on Cassette."

"First of all," she replied,"who listens to cassettes? Cars don't exactly come with tape decks anymore Grandpa."

The *grandpa* clearly thrown in to twist the knife.

"There are apps for this stuff now. And second, I didn't know you spoke Spanish." She looked over at him. "Something you picked up in the army?"

He laughed. "Oregon, actually. It might have been a small town but we had people from all over the world. My best friend in high school was from a small town on the Tex/Mex border, so it kind of stuck."

They both fell silent, letting the soothing strains of a heavily-accented Latino man flow around them. Logan leaned into the back seat and grabbed a soda out of the plastic bag.

"We need to grab a cooler the next time we stop. It's going to be a long drive and I wouldn't mind some ice."

"Speaking of, I don't suppose you'd fill me in on a destination?" She turned those big eyes his way. "This aimless driving is getting a little old."

Point taken. "Sorry about that. I don't want to lead these guys to Dr. Garrison. He's firmly off the radar and I'm not about to put him back on it." He thought back over the previous night. "And I'm a little concerned about how Brandon managed to track us to the motel. He obviously didn't know what car we were driving since he was looking through the windows of all the cars in the lot. So how did he find us?"

It was a good question, one that had been bothering him since their near miss. He had agreed to let Quincy drive because he knew she was right - he needed some sleep if he wanted to be on top of his game. But he also agreed because he thought, if he got some rest, he might be able to figure out where he'd slipped up. But he still didn't know, and that was dangerous.

"I've been thinking. The shot came from across the street and above, meaning probably one of the lofts above the ice cream parlor. With all of the panic, the people running and blocking his view, he probably wouldn't have been able to see where you went. Plus, the police were en route pretty fast. He would have packed up the second he started to hear sirens."

"How long does it take to 'pack up' from trying to kill someone?" she asked.

Logan did some quick mental math. "The shot sounded like it came from a large caliber rifle. If he's a professional, and I think we can assume he is, then he could have been out the door in less than two minutes." He reconsidered. "Much less, if he was in a hurry."

"So, it's possible he could have gotten down to street-level and saw us take the car?" Quincy asked.

Logan shook his head. "Possible? Technically, yes, I guess it's possible. But he would have had to get out of the loft, down to the ground, and across the street. Then, he would have had to know which alley we took and watched us drive the car off the lot. With the amount of people crowding the street, I doubt he would have been able to get there in time."

"Okay," she said. "So what other options are there?"

"I don't...," he started, trailing off as an idea started to take shape.

"What was it you said earlier?" he asked. "About cassette tapes?"

She looked over at him, confused. "Cassettes tapes? What, that cars don't have decks anymore?"

He shook his head. "No, the other thing. About - "

She cut him off. "About how there are apps for that now," she said in excitement. "There are apps for almost everything anymore. You don't think..."

Logan interrupted her. "That Brandon downloaded a lo jack app to your phone? Yeah, I kind of do." He reached up and grabbed it from the dashboard. "But if he's tracking it, how would we even know?"

He was flipping through her system settings and apps but nothing was standing out.

"Does it matter?" she asked. "If he is tracking the phone, he's probably behind us right now. He can hang back an hour, two hours, and it wouldn't matter. The second we stop, he'll have us."

She hit the turn signal and took a hard, sudden right onto an off ramp that was already too far behind them to safely take. Several honking horns and two turns later, Logan pried his hand off the door handle and turned to her, a silent question on his face.

"Give me the phone," she said. "I have an idea."

She held out her hand and he slapped the phone into it. She pushed the door open, hopped out, and shook her arms and legs. Then she started to walk, seemingly wandering around the parking lot with no clear purpose or destination.

Logan decided to give her the benefit of the doubt and pushed himself out of his own seat. He begrudgingly admired how easily she'd been able to shake off hours in the car on little sleep because his body wasn't quite as spry as hers seemed to be. He rolled his shoulders and slanted his face up towards the sun.

It was warmer here than in Sheraton but he could feel fall in the air. It wouldn't be much longer and the chill would be here, too.

"Okay," she said, slapping the hood of the car to get his

attention. "Let's go."

"What did you do with the phone?" he asked, leaning his forearms on the hood and looking across the car at her. She had the driver door half open but stopped, looking up at him with a grin.

"Tossed it into the open window of that truck over there." she said, nodding towards a big rig with Illinois plates. "Silenced it, just in case he got any bright ideas about calling. But I heard the driver say he was heading to Maryland, which should be enough of a wild goose chase that we can slip away pretty easily."

Logan whistled appreciatively. "That's smart." He raised an eyebrow speculatively. "How did you come up with it?"

She had the grace to blush. "I may have read it somewhere. Maybe."

The blush got deeper. "Whatever. It works, doesn't it?" She threw herself back into the car and slammed the door. Logan laughed, taking his time before climbing back into the car himself. She really was a handful.

39

Chapter 39

The Colonel

He sat at the bar of his four-star hotel, nursing his drink and watching the news footage reporting live from the downtown area with the other patrons. Some were locals and he could hear them talking animatedly about the excitement. Apparently, shootings were few and far between in the charming little college town.

He overheard one man speculating about the heretofore unknown mob presence possibly making itself known while another dismissed it entirely as an accident. He suppressed a laugh.

It was a high caliber bullet shot with extreme precision from the roof of the building across the street. It never failed to amuse him how the common man could cover up blatant violence with a shrug and an explanation.

Not that he minded. He'd relied on blind eyes and willing trust too many times to count. He sighed and signaled the bartender for another.

The situation was inexcusable. He had given explicit orders for his man to keep the situation contained and now he had a very public spectacle on his hands.

He should have never trusted Auberdeen to handle something sensitive. He'd had a feeling about the man but he'd come so highly recommended that he'd hired him anyway. The man hadn't even called him to report. It was unprofessional and unforgivable.

Well, bygones and all that. He didn't have time to sit and ponder what he should have done. He would have to deal with what was. And what was, was something that would require his personal intervention.

He finished his drink in one swallow and pulled out his wallet. He tossed a couple of twenties on the bar and heaved himself off the stool. He had another long drive ahead of him and he thought blandly that he might just be getting too old for this.

Unfortunately, the only way out was one he wasn't ready to take himself just yet. No, for now, he would finish the job. And then he would ensure that Mr. Auberdeen found his way to that one-way exit.

40

Chapter 40

Quincy

Quincy lay in bed that night, staring at the ceiling. The day had been uneventful after their unplanned stop to ditch her phone and the drive had been monotonous. She was exhausted though, if not from sitting in a car for six hours then from the conversation.

It had been a heavy day. But sleep wasn't going to come tonight, no matter how much her body needed it.

For starters, she had gotten almost four hours of sleep the night before, courtesy of the migraines that always forced her mind into an uncomfortable sleep. But mostly, she was just unsettled. Her mind was spinning, but not in the usual way. She was used to her thoughts jumping randomly from one subject to another, without rhyme or reason.

Trapped in the car with Logan, sometimes talking about their situation, sometimes talking about nothing, and sometimes not talking at all - but never talking about why *exactly* they were on the road, had created a razor-sharp focus and she could think of nothing else.

Most of the story he was telling made sense. She had known from the start that he was military. His build and posture gave him away, if nothing else. He had been open about his service from day one. He had told her that day in the park that he had lost people he cared about, so Logan's experiences overseas wasn't a big surprise.

Yes, the IED explosion, the trauma, both physical and mental, she got that. But there were parts of the story that just didn't make sense. Super hearing? This wasn't a movie. Things like that didn't happen in real life. But she found herself believing it anyway, because she had felt his sincerity.

Logan was telling her the truth. As the great Sherlock Holmes liked to say, when you have excluded the impossible, whatever remains, however improbable, must be the truth.

She smiled to herself. Logan was right. She really did read too much. The smile faded quickly, though. What Logan was telling her about Jones's injuries, his recovery and his hearing, was improbable. But it wasn't impossible. Not technically. She was pretty up-to-date on current trends in neurology thanks to a book she had found tucked haphazardly under a bookcase at Sit-a-Spell.

The human brain had built-in safeguards to filter the amount of input they consciously register. The thalamus was responsible for sifting through incoming information and eliminating what was unnecessary because too much stimulus would cause mass chaos in the nervous system.

It was a system of checks and balances that the body seamlessly employed to protect itself. It was possible - improbable but certainly possible - that Jones's thalamus could have been injured in the attack and healed, but incompletely, leaving him without his filter.

But she always circled back around to her initial concern - this story had something to do with her. Or Logan thought it did, anyway. The mere fact that Logan had sought her out, going so far as to enroll in college classes to put himself in closer proximity to her, indicated he believed, strongly, that she was connected somehow.

People like you, he had said, first in the alley and then again in the car Friday afternoon. Those words kept playing over and over again in her head.

People like you. Who were people like her, she wondered. He was grouping her together with Jones certainly, whose defining characteristic was his brain injury and the resulting side effects. But she didn't have a brain injury. And unless he was counting a great memory and super insomnia as her super powers, she didn't have any improbable side effects, either.

The pounding she had shoved to the back of her head earlier returned full force, pushing painfully against her thoughts, making her feel anxious and jittery. She threw back the covers in frustration, kicking her legs free and making the old bed creak and groan as she moved. She was being petulant and she knew it. But if she couldn't sleep, why should Logan get to?

Apparently the man, when he slept, slept like the dead. She rolled onto her side facing Logan, tucking her hands under her cheek. She watched him a little wistfully as he snored softly. What would it be like to sleep so soundly? Or to sleep all night? It was probably really nice. It would explain why she had never seen him with dark circles under his eyes. Lucky duck.

She needed to run. The second it crossed her mind, it became a painful, burning urge. She was a runner by necessity more than sheer love of the sport. The physical exertion helped clear her mind more than anything else and it served the added bonus of wearing her body out too.

If her body was exhausted, she could usually get at least a couple hours of sleep throughout the night, which was probably adding to the problem. She hadn't run in almost 48 hours, which meant her body was rested; her brain, however, was not. If she could just get a few miles in....she glanced over again at Logan. He was breathing deeply, still sound asleep. It had been hard to convince him to sleep He wasn't satisfied that Brandon had taken the bait with the phone and was on his way to Maryland instead of hot on their trail.

He had compromised by swapping cars again. They had driven through a town on the Texas/Kansas border and parked their 'borrowed' Focus in a two-hour paid public lot. When the car was flagged as being delinquent, it would be towed and the owner contacted.

They had wiped it down as well as they could and Quincy had insisted on topping off the tank. Leaving it empty would've been adding injury to insult and Patricia deserved better than that. Then they had walked to a nearby rental agency and put a Honda Civic on Logan's super special credit card, which apparently came with its own handy fake i.d.

Before jumping back on the interstate, they had swapped out the rental plates with a minivan parked in the lot of a run-down motel. Quincy could see shoes and a tiny pink Barbie jacket through the Baby on Board sun visor stuck to the window. First they rip off a small business owner, now a family-friendly soccer mom. She was living the dream.

Finally convinced they were as safe as he could make them, Logan had collapsed his ten-foot tall frame onto the hard mattress and hadn't moved since. So it was completely plausible that she could sneak in a run and he would never even notice she was gone. Because if he did, she had no doubt all hell would break loose. She knew why he was being so protective, for lack of a better word. And she appreciated his tight reign on security. Her life did seem to be in danger, after all. But they had taken Brandon out of play hours ago and it was still the dead of night. She didn't know the terrain but if she stuck close to the building, maybe jogged through the residential area right behind the motel, she would be fine. But if Logan woke up, there was no way he would let her go.

He was probably right, but the burning in her legs and her mind wouldn't let her give up the idea. She rolled slowly, taking care to avoid the more creaky parts of the mattress, and landed on her feet on the opposite side of the bed.

Luckily, she was very accustomed to getting dressed in the dark. Her shoes were lined up beside the bed waiting for her. Out of habit, she had laid out her clothes for the next day in the chair beside her bed. She shot another quick glance Logan's way before slipping out of her current clothes and into the leggings and t-shirt she had bought at the department store several towns back.

She had noticed a chill in the air that evening so the leggings would be perfect. She turned to grab her phone out of habit but checked the impulse quickly. If all had gone according to plan, her phone was still in a big rig heading for the East coast. She wasn't used to running without it, but no matter. The jog alone should be enough to clear her mind and help her unwind.

She took a moment to contemplate her backpack. She didn't usually run with it because there was no waist strap to keep it in place. But these weren't usual times. She debated a second more before turning away. She'd only be gone for a little while. One hour, tops.

Now for the tricky part. She moved slowly, so very slowly, passed Logan's bed, stopping every few steps to make sure his breathing was still deep and easy.

When she reached the door, she stopped again, turning to check him one more time. She felt a twinge of guilt at leaving him.

What if he woke up and she was gone?

There was every chance he would think she had decided to skip out on him. She debated for just a moment before turning slowly back towards the desk in the corner of the room. There was the standard motel pen and a pad of paper and she jotted a quick note with the time - 1:30. *Went for a run. Back by 2:30.* It would have to be enough.

She grabbed a room key off the desk and slipped quickly out the door, fading silently into the night.

41

Chapter 41

Logan

Logan woke with a start. Something was wrong, but he couldn't pin it down. He was still soldier enough that his instincts kicked in without thought, holding him completely still until he could pinpoint the danger.

He took in his surroundings, trying to remember what was and wasn't there last night when he'd gone to sleep. The air conditioner banged and clicked outside the room. There had been a brief but heated debate over whether the air conditioner was necessary in 60 degree weather.

Quincy had thought not, Logan had disagreed. He had settled the argument by volunteering to sleep naked, so as to avoid getting too hot. He had a moment of worry that she might actually call his bluff. It wouldn't be the first time he'd lost his clothes on a dare but he had no intention of sleeping on a questionable motel bed without the already insufficient protection of his clothes. None whatsoever. But she didn't know that and he tried to maintain a good facade.

She finally caved and stole the quilt off his bed to compensate.

Even with his eyes shut, he could tell it was still dark outside. This particular establishment didn't just skimp on bed sheets and maintenance. Much like their room the night before, the curtains here were thin and not especially successful at blocking the light from the parking lot.

So he was sure it was either very late or very early. Other than the air unit, it was completely quiet. No one was moving around outside or inside. If there had been someone else in the room with them, he would have felt it.

A movement, no matter how slight. A breath, no matter how silent. Something would have alerted him to their presence. But there was nothing.

Logan finally opened his eyes and glanced at the clock. Just after two in the morning, which meant they still had a good four hours before they needed to be up. As much as he hated to admit it, especially to her, Quincy was right.

That trick with the phone had been genius. Brandon was out of the picture, which gave them a little more breathing room to operate. He closed his eyes and rolled onto his back, stretching out his arms and legs to their full extent. It felt good to sprawl, having spent hours in vehicles not meant for a man his size over the last two days. And the cold air blowing from the wall unit felt good as it breezed over him.

They were almost halfway back to Louisville. If they kept up the pace, they should be back at base in just over 48 hours. He could sleep in his own bed, such as it was. Take as long of a shower as he wanted, without the threat of catching an unfortunate foot disease in the process. He could ride his motorcycle again.

No more tiny cars in his future. Not for awhile, at least. He let his mind float, wandering back towards sleep. The air conditioner banged and clicked, the cold air washing over his face and legs. There was no other sound in the room. No other movement.

There was no other movement. Logan sat bolt upright and jerked his head towards Quincy's bed, disbelieving. She was gone.

Logan hit the light on the bedside lamp as he swung himself upright. He pushed the bathroom door open hard enough that it banged off the wall.

Empty. He stepped back out into the room and took stock. Her backpack was still leaning against the wall, so he knew she wasn't gone for good. She would never disappear without her lifeline. The shoes and clothes she'd bought the day before, however, were.

He tried to think of where she would go. She hadn't mentioned being familiar with the area so he doubted she had somewhere she wanted to visit at two in the morning.

As he looked around, he noticed the pad of paper on the desk. It had writing on it. Well, he thought wryly, at least she left a note before risking her life.

1:30. Went for a run. Back by 2:30. Logan picked up the note and flipped it over, thinking surely she'd left more than that. But no. That extremely vague and short note was all there was. He blew out his breath as he thought. 1:30. She'd been gone for half an hour. It was true that Brandon was probably off their backs but even so, what was she thinking?

He thought he had convinced her of the danger she was in. Or at the very least, the bullet shattering the glass store front beside her head should have. But apparently not. The more he thought about it, the angrier he became. He fumed as he jammed his feet into his shoes.

And he fumed as he grabbed their backpacks and the remaining room key off the desk. He expelled some of his steam when he slammed the door to their room, and again as he slammed the door of the car. But as he circled the lot, it came back full force.

She could have gone one of two ways. Left would take her out to the highway and eventually back to the interstate. Right wound through a residential area, with multiple streets and blocks. The highway would be darker but the residential area would be safer. Probably. But who was he kidding? If she was that concerned about safety, she wouldn't have gone for a run while she was on a hit list. He turned right.

And soon began to worry he had made the wrong choice. He had worked his way through the streets and still hadn't found her.

It was completely possible that he had missed her. He could have turned down one street as she had turned up a different one. Or he could have pulled off of a street that she was just turning on. But it worried him just the same. Brandon wasn't the only psycho he was worried about. Kidnappers and killers came in all shapes and sizes. And they weren't the only dangers.

In unfamiliar territory, in the dark, it would be easy to miss a step. She could have accidentally stepped off the curb, or even stepped on something she wasn't expecting. She could so easily be hurt or lost. As he circled the next block, the swell of anger that had built up against her slowly started easing back out to sea. He knew she liked to run. Or at least ran a lot. But he couldn't imagine why she couldn't sacrifice a few days of running while the danger was so high. Or why she wouldn't have woken him up and asked him to go.

It would have still been dangerous but having him along would have reduced the risk. As would a daylight run. So, why make such a sloppy, stupid choice? He turned another corner, moving slowly so he could see through the murky blackness.

Unless she wasn't jogging just to jog. Maybe for her it was more. Maybe it was a way of combating the insomnia and the continuous noise in her head.

Did she run so she could have just a few minutes of peace? What would that even be like? To never be still. To never have quiet inside your own head. To never sleep soundly. To never have peace, even for a minute. Did Quincy use running as a coping mechanism, a way to gain peace? Even if just for an hour or two at a time? Possible.

No, he realized. Probable. Very probable. The thought made him a little wistful. Dr. Garrison had been optimistic that, given time, Jones would be able to do the same. To find a way of coping with his hearing abnormality. To be able to live a full and productive life. Jonesy hadn't believed him even though Logan had, and here was the possible proof right in front of him.

Again, he couldn't help seeing Quincy and imagining what could have been. He took a deep breath and blew it back out. He couldn't worry about that right now. Jones was beyond his help but Quincy was right here. Or she should be. Where was that girl?

Logan turned back onto the highway and headed towards the motel. It was after three by now. It was possible he had missed her completely and she was back at the room. Where he would kill her. And then kiss her. Maybe. Or maybe that would just muddy the waters. Man, was he tired.

But all thoughts of killing her disappeared pretty quickly. He parked right in front of the room this time, knowing he would be leaving again whether she was in the room or not. If she was, they were hitting the road. Despite how tired he was, he knew he wouldn't be able to go back to sleep and figured they might as well capitalize on it.

If she wasn't, well, he didn't know what he'd do but he doubted it would be staying in the room. But he knew before he opened the door that she wasn't there. He stood in the open doorway, eyes closed, more worried than he knew how to say.

She wouldn't be almost an hour late without reason. It was stupid to leave the room at night without him but he could maybe understand her reasoning. What she wouldn't do was say she was coming back at a certain time if she wasn't going to stick to it. She left that note to try to keep him from worrying. Being late would only amplify his worry.

No, she was late because she couldn't get back. As he stood in the doorway, running possible scenarios through his head, a car passed the motel, heading for the interstate. At the sound of the engine, Logan automatically glanced over. A dark mid-size, possibly a Sebring, headlights off. The windows were tinted, keeping Logan from getting a clear line of sight into the vehicle. But it didn't matter. There were precious few reasons to drive at night without headlights.

Quincy was in that car.

He didn't know how these guys had caught up with them again and he didn't care. He could figure that out later. Right now, he needed to keep a visual on that car. Leaving the door to the motel room open, he bolted back to their rental and squealed out of the parking lot in the same direction.

42

Chapter 42

"We feel free when we escape – *even if it be but from the frying pan to the fire.*" *Eric Hoffer*

The need to escape, to breath, is intrinsic in nature. Built into each individual soul. The girl's soul is no different.

Her mind, yes. But not her soul.

* * *

Quincy

Quincy's feet pounded against the pavement in a slow, steady rhythm. She usually had trouble finding her pace at the beginning of a run but as the minutes stretched out, her mind would slowly begin to clear and her stride would gradually lengthen until she found that middle ground.

Tonight was no different. As stressed as she was, the familiar routine of running started working its magic and she settled into that easy pace, and although her feet still beat to the phrase *people like you*, it was growing fainter with every step.

It was a beautiful night for a run, with a sky clear enough to see stars. Away from the main hub of the city, they lit up the night like a beacon, providing her with plenty of light to see the road in front of her.

It was also quiet. So, so quiet. Once you made it far enough away from the interstate, it was almost like you were alone. For the first time since this madness started, she was alone and she could think. Could breath. Logan had been great, what with saving her life and all. His concern for her seizure-like headaches and his kindness and patience in not pushing her to talk were both endearing and appreciated. But she was used to being on her own. And even when she wasn't alone, so few people noticed her that she felt invisible.

Sharing a car, sharing a room, had been more together time than she was used to. Even though Logan would blow a gasket if he knew she had gone out alone, especially at night, she had needed this badly. The jog, the quiet of the night - she could finally let her guard down and think. And what she was thinking about wasn't the assassination attempt. Or the long, monotonous drive. Or her weird headaches. Or even Logan.

She was thinking about Kara Scott and Gracie Elliot.

It had been easy jumping from one alias to another. Seamless, really. Grace, Kara, even Quincy, were all very much alike. Part-time college kids working their way through school. Low-rent apartments, no personal belongings. They were walk-aways.

She hadn't really even needed much in the way of documentation to accomplish her goals. Applications to college were ridiculously easy to fake. Both the diner and the bar had been a breeze. Old Gus hadn't even gotten around to making her fill out paperwork until the third or fourth week she had worked for him.

She had been a little worried about the library at first. It was an upscale place, academic and above board. But they had accepted her college-issued i.d. without question. She wondered what they must think. Or if they'd even thought of her at all. She had missed her shift yesterday. And she obviously wasn't going to be there today. She could understand the bar in Chicago not alerting the police. Bartenders were a dime a dozen and she got paid under the table. She probably wasn't the first to walk away from that fine establishment and undoubtedly wouldn't be the last.

Even the diner in Boise probably hadn't made too much noise. She was shockingly well-liked there, despite her penchant to keep to herself. The waitresses and Dave the fry cook treated her like their little pet and the truckers had quickly developed a protective streak, which she deeply appreciated. But again, people moved on. Sometimes with no warning.

She did feel a twinge of guilt. Doris and the others had probably worried over her. She should send them a postcard, let them know she was fine. Fine-ish. But the library was a respectable establishment. They kept proper paperwork and employment records. She assumed. Surely someone would notice if she didn't show back up.

Or what about the Boatrights? Wouldn't they worry if she

stopped coming around suddenly? Some of the other shop owners, too, had become used to seeing her. And what about the shooting? Would anyone think to link that to Quincy's disappearance? It was kind of depressing to think they might not. That she could disappear and no one would even blink an eye.

She had deliberately created that distance, though. She had encouraged invisibility. So she had no one to blame but herself. Although Brandon disappearing at the exact same time as she did might ring some bells. Or make her that much easier to write off, she realized.

The gossips down in Circulation would no doubt spread the word. They had overheard Brandon asking Quincy out and now they were both MIA. Wink, wink. Giggles all around. It did have a sort of symmetry, though. Brandon did, after all, have a secret rendezvous planned for her, although she was pretty sure he was the only one meant to enjoy it.

The road between the motel and the small neighborhood a few blocks away was level, with few cars going back and forth this time of night.

The city apparently felt that street lights out here were either A, unnecessary, or B, an expense no one cared to pay. Probably a little of both. And without street lights, it was sometimes difficult to see, despite the light from the stars. But there was no sidewalk either so in the event a car did come along, she was going to have to take her chances.

Since she didn't have her phone with her to play music or one of her audio books, she counted to herself. *One, two, three, four, breathe, one, two, three, four, breathe.*

As much as she didn't want to, she was going to have to ask Logan, point blank, what he had meant with this little quip.

It would drive her crazy otherwise. And she needed the full version. She needed to know how Jones's story connected to her. Why Logan had been looking for her. Why he felt the need to get close. Why he would risk his life to protect hers.

She had a feeling, if she asked him directly, he would tell her. Which was maybe why she hadn't done it yet. It was easier to ask vague questions and get vague answers back. But that wasn't going to help her with whatever strangely surreal situation she'd found herself in.

She could hear the sounds of the night as she ran towards the housing development and it was oddly comforting. It sounded and felt so much like her route back home. Sheraton. She slowed a little as she realized she did kind of think of it as home. How she had allowed that to happen, she didn't know. Friendship wasn't the only thing she'd let slip under her guard these last few months.

And speaking of that friend, she was starting to feel kind of bad.

If Logan woke up, which he probably would, and she wasn't there, he would not be amused. It was worry for her, she knew, but after this afternoon, he might think the worst.

The conversation in the car had gone from silliness over radio preferences to something more dark and intimate than she was ready for and she had shut him down pretty hard. She would hate for him to think she had ditched him after everything he had done for her. The note she'd left had been a pretty paltry effort and didn't really assuage her conscience.

She really didn't know why she couldn't answer his questions.

He wasn't asking for access to all her darkest secrets. He just wanted basics. Name, rank, serial number - he was a soldier, after all. But every time he asked a question about her past, something inside of her pushed back, hard, and she didn't know why.

Logan had been tapping his fingers against the steering wheel for 17 minutes and it had become more than simply annoying. She was getting jittery, her nerves pulling even tighter than they already were. He was spreading his restlessness around and she didn't appreciate it.

They had swapped out driving when they stopped for lunch. Instead of fast food, Logan had suggested an actual sit-down restaurant and Quincy had readily agreed. She wasn't used to spending so much time in a car. She ran and walked everywhere she went and this constant, prolonged inactivity was going to be the death of her. And Logan too, if he didn't stop drumming those fingers.

They hadn't spoken since they left the restaurant over an hour ago. Quincy chalked it up to the post-lunch wind down, which was fine by her but she didn't figure Logan had ever gone so long without talking. It had to be a record, but it looked like he was about to snap.

She leaned forward and flipped the radio on, for background noise if nothing else. Anything to distract from that infernal tapping. His fingers stilled and Quincy leaned back in her seat and closed her eyes, relieved. Momentarily. It wasn't long before she could feel his eyes on her.

"What?" she asked, not bothering to open her eyes.

"Are you serious?" he asked. "This is what you want to listen to?"

She shrugged her shoulders dismissively and could practically feel the eye roll. She hadn't been listening at all but since it obviously bothered him so much, she tuned in. Some kind of political shock jock, spewing angry nonsense for ratings and little else.

She felt him shift in his seat as he leaned forward, flipping rapidly through stations before settling on something that sounded like country music. From the 80s or 90s.

"Oh yeah, this is much better Grandpa," she teased.

"You don't like it?" he asked.

It was a question asked rather for appearance than anything else, as he didn't seem inclined to change the station regardless of her answer.

"Well, it's no talk radio but whatever makes you happy, I guess," she answered without any real heat.

"You can't really tell me you like talk radio, right? I mean, you had to be going for background noise and not listening pleasure. Come on, 'fess up."

Eyes still closed, she smiled against her will. Like a dog with a bone, he spotted it and pounced.

"Yes! There. Right there. I knew it. You don't like political shop talk anymore than I do."

"No," she reluctantly agreed. "I really don't. What I do love, though, is just how much you hate it. Your rage brings me joy. Go figure."

Logan laughed. "Serving in the military kind of ruined me on talking politics."

"I can see that," she said, tucking that helpful little nugget away for future reference.

"So really," he said after a few minutes of silence, "what do you like to listen to?"

She paused to think about it. "I don't know," she said after a beat. "I guess I don't really listen to much music."

"Yeah, but there's got to be something you prefer."

"I don't know," she said again. "I just don't care much about music. What can I say?"

But Logan was a dog with a bone now. "What about when you run?" he pushed. "I've seen you with your headphones in, running around downtown. What are you listening to?"

"Audio books mostly." If she was correctly interpreting the look on Logan's face, and she was fairly certain she was, he was both shocked and slightly disgusted.

"Seriously?" He shook his head, like maybe he hadn't heard right. "When you run, and you're at mile whatever, and it hurts and you hit a wall, what you rely on to dig out and push through is – a book? On tape?"

"Hey now," she answered mildly. "First of all, we've been down this road before. No one listens to cassette tapes anymore, remember? And secondly, I like books. I like stories. And for your information, you never hit that wall if your mind is in a completely different place and time." She sniffed arrogantly. "Just doesn't happen."

"How many miles do you usually get?" he asked.

Quincy blinked. "What?"

"When you run. How many miles do you usually put in?" He segued so smoothly between topics that she answered almost automatically.

"Somewhere between six and ten, usually. Depends on the day."

"Huh. So, how do you pace yourself without music? Even if your mind is occupied, what do you set your breathing to? That many miles, you've got to use something and an audio book is too slow. It's got to be."

Quincy sighed, accepting defeat. "You know how I told you my brain works rapid fire?" He nodded. "Well, I run to bleed off all that excess energy."

How to explain it? "When I first start a run, I'm all jittery, like a light bulb with a short in it. But as I run, I relax and the shorts get fewer and farther between. That jumble of noise quiets and I find my stride. I don't know." She shrugged. "It's never been any more complicated than that."

Logan was quiet for a minute. And then, "Yeah, okay. I can buy that. And how old are you again?"

Quincy laughed out loud that time. "Nope. Not going to work a second time. Pick another question."

"Okay. Where did you grow up?"

She shot it back at him automatically. "Where did YOU grow up?" And then mentally kicked herself. She already knew where he grew up.

Logan grinned. "Nice try. Where did you grow up? Do your parents still live there?"

She wasn't quite ready to give it up. "Do your parents still live where you grew up?"

"No idea. My dad died when I was in high school and I haven't seen or heard from my mom in years. Why won't you tell me anything real about yourself?"

Well that was a pointed and difficult question to avoid. Quincy twisted around and reached into the back seat for their bag of snacks, trying to hide how uncomfortable his questions were making her. They shouldn't be, she knew that. Logan had earned her trust, after all. And it wasn't like he was asking for her social security number or nonexistent financial information.

But still, she couldn't bring herself to answer. And the more she thought about it, the more stressed she became. Her head was throbbing in time to the beat of the music and if she wasn't *careful, she was going to have another migraine on her hands.*

"It's not a hard question. You don't even have to tell me their names. I just want to know something about you that wasn't created in the last six months or so. Why is that such a problem?"

"Because I don't want to talk about it, okay?" she snapped back. "We've been down this road before. I don't talk about my past with anyone. So drop it."

"Fine," he answered coolly. "I was hoping I had made it past being just anyone but no worries. It's dropped." He turned the radio up loud enough to drown out the silence and left her alone with her guilt.

Logan drove straight through until pulling off the interstate around 10:30 without ever asking if she needed a break. The army must train its soldiers to have bladders of iron because she was dying by the time they pulled into the seedy motel but she wasn't about to be the weak link in their little standoff. He pulled around to the back of the motel like last night and didn't wait for her before heading for the room.

If he was going to play that game, so be it. She took her sweet time getting out of the car and stretching before reaching in the back and grabbing her backpack and a couple of waters.

She hesitated for a few seconds and then grabbed his bag as well. It was possible she had been a little harsh and maybe it wouldn't hurt if she offered him something, even if it wasn't the information he wanted. She tossed his bag onto the bed next to him when she walked in but he didn't even glance over. Apparently bringing in his bag wasn't enough of an apology. But it was the only one she was prepared to give at the moment so she just rolled her eyes and headed into the bathroom. She needed a long shower because she could already tell it was going to be a long night.

That had been the last they had really spoken.

So maybe she shouldn't have left like she did. And maybe she should have actually apologized. She sighed in annoyance. Running was supposed to calm her down, not make her cave to a guilty conscience. But nevertheless, there it was. There was a cul-de-sac up ahead. She'd circle it and head back towards the motel. She might as well face the music. She would owe him an apology for more than her attitude when she got back.

She was almost halfway back up the main road when lights flared to life across the road. It was so sudden in the darkness that she was completely blinded. She staggered back, head down and eyes clenched against the onslaught. The lights were pointing right at her and she was helpless to get away from the glare.

The sound of a car door slamming caught her attention and she struggled to open her eyes. She could hear footsteps crunching over the gravel and she instinctively knew it wasn't Logan. He might be mad but he would never try to scare her. This was an intimidation technique, which meant she was in hot water.

A deep voice sounded right in front of her. "Finally we meet."

Quincy's eyes were watering and all she could make out was the silhouette of a man, medium height and build, in the headlights. But the click of a gun being cocked was all too obvious.

"Do you prefer Kara, Grace, or Quincy?"

43

Chapter 43

The Colonel

The Colonel was a confident man and didn't mind saying so. He was very good at what he did. He had been a highly-sought after asset in the military, though he received no official recognition for what he accomplished, and it was his special skill set that had landed him on the agency's radar. He was given a mission and he accomplished it. He had never failed an assignment. Losing Kara Scott, twice, was nothing more than a minor detail. Acquiring her tonight had restored his perfect record. Everyone got lucky now and again, which was all this had been - a scared girl with a string of good luck.

He had been tempted to simply eliminate her. That was the order he had given his associate in Sheraton, after all. He couldn't afford to lose her again, not with the agency breathing down his neck for a resolution.

She had been foolish enough to leave a protected environment in the middle of the night and enter an unfamiliar, remote location. She had obviously slipped past her guard dog, because she would never have been out otherwise.

The Colonel had watched the girl jog away from the motel, heading down the road towards a housing development that looped around on itself. The only way in or out was that one road. Once the girl had disappeared from view, he had followed, pulling the car over to the side of the road about halfway down the hill, out of sight of both the motel and the development. She would have to come back this way in order to get back to her room. As he sat in the dark, he contemplated his options, tapping the gun idly against the steering wheel. One shot was all he needed. The suppressor he'd screwed onto the end of the barrel ensured no one would hear a thing, even the girl. There would be no witnesses, no panic, and no way to trace the crime to him, an invisible man.

He would be gone before her body guard even knew there was a problem. He shook his head. What kind of soldier let the target sneak away from him? Lt. Davies must be slipping.

But what if he didn't need to eliminate the girl? In complete seclusion, there was no reason a snatch shouldn't work just as well. He had only ordered the elimination because she had proven to be resourceful in a populated setting. But out here, alone and without witnesses, she was playing with a short deck. The agency would much prefer a living specimen to a dead one.

When the girl came jogging back up the hill, barring any complications, it should be easy enough to force her into the car. He was always prepared to take a living target - zip ties, sedatives, deactivated door locks. He should have no problem containing her.

Headlights topped the hill behind him and he tensed. The

car, an older model compact, drove slowly by, turning down the first street, and the Colonel cursed. Davies. Slipping or no, if he caught up with the girl there would be no chance for a clean shot. Most likely, the Colonel would be subject to yet another long day of driving across America, presumably towards wherever the doctor was holed up and waiting. He considered that option briefly. If he allowed the lieutenant to take the girl, he could potentially trail them all the way back to Garrison. It was tempting, yes. But there was no guarantee he could stay on them. Davies was good. He'd managed to keep Garrison hidden all these years, after all.

He watched as the car turned down the next street, still moving slowly but never stopping, and the Colonel started to hope. In the dark, with the girl being cautious, it might be difficult to find her if he didn't know for certain she was there.

The minutes stretched and the car finally drove back by. The Colonel wavered. Should he follow the car back to the motel? He knew where they were staying, even if he didn't know the exact room. And he knew the car now.

If Davies did have the girl, it was unlikely they would keep driving. There would be no reason to believe their cover had been blown so he decided to give it a few more minutes, see if the girl would appear.

And eventually, his patience was rewarded.

44

Chapter 44

Q**uincy**

It wasn't Brandon. That was Quincy's first thought. This man was shorter and thicker, and his voice was deeper. He also spoke with a slight accent that she couldn't quite place. The man moved slightly to her right, out of the beam of the headlights, and gestured towards the car.

"Please," he drawled, "After you."

Quincy hesitated, considering her options. She could try to make a move on him. Maybe startle him enough to shake the gun loose. But he had a good hundred pounds on her. And that gun was rock steady, trained on her left leg if she wasn't mistaken. So he wasn't intending to kill her outright.

Not here, at least. It was entirely possible he was intending to drive her somewhere, kill her, and dump the body. A cheery thought. Or she could just make a run for it. If she could make it out of the glow of lights, she would be much harder to see. She could take her chances in the woods, hoping to lose him in the trees or at least be much harder to hit. The man was watching her patiently, a half smile on his face.

He seemed amused, like he knew what she was considering and was waiting to see how it would play out. He was indulging her, giving her time to choose how she wanted to play it. But he wasn't worried, that much was clear. Whichever option she chose, it wouldn't matter. He was confident she would be coming with him, one way or another.

Quincy took a step forward, and then another. The man stepped back even further, allowing her to move towards the car while keeping a polite distance between them, the gun never wavering. She reached for the back door but the man stopped her.

"Now, now. I would very much appreciate it if you would sit up front with me." He opened the front door with a flourish and waited until she had slid onto the seat before leaning down. "Don't forget to buckle up. Safety first."

The car door swung shut and the man moved around the car towards the driver's seat. Quincy glanced around, trying to get a feel for the car. She slid her hand slowly towards the door handle but found it locked. He must have engaged the child safety locks. She wouldn't be able to open a door unless he allowed it. She really didn't have much else to work with.

The car was pristine. The man had kept the keys in hand, there was one flat of water bottles on the back bench seat, and nothing else. When he opened his door to get in, Quincy noticed the overhead light didn't come on. Logan had said that was a trick used by professionals. But she got the feeling that this wasn't just some collector sent to bring her in.

"Do you recognize me?" he asked as he started the car.

"I'm sorry. Do we know each other?" she replied innocently. "If you hadn't blinded me, maybe I could say."

He just smiled. "Sarcasm has very little effect on me. As does goading or guilt. This will go much more smoothly if we can speak to each other in a civil manner."

"I'm not super interested in making *this* go smoothly for you. So be aware, my sarcasm meter is on overdrive."

"Noted," he said, "But as I asked before, do you recognize me? You should. You've seen me twice before tonight."

It was still too dark to make out features, especially without street lights, but there was something familiar about him. He said she had seen him before.

"You were in Boise, at the truck stop. And in Chicago."

"That's right," he said, seeming pleased with her answer. "The first time you burned me, I was surprised and a little impressed. Very few of my targets get away. But the second time, I knew you were special." He seemed to mull his words over. "But of course you're special. It's why I was sent for you. All of my targets are special. But you seem to be more aware. Of your surroundings, of the need for caution, of the danger you're in. The others had no idea. They were easy pickings. Their gifts didn't protect them as yours did. Even if it was only on a subconscious level."

The man made a turn onto the interstate in the opposite direction that Logan's route had been taking them. She did her best to not look back.

"You never did answer my first question," he said.

"What question was that again? This whole kidnapping business has left me a little frazzled."

He smiled indulgently. "I asked what you would prefer to be called. I've known you as Kara Scott, Grace Elliott, and not Quincy O'Connell. All three lovely names, of course. But surely there's an identity you prefer?"

276

She hesitated. "Quincy. I go by Quincy now."

"Of course. You've stuck with Quincy far longer than your other two aliases, which I find very interesting. But we've no time for psychology now. You may call me Colonel."

"Okay, Colonel. Riddle me this – what's so important about me that you've tracked me across the country and through three different aliases? And why take me alive? I assume the sniper a few days ago was yours?"

The Colonel opened his mouth but Quincy beat him to it.

"I'm not done. Who are the other targets you mentioned? Who wants a bunch of random people so bad they'd hire a wet work mercenary to take care of it?"

He tried to speak again but she had one more. "And what *gifts* do you think I have? If it's the gift of dry wit and a caustic attitude, sure. But that's all I come armed with."

"Is it my turn now?" he asked. Apparently two could play the sarcasm game, although his still sounded more amused than anything. "I will answer all of your questions openly and honestly. Unlike your friend."

Quincy went cold. "My friend?" she asked, hoping he was just bluffing.

"Your young man. Mr. Auberdeen mentioned he was with you when the shooting occurred and was mysteriously missing afterward." The Colonel seemed to sense her fear. "Not to worry. I have no real interest in the Lieutenant, provided he doesn't continue to complicate my mission. He is a direct link to Dr. Garrison, true, who is an important resource to my company but my mission is you, not him. I left him alive."

Quincy sagged in her seat, relieved. Logan didn't deserve any of the trouble she had brought on him, and she had brought him a lot.

"But if I were to guess, I would say he didn't really tell you much about your role in all of this. He would have tried to ease you into it. Am I right?"

She stared stonily ahead, refusing to play his game.

"Well, I won't do that. I've read your medical file and I'm eager to see exactly how it works."

45

Chapter 45

Quincy

"I'm sure Lt. Davies was trying to be gentle but I do not suffer the same affliction," the Colonel said.

"If by *affliction*, you mean *empathy* or *human decency*, then I completely agree," Quincy answered snidely. The Colonel simply smiled.

"That is exactly what I mean. I am paid to perform a certain job or service. It matters very little to me what that job or service is. Human decency, as you so delicately put it, does not factor into the equation." He paused to glance at his phone, and then texted what Quincy could tell was a short set of numbers. Coordinates possibly.

"Now, the truth about your situation is this - you have a condition Dr. Garrison refers to as Reflexive Neurological Bias. It's a theoretical medical condition that the agency who pays me has been paying Dr. Garrison to research and develop for the last 10 years.

Not much is known about RNB. Few experts in the field

even believe in its existence. In fact, Dr. Garrison has been summarily laughed out of the profession because of his research and his insistence that this condition does in fact exist."

Quincy broke in. "Then why would your agency buy into this theory, if no one else does? Why is the word of this one man so compelling?"

The Colonel nodded approvingly. "An excellent question. With a beautifully simple answer - Dr. Garrison is a brilliant man. But you aren't wrong - the field of science is full of brilliant men. What makes Garrison special is the irrefutable fact that he is an idealist. Most research doctors seek fame, fortune, publishing credentials. The research is always secondary to the recognition it might bring."

The Colonel checked his phone one more time, nodding his head in approval, before tucking it away into his jacket pocket. "But Garrison already had all of that. He had the fame - he was widely sought across the globe and had his pick of cases on which to consult, as well as the money that went along with it. Instead, he simply saw a need - lives that could be saved, people that could be healed - and he wanted to fill that need wholeheartedly.

The agency had been watching him for some time, reading his research, seeing the possible applications. That is why they hired him. Why they gave him the money and autonomy he needed to pursue and develop his theory. And why we are having this conversation right now. Garrison identified you as one of the precious few who developed RNB following a traumatic brain injury. Not every injury results in RNB, you see. Garrison has some ideas on what might contribute to it but he hasn't been able to isolate a specific contributing factor."

Quincy sat quietly, watching and listening to the Colonel in a state of skepticism as he continued.

"One of the main difficulties in proving its existence has been how difficult it is to diagnose. It manifests differently in each case. Signs and symptoms are unique to each individual patient and often depend on the severity of the original injury."

Quincy shook her head. "You're insisting I have this...RNB... but based on its very definition, I can't possibly."

The Colonel glanced over. "How do you mean?"

"You told me RNB develops after some sort of head injury. A very specific type of traumatic brain injury, most likely. But I've never had a brain injury. That's something that can't be faked. I'm not sure what medical records Dr. Garrison is basing this 'diagnosis' off of, or that it's even legal for him to have medical records without the patient's permission," she threw in caustically, "but they can't be mine. A brain injury isn't something a girl would forget."

The Colonel smiled indulgently, which was more than a little disturbing. "You wouldn't think so, wouldn't you?"

He signaled and smoothly merged onto an obscure exit ramp, taking the first right into a small, dark parking area. He put the car in park and turned it off. Creepier and creepier. But Quincy didn't think he had brought her all this way to kill her, not when it would have been easier and less messy to do so before he forced her into his car, so she turned towards him, waiting for him to continue.

"As strange as it may sound, I'm beginning to believe you when you say you don't remember having a brain injury."

"That's not exactly what I said," she pointed out. "I said

I've never had one, not that I don't remember it."

"Did you know," the Colonial asked suddenly, "that brain injuries are permanent? The tissue can heal and function can be restored, but the injury will always be there. Always be a part of the brain's anatomy and chemistry. Isn't that interesting?"

Quincy herself didn't find it particularly thrilling. This whole thing had been one intense nightmare. She might believe it really was a nightmare except for one thing - the pain building inside her skull.

She had been pushing it down ever since she had climbed in this guy's car but the more he talked, the louder the noise was becoming. At least it was just one of her normal headaches, if such a thing existed. She should still be able to function.

Of all her fears and worries, having a migraine and being incapacitated as her enemies closed in was her worst. But conversely, she found she didn't want him to stop. Logan answered all of her questions with more questions. At least the Colonel was giving her the answers she was asking for, despite the fact that they were completely off-base.

"Listen," she began but the Colonel cut her off.

"No. It's time for you to listen," he said, pinning her with a look. "Here it is. Eight years ago, you were involved in a hit-and-run accident. There were no witnesses and you were carrying no identification. You spent just over a month in a coma with a traumatic injury to your right temporal lobe, in the region of the thalamus specifically, and when you woke up, you had no memory. Of the incident. Of yourself. Nothing."

Quincy wanted to interrupt but he was still staring her down, his eyes missing nothing in their penetrating appraisal, watching for some sort of recognition.

"You spent another month in the hospital, spending most of your time with physical therapists for your physical injuries and psychologists for your amnesia. Numerous imaging studies were done that showed a healing brain injury but nothing that should have resulted in long-term memory damage. And then one day, you disappeared."

He leaned back against the car door, silent and watchful.

"Look," Quincy tried again. "I don't know how much clearer I can be. This girl that you're describing, that you're looking for, she's not me. Eight years ago I was," and here she faltered. But only for a moment. "I wasn't in a coma, in a hospital with no memory. It just wasn't me."

She was surprised to hear how desperate she sounded but she supposed she shouldn't be. This man had kidnapped her in the middle of the night, had stalked her across America and set a sniper on her, because he thought she was this amnesic girl with a weaponizable brain. This couldn't be real.

"Then where were you eight years ago?" he asked calmly. "If you can prove to me now that you weren't comatose in a hospital in Sacramento, then I will let you go."

Quincy laughed a little hysterically. "How exactly do you expect me to prove that?"

The drum beat in her head was approaching its crescendo but she stubbornly pushed back.

"I have proof," he said quietly. He took her sudden silence as permission and reached into the back seat for a small tablet. It took him a moment but when he flipped it around towards her, she could see a black and white still, enlarged and slightly grainy.

"Surveillance cameras caught you as you were leaving the hospital. I ran facial recognition on Kara Scott in Boise. And I

283

ran it again off a picture Mr. Auberdeen sent after he made contact."

She took the tablet and held it closer to her face. She couldn't look away. Because it was her. It was her, leaving a hospital in some town she didn't remember ever being in, wearing a hairstyle she didn't remember having, in a ripped, torn jacket she definitely didn't remember owning.

"What is this?" she whispered. When she got no response, she looked up. "What IS this?"

"It is exactly what it seems," the Colonel answered serenely. "This is proof that you are who Dr. Garrison thought you were. Case file number twelve, RNB patient Jane Doe from Sacramento University hospital. Whether you remember or not, this is you."

The noise in her head, the clanging drum beat that had been building in intensity for the last two hours, died instantly. The absence of it was almost as painful and shocking as the noise itself. Her head suddenly felt empty, like it had too much space to fill, and a wave of dizziness swept over her.

Quincy handed the tablet back to the Colonel and turned away. She didn't want to have to look at him and see his absolute certainty. She didn't want to see anything at the moment.

She didn't understand. That picture, she couldn't argue with it. She wanted to, but something deep inside of her seemed to acknowledge the truth of it, even if she couldn't quite admit it to herself yet.

She leaned her head back against the headrest and closed her eyes. It was still night but there was just a faint brightening on the horizon to her right. East. So they were traveling west. Quincy could only assume the Colonel was taking her to wherever his agency stored these RNB patients the Colonel had been hired to round up.

She spoke without opening her eyes. "How many of us?"

"I beg your pardon?" he asked politely, either misunderstanding or pretending to misunderstand the question.

"How many of these patients have you kidnapped and turned over to the agency?" She took in a steadying breath and turned her head to look back at him. "You said I was case file number twelve. I assume that means there are at least that many of us. Am I the last one or are you still looking for others?"

"Ah," he said. "Another valid question. I'm glad to see the shock of the night hasn't diminished your reasoning abilities. I can't say the same for some of the others who've sat where you are now." He glanced at his watch. A very slight tightening of his lips suggesting he was frustrated. They must be waiting on someone, Quincy realized. Someone who was running late.

"When Dr. Garrison left the agency, he took as much of his research as he could get away with. The rest, he attempted to destroy. We were able to recover the majority of the patient files he had accumulated. Unfortunately, they have been transcribed from their original into Dr. Garrison's own shorthand. A very difficult thing, trying to read a doctor's notes.

But slowly we have been piecing together the information. Enough to help identify some of the patients. We have people trying to crack more of the files now and others searching for unknowns who fit the profile Garrison put together."

The back passenger door of the car jerked open and Quincy jumped. The Colonel, however, merely glanced at his watch again.

"You're late," he said quietly.

"Well, I was halfway to Baltimore, wasn't I?" Brandon snapped back.

"Mind your tongue boy. The girl outsmarted you. Take the lesson and move on." The Colonel allowed a faint trace of iron in his voice when he spoke, enough to remind everyone in the car who the authority belonged to.

"Miss O'Connell, I believe you know my associate Mr. Auberdeen." Quincy suppressed the shudder. She could feel him behind her, staring. Seething. He apparently didn't appreciate being made to look the fool in front of his boss.

"We've met," she said shortly. Having the sniper that tried to kill you sitting in the seat behind you was unnerving, to say the least, but she'd rather kiss the man than let him know he was getting under her skin.

The Colonel put the car in drive and headed back onto the interstate. "Mr. Auberdeen is relatively new to our organization, though he came highly recommended. He's one of our trackers. When you managed to disappear for the second time, I turned my attention to others on the list. But I assigned your case to Mr. Auberdeen and I must say, despite his rather lackluster performance over the last week, he located you with respectable speed."

"If he found me so fast, why did it take three months for him to try to take me out?" Quincy asked, more curious than she probably should be.

"Because we needed proof. You fit the profile of patient twelve, but so did several others. And I only identified you in Boise and Chicago because you ran. You disappeared so quickly, and so completely, and that was all the proof I needed."

"What do you mean by that?" Quincy asked. "Why would running confirm my identity?"

"Because it isn't the normal response," he replied. "The normal response would be a complete lack of response. I'm very good at blending in. So the fact that you noticed me, that you sensed the threat I represented, and that you were able to mobilize quickly enough to escape told me everything I needed to know."

He glanced in the rear view mirror, checking a car that was passing on the left. "I didn't want you to run again but I did need some sort of reaction."

"Which is where I came in," Brandon added blandly from the backseat.

"You didn't look anything like Kara Scott or Grace Elliott," the Colonel added, "so we needed something else. Most of the RNB patients we have collected exhibited their abilities on a daily basis. We just had to watch and listen. You, my dear, have been an entirely different story."

"I watched," Brandon said. "I watched for weeks. But there was nothing."

"You didn't appear to be sensitive to external stimuli," the Colonel said. "Those are the usual symptoms - sensitivity to loud noise, light, smells. Even being touched. But you didn't share any of those concerns, at least that we could observe. So we had to get in closer. But how to do that without tipping you off?"

Quincy picked up the story. "So you insert someone into my life in as natural a way as possible. Someone who would blend in."

She nodded her head, because it all made perfect sense.

"He gets a job at the library. Not in the same department, but close enough to be able to watch without seeming out of place. And once that didn't trip my danger sensors, you had him approach me directly. You know," she said dryly over her shoulder, "stalking isn't just a crime. It's creepy, too."

Creepy was the word some of the other library employees floated around about Brandon. She never knew if it bothered him but she pulled at that thread, hoping it might reveal a weak spot. If his job was to observe, he would have heard the things the other employees said about him, especially since the gossips didn't make a secret of it. That he was weird. A loner. A creep.

There was a quiet rage in his voice when he spoke, so apparently she was right. "I don't get paid to make friends. I get paid to do my job. And my job was you."

She could practically hear his teeth grinding together. She imagined his face, flushed with anger, and smiled. The Colonel might be unflappable but his employee was not. She could work with that. But the anger was gone almost as quickly as it came and he leaned forward casually, draping his arms over the back of her seat, hands resting near her shoulders.

"You know, this could have all been avoided if you'd just gone out with me," Brandon said silkily. "A nice dinner. A romantic walk beside the lake. A quick twist." He mimicked his hands around her neck and gave a quick jerk. He smiled. "And then on to the next target by breakfast."

It took all she had but she didn't respond to the threat or the desire in his voice. He might have tried to kill her back in Sheraton, might have even looked forward to it, but the Colonel had made it clear the orders had changed. He was no threat to her right now. No lethal threat, at least.

The Colonel cleared his throat and Brandon leaned back slowly, settling in.

"As I said before, Mr. Auberdeen is rather new to our organization. He's still a bit wild. Unrestrained. At the moment, I have no desire to kill you Miss O'Connell. You're worth more to the agency alive than dead. But make no mistake." The Colonel continued to drive, not bothering to look at her. But she could hear the warning in his voice. "I will not risk losing you again. If you attempt to escape, you will be killed. There will be no more chances. Do you understand?"

Quincy turned back to the window. "I understand," she murmured quietly. And she did understand.

Didn't mean she was going to listen though.

46

Chapter 46

Auberdeen

Brandon Auberdeen was angry. He came by it very easily, being angry by nature. But this wasn't the usual anger. This was a slowly burning rage. A fire that crept over him quietly, crawling through his thoughts and sinking deep into his skin.

He would not be bested by some nothing of a girl. He leaned forward, draping his arms along the back of the seat in front of him, barely brushing her neck with his hands. He was careful to stay just out of her line of sight. The fear response increased exponentially when you took sight out of the equation. What one imagines is always far worse than the reality, and Brandon wanted her to imagine the very worst. She had made him look the fool in front of his boss twice now, never mind the Colonel had lost her twice himself.

"You know, this could have all been avoided if you'd just gone out with me," he said conversationally. "A nice dinner. A romantic walk beside the lake. A quick twist."

He briefly wrapped his hands around her neck, ghosting over her throat and jaw as he did so. "And then on to the next target by breakfast."

Brandon was well-aware the deck was stacked against him. The Colonel had never quite taken to him, preferring to use other operatives for important assignments and keeping closer tabs on him than the others. But that hadn't mattered to Brandon. Every man had to earn his stripes and he knew he would eventually prove his worth.

He felt like he had been making good progress, too. He had located the girl, who was working in a library and calling herself Quincy this time. He hadn't been offended when the Colonel had ordered him to observe but not engage. Reconnaissance was important - know your enemy.

The Colonel wanted to be absolutely sure this was case file number twelve, alias Kara Scott, alias Grace Elliot. And she had proven herself with every test Brandon threw at her. He had rather enjoyed that part, to be honest. Yes, he could admit that hurting the woman at the bus station had been extreme but it had also been exceedingly satisfying. And the large payout had been worth the risk in the long run.

Watching the girl snap into 'brain mode' had fascinated him. It was part of what had initially convinced him she was his target, in fact. Watching her transform from shell-shocked bystander into blood-soaked hero-of-the-day at the bus station had been almost alluring. Seductive.

The violence in him had responded ferociously to the tension in the atmosphere - the blood, the fear, the chaos. He had fully expected his victim to die. He had sliced very cleanly through her jugular, after all. The fact that the girl had managed to save her was testament to how vast her condition really was. How useful it could be.

But useful could only go so far. He understood the agency's desire to study the condition and explore the possible military applications. And RNB, from what little information he had been made privy to, had the potential to be vastly weaponizable. But only if the subject was compliant.

Brandon had been observing the girl for three months now and felt like he had a pretty good handle on her.

She was a loner by nature. Intensely suspicious of her surroundings and deeply distrustful of anything that disrupted her well-ordered routine. As was he. Which was part of the reason it burned him so much that she'd taken to the other guy so strongly.

Brandon had been cautious. He'd been respectful. He'd allowed her space. The soldier had done none of those things, yet she'd still been drawn to Logan. In retrospect, he thought, maybe it was nothing more than her survival instinct at work. Brandon was a threat, after all. Maybe the part of her brain that had been damaged and formed into something new was working overtime to keep her alive in every sense of the word, even subconsciously.

Despite their similarities, Brandon knew there was one big difference between them and that difference was going to be what killed her in the end.

Quincy seemed to have some sort of moral compass, despite the damage she'd suffered. He was not burdened by that same affliction.

Yes, he was quite sure Quincy would follow wherever her compass pointed. And if her compass pointed towards saving the life of an unknown woman in an out-of-the-way bus station, exposing herself to danger in the process, the odds were good she wasn't going to fall in line with the agency's plans for her. Which made the only viable choice elimination. Brandon leaned back in his seat and smiled grimly. The time would come.

He would just have to be patient.

47

Chapter 47

Quincy

The car hit a bump, startling Quincy awake. She honestly hadn't believed she'd be able to sleep considering her somewhat dire situation and yet, here she was, being shocked back to consciousness. She didn't think she'd really slept since this entire debacle had started. If she had, she couldn't remember it. Although according to the Colonel, that sounded about right.

It was light outside but only just. She estimated they had been traveling for about three hours. It must be close to 6:00 now. It looked like it was gearing up to be another mild, sunny day, perfect if you were outside. Less so when stuck inside a car. If she had only known yesterday who she would be traveling with in less than twenty-four hours, she might have been nicer to Logan.

Logan. What must he be thinking?

Quincy had no doubt he would have woken up to find her missing hours ago. She really hoped he had gotten her note.

She knew he would be upset that she was gone but she hoped he didn't think she'd run out on him.

Despite her recent behavior towards him, or all of her behavior towards him since they'd met, actually, he was her friend.

She'd been so angry when she'd realized Logan had lied to her. Hurt, if she were being honest with herself. But even if she hadn't realized it before, seeing Brandon and being abducted by the Colonel had solidified Logan's presence as a point of safety in her mind. He had only been trying to protect her from the people who were trying to hurt her, like he'd said. The difference between them was now perfectly obvious. But as to why these people were trying to hurt her, that was still up for debate.

She frowned out the window. It was a ridiculous theory. That she could have no memory of who she was or where she'd come from was absurd. Quincy O'Connell was an alias. She knew that. She had created her after Gracie Elliot had been burned.

She had created Quincy's entire story, just like she had Kara Scott and Gracie Elliot.

Quincy's birthday was June 5. She had gone to high school in White Falls, New York. She was an only child whose parents had passed years ago. Gracie Elliot had been a glorified therapist, slinging drinks and turning a listening ear to drunk businessmen pouring out their troubles over hard liquor. Kara Scott had been a poor little rich girl, working for no other reason than to prove a point to mommy and daddy.

Quincy knew everything about these women. They were real to her. They had to be, in order for them to be real to everyone else. But before Kara Scott, there had been...who, exactly?

Odd. Quincy closed her eyes and leaned her head back against the seat.

Who *had* come before Kara Scott?

She could remember Kara clearly - creating her, memorizing the details of her life, creating the necessary documentation. But everything was a little fuzzy before that. Her name had been... something else. Her head ached as she strained to think. She tried to remember who she was, who she had been before the running and the hiding, but her mind kept sliding forward to Kara or Grace or Quincy. It felt like she was trying to run up an icy hill and every time she came close to the top, she would slip and slide all the way back down.

As ridiculous as it sounded, she really couldn't remember anything before Kara Scott. How had she never realized that before? The Colonel's story couldn't be right. It wasn't even remotely plausible. But she couldn't come up with anything that made any more sense. That old, familiar buzzing invaded her mind again, making its reappearance after a blissful reprieve. She needed a distraction. Something else to think about. So she turned her mind to more practical things.

"Tell me about this agency you work for," she asked the Colonel. The more he talked, the more information she'd have and information was power. She heard a snort from the backseat.

"You might as well," she said. "If you're right, it's not like I can do anything about it anyway. Who am I going to tell, considering you'll kill me and dump my body if I try to make a break for it?"

The Colonel smiled, almost indulgently, like she was a child pretending to be an adult. Quincy smiled back. He wasn't the first man to underestimate her. "I suppose it wouldn't hurt. You'll most likely be spending the rest of your life with them, in any case. A little background information wouldn't be out of line."

She could practically feel the heat of Brandon's anger radiating through her seat.

"Background information, sure," she said. If he was willing to talk, she'd listen. Hopefully she would pick up something that might help once she was there.

"The agency," the Colonel said by way of introduction, "has a long history. Very little of it is important. Only a little relates to you."

The agency came from humble beginnings. The man whose name still hung on the building had had a vision, all those many years ago – a better world. A kinder world. Or something like that. Healthcare for the masses. Dignity for even the most modest of citizens. Cutting edge technology to benefit those most in need. He had been a business man with the soul of a philanthropist, a rare combination indeed. Oil and water, but he'd made it work. The intervening years had all but erased that starry-eyed idealism from the history of the agency, though.

The great grandson had little knowledge of, and even less interest in, his great grandfather's vision. His father had started the inevitable march toward capitalism. Under the direction of his old man, the company doubled down on Big Pharma and raked in millions. But the kid had different ideas. Big Pharma had run its course; pharmaceutical companies were a dime a dozen these days. He was interested, generally speaking, in the practice of innovation.

Specifically, government contracts held his attention. Military applications were where the real money was. The weapons market had already been cornered and private security companies numbered in the hundreds, if not thousands. No, neither of those would be profitable without years of effort. The agency already specialized in medical research. It was a simple enough endeavor to turn that research into contracts with the government to create a bigger and better fighting force.

It took very little effort, really, in the long run. The agency was already successful in bio-pharmaceutical research and sales. A couple of strategic pitches and greased pockets later and the contracts were rolling in.

His success had been predictable and satisfying, but the subsequent fight to stay on top had not been. When you were on top, there was nowhere to go but down, a fact which necessitated and justified the addition of the Colonel, whose presence had allowed him to breathe easily for the first time in years. And it was a partnership that had worked out beautifully.

He simply communicated the outcome he desired and the Colonel acted in whatever manner he saw fit. As long as payments were made generously and on-time, the machine worked perfectly. And he was able to ignore the small voice in the back of his mind that warned nothing lasts forever.

"Those government contracts are the reason you are here, Miss O'Connell. My employer has been working with the military for years but he's always looking for new avenues to explore."

"Exploit, you mean?" she countered.

"Are the two really so different?" he answered rhetorically. "In any case, my employer happened to attend a symposium on neurobiopathology and heard the renowned Dr. David Garrison speak. Dr. Garrison was in the process of systematically destroying both his career and reputation by publicly advertising his theories on traumatic brain injuries and the brain's ability to find alternate pathways for damaged areas. The science escapes me," he admitted without embarrassment.

"But my employer saw the possibilities and invited Dr. Garrison to work exclusively for him. He provided everything Garrison needed to investigate his theory to the fullest extent. And so much the better that the rest of the world thought the good doctor was deluded. Less competition that way."

"So," Quincy said, mulling the information around in her head, "somehow, Dr. Garrison's research led your employer, led you, to me?"

The Colonel nodded in affirmation.

"Because you, or he, thinks I have amnesia and don't know it?" Quincy wanted to laugh but couldn't quite bring herself to do it. "Even if that were true," she said, savagely shoving her inability to remember anything beyond eight years ago to the back of her mind, "why would traumatically-induced amnesia have any relevance to the military? How could it possibly help with building super soldiers, or whatever it is the government wants?"

"It isn't your amnesia that is of interest to the company. That's simply a side effect of the trauma. But it isn't the only one and that is where you become valuable."

Valuable. It was the kind of word that should be flattering. It implied worth. Implied desire. But Quincy didn't feel desired. She felt, in fact, thoroughly repulsed. The Colonel was talking about her like she was nothing more than a commodity to be traded. But she didn't want to run the risk of alienating him. Not while he was inclined to share. The more information he leaked, the more ammunition she had.

So she pressed on, throwing out the first question that came to mind, pushing through the building pain.

"What do you mean, *it isn't the only one*? What else do you think is wrong with me?"

"This is where it gets interesting," the Colonel said with relish. "It took quite some time to find you. You know this, of course. And you know that I hadn't confirmed your identity, that you were the case file I was looking for, until you ran. Why would someone with nothing to hide and no reason to be fearful disappear?"

He tapped his fingers lightly against the steering wheel. "And then, to disappear so completely? I am a very difficult man to elude and you managed it twice. Yes, you all but confirmed your identity with nothing more than your behavior. But then," he said, almost as an afterthought, "that's how most people give themselves away."

"I didn't disappear this time," Quincy argued.

"No. You didn't. We were smarter this time. I had learned not to underestimate you or expect a normal reaction. Which is why I embedded Mr. Auberdeen into your life, such as it were."

Such as it were? "Really, Colonel. There's no need to be rude," she said imperiously. "And *Mr. Auberdeen* wasn't in my life." She turned her head and smiled sweetly at Brandon. "He's just not my type."

"I don't know," Brandon replied snidely. "I'm tall. Military. Seems exactly like your type."

"Maybe," Quincy shot back. "But the whole *trying to kill me* thing really lost you some points."

He smiled at that, a vicious smile, and turned back towards

the window. Probably trying to spot a tail, she figured.

"Mr. Auberdeen got close enough to you to evaluate your abilities. That is all I required of him," the Colonel continued mildly.

"Abilities?" Quincy asked. "What abilities? What is so wrong with all of you that you think there is anything even remotely special about me?" she asked in exasperation. "What have I ever done to make anyone look at me twice?"

"You are quite good at blending in," the Colonel agreed. "You do everything you can to go unnoticed. But tell me, is it normal to be able to perform field surgery, without tools, after reading about it? You saved that woman's life. Without immediate intervention, that wound would have been fatal."

Quincy went cold.

"I read the medical report. The artery was almost completely severed. Simply applying pressure would have resulted in death. But you opened the laceration and applied force to both ends of the artery itself. Tell me Miss O'Connell, how does a library assistant know to do that?"

Quincy swallowed, attempting to force moisture back into her mouth. She'd gone dry during the Colonel's little spiel.

"So, it was you then?" she asked, although it was really more of a statement than a question.

"Of course," Brandon answered. "I had followed you to the train station enough to know where you were going when you left that morning. I knew you would go and sit, observe the security and the routes available. You were running through your escape plan." He shrugged. "You're not the only one who can spot holes in security."

"So you waited in the hall behind the women's restroom and attacked a random girl, all to see how I would react?"

she asked, horror leaking through her words. Psychopaths. That's who did that kind of thing. And sociopaths. She was dealing with psychopaths and sociopaths.

"Of course," he said again without hesitation. He seemed amused that she would think otherwise. "Collateral damage is acceptable, as long as it's manageable."

Quincy was aghast, shocked at both his callousness and his complete lack of sentiment for human life. She had figured out pretty quickly that he was cold. He would have to be to play his part so effectively. But it was hard to understand the complete lack of conscience.

Even the Colonel, pragmatist that he was, allowed room for feeling. He might not allow it to affect his actions, but he still valued human life. Brandon was not afflicted with the same sympathy.

She needed to remove herself from this situation. Immediately. Whatever the Colonel promised, she had no assurances that he could control Brandon.

The Colonel might kill her if she tried to escape, but Brandon would kill her if she stayed.

48

Chapter 48

Auberdeen

Letting the girl out was a mistake. Of this, Brandon had no doubt. Stopping for gas was a necessity, unfortunate but unavoidable. But to let Quincy go inside... Brandon had suspected the Colonel of slipping lately but this was madness. It was a completely unnecessary risk.

True, he had no real desire to listen to her whine about the insanity of kidnapping a girl without having made proper bathroom arrangements either but she was a proven flight risk. She could stand to suffer a long drive as far as Brandon was concerned. The Colonel hadn't even hesitated when he voiced his objections.

"Go with her Mr. Auberdeen," he'd said dismissively. "Surely you can control her, now that we actually have her in hand."

Brandon had burned from the dig. He'd grabbed the girl by the arm and jerked her close to his body.

"If she makes a move, kill her. A body is better than nothing at all."

Brandon stopped and looked back at the Colonel. The man had already turned away to begin fueling the car. "It would be my extreme pleasure," he hissed in her ear. He smiled as he felt her tense under his hand, but she didn't try to pull away. In fact, she leaned into him and slipped her arm around his waist.

"What are you doing?" he growled into her hair.

"My life's on the line, *Mr. Auberdeen*." she hissed back. "Just trying to make it look real."

The drive had slowly but surely clawed through Brandon's last nerve. Maybe if he had been driving he wouldn't be so unsettled but as it was, his muscles burned with inactivity and he was tenser than he should be. He didn't do well with stillness.

The need to do, to act, drove him and being forced to wait, to sit behind the girl and listen to her bait him but utterly unable to do anything about it, left him with a fatal loss of control. And he desperately needed his control.

The Colonel seemed content with the outcome of the pursuit, at the moment. Brandon hadn't known he'd harbored any hopes of taking her alive given the kill order, but he must have seen an opportunity and decided it was worth the risk.

Which was exactly what Brandon had done when he'd cut that girl's throat at the train station. And when he'd made the assassination attempt. He'd taken the risks of both actions into consideration, as well as the potential benefits, and decided it was well worth the cost.

He called it initiative. The Colonel called it insubordination. He'd been reamed by some of the most intimidating officers the military could produce but the Colonel was playing in a league of his own. Failing his C.O. had come with some harsh penalties but he had a feeling failing the Colonel again would be lethal.

He had tried to keep an ear on the conversation happening up front while he scanned their perimeter. The man Quincy was traveling with was going to be a problem. Brandon had noticed him in his surveillance of the girl, noticed how he always seemed to appear when she was alone.

The Colonel had confirmed the man, Logan Davies, was former military, something Brandon had pegged the first day he'd seen him.

His build, his walk, his posture – it all screamed service. His hair was far from regulation but still, Brandon could spot a fellow soldier. He hadn't minded so much when Quincy shot down his first dinner invitation. But she had jumped right on board with this other guy, going on walks with him, letting him buy her dinner. She clearly had a thing for him and it scraped Brandon's pride like a dull knife.

It had always been that way with women for him. He never seemed to be good enough for them. Not tall enough or smart enough or strong enough. Even his mother didn't respect him. Until he made her. And now, with Quincy in hand and under control, he would make her show that same respect.

She would know exactly how much better he was than Davies when he killed her. If he'd been feeling charitable, he would snap her neck. Clean, quick, efficient. But now? She didn't deserve clean or quick or efficient. He would do it slowly, so he could watch the fear in her eyes, followed by the slow realization that she was going to die. And once her breath was gone, he would scoop her up and drop her body out the back door.

It should be easy enough to find the alley that led to the back of the store.

He would inform the Colonel that she'd tried to alert the cashier and that he'd followed orders like a good little soldier. They could pick her body up out of sight and continue on to the agency to make their deposit.

Quincy pulled to the right, jarring him from his thoughts and he jerked her back. "What do you think you're doing?" he hissed at her.

"Going to the bathroom, genius. That was the point of this whole trip." She pointed toward the far right corner of the store. "It's back there."

Brandon glanced around, hoping no one had noticed their little tug-of-war. "Fine. Let's go." He nodded at the cashier and gave him what he hoped was a friendly smile.

"Oh yeah," Quincy mocked. "That was believable."

He shoved her toward the bathroom, frog-marching her down the aisle between bags of chips and battery cables until they reached the door. Quincy stiffened, pushing back as he started to push her in, but he'd been expecting that. He smiled and slipped the K-bar he kept strapped to his back from beneath his jacket.

"I didn't really need the excuse but I'll take it," he said.

He forced her through the door with one hand and slammed her back against the wall of the stall, effectively pinning her in place. He twirled the knife in his hand and grinned, enjoying his moment. He hadn't had to be nearly as patient as he thought. He brought the knife towards her slowly enough for her to see her death coming and know there was nothing she could do to stop it.

He had just enough time to notice the shift in her eyes before the control he'd worked so hard to reclaim was ripped out from under him once again.

Chapter 49

"*E*xtinction is the rule. Survival is the exception.*" Carl Sagan*

What is 'normality'? And what has it to do with survival? Can it feed the girl? Can it rescue her, heal her? Can it save her? No.

But I can.

* * *

Quincy

She was playing this one totally by ear. She had survived to this point in her life by having a plan and plotting every move methodically. But that option was gone and she was operating on nothing but instinct now. And instinct told her she had to get away. Right now. The gas stop was merely fortuitous in its timing.

So, with no plan, no escape routes marked out, no backup plan, she blurted out the first thing that came to mind.

"I need to use the restroom." The Colonel didn't even look her way.

Brandon laughed from the backseat. "You'd have to be crazy to think we'd actually let you out of this car. Deal with it."

She spun in her seat so she could look him in the eye. "It's not just my problem, moron. If you want me to 'deal with it', it's going to be all of our problems. Plus," and here, she tossed her hair in that way he seemed to really hate which would have, admittedly, been more dramatic if it hadn't been pulled up in a ponytail, "ladies have special bathroom needs. If you *gentlemen*," she put special emphasis on the word, "need me to spell it out for you, I can. I'm..."

"That won't be necessary Miss O'Connell," and here, finally, the Colonel broke in. "We quite understand." Quincy hid her smile. It worked every time.

He sighed. "Mr. Auberdeen, go with her."

"What?!" Brandon spluttered from the back. "You can't be serious. Sir..."

"Enough," the Colonel said mildly. "She knows the cost of trying to run. My order stands. Go with her. Surely you can control her, now that we actually have her in hand."

Quincy couldn't help but smirk, just a little, at the Colonel's obvious slight. Brandon had more than picked up on it and was fuming. And the angrier he was, the more likely it was he'd make a mistake.

She hopped out of the car but startled when Brandon

grabbed her viciously by the elbow, jerking her against his body. He started to say something but the Colonel beat him to it.

"If she makes a move, kill her. A body is better than nothing at all."

Quincy tensed. The Colonel had just given Brandon carte blanche to kill her in that gas station so maybe she had overestimated her worth to the man just a bit.

"It would be my extreme pleasure," he hissed into her ear.

She had no doubt. She slipped her arm around his waist and leaned into him, ignoring the way her skin crawled at the contact.

"What are you doing?" he growled, surprised and appropriately suspicious.

"My life's on the line, *Mr. Auberdeen*," she said, pouring as much venom into her voice as possible, disappointed when it had no effect on the man. "Just trying to make it look real."

The gas station wasn't very crowded, making them more visible than she would have liked. Brandon wasn't playing his part all that well, making it fairly obvious that something was off about them. If she had been willing to make a scene, it would have been fine. But she wasn't interested in putting innocent people at risk.

She had no idea what her next move was. Brandon wasn't going to let her out of his sight. There was absolutely no way she was going to actually use the bathroom in front of this creep, but she doubted she would even get the chance. Quincy was pretty sure he would kill her as soon as the door was locked.

She surveyed the place, trying to come up with something. Anything. The restrooms were in the back corner of the store, single stall by the look of it. Great. Brandon could drag her in there, kill her, and smuggle her body out the back.

She doubted there would be a window in the tiny bathroom. Not that a window would help if Brandon was inside with her. The back exit was only 10 feet past the restrooms, though. On the very limited chance she could distract him, that might work. She moved to the right toward the hallway, but Brandon jerked her back hard. Quincy noticed the cashier look over in concern. She gave him a weak smile.

"What do you think you're doing?" he hissed.

"Going to the bathroom, genius. That was the point of this whole trip." She pointed toward the far right corner of the store. "It's back there."

"Fine. Let's go," he snapped. He nodded toward the cashier and shot him what she thought was supposed to be a reassuring smile.

"Oh yeah," Quincy mocked. "That was believable." *Push his buttons, push his buttons, push his buttons.*

He shoved her toward the bathroom and she started to panic. There was no way he was going to let go of her. Once they were in the bathroom, she was going to die. She couldn't go in but she couldn't stop it, either. Brandon opened the door and Quincy stiffened, pushing back as he started to push her in. He smiled and pulled a six inch knife from under the back of his jacket.

"I didn't really need the excuse but I'll take it," he said. He forced her through the door with one hand, slamming her back against the wall of the stall, effectively pinning her in place. He twirled the knife in his hand and grinned, bringing it toward her slowly enough that she had plenty of time to see her death coming and know there was nothing she could do to stop it.

Quincy squinted her eyes as the buzzing in her head stepped up a notch. The whole world narrowed down to nothing but that knife.

As Brandon advanced on her, several things happened at once. The noise in her head increased to frantic levels, and she couldn't help but wonder why it always seemed to get worse in moments of stress. Was this part of what the Colonel had been talking about? Was this violence raging in her head caused by some sort of unremembered trauma? Was she about to have an epiphany and remember some sort of lost knowledge that would let her escape certain death?

It seemed unlikely and she shook off the crazy, coming back to the matter at hand.

Namely, her imminent death. She may be about to die but she refused to give him the satisfaction of seeing her scared or powerless. Even if she didn't have hidden jujitsu skills, which would have been extremely handy at the moment, she wouldn't go down without a fight. She braced herself to do ... something, despite not knowing what that something would be, when silence descended.

Immediate and complete silence, replacing the noise inside of her head. And as the tornado in her head vanished and her body took over, multiple sirens erupted from outside.

Brandon jerked at the sound and a second later, her knee connected with his groin. If he had been focused solely on her, she doubted she would have gotten in the hit or that it would have been enough to phase him. But Brandon, startled by the sirens, flinched and Quincy's low blow took him by surprise. He keeled over and she threw the elbow he wasn't holding at his face, slamming into his nose.

When his head jerked back, she grabbed his collar with one hand and the back of his head with the other and slammed him face-first into the concrete wall. So, maybe not a jiujitsu master but she did apparently know something. What she didn't know was that a man could make that particular sound. But she didn't stick around to question it. Brandon didn't go all the way down but he did stagger away from the wall, curling around his injured anatomy and trying to catch his breath, a feat made all the more impossible by his broken nose and the blood streaming from it.

Quincy spun and threw herself out of the bathroom and glanced to the left. The cashier had moved out from behind the register and was looking out the front door to where the Colonel's car was surrounded by police cruisers. Again, she didn't question it. She could hear movement in the bathroom and spun toward the back exit.

She hit the door at full speed and it gave easily, catapulting her toward the dirty sidewalk behind the store and straight into a pair of waiting arms.

50

Chapter 50

Logan

Logan had been following the car as discreetly and distantly as he possibly could. There were a few times he'd been afraid he'd lost them but as the light began to grow, he grew more confident. He had no doubt Quincy was in that car. What he did doubt was who she was with.

They'd pulled off onto a commuter parking lot shortly after she'd been picked up and he'd waited on the off-ramp, worried that whoever had her was just going to kill her and dump her in this remote place in the middle of the night. But he hadn't moved. Quincy didn't seem to be putting up a fight, so he'd waited. And as he'd waited, he'd fumed.

Why? Why would she go for a run, by herself, in the middle of the night, when she knew she was being hunted? He had managed to convince her, hadn't he? She trusted him now, at least to a point. He knew she did. So why would she do something so stupid?

This condition Garrison claimed she had was supposed to

make her super smart, or something like that. A super smart idiot, maybe. Oh, Logan knew good and well that he wasn't really angry. He was worried. Panicked at the thought that these guys, whoever they were, had their hands on her. He had lost Jones. He had been too late to save any of the other victims of this agency. But he hadn't been too late with Quincy. Not too late to get to know her. To let her get to know him. To get invested in her. She was more than a mission, had been since he'd first met her, and just because he didn't know exactly what she was, didn't mean he wasn't terrified at the prospect of never getting the chance to figure it out.

And then Brandon had shown up. Logan clenched his hands around the steering wheel. He'd known the guy was trouble from the get-go. Always watching her when she was at work, running into her randomly when she wasn't. Not that he hadn't done the same thing, but that was exactly why he should have figured it out sooner. One stalker to another, he was so looking forward to wiping the floor with that guy.

Logan watched as Brandon climbed into the backseat of the car, which immediately pulled back into drive. Logan slid smoothly back onto the road behind them, headlights still off, as invisible as possible.

He followed the car for hours. They were heading away from Colorado, away from the limited safety Dr. Garrison's clinic would offer. But other than direction, Logan had no idea where they were going. Brandon was clearly just the flunky. The guy that got sent out to collect the target. He'd failed multiple times so the boss had finally stepped in.

But who was the boss? Who was calling the shots? And how much rope did he give them before he stepped in? He couldn't let this go on much longer. The danger to Quincy increased with every mile they traveled. He didn't know how long he had until they got to where they were going. And once they got Quincy inside the system, it would be impossible to get her out. Not that he wouldn't try. But he wouldn't succeed and he couldn't live with that.

When he'd seen the car pulling off the interstate, he realized this might be the only chance he'd have to act. The town was some no-name pit stop on the side of the road so he doubted it was their final destination. They would just be stopping for gas or food. If it was food, he was screwed. If it was gas, at least one of them would have to get out of the car.

And he needed them to get out of the car. If Quincy were smart, and he knew she was very, very smart despite his recent realization that she was also an idiot, she would figure out some way to get out of the car. If she could just convince them to let her go inside, maybe he'd have a chance.

But if she did her part, he would have to do his. Logan breathed a sigh of relief when the car pulled into a busy gas station, the only one in town by the look of it. He turned off at the restaurant before the gas station and pulled around back. Most of these businesses had adjoining lots. If he could just get lucky...there.

He cut down the back alley and slid the car neatly behind a dumpster. There was a private exit at the top of the loading ramp. He could easily enter the store without being seen but then what? Even if Quincy could convince them to let her go into the store, she sure wouldn't be allowed to go alone. Brandon would recognize him from being around Quincy at the college, at the very least. He might react badly and there were civilians in the line of fire. He needed a distraction.

He snuck to the edge of the building and peered around.

The pumps were fairly busy and they were a few cars back in line. From where he was standing, it looked like Quincy was talking to the man in the driver's seat, a large, well-built older man. Brandon was in the backseat, looking like he was about to have a stroke.

Logan smiled. At least he wasn't the only one she had that effect on. He slid his hand into his pocket and pulled out his phone. He luckily had some experience in spur-of-the-moment distractions. He dialed 911 and put the phone to his ear.

"911. What is your emergency?"

He lightened his voice, adding a little hard-working southern honesty to it. "Yes ma'am. I'm at the filling station on Broadway and Chestnut and I think there's something wrong with the car in front of me. There's something smeared all over the back of it, looks all wet and rusty. And, well, I think I can hear something coming from the inside of the trunk. Hollering, maybe. I'm worried there might be someone in there."

He threw as much concern into his voice as he could and topped it off with wholesome southern twang. He'd learned a long time ago that people tend to trust a southern accent.

"Sir," the operator said, "I need you to take a breath." She waited while he exhaled noisily through his mouth. "Okay now. Can you tell me what this car looks like?"

"Oh, yes ma'am. It's a black Mercury Marquis, license plate NW9-7B1."

"I have a police car en route. Please stay where you are and do not try to approach the car."

"You might better send several cars ma'am," he drawled. "There's two guys in the car, both big, burly types. It looks like the guy driving has a gun in his belt."

He dropped the call, leaving it at that. Cliffhangers tended to enhance the sense of emergency and the sooner backup arrived, the better.

The passenger door flew open, Quincy stepped out, and Logan took his first full breath since she had disappeared. He hadn't realized just how worried he was but seeing her here, alive and unhurt, caused something in his chest to relax for the first time in hours. But it clenched back when Brandon grabbed Quincy by the elbow, hard, and jerked her back against him. She flinched and Logan could see the pain on her face, brief though it was.

He gritted his teeth. Yep. He was going to enjoy wiping that smug, leering look right off the man's face. Soon. But Brandon and Quincy were walking quickly towards the store and Logan needed to get into position. He still didn't know what his play was but he was fairly certain he'd only get one chance.

Logan was just loping up the ramp of the loading dock when the sound of sirens burst from the front of the store. He smiled. Perfect timing. He grabbed the door handle, intending to ease it open and slip quietly inside, but the door exploded outward before he had the chance.

He stepped back in surprise as Quincy slammed into his outstretched arms.

51

Chapter 51

Logan

Quincy catapulting suddenly into his chest hadn't been part of the plan but Logan would take it. She hit him hard enough to force him several feet back down the ramp and he wrapped his arms around her to keep her on her feet. The fist she swung was unexpected and well-placed, knocking his head back, no doubt intended to make him drop his hold but having the exact opposite effect. Logan tightened his grip around her waist.

"Ow! Quincy." he whispered. "Quincy! Stop fighting. It's me. It's Logan."

She bucked in his arms, fighting to get free, but he kept her wrapped tight. "Quincy! Quincy, come on, we don't have time for this. Look at me." He doubted his words were making any impact but she must have recognized something in the tone of his voice. The fight started to die out of her and she finally looked at him.

"Logan?" she asked in disbelief. "What? How? I..."

He let her slide to the ground and grabbed her hand. "Details later. We need to go. Now."

He started to pull her towards the dumpster, back toward the car before Brandon, wherever she'd left him, came looking but she dug her heels in.

Logan shook his head. "Seriously?" he asked. "Are we really going to do this again?"

One more alley. One more life-and-death situation. One more tantrum when they didn't have time for it. At least this time she had the grace to look contrite.

"Where's Brandon?" he asked pointedly, looking over her shoulder.

Quincy finally picked her feet up and started hoofing it towards the car. "On the ground spitting blood and growling in a pitch higher than usual, last I checked."

He couldn't help but grin. The higher the danger, the higher the snark apparently.

The sirens had quieted down but Logan figured the police were still detaining the driver of the Marquis. He hoped so, at least. He could only assume that any man who would kidnap a girl off the street would hesitate before letting local cops search his trunk. They should be fine from that angle for awhile but what about Brandon? Whatever Quincy had done, she seemed to feel like he was down but certainly not out. She ran around to the passenger side of the car and jerked the handle but nothing happened.

"You locked it? Seriously?"

"Sorry, sorry." Logan dug in his pocket and pulled the keys. "Force of habit." A seriously stupid habit. He knew better. Locking the door and pocketing the keys when a quick getaway was required was a rookie move. Quincy rolled her eyes and slid into the seat.

"Get me out of here," she said and he cranked the engine.

Logan reversed from behind the dumpster and inched back the way he'd come, pulling through the restaurant parking lot. "This is the tricky part," he said. "Do you know if they made the car before picking you up?"

Quincy shook her head. "I don't know for sure, but it didn't sound like it. I think he got lucky," she said sheepishly. "Totally on me, by the way."

"Oh, it's definitely on you. Maybe now's not the time to say it, but you went running. Alone. At night."

Logan didn't even bother looking at her. He pulled the car forward just enough to see the swarm of police cruisers surrounding the black Marquis and the man standing in the middle, talking calmly with officers. Still no sign of Brandon. They needed to go now, while everyone was still occupied. Quincy sighed.

"Why would you do that?" he asked. "You knew the danger you were in." He didn't understand. He probably wouldn't even after she explained but he still felt like he deserved the explanation. "You're not the only one on their radar anymore you know."

"You're right. I'm not and I didn't even consider I might be putting you in danger too. I'm sorry. I left a note," she said, almost as an afterthought, without any real hope that would mollify him.

"Oh yes, that's right," he snapped. "My mistake. The note makes it all better." Logan put on his turn signal and pulled left onto the road, heading away from the gas station and back towards the highway.

"I think we should keep going east," Quincy said. "At least

for awhile."

Logan had already been planning to do just that but was curious, despite himself, why she was thinking the same thing.

"Because he'll expect us to go back the direction we were heading, not keep moving towards his goal. Wherever that is," she said in response to his unasked question.

Logan quirked an eyebrow. "I didn't say anything," he said dryly.

"Please," she said. "You were practically shouting."

He laughed. "Fine, fine. So, we agree to go east and we agree that you are to blame for this unplanned and wholly unappreciated detour. Let's find a ball game on the radio and you can tell me about the mystery man and the Energizer Brandon."

She looked over at him in question. "You know. Because he keeps coming and coming and coming." He thought it was funny at least.

52

Chapter 52

The Colonel

He sat in the car, considering. The police had been a surprise. It took a lot to throw him off his game and the soldier had succeeded. He could only assume it was the soldier. The girl hadn't had access to a phone or a computer and had had no prior indication they would be pulling off in this specific town. Unless Auberdeen had allowed her to slip away long enough to borrow a phone, which was not altogether unlikely at this point.

But still, he doubted she would have had enough time. The police had shown up a scant minute after they went inside.

No, somehow the soldier had found them. The Colonel sighed. He had to admit, if only to himself, that he had made a mistake. He should have just eliminated the girl. The company might prefer living specimens, but a body was better than nothing. It would have been simple and posed less risk, certainly. She had no identification on her and he couldn't be traced to the town.

But he had seen an opportunity. And maybe his pride had played a role in the decision to take her as well. She had eluded him twice. No one had ever done that before and the failure stung. She was just a girl, after all, with no special training or skills. Had she been trained, she might have used her condition and the advantages it provided to aid in her escape, yes. But she was still in denial so actively using it would have been a stretch.

He shook himself and refocused. Steps needed to be taken. Firstly, the girl was now outside of his immediate reach. If the soldier had come for her, and after a quick examination of the store and surrounding area had come up empty, he was sure he had, then they were gone. The simple tracking device he'd planted on the girl would give him the tether he needed to find them again so he had the luxury of giving them a head start. The company need never know about this debacle.

But Auberdeen. He would need to be dealt with. He had disappeared as well and the Colonel had no doubt the man knew he was finished.

The Colonel didn't know exactly what had happened inside the store while he convinced the local law enforcement, every single one of them in this god-forsaken town if he were guessing, that the call had been a hoax, but Auberdeen had effectively vanished. Fresh blood on the bathroom floor told him there had been a struggle of some sort but the room looked remarkably untouched otherwise, which meant it had been a short one. Something fast and unexpected. Something that would allow someone untrained to outmaneuver a bigger, more skilled opponent.

The girl had used the sirens as a distraction and broken Auberdeen's nose. She'd most likely escaped out the back, where the soldier was probably waiting. And Auberdeen, knowing the Colonel would brook no further mistakes, had slipped away like the coward he was.

Well, there was nothing he could do about Quincy O'Connell at the moment, but he suspected he would pick up their trail, fresh as it was, easy enough. Auberdeen, on the other hand, could not be allowed a head-start. The man wasn't as smart as he thought he was but it was best to end that particular threat immediately. One didn't simply walk away from employment like theirs. To ensure the safety of the agency, the Colonel would find Auberdeen and make sure he didn't become an issue. And then he would find the girl.

He would not allow her to disappear again.

Chapter 53

Q**uincy**

The car was quiet as Logan drove, keeping a careful eye on the rear view mirror to make sure a black Mercury Marquis wasn't on his tail. Not that the guy couldn't have ditched the car for a new one by now but he felt better staying focused.

"I'm pretty sure we're good," Quincy finally said. "The Colonel didn't have any idea you were behind us."

"And we didn't have any idea they were behind us either," Logan clipped back. "I think I'll stay alert."

Quincy sighed. He was mad. Not that she didn't deserve it, but still. She had escaped a seemingly fatal trip to the bathroom. Why couldn't they celebrate a little?

"We will need to switch cars again," she said instead. "He knew about you and he'd cased the motel. Better to be safe than sorry."

"Ironic, coming from you," he quipped. Then he sighed. "I agree but I don't think our usual tricks are going to work again". He nodded to his phone lying on the dashboard. "Can you look and see where the nearest bus station is?"

"Really?" Quincy grabbed his phone. "Won't that be a little obvious when he tracks our car to the parking lot?"

"He won't," Logan said. "He'll track our car to the nearest rental agency. And then he'll track our new rental. Or he'll try."

Logan finally looked at her and smiled. It wasn't a patented, thousand-watt Logan Davies smile, but it would do for now. "And then he'll lose us. Because our new car won't be on the highway. It'll be in an alley behind some abandoned building. And it will be missing its GPS. I think that should buy us the time and distance we need. He doesn't know where we're heading, does he?" Logan asked as an afterthought.

"How could he?" she answered. "I don't even know where we're heading."

"Did you find that bus station?" Logan asked. If he thought he could distract her that easily, he was quite mistaken.

"Would a train work?" There hadn't been a bus station for another hundred miles but maybe that wasn't the only option. "There's a scenic railway tour that runs northwest out of Idaho city. It's a two-week tour if you ride the whole thing. It looks like it goes all the way to San Francisco."

"Book it," Logan said. "There's a card in my wallet under the name Brad Montgomery. Use it and book us two tickets to the end of the line."

"Brad Montgomery?" Quincy scoffed. "You just happen to have an alias lying around?"

"I would think that's something you'd approve of, Miss O'Connell. Or, I'm sorry, would you prefer Miss Scott or Miss Elliott?"

"Fair enough," she conceded. "Okay, two tickets on the train leaving at 4:00 p.m. this afternoon. Once we check in, we'll be treated to a gourmet dinner and then escorted to our sleeping car. I booked the deluxe luxury compartment, by the way. Brad Montgomery owes $2600 dollars."

"For a train ride?" Logan asked in shock. "That's just plain robbery."

"Oh come on," Quincy said. "For five days and all the meals to go with it?"

"And don't forget the fancy bedroom," Logan reminded her wryly.

"I'm looking forward to that fancy bedroom. After the rooms we've stayed in? Believe me, we've earned it."

Logan glanced at her, eyebrow raised. "Really?" he asked.

"Insinuation noted and ignored. If I'm feeling generous, you can share the bed. If not, you can have your pick of the floor or yet another teeny tiny armchair".

Logan sighed. "A guy can dream."

"Not if he wants to share this bed."

54

Chapter 54

Logan

He had noticed the blood on her arm about two hours ago, once everything had settled down. But she hadn't seemed hurt and it was a pretty minor amount of blood so he'd let it go for the moment. But now that Quincy had nodded off, he couldn't stop thinking about it.

Brandon had gone into the store with her but only Quincy had come out. It stood to reason the blood was his. There was a story there and he wanted to know it. Quincy was small by female standards and while Brandon wasn't as big as Logan himself was, he was still a big guy. He had at least six inches and 100 lbs on her. What kind of skills was she hiding in that messed up head of hers?

When Jones had been injured, he'd at least known something was wrong. There had been the explosion, the surgery, and then the recovery that was supposed to happen but never actually did. But Quincy seemed to not have any of that. And she also seemed to be in control of her symptoms, for the most part. Logan didn't claim to have figured out exactly what form her reflexiveness had taken but he was pretty sure it had to do with memory. He wasn't sure it was a normal function of the brain to be fluent in multiple languages after listening to an audio lesson or perform trauma surgery on someone bleeding out after reading a book.

Jones could process sound far above and below the levels allowed by a regular brain but he never did learn to harness it. Or maybe he just didn't want to. That was something Logan tried not to think too much about.

But Quincy absorbed information and used it, almost un-consciously. He'd been watching when she'd hot wired the car. She had been skeptical at first and then she'd looked confused when she finished, like she didn't know exactly how it had happened. He wondered if she even remembered what she'd done.

The headache had taken him by surprise but it shouldn't have. Not after everything that had happened with Jones. Quincy had just never shown him that side. It didn't look like something she would have been able to hide easily. If Logan were guessing, he'd say the headaches, insomnia, and constant noise in her head were all symptoms of the injury. Jones's brain responded to the increased levels of sound much the same way.

But she hadn't self-destructed the way he had. She was still here. Still alive. Why? Why Quincy and not Jones? The man had been army tough. But he still hadn't been able to deal with the pain and the confusion that came from not knowing *why*. He'd allowed it to drive him over the edge and it had ultimately killed him.

Just like it had killed several others that Dr. Garrison had identified as possible RNB patients. Logan didn't know why it hadn't killed Quincy but he knew he didn't want it to. He needed to get her safely to Dr. Garrison. Failure wasn't an option.

He had driven another thirty miles when Quincy bolted upright in the seat, breathing hard.

"Easy there, soldier," he said, making sure not to touch her. "You're okay. We're good." He kept his hands on the wheel, making sure to not make any sudden moves. He'd woken up to flashbacks before. Heart pounding, caught in a memory, it always took a few minutes to process reality. So he kept driving, giving Quincy the time she needed to get her bearings. After a couple of minutes, she relaxed back into her seat.

"How long have I been out?" she asked.

"Not long. An hour maybe. We're about a half hour outside of Idaho City."

Quincy nodded. "No sign of a tail?"

"Nope. I think we're clear for the moment. If by chance he really did make the car, he's probably keeping his distance, relying on the GPS to keep us in sight. Once we ditch the car, we should be good."

"Great," she said, looking out the window.

"Listen," he started, but she cut him off.

"Could we table this whole discussion? Just for now? I know you have questions, and I definitely owe you answers. But can it wait? At least until we get settled on the train. I'm still kind of sorting through it myself."

Logan glanced over. She was looking ahead, staring out the windshield. She looked tired. She always looked tired, but his was more than that. This was exhaustion - and something

331

else.

"Sure," he said, relenting. "Take all the time you need."

Chapter 55

Q**uincy**

She was exhausted. There was really no other word for it. She never really slept but she hadn't even shut her eyes in 48 hours. The cat nap in the car with Logan only seemed to make it worse. She knew he had questions and she knew he deserved answers. And she really wanted to give them to him.

She just didn't have it in her to do it just yet. Where was she supposed to start? With the kidnapping? Or Brandon trying to kill her in the gas station? Or maybe she could tell him the Colonel had shared Dr. Garrison's theory about her.

Now that she wasn't in immediate, life-threatening danger, she couldn't seem to shake what he'd said. Her having a super brain was ridiculous on so many levels. But why couldn't she remember anything from her life before Kara Scott? She could explain away the rest of it but that one was tough.

She closed her eyes again and tipped her head against the window of the car. She had parents, right? She must. Or must've at some point, at least. But there was nothing there. Siblings? Nothing. Just a big, blank space.

Suddenly, something hit her. A recent memory. Her and Logan, walking through the park. He'd asked her to tell him something about herself. Parents, hometown, birthday - anything. She had ducked the question, using the stranger danger argument as a deflection, compelled by something deep inside to change the subject and steer Logan away from those little personal details. Maybe she was unconsciously steering herself away from them, too. Shielding herself from the realization that she didn't actually know any of those things.

One thing was perfectly obvious, though. Logan knew. He had been subtly probing and she'd never picked up on it. Which meant that the Colonel wasn't the only one with ridiculous theories. Somehow, it was harder dismissing Logan's opinion.

"Hey."

She felt a light touch against her shoulder, shaking her from her thoughts. "Yeah," she said, bringing herself back to the present. She sat up and stretched, looking around. "Is this it?"

"It is." Logan pointed to his right. "We're going to switch rental cars there and then ditch the new one about a mile from the Grey Hound station. Then it's a quick four mile walk to where we're joining up with the railway tour."

"The first thing I'm going to do is take a shower. A very long, very hot shower," Quincy said. "And change clothes. I forget just how long I've been wearing this."

Logan grinned. "Your bag's in the back. You're lucky I grabbed it before going off to look for you last night."

"Yeah, well..." She sighed. "Thanks for that, by the way. I know I put us in a bad spot."

"You put us in a very bad spot," he agreed. "But we're both fine and this is going to work. Once we're on that train, we should be off your Colonel's radar. Come on."

She hoped that was true, but she wondered. The Colonel had been so sure of himself, so unflappable. Quincy doubted he was the kind of man to be shaken off so easily. Logan grabbed their bags and pushed out of the car. Quincy followed him out but paused beside the building. "Go on," she said when he paused to wait for her. "I'll wait out here for you."

Logan hesitated, obviously debating the odds of that.

"I'm not going to disappear again," she promised.

"I'm not worried about you running off. I'm worried about the other kinds of trouble you seem to find."

Well, he wasn't wrong but she rolled her eyes so he wouldn't know it. "I'll be right here, in your line of sight the whole time," she said impatiently. She needed him to go inside. She needed a few minutes to collect herself. She was in pieces on the inside and she needed to patch herself back together if she was going to be able to hold a rational conversation about everything she'd learned.

The sun was warm on her face so she tipped it up, leaning her head back against the wall. The buzzing had come back at some point but it wasn't as bad as it sometimes was. It had been nice, those few hours without it. She wondered just how far away the Colonel and Brandon were. An hour? A few minutes? Could they see her right now, maybe watching from a distance? If so, this plan of Logan's wasn't going to work.

But she had a feeling the Colonel was giving them some space. If she were within eyesight, she would be dead. He had made it perfectly clear there would be no more chances. He would rather put a bullet between her eyes than risk losing her again. So at the moment, they appeared to be fine. They just needed to keep it that way.

The door jangled beside her. "Everything okay?" Logan asked, bumping her softly with his shoulder.

"Yeah," she said, opening her eyes and looking up at him. "Just tired."

He wrapped an arm around her shoulders, pulling her against him. "I know," he said, glancing down at his watch. "Give me two hours to get us safe and you can rest for as long as you need."

Quincy smiled. He really could be sweet. She doubted she'd be able to get more than her usual broken sleep but it was nice that he tried.

"Yeah," she agreed, humoring him. "Two hours. So," she looked around, shading her eyes with her left hand. "Which one is ours?"

Chapter 56

Logan

Getting to the train was a non-event, as it turned out.

Despite his relaxed attitude, Logan had been alert, ready for an ambush. Quincy hadn't said as much but he suspected this Colonel had made a strong impression on her. There wouldn't be another attempt to take her alive. She was too much of a flight risk, especially with a partner.

No. The next assault would be fatal. So he kept his eyes open for decent sniper nests and roadblocks that could be deadly. But there had been nothing. So maybe the Colonel really was staying back, watching to see what their next move would be. If so, that would play right into their plan.

The four-mile walk to the train depot had turned into a four-mile run, which had been all the better. Quincy had looked up at him with those ridiculously big green eyes of hers and he had caved. After all, the quicker you moved, the less chance someone had to take you by surprise. She was in good shape and he had a feeling that had come in handy doing whatever she had done to shake Brandon at the gas station.

But he didn't think she ran because she liked it. It had something to do with what went on inside her head. Logan wondered briefly if the Colonel had told Quincy why she was on his hit list. If he had gone into detail on Dr. Garrison's research or her value to the wrong kind of people.

It was possible the Colonel himself didn't even know why she was a target. He could simply be hired help, contracted to eliminate targets. And then he decided it didn't matter right now. Quincy would tell him. They would deal with it once they were in the relative safety of the train. And he would do the same. He would tell her everything this time. There was no reason to hold back now.

"Wow," Logan deadpanned when Quincy opened the door of their compartment. "You weren't kidding with the luxury suite, were you?"

"It's luxury for a train."

"Luxury must mean tiny," he said, stepping into the small space and sitting their bags down on the bed.

"I prefer cozy," she said. "Makes it seem small on purpose."

He couldn't argue with that. "I know you want to grab a shower," he said, looking doubtfully into the cut-out space that held the walk-in shower, "but can you wait long enough for the train to pull out?"

It was unlikely the Colonial would figure out their scheme in time to catch the train but he didn't want to take any chances. "I'd like to be mobile, just in case we have any unwanted company."

"That's smart," she said tiredly. "How long do we have?"

Logan glanced at his watch. "Another half hour. Why don't

338

we head down to the drink car. It has a good view of the platform and I wouldn't mind a soda."

"Sure." Quincy smiled tiredly and held out her hand. Logan just stared.

"Come on," she said. "We're supposed to be married. We better act like it."

Logan was beginning to be able to read her pretty well and her exhaustion was bleeding through the cracks in her usually flawless walls. If she needed a little extra security, he wasn't about to deny her. Besides, no army man worth his salt would turn down the opportunity to hold hands with a beautiful woman.

"Yes ma'am," he said, taking her hand in his and pulling her closer.

Logan had been right. The view from the drink car was perfect. He could see the entire boarding platform and the parking lot to boot. No one could get on or off the train without him seeing.

He ordered a coke for himself, a large black coffee for Quincy, and waters all around. He threw on a bottle of wine, winking at the waitress and telling her it was their honeymoon. It was far too conspicuous being the only couple in the drink car not drinking alcohol. He watched Quincy gaze out the window, lost again to some place far away. It was time to find out what exactly had happened during those hours she had spent with the Colonel and Brandon.

"So," he started. "Want to tell me how you managed a joy ride with the Dynamic Duo when, last I knew, you were sound asleep in the bed next to me?"

"I'm never sound asleep," she said idly.

Logan waited. He would let her tell the story however she

wanted.

"I don't sleep. Not really. A few hours here and there, but rarely anything substantial."

Logan rolled that around in his head. "That sounds exhausting," he finally said.

"It is," she agreed, eyes still trained out the window but not really focused on anything. "It is completely exhausting. I just can't stop. My brain jumps around, running through idle and random information that I've read or heard or seen. And then there's the constant white noise in the background that I can't seem to get away from."

She finally glanced away from the window, down toward her hands that had wrapped around her mug of coffee. "That's why I run. It's one of the only times my mind can relax. How do I explain it?" she wondered to herself.

"When I run, the gears in my brain seem to tune themselves to my body, instead of my body to my brain. The more I settle into a run, the more my mind lets go."

The dark circles under her eyes took on a deeper meaning. Logan had noticed them the first time they'd met. Well, maybe the second. The first time they'd met, he'd just noticed her eyes.

"So much had happened in the last 48 hours. Finding out you weren't exactly who you said you were set off my survival instincts." Not exactly an accurate description of events, but he'd give her some leeway.

"Having a shot taken at me in broad daylight didn't help. And then stealing a car and embarking on a cross-country road trip with someone I didn't know if I trusted." She sighed. "I do now, of course. But the headache was the final straw."

Logan broke in. "Do you have them often?"

"The headaches?" she asked. "No. Yes." She mulled it around. "What's 'often'? I get them when I get stressed and the last few days definitely qualify. Ironically, that's the best sleep I ever get, after those headaches."

"Not really worth it, if you ask me," Logan said drily.

"Try living through one," she snarked.

"Try watching someone you love live through one," he shot back.

She looked nonplussed for a moment, not sure what he meant by that, before understanding dawned. "Jones?" she asked.

Logan just nodded, trying not to think about it too hard.

"Was that Dr. Garrison you called? When you thought I was stroking out?"

"It was. Not that he could do anything, hundreds of miles away." He let the silence stretch, waiting for her to look at him.

"I told you about the pain Jones was in before he died." Quincy nodded. "He would get headaches just like that. Agonizing. They would roll over him in a wave and there was nothing I could do to help." It was his turn to look out the window. "I don't like being helpless."

"I'm sorry I left," she said quietly. "I should have woken you up. I know that. I knew it then, too. I just didn't do it. I needed the space. The silence. I thought running would help me gain some sort of perspective. I felt, I don't know…"

She tightened her grip on the mug, frustrated. "It was compulsive. I had to run and I knew I would never sleep until I did." She shrugged. "Doesn't make it right."

"No," he said slowly. "But it does make it understandable."

Quincy shook her head, not quite willing to let it go so fast.

"You would never let one of your soldiers get away with going AWOL."

"Please," he said. "I would never mistake you for a soldier." There it was. He'd been waiting to see that smile. It was tired, but it was real. The train whistle blew and the conductor gave the old-fashioned "All aboard!" The train jerked into motion and they looked at each other and smiled.

Within seconds, they were rolling down the tracks and away from the Colonel and the company he worked for. He hoped.

Chapter 57

Logan

The shower had been running for almost an hour without a word or sound from Quincy. Steam was billowing out from around the glass door from the heat of the water, filling their compartment. Logan was sure there was a quota per cabin - a max cap on water usage - but he let her be. She deserved a break after the week she'd had.

Their scenic getaway had gotten started without a problem, which seemed almost suspicious after the last 48 hours. No one matching Quincy's descriptions of the Colonel or Brandon had boarded after them. He couldn't rule out the possibility that the company bankrolling the Colonel had another agent on them, one they hadn't seen, but it seemed unlikely.

The Colonel had to be the driving force behind the disappearance of Dr. Garrison's suspected RNB patients. He was obviously former military, probably special ops. He'd tracked Quincy like a bloodhound. He'd only needed to catch the scent, which Brandon had been lucky enough to find. Logan worried the man might be inside their heads. If he knew how they'd given Brandon the slip at the truck stop, dumping Quincy's phone in a truck headed the opposite direction, he might have guessed what they'd do now. If he found them again, he'd put a bullet through Quincy's head without hesitation and walk away.

It was a troublesome thought but one he had no control over. The Colonel would find them or he wouldn't. Logan had done everything he could to shake the tail and now all he could do was keep calm and keep watch. Quincy was smart and had proved she worked well under pressure. He could count on her to keep her head and not freeze up when the time came. That was more than he could ask of most people.

Quincy really was smart, he mused. He'd guessed she was intelligent based on her ability to stay unidentified and off the radar for so long but the first time he'd seen her had confirmed it. It had been more of a gut feeling than scientific proof, considering they hadn't even spoken that first time out on the quad. But they'd locked eyes, if just for a moment. Long enough for him to see.

Logan decided to rustle up a game of Frisbee with a bunch of undergrad jocks, knowing it would give him a valid reason to be there and knowing he would need one to stay off her radar. She had been near-impossible to track down and it wasn't by being unobservant.

The college kids were athletic and energetic but he was a trained army lieutenant. He had no trouble keeping one eye on the game and one on the walkway leading past. So he'd seen her the moment she'd shown up at the coffee kiosk. He thought he'd known what to expect but he'd been unprepared for the reality.

He'd pulled her profile picture from the college database so he knew who he was looking for. A little on the small side, casually dressed, blending in with the students around her.

But then the sunlight hit her and his impression changed. In the picture, her hair was a dark brown but standing outside in the sun, she lit up, the auburn of her hair turning to flame. How she'd managed to be invisible for so long, he didn't know. That hair was sure to attract attention and her eyes...those big, almond-shaped eyes. So distinctive. More green than anything had a right to be. And the intelligence. She had noticed him almost immediately and he could practically see her mind turning, processing the scene. Wondering why a thirty-something year old man was messing around with a bunch of undergrads.

Survival was her top priority and he was afraid, in that split second, he'd pushed too hard. Afraid she'd disappear. He'd worked hard to get this close to her and he didn't intend to lose her now. He hadn't been entirely convinced the smile he'd given her would be enough to throw her off but he poured every ounce of charm he had into it.

And now here they were. The shower shut off, jarring him out of his stupor, and Quincy stepped out, wrapped in one of the soft, oversized robes provided for their suite. At least something in this *luxury* compartment fit the bill.

"I didn't realize how long I was in there," she said after a quick glance out the window. "Sorry."

"No worries," Logan replied. "You needed it."

Quincy cocked an eyebrow and Logan felt his face heat up. "I didn't mean it like that. I just...you've been...it's not..."

Quincy finally raised a hand, mercifully ending the torture. "It's fine. I really did need it. I had been in the same clothes

345

for almost 24 hours." She sank down onto the bed and leaned against the window, cupping her head against her arm as she looked out. "Dr. Garrison thinks I have some sort of head injury?" she asked.

It was a blunt observation, with no lead in or preamble. Logan absorbed it and considered the sudden subject change, not quite sure what to say.

"I take it the Colonel had some things to say?"

She nodded her head, still looking out the window.

Logan sighed. "You know, I'm really not good at this part. Dr. Garrison is the one who understands the science."

Quincy shifted around so she was facing him, sitting cross-legged on the bed. "But you're the one who's here."

Logan hesitated, but only briefly. She was right. She deserved to hear the truth. Or as much of the truth as he knew how to give her.

"Dr. Garrison knows all the technical stuff. I'm just the muscle." He thought for a second. "Like the Colonel, I'm guessing. But I can tell you what he told me when he was working with Jones. And what he told me after."

Logan leaned forward, resting his elbows on his knees and looking at the ground, trying to think. This was difficult enough when the patient knew about the head injury. But how do you convince someone with no memory of it? He needed to get his head on straight, frame it right. But he shouldn't have worried. Quincy jumped right in.

"I have amnesia. But you know that already, right?"

Logan shook his head slowly. "I didn't know. Not for sure. But I suspected." He sat back up, propping his feet up on the bed next to her. "It was the little things. The lack of even the smallest of details. Usually when someone is spinning an alias, there's something. Mundane details that make it seem more realistic. But you had nothing. Nothing on your family, where you were raised, anything from your past."

"I told you my birthday," she protested.

"No, you lied about your birthday". He smiled. "You won't tell me your mom's first name but you'll tell me your birthday? I don't think so." She looked like someone who wanted to protest but knew she didn't have a leg to stand on. "And you really seemed to have no idea."

"No idea about what?" she interrupted. "What don't I know? Why don't I know it?"

He could see the frustration bubbling up, seething right below the surface. "Why can't I remember anything past a couple of years?"

"Listen," Logan broke in. "I know you're frustrated, and I'm going to tell you everything I know. You just have to hang with me." She blew out a big breath, fluffing her hair away from her face, which was drying and getting alarmingly large as it did so. "And maybe brush your hair or something," he suggested.

She grinned. "Who am I trying to impress? My fake husband? He's seen worse."

He rolled his eyes but had to laugh. "One fake marriage doesn't mean you should just give up."

"Anyway...," she prodded.

"Right. Back on track." Logan leaned his head back against the wall, trying to get more comfortable. "This is what I know - eight years ago, a Jane Doe was found on the side of the road, a victim of a hit-and-run. She had no identification on her and spent over a month in a coma. She was never identified."

He glanced at Quincy, trying to gauge how she was taking

the news but she wasn't giving him much to go on. "A month after she woke up, she walked out of the hospital. Four years later, Dr. Garrison published his first paper on what he called Reflexive Neurological Bias. And four years after that, we believed we'd finally tracked Jane Doe to a college campus in Sheraton, Arkansas, living under the name Quincy O'Connell."

"That's basically the same story the Colonel gave me," she said. "But why were you trying to track this Jane Doe down? What brought her to your attention?" Quincy asked. *Her*. Not *me* or *I*. She was distancing herself, not quite ready to buy in.

"In his research, Dr. Garrison collected medical records from around the country, attempting to identify patients he believed might be suffering from RNB. If I hadn't read one of his papers on traumatic neurological pathology and contacted him first, he would have found Jones eventually on his own."

"If he was looking for patients with RNB while he was still working for the company that sent the Colonel, that would explain how my name made their list. If Dr. Garrison believed I was one of these patients, he would have given my name, or at least my information, to this company."

"No," Logan disagreed. "Dr. Garrison wouldn't do that. He was compiling data for his research but he would never have violated patient privacy by disclosing personal medical information. He was trying to help people, not make a buck. When he ran, he eliminated as much identifying information from the files as he could. And besides, you were just 'Jane Doe'. It took us... and the company, apparently... four years to find you."

"That's not completely true," she admitted. "I've seen the Colonel twice before. I recognized him from when I was Kara

Scott and Grace Elliott. He found me both times. I was just lucky enough to see him before he saw me."

"This has happened before?" Logan asked, incredulous. She had managed to go up against this guy three times now and escape? She really was special.

"That's why I panicked that day at the cafe. I thought he had sent someone else this time." She grinned wryly. "Turns out I was right after all, just not about you."

Logan found the fact that she had considered him suspicious and dangerous, but not Brandon, slightly offensive but he decided to let it go for now.

She ran her hands through her hair and tugged on the ends absently. "I'd known for awhile that I'd stayed too long. I have a rule - nowhere longer than a couple of months. But I really liked Sheraton," she said wistfully. "I like Mr. and Mrs. Boatright. I like Sit-A-Spell. I love the parks and the squares and the feeling that I almost fit in." She was quiet for a minute. "Do you think they even notice that I'm gone?"

Logan could sympathize. "I could tell you that, yes, of course they notice. That they liked you as much as you liked them. But that's not really going to make you feel any better, is it?"

Quincy looked away.

"It's hard, being somewhere, making friends and living a life one minute, and then having to burn it, abruptly and with no notice, the next. Believe me, I know." He ran a hand through his own hair, brushing out his tangle of curls. "And it never really gets any easier."

Logan leaned forward and gripped Quincy's knee, squeezing until she looked at him. "But you did what you had to do to survive. Mr. and Mrs. Boatright wouldn't have wanted you to do any different." He held her eyes until she nodded, resigned to what was, and then leaned back. "Besides, who knows? Once this is all cleared up, maybe we'll go back to Sheraton. Let everyone know you're okay."

She looked at him, mildly amused. "We?"

He grinned. "You're stuck with me now kid. Like it or not."

They sat like that for a moment, grinning at each other and comfortable in the silence. Until Quincy broke it. "So, what superpowers does Dr. G think I have?"

58

Chapter 58

"Tired, tired with nothing, tired with everything, tired with the world's weight he had never chose to bear." F. Scott Fitzgerald

The burden is heavy. It weighs more with every revelation. Every discovery. How long can she stand to bear it? How long can she fight?

How long until she chooses?

* * *

Quincy

"So, what superpowers does Dr. G think I have?" Quincy laughed at the look on Logan's face. She had clearly caught him off-guard with her spur-of-the-moment backhand.

"Why," he finally asked, "do you think you have superpowers?"

"Because the Colonel said so."

He seemed taken aback. "The Colonel said you have superpowers?"

"Well, he said something along those lines. I believe the term he used was *weaponizable talent.*"

Logan shook his head. "That's a little different than superpowers."

"Tomato, tomatoe," Quincy said. "I want to know what they are."

"Other than your super powered ability to annoy and frustrate?" He shrugged. "Who knows?"

"Seriously?" Now Quincy was annoyed. "You search high and low for years, trying to find me because I have some condition Dr. Garrison wants to study or document or whatever, but you don't even know why?"

Logan rolled his eyes again. That seemed to be his preset response lately. She wondered if he did it to everyone or if she was just special. "Let's dial your *drama queen* phasers down from kill to stun, shall we?" he said dryly.

Quincy pushed herself up from where she sat cross-legged on the bed and bounced herself over towards Logan, grabbing his feet and making him look, really look, at her. When he did, when she was sure she finally had his full attention, she asked what she really wanted to know. "Can he fix me?"

Logan cocked his head to the side, studying her suddenly serious eyes and tone. When he didn't answer, she inched her way up his legs where they were sprawled across the bed until she was sitting on his lap, as close as she could possibly get, and gripped his shoulders. She needed him to get how important this was.

"Logan. Can Dr. Garrison fix me?"

Something in Logan's eyes softened, saddening ever so slightly, and she had her answer.

"Quincy," he said, reaching up to hold her face between his hands as she tried to pull away. "There's nothing to fix."

At that, Quincy tore away from him like she'd been slapped. "What do you mean, there's nothing to fix?" she cried as she pushed away from him, retreating to the farthest corner of the bed.

"How can you say that? It never stops! I don't sleep. I know how to perform field surgery but I don't know my own birthday. The pain." She paused for breath. Logan looked like he wanted to reach back out to her but was stopping himself through brute force.

"I just want to sleep," she finally said quietly. Her voice sounded broken to her own ears. "I just want it to be quiet. I need it to be quiet. Is that so hard to understand?"

"No," he said quietly. "It's not hard to understand at all. And I don't know. Maybe Dr. Garrison can figure out some way to help you cope. But you have to know that the condition is permanent. You were dying. Your brain couldn't heal the trauma so it found a new way to function. This is your normal and there's nothing anyone can do to change that."

He looked so earnest. So raw.

"Jones didn't want to accept it either. It hurts. I know it hurts. But it saved your life. The noise, the pain, the exhaustion? They may just be the price you have to pay to live."

"Yeah, well, Jones didn't exactly buy your party line either, did he?" she spit out.

Now it was Logan who looked like he'd been slapped. She hadn't realized it until she'd said it, but it made perfect sense. Jones hadn't died from complications of his injury. He'd died because he couldn't live with the results. How many times had she had those same thoughts? Those same doubts? Thoughts about just ending everything and hoping there was something better in death. Something quieter. Something...else. If she and Jones were the same, and she could see now that they were, then she could understand why he'd decided to end it himself.

Logan had gone pale. She watched as he opened his mouth, hesitated, and then closed it again. He shut his eyes, clearly trying to find words. Quincy wanted to feel sorry. That was a low blow and she knew it. But she just couldn't. Not yet. She hadn't realized she'd been slowly building up hope until it was yanked away.

Finding out there really was something wrong with her, that there was a reason she was suffering, made her wonder if a future might exist where she didn't have to live with the fear, anxiety, and pain anymore. Losing it, losing that small bit of hope she didn't even know she had, broke down every wall she'd built up and in that moment, she understood Jones and the choice he had made perfectly. Because honestly, how could she keep living like this? How could anyone live like this?

"You're right," Logan finally said, voice raw with grief. "Jones didn't buy it. Or wasn't willing to. And so he didn't. And I didn't know how to help him. But I do now."

Logan seemed to hear his own words and draw strength from them. "I didn't know what to do before but I do now. And between me and Dr. Garrison, you don't just have to learn to live with this, you can help others learn to live with it too."

That caught Quincy's attention.

"What do you mean?" she asked skeptically.

Logan pounced, looking like a dog who'd finally found someone to throw him a ball.

"There are others out there and we're going to find them. We're going to help them hide before the agency can get to them and then we're going to help them understand and deal with whatever symptoms of RNB they have."

"So no one else has to become a Jones," Quincy said quietly.

"So no one else has to become a Jones," Logan echoed.

Chapter 59

Logan

Had she bought it? Logan wasn't sure. Quincy had left the compartment hurriedly after stepping back into the small bathroom to toss her clothes on, saying she needed some fresh air. He hadn't offered to go with her. He couldn't. He'd been too stunned. She'd made that comment about Jones, and it had been mean and low and meant to hurt him, which it did.

But it also told him, in not so many words, that at some point over the last eight years, she had considered that option, too. After they'd met, he'd never even considered it. But he should have. One of the statistics Dr. Garrison had cobbled together from his hodgepodge of notes and deceased patient files was the probability of a high suicide rate for patients with RNB.

But Quincy had seemed so solid. So confident. Sure, she usually had circles under her eyes but so did he. He guessed the difference was that he didn't sleep because he was usually on the move. She didn't sleep because she honestly couldn't. She'd never let on before. She'd mentioned the noise in her head, and he'd seen first-hand the headaches and their aftermath, but she hid her feelings so completely. Jones wore his despair and self-loathing like a banner, announcing to all who would hear the misery he felt.

But Quincy wasn't like Jones, not completely at least. She had survived for eight years, battling the condition and its painful side effects on her own, all the while dodging the company's lead hunting dog and learning to disappear. She was stronger than Jones had ever been, which was difficult for Logan to concede. Jones had been his friend, his partner. They had fought together and laughed together and saved each other's lives more times than he could count. He had thought the man was made of steel.

"Well?" Jones demanded angrily. "What did he have to say?"

Logan hadn't felt this optimistic in a long time. "It's good news. Dr. Garrison says you fit his theory. He thinks you have this Reflexive Neurological Bias he's been studying." Logan stumbled, the medical jargon twisting his tongue on the way out. No wonder Dr. Garrison had taken to saying 'RNB'. The whole name was too big of a mouthful.

"What's that supposed to mean, exactly?" Jones demanded. "Can he fix me?"

Logan paused, not sure how to answer. He had been thrilled that they finally had a workable diagnosis, even if modern medicine wasn't entirely on-board. Logan didn't much care what modern medicine thought anyhow, considering they had come up empty and then quit trying altogether.

He finally settled on, "He thinks he can help you."

"Help me what?" Jones retorted. "Help me clean the blood out of my ears after an eardrum explodes? Help me walk without tipping over? Help me sleep? Help me over the side of a bridge? Tell me, Davies, what exactly is he going to help me with?"

Jones had bounced from confused to determined to depressed after his hearing had failed to go back to normal before finally settling on angry. And he had parked himself quite firmly in that position and determined not to move. Logan had made excuses at first. After all, whatever this was wasn't just affecting Jones's ears. His balance was off. His other senses were going haywire in response to too much sound. He struggled to eat, to follow a conversation.

And all of these things made it impossible for Jones to resume full or even partial active duty. Logan considered how he would respond if he was told he was going to be discharged from service, whether he wanted to be or not. It felt a little premature to Logan, giving up on a man whose injury had happened in service to the very country who was dismissing him. But that wasn't something they could change. Dr. Garrison thought there was a chance they could give Jones his life back, though, and he intended to throw his full weight behind the man.

Looking back, Logan knew there were plenty of signs he should have picked up on. He just never thought he'd actually... no. Logan cut that train of thought off. Jones was gone. Whatever he could or should have done, it was too late now to change anything.

But Quincy was still here. She was still within his reach. And he'd rather die himself than let someone else he cared about go down that rabbit hole. He pushed himself up from the chair and rubbed his hands hard over his face in an effort to erase the emotion stamped all over it. Then he turned and headed out to find Quincy. He wasn't willing to let that be the end of the conversation.

60

Chapter 60

Quincy

The air was cold as it whipped past Quincy but she didn't mind. In fact, she leaned into it, letting the wind catch and throw her hair around her face. She had gotten out of the room as quickly as she could, honestly surprised when Logan didn't even attempt to stop her. She had needed air, and she had needed it fast. She had wandered aimlessly through the different compartments, finding her way to the dining car and some kind of social club car, definitely not for her, before she'd come across the balcony car.

She had been curious so she'd pushed open the door and found exactly what the name described – a car with a balcony wrapping around it. A part of her wondered if that was even legal and whether the railway company suffered through many lawsuits on its behalf, but then she decided she didn't care. She didn't even care that her hair was going to be a tangled mess when she went back inside. If she ever went back inside.

Honestly, she wasn't entirely sure there was much point anymore in soldiering on. Had there ever really been? All she had had in her life that she could remember was long, miserable nights and lonely, paranoid days, pain and exhaustion her only close companions.

Of course ending it had occurred to her before, mostly during severe migraines and those days when no amount of running could give her relief from the noise. That constant, relentless noise. A symptom, or so Logan and the Colonel seemed to think. Calling it a symptom made it seem so ambivalent, didn't it? Like it wasn't this living, breathing thing that crept through her mind, bedding down and waiting to attack when she was at her most vulnerable, keeping her from ever being fully at peace.

She sighed, tipping her face up and letting the air rush across it. And now it was worse than she'd thought. It was one thing to spend your life on the run, trying to stay one step ahead of danger. It was another to realize the danger revolves around the fact you don't know who you are.

How on earth could she not know? Or not know that she didn't know? How had she gone eight years, if not longer, without realizing she didn't have any memories of her past? Was she moving around, creating aliases, not to keep herself safe and hidden, but because she didn't know who she was in the first place? How messed up was that?

Logan would have her believe that Dr. Garrison could help. Not heal her, of course. No, no. There was nothing to fix, after all. Quincy squeezed her eyes shut, seeing Logan look at her, hearing him tell her she wasn't broken. Pretending that she was stronger than she really was.

What was it he'd said? *You don't just have to learn to live with this, you can help others learn to live with it too.* She supposed he had to believe that, knowing what she did about his partner. He was only here to finish a mission that had started with Jones and he would see her failure as his own.

What would it be like, she wondered, to die? She had almost died eight years ago, or so Logan believed. She didn't remember anything from that time, but maybe there was nothing there to remember. Maybe sliding into death would be like sliding into a deep sleep. It sounded peaceful. It sounded quiet. It sounded like giving up. She didn't like to think she was a quitter but sometimes she wondered if that would be such a bad thing.

The door slid open and shut quietly behind her and she felt someone lean heavily against the rail beside her. She didn't say anything, keeping her eyes closed and her face tipped up to the sky, needing him to go away but also needing him to stay. Such a funny thing, she thought, to need so many things from one person and expect he could give them to her. But at this point, Quincy knew Logan well enough to know he wasn't going to let the conversation drop. Not like that. And she needed to apologize. She might have been devastated but that didn't give her the right to lash out at him.

She dropped her head onto her arms where they were crossed over the railing. Without looking at him, she said, "I'm sorry."

"I know," he replied, forgiveness lacing easily through his voice.

"How do you do that?" she asked, finally turning her head to look over at him. He was standing in the same position she was, arms crossed over a coat he had draped over the railing, body braced over them, but his head was up, looking out at the landscape as it sped past them. He always seemed to be looking.

"Do what?"

"Let things go so easily," she said, amazed and frustrated all at once. "What I said about Jones – that was wrong. And mean."

"Well," he glanced over at her. "Are you sorry?"

"Yeah, but..."

"Then no 'buts'. It's done." And he turned back out to the landscape again, not seeming bothered in the least.

"Okay," she said, raising up and turning to prop her back against the rail. "But you still followed me out here and I know you have something to say. So just go ahead and say it."

He sighed. "I don't want to upset you. Or make it worse than it already is."

"But?" she said, knowing that wasn't going to stop him.

"But," he agreed. He seemed to gather his thoughts, rolling them around in his head a little to see if they were right. "You and Jones might have the same condition but you're not the same, not really. I need you to know that. I need you to know that you're so much stronger than he ever was." Logan said.

"That's just not true," Quincy replied softly. "Jones was your partner. Your best friend. He was a soldier who saw and did terrible things. You both did. Of course he was strong."

She could tell it had been hard for him to say, but he pressed on. "He was strong when he was strong, if that makes any sense."

Logan looked down and smiled. "I remember this one time, we were in Kuwait, maybe? We had this car we had cleared of mines and explosives and brought into camp where it promptly died. Nothing the mechanics did made a difference. A bunch of the guys were messing around off-duty and joking that maybe we could just pick it up and carry it out of the way."

Now he laughed. "It was this big, rusted bucket of bolts and metal, ugly as sin and just as heavy. No one could pick that thing up. But Jones? He decided he could do it. The guys gave him a hard time, said if he could pick it up, they'd take his mess duty for a month. And that was that." Logan looked over at her. "Jones was competitive that way."

"And did he do it?" Quincy asked. "Did he manage to pick it up?"

"He did," Logan said. "He got the front end up about three inches." He was silent for a minute, lost in the memory.

"Physically, Jones was maybe the strongest man I knew. He could tackle any challenge. But the injury, the way it impaired him? Mentally he just couldn't take it. He couldn't stand how his hearing had changed, how it affected everything else in his life. He didn't want to work on it, he didn't want to learn to use it. His purpose was to be a soldier and without that, he wasn't interested in going on.

"That's not strength," Logan said fiercely. "That's stubbornness and selfishness. He was too stubborn to even try to adapt and selfish enough to not care about how his death would affect me. And I don't think you are either of those things."

Quincy looked away. "You don't think I can be stubborn and selfish?" she asked, unable to meet Logan's eyes.

"Oh, I know you can be both. Just look at what brought us here." Quincy flinched, knowing he was right.

"But you care about things. You see people and you get to

know them, even when you don't let them get to know you. Just look at the friendships you made in Sheraton. And the girl you saved at the bus depot? You could have walked away but you didn't. If there's even the slightest chance you can use your own pain to help save someone else from a terrible fate, you will."

Well, he had her there. She wouldn't wish the Colonel or his company on anyone else.

"And you care that you hurt my feelings with your comment about Jones. If you care that much about causing me a little pain, you care too much to kill yourself and put me through that kind of hell all over again."

He let his words drop like stones and Quincy absorbed the impact like ripples through water. He handed her the coat he'd brought with him and when she took it, he put his hand on her shoulder and squeezed gently before turning and going back inside. She hadn't even noticed she was cold until then. She pushed her arms into the sleeves of the coat, zipping it up and letting it swallow her before turning back to the railing, closing her eyes again.

He was right, of course. He always seemed to be, though. They hadn't known each other long but she did know he shared himself freely with others. Her exact opposite. By spending time with her, saving her life over and over, he had given her a piece of himself, just like he had with Jones. And Jones had taken that piece of Logan with him when he died.

No. When he killed himself. Dying in the war or in some kind of accident, or even cancer, would have been different. Logan could have grieved and moved on, knowing there was nothing he could have done for his friend. Choosing to end his own life was much worse for Logan because he would never know if there was something he could have done differently and, without knowing that, he would never be able to move on.

And she would never be able to force that pain on Logan again. She took a deep breath, letting it out slowly. Which meant she would need to resign herself to a life, however much she had left, of dealing with her issues, no matter how painful and or exhausting they might be. But she wasn't convinced she would be able to do that either.

The door behind her slid open and closed again. "What does a girl have to do to get some space, huh?"

When he didn't answer, she rolled her eyes. "I don't really feel like talking about this anymore."

"That's alright," the Colonel answered. "There's nothing left to say anyway."

Chapter 61

The Colonel

Finally this would be finished. He should have finished it last night when he'd found her jogging. She had been alone and vulnerable, with no avenue of escape. He realized now that it had been a mistake to try to take her alive. She had been slippery from the first and his pride had been wounded, causing him to make choices he wouldn't have normally made.

But no matter. He would rectify the situation now. He had waited for hours, watching as they had their drinks, and then waiting as they went into their room and stayed for hours.

He didn't bother considering what they might be doing. It didn't matter. All that mattered was that they come out. His plan was to wait until they left the train when it made a stop. Once they were off, he could follow them to whatever escape route they had planned next.

There were always ways of drawing someone off the well-beaten path. The girl had proven she was empathetic. He could easily use that against her. Empathy was weakness and innocent bystanders were sharp weapons that could be wielded with ease. The soldier would be more of a problem, the Colonel knew. He would need to be dealt with first but he wasn't concerned. He would adapt and fit his plan to the circumstances, just like always.

He had taken it as providence when the door of their compartment had opened and the girl had rushed out alone. Where was she heading? The Colonel made his way after her, making sure to stay well out of her line of sight.

He ducked into a side bathroom when she stopped and he watched as she slid through a door and stepped out onto what looked like an outdoor platform. Who knew this train had a balcony car? He wondered idly if they experienced many lawsuits because of it.

Regardless, it was an unexpected opportunity, one which he didn't plan to miss. He watched as the girl leaned over the railing, head tipping up and eyes closing. She was perfectly, completely unaware of her surroundings.

The Colonel slid his own door open, preparing to step out, when the soldier came striding down the hallway. Of course. Could the man not leave her alone for five minutes? The Colonel watched impatiently as the soldier went out onto the deck, noting the almost silent slide of the door. Helpful.

The soldier's body language gave so much of what he was thinking and feeling away, the Colonel noted clinically. Inefficient for undercover ops or wet work. He must have been a grunt. Or one of the brute ground forces that operated as battering rams wherever they were sent. The Colonel had uses for those men, of course. But all the better when they came to him with both skill sets. The soldier straightened and handed the girl a coat and then...he walked away.

The Colonel could barely believe his luck. The man was actually leaving her alone. Outside, where no one else could see her. He waited until the soldier disappeared down the hallway before slipping out of the bathroom. He stopped long enough to slide out his knife and cut the long silk cord holding the curtains, winding a length of it around his hand and letting the curtains cover the doors before stepping out onto the balcony. It was just one more stroke of luck, he thought, that no one else was utilizing this car. The chill of the day helped, he supposed. The girl heard him but didn't turn. She seemed affectionately annoyed though, when she spoke.

"What does a girl have to do to get some space, huh?"

He didn't answer, using these last few seconds before he was exposed to move closer. His silence seemed to spark something in her.

"I don't really feel like talking about this anymore," she said and he took the opening.

"That's alright," he replied smoothly. "There's nothing left to say anyway."

The girl spun around, instinctively trying to put some distance between her and the closeness of his voice, but it was in vain. He was only feet away and she had nothing but railing and open air at her back. His priority was speed and silence and he stepped the rest of the way up against her, wrapping the cord smoothly around her neck, instantly cutting off her oxygen supply.

The girl made a gasping sound, hands reaching up to claw at the cord. Strangulation could be quick, when done correctly. Using his knife would have been even faster but the evidence trail would be difficult to cover and he'd rather not give cause for alarm. He was trapped on this train until it stopped, after all.

So he watched as the girl struggled, hands leaving the cord and reaching out for him, searching for some kind of purchase, some weakness to exploit. Tears rolled from her eyes, soaking into the cord and leaving a trail of wetness down her face, which was turning a very unnatural shade of red. It would be over soon, he knew. It was a difficult thing to watch the life bleed slowly out of someone under your own hand but he had shed that weakness long ago. To him, it was nothing more than the passage of time.

"You know," he said, "you should take pride in the fact that you have been the only one to ever elude me. And I should thank you. You revealed a weakness in my organization that I have since eradicated."

She made a noise, the sound gurgling around the cord at her throat, barely audible over the rush of the wind and the noise of the tracks.

"Mr. Auberdeen was never a good fit anyway. I suppose I allowed sentimentality to rule when I hired him. But he won't be a problem anymore."

The girl's hands slapped weakly at his wrists, begging for air.

"You should know it took him much less time to die than you. Again, you should be proud."

He stepped forward, pressing the girl's body against the rail. Once she was dead, her body would topple over the balcony and disappear. The soldier would likely realize what had happened but the Colonel planned to be long gone by then.

"It was a good game," he said, watching as her eyes slowly

closed.

62

Chapter 62

The Colonel

When the pain came, it was unexpected. The Colonel was watching the life drain slowly from the girl's eyes, planning his next steps, when something hard and heavy slammed against his head. He staggered but managed to maintain a one-handed hold on the cord. At least until he felt the second blow, this one shattering the crystal decanter across his head.

It was a testament to the strength of the swing and not the hardness of his own head, he thought, that caused it to break. He had made note of those as possible weapons himself, thanks to their sturdy, expensive design. He rolled fluidly to his feet, sweeping up a large shard of the decanter in his left hand. It cut into his palm but he ignored it. The girl was on the ground, silent and still, and the soldier stood between them, bracing for a fight.

"Colonel," the soldier said, more a statement of fact than a question.

The Colonel sighed. "You just can't leave her alone, can you?" he remarked dryly.

"I keep trying," the soldier answered, adjusting his position as the Colonel stepped to the side, looking for an opening. "But she just seems to keep finding trouble without me."

"Hmm." The Colonel slid his free hand into his pants pocket, coming up with his knife. "No, I don't think that's it." The soldier didn't respond, just watched as the Colonel shifted the opposite direction.

"I don't think you *can* leave her be. I think you just can't let go of the past."

"What do you know about my past?" the soldier asked curiously.

"I can make some educated guesses. You were a soldier, served several tours overseas. You've seen combat," he said. "Some things are obvious when you know what to look for."

"I've never tried to hide my service." The soldier shifted back slightly, enough to nudge the girl with his boot. "Quincy?"

"She's still breathing, if that helps. For now."

The soldier looked back at him. "I plan to make sure it stays that way."

"No," the Colonel said, shaking his head slowly. "I'm afraid not. She's unfortunately outlived her usefulness. My agency will have to move on without her. It is a pity, though. She did make things interesting."

The girl made a noise, a small, soft cough followed by a wheeze, the soldier relaxed infinitesimally, and the Colonel narrowed his eyes. He needed to finish this. Now.

"I did some research on you Lt. Davies." He tilted his head to the side. "Your Lt. Jones would have been on my list, too, if he hadn't taken the coward's way out."

The soldier narrowed his eyes but didn't respond. Inter-esting. And unfortunate. This one wouldn't be goaded into a confrontation. Instead, he lowered himself down next to the girl, making sure to keep his eyes on the Colonel at all times, and reached for her shoulder. She was still wheezing, but her hands were fumbling weakly at the cord still wrapped around her neck. The Colonel waited until Lt. Davies had his hand on the girl, his attention divided, and then he surged forward.

63

Chapter 63

Logan

The Colonel surged forward, aiming a steel-toed boot at his face. Logan was out of position to avoid the attack and he refused to allow the Colonel to maneuver into Quincy's space. He managed to block the kick with his body, taking the brunt of it on his shoulder. It set him back on his heels but he managed to stay upright. The Colonel used his off-balance position to swing his knife around, burying it in the same shoulder Logan had taken the kick in.

Suddenly, the old guy didn't look so old to Logan. He swept out a leg, missing the Colonel's ankles but managing to force enough of a retreat to give him some breathing room.

Logan jerked the cord away from Quincy's neck, relieved to see she was starting to come around, and turned his full attention to the Colonel, who had backed off and was sizing up the situation. Logan was doing that himself. He had his own knife, of course, but he didn't know if it was smart to bring it into play. There were already two sharp objects in the room, although it would be nice to have one of his own.

But if he used the knife, he would leave a blood trail. His own blood was already soaking into the wood of the balcony of course, but it could be cleaned up easily enough. If either of them struck a killing blow with the knife, there would be no way to hide it. Not that the Colonel seemed to care much about that. He looked like he was okay with any option.

"You know," the Colonel said blandly, "you're wasting your talents with the doctor."

The Colonel shifted and Logan mirrored the movement, not bothering to respond. "You have exceptional training, I can see that. The agency I work for pays well for your brand of talent and skill set."

He tried one more time. "Is the good doctor even paying you for your services? I would doubt it very much. He's on his own, with no resources. You're still young. You could do very well on my team."

The Colonel's eyes dropped to Logan's knee, assessing for weakness there. Evaluating whether it was a good point of attack.

"I don't need to do 'very well' on a team of assassins."

The Colonel's eyes wandered back up. If he was surprised by Logan's decision to participate in the conversation, he didn't show it.

"The army can't pay you much in the way of a pension. You're too young to have put in your twenty. Or was it the Marines?"

"Army," Logan clipped out. "And we don't work for money."

"Ah. I see," the Colonel murmured. "An idealist. Was your partner an idealist too? I wouldn't think so, considering his actions at the end. I wonder," the Colonel said, head tipped slightly to the left, "what he would have done if the situation were reversed.

"If you'd been the one injured and left in agony, unable to go back to the country who abandoned you. Would he have searched tirelessly for an answer? Would he have doggedly pursued a solution? Been a stable source of support and encouragement? Or would he have gone back to his unit, wishing you well and promising to check in when he could? Considering the fact you didn't make much of a difference in his choice to die, I would assume the latter."

Logan shifted again, continuing to mirror the man's movements. The Colonel wasn't just assessing Logan's physical strengths and weaknesses. He was assessing his mental stability. Poking, prodding, seeing if he could use Jones to push him off-balance.

But this wasn't about Jones. It couldn't be. It wasn't even about Quincy. This was about Logan, about his ability to put his feelings aside and be nothing more than a soldier. It had been awhile, but it wasn't something you easily forgot and he felt himself slide seamlessly back into the habit. The Colonel must have come to the same conclusion because he sighed.

"What a waste," he said, almost sadly. "What a bloody waste." And then he attacked.

64

Chapter 64

Logan

Logan didn't have time for thought or planning. He simply reacted. His instincts, honed by three combat tours, took over. The piece of glass the Colonel was clutching in his left hand glinted as it swung, carving a path down Logan's left cheek, before Logan ducked and flung himself forward, colliding with the Colonel's midsection and taking him down in a classic football tackle.

He had just enough time to think about how proud Jones would be of that one before the Colonel was using his momentum to roll them, pinning Logan to the floor and wrapping his hands around Logan's neck. This guy clearly had his own special forces training and if he let him get a good grip, it would be over.

Logan threw out his elbows, creating too much space for the Colonel to close around, and then bucked his legs, tossing the other man forward and allowing Logan to land a solid palm thrust to his nose. The satisfying crunch let Logan know he'd found his mark and the Colonel jerked back, blood spraying across Logan's shirt and face.

"Very good Lieutenant," the Colonel said, using his sleeve to wipe some of the blood from his face. "It's been too long since someone gave me a decent fight. Shall we end this?" he said, glancing meaningfully over Logan's shoulder towards the door. "I've a feeling we're on borrowed time."

"No need to finish something that never should have started," Logan replied mildly. The Colonel would never take the out. Logan knew that. Knew the type of man he was dealing with.

But he couldn't not make the offer. Couldn't not try to avoid the inevitable. Because the Colonel was throwing down an ultimatum. It was going to be them or him. And despite the amount of death Logan had seen, had even been responsible for in his time in the service, he never enjoyed it. Killing was always a choice. It might also be a necessity, but it was still a choice.

Logan just never wanted it to be his first choice.

The Colonel almost smiled. "Now Lieutenant," he said in amusement, "you know that's not possible."

"Why?" Logan asked. "Because of the money? I know the agency must pay you pretty well to be their hunting dog."

"It has nothing to do with the money," the Colonel answered. He seemed almost surprised by the question. "Yes, the agency pays me very well. But I live by a code. I accept a job. I finish a job. It's as simple as that."

"And it doesn't matter what that job is, so long as you complete your mission?" Logan asked. "I'm not sure that moral compass is worth bragging about."

"A moral compass has nothing to do with it," the Colonel

replied calmly. The older man casually began to circle the balcony, running his hand along the railing as he did. Logan tugged Quincy back a little further, trying to make sure she would be out of the way when the fight started again.

"A job is a job," he said. "I don't allow emotion to drive my actions. Something you might want to look into." He reversed direction, wandering back the opposite way. He was looking for an opening, studying Logan for weak points. But Logan was doing the same.

"No," Logan shot back. "I'm good. I think I'll stick with the caring and sharing. Might make things harder sometimes," he admitted, "but it also keeps me on the right side."

"The right side of what, I wonder?" the Colonel mused. "From what I can see, all it's done is caused your death." And he surged forward.

Chapter 65

The Colonel

The Lieutenant was good, the Colonel would give him that. It had taken longer than he'd like to admit to catch his breath after Davies had caught him with a palm strike to the face. Five years ago, something like that wouldn't have phased him. Now, he admitted wryly, if only to himself, the pain and blurred vision was harder to ignore.

So he'd engaged the man verbally. He'd used it as a distraction to move and watch as the Lieutenant countered. The shoulder injury would certainly come in handy. And unless he was mistaken, the left knee was a considerable weak point as well. But Davies's physical weaknesses weren't his biggest problem. He tuned back into the conversation.

"A job is a job," he said. "I don't allow emotion to drive my actions. Something you might want to look into." He reversed direction and watched as Davies mirrored his movement. For a soldier, Davies was remarkably involved with the girl's welfare. She was his mission. She shouldn't have become more than that. Not if he wanted to successfully protect her. Feelings clouded the mission.

"No," Logan shot back. "I'm good. I think I'll stick with the caring and sharing. Might make things harder sometimes." Well, at least the man knew it wasn't the optimal way to run a mission. "But it also keeps me on the right side."

"The right side of what, I wonder?" the Colonel mused, finished with the dialogue portion of the fight. He'd gotten the intel he needed about his opponent. Now he was prepared to finish it. "From what I can see, all it's done is caused your death."

He surged forward.

Chapter 66

Logan

The Colonel came at him and Logan stopped thinking.

He had done what he could to spare a life. But this man was determined to kill Quincy and Logan wouldn't allow that. It was how he had survived on the ground in so many war zones.

He simply eliminated failure as an option. Once that was off the table, the fear always vanished and his instincts took over. It was the same now.

The Colonel came at him from the left and shot an arm towards Logan's face but it was a feint. Logan had seen him zero in on the knee he'd injured a few years ago after a jump gone bad. So Logan turned into the punch, allowing his momentum to carry him away from the Colonel's leg sweep and pulling the man up and over. As the Colonel landed on his back, Logan rolled with him, pinning him in place and aiming another palm thrust towards his nose. He might have shaken off the first strike but landing a second hit to an already broken nose would be harder to ignore.

But the man caught his arm, using Logan's own momentum against him to tug him closer. The Colonel's hand wrapped around the cut in Logan's shoulder and squeezed, causing Logan to flinch and clamp his teeth together to keep from howling while the Colonel delivered his own palm thrust to Logan's face. He missed his nose but it was still enough to shake Logan's grip and the Colonel to roll free.

The Colonel was on his feet again in an instant, the knife back in his left hand. He came at Logan without hesitation, not giving him a chance to regain his own feet. The knife came down swiftly but Logan managed to catch the Colonel's arm with his own. He struggled to his feet under the weight of the other man's force.

He needed to end this. Now. The Colonel was a skilled fighter and, if failure had been an option, Logan might have been worried. But as it was, his main concern was how long it would be before someone else on the train, another passenger or even one of the dozen staff serving aboard, found their way to their car. He might not be worried about failing but he was concerned about the fallout from being caught in a deadly fight.

The Colonel shifted suddenly, pulling the glass shard he'd used previously out of thin air and bringing it towards Logan's unprotected left side. Logan dropped like a rock, the movement sudden enough that the Colonel was caught off guard. He stumbled forward and Logan took advantage of the momentary lapse, pulling both legs in tight and launching them up, catching the Colonel high in the chest.

The Colonel flew back, slamming into the railing and clutching at it to stay on his feet. Logan was on him in an instant, not as steady as he preferred, maybe, but steady enough. The uppercut he threw connected with the Colonel's jaw at the same moment the man pitched forward, the force strong enough to carry the Colonel up and back.

He caught the railing on his lower back and toppled backwards, disappearing from view.

67

Chapter 67

Logan

Logan doubled over, out of breath and hurting, and stared at the place the Colonel had disappeared from. Was he...did he really... Logan stood and shuffled over to the rail, peering over. There was a service platform about five feet wide running the length of the car but it was empty, save a small smear of red along the outside edge of the back corner. Below the platform was nothing but air.

They were going over a bridge, hundreds of feet in the air, and Logan shoved back quickly, breathless from the height and from the beating he had just taken. The Colonel had worked him over good and he swiped his hand across his face, grimacing when it came away bloody.

He glanced over at Quincy, who still hadn't moved since she'd fallen. He had managed to slide her out of the way of the fight and the coat he'd given her earlier was wrapped protectively around her, mercifully blood-free.

He crouched down beside her, feeling her pulse again to

reassure himself, and then slipped the coat from around her, being careful not to get any blood on it.

He pulled his shirt off and turned it inside out, using it to clean the blood off his face as best he could, and then pulled the coat on, zipping it up high. It would have to do for now. If their luck held, no one would come out to the balcony tonight, the cold only increasing as the sun sank. He'd get Quincy back to their sleeping car and come back if he could to clean up the mess.

He scooped Quincy up as gently as he could, adjusting her hair to cover as much of her bruised neck as he could and eased the door to the balcony car open quietly. No one in the compartment. Knowing his luck couldn't hold much longer, he carried Quincy through.

He stepped back into the hall and shifted her in his arms, pulling her as closely against him as he could. He could feel her heart beating weakly against his own chest and he whispered soothingly in her ear. What he actually said, he couldn't say. It was really more for his own benefit than hers, considering she was unconscious.

He had come so close this time. So close to losing her. If he hadn't gone back for his phone. If he had decided to wait for her to come to him, she'd be dead. He felt sick with the knowledge and more than a little lightheaded, though both could be explained away pretty easily by his injuries. He figured he had a concussion and bruised ribs at the least, and he hadn't even looked at his knife wounds yet.

But that could come later. Quincy was the priority. Strangulation, even unsuccessful, was traumatic. Her trachea wasn't crushed because she was still breathing but it could very well be constricted or the cartilage inside fractured. She could have damaged or paralyzed vocal cords.

At the very least, the swelling in her throat would keep her from talking above a whisper for several days. She would be able to hide the angry welts and bruises on the skin around her neck but there would be no hiding her eyes, the whites red with blood from burst capillaries. Petechial hemorrhaging, the doctors called it.

And then there was the emotional trauma. Strangulation was slow. It was violent. And it was personal. By its very nature, it elevated the terror of the situation and allowed the victim to understand and feel what was happening for minutes before they lost consciousness.

It was callous and cruel and Logan was very much afraid that this would be the last straw. How much more could she take before she cracked? She'd handled everything that had happened over the last several days so well – the sniper, the migraine, being kidnapped and confronted with the reality of brain injury and amnesia. And now this. Would she feel safe with him anymore? She'd been attacked three times on his watch.

This might just be the push she needed to disappear again, this time for good.

Chapter 68

Q uincy

Awareness came slowly, like swimming up through the deep end of the pool. The clickety-clack of the train rolling over the track was oddly soothing, the slight movement of the cars enough to lull her back to sleep. It was warm here, and quiet. And it wasn't often she slept so deeply, so she didn't feel like moving quite yet.

She could smell coffee brewing and the faint clatter of pots and pans in the distance told her it must be close to breakfast. She didn't remember going to bed last night but she was feeling too relaxed to worry about it. A sound to her left, like a door opening and closing, caught her attention but she ignored it. The faint scent of pine and sea salt drifted to her, overlaid by the suddenly stronger smell of coffee. Logan must have gone down to the breakfast car and picked up drinks.

She wondered if he had brought any doughnuts too, then decided she didn't care. She didn't want to wake up and doughnuts weren't a strong enough bribe to make it happen.

She wanted to stay exactly where she was. It was peaceful. And safe. And no one wanted to talk about things she'd rather ignore.

But the coffee...oh, the coffee. Coffee was more difficult to ignore than doughnuts and Logan knew it. Which was probably why he'd brought it. Shameless, letting coffee do his dirty work for him. She could hear him moving around, unzipping and zipping his bag, pulling open cabinet doors and closing them quietly, and a few seconds of silence before the shower kicked on. A shower sounded nice right now. Hot shower, hot coffee...maybe she could be convinced to roll herself out of bed after all.

Quincy moved to stretch and yawned, gagging suddenly as pain shot through her head, neck, and chest like fire. It was so unexpected and so intense that she coughed reflexively, lurching up in bed in an attempt to force air down a windpipe that just wasn't having it.

Her hands grasped at her neck but jerked back quickly as she realized the pain wasn't just on the inside. She could feel the swelling and burns around the skin of her throat and when she tried to turn her head to control the coughing, it didn't want to move.

She grabbed a pillow from behind her, holding it to her chest and burrowing into it, trying to control her breathing. She didn't know how long she sat there, tears streaming from her eyes, but eventually her body unwound, the muscles in her chest and throat uncoiling as the instinct to cough slowly fizzled out.

She sat, hugging the pillow like her life depended on it, trying to think through the haze of pain. What had happened? What could have caused that much pain? She reached back, trying to comb through recent memories but nothing stood out.

She noticed Logan's phone where it sat on the dresser behind her and slowly, oh so slowly, reached back and felt around, bumping the phone and almost sending it crashing to the floor before her hand closed around it. She brought it around and tried to open it, hoping to use the camera to see what the damage was. Locked. She grit her teeth in frustration, sending another wave of pain through her upper body. What was the deal?

She was afraid to get up, afraid of what other kinds of pain she might find. It would be so much easier if she could just unlock Logan's phone. She stared at it. What would Logan use as a pass code?

Most people used numbers that meant something to them, something they could easily remember. Logan had told her his birthday once, back on that walk they had taken through the park. It had been his way of trying to cajole some kind of personal information out of her. A ploy to see how far back her memories went, she knew now. If it had been irritating at the time, it was maddening now.

She fought the urge to shake her head, knowing she would regret it, and focused back on the phone. As she stared at it, trying to piece together numbers that might mean something to Logan, her mind started to narrow, fading a little around the edges. Soft, almost like her brain was wrapped in cotton; the buzzing in her head intensified briefly before going completely mute...

Quincy jerked her focus away from the phone. She knew what this was. She recognized it, now that she understood. This was what the Colonel was talking about. What Logan had been trying to tell her. This was RNB. Reflexive Neurological Bias. It was the feeling she got before she did something crazy, like stitch up a torn artery.

The Colonel had told her the company he worked for wanted to weaponize her, to use whatever weird brain activity she had to build better weapons, or be a better weapon, or something like that. But Logan had said Dr. Garrison could help her learn how to control it, so she in turn could help other people who were going through what she was going through.

So maybe it wasn't all bad. Maybe she could learn to channel it, whatever *it* was. But how? It was a good question, she thought wryly. If only Logan's super special doctor friend was here to answer it.

Quincy thought back. Every time she could remember it happening, she had been focused pretty singularly on one thing, whether it was wires in a car, a gaping injury, or a musical instrument. And just now, she'd been thinking about Logan and numbers that might be important to him.

She looked back at the phone still clutched in her hand and allowed her thoughts to lock on that one thought and then scatter. Logan. Numbers. Logan. Numbers. The edges of her mind became blurry, soft and out of focus again, but this time she didn't pull back. She heard the shower turn off in the back of her mind but it barely registered. Logan. Numbers. Logan. Numbers. Logan. 5625. Logan. 5625 Logan 5625 Logan 5625. Without thinking, she entered the number into the security screen and the phone unlocked.

Quincy sat staring at the phone for a minute, trying to process what had just happened. Idly she wondered if the headache would follow. She hadn't had time to piece together that aspect of her drama but she could worry about it later, she supposed.

The number, it was the middle four digits of Logan's military i.d. She had seen it once, that very first day on the quad at school. He had been playing Ultimate Frisbee with a bunch of teenagers and had gone down hard, his dog tags slipping out from under the collar of his t-shirt.

She shouldn't be able to remember the number. She had only seen it for a second, at a distance, before she even knew him. She didn't think the number itself had even registered so much as the fact that there was a number.

So how had she pulled it back up? It was one thing to figure out how to break the code; she'd read that book on cryptology a couple of years back.

But to do it in seconds, using a number she didn't even know she knew? In computer terms, it was a lot of processing power in a ridiculously short amount of time. It was crazy, was what it was. It was also a pattern, one she hadn't noticed before. But she hadn't known to look before, either.

Now that she knew about Dr. Garrison's theory, now that she had accepted it as fact, there was so much that could possibly be explained. Why she couldn't sleep. Where the noise in her head came from. How she could do such random, unlikely things.

She suddenly wanted to meet Dr. Garrison so badly. To sit down and talk with him, let him explain to her the way Logan said he'd explained to Jones - kindly, like someone who actually cared. She needed so desperately to understand. And she wanted so badly to be understood.

Logan's phone was still clutched tightly in her hand. She unlocked the screen again and started scrolling through the phone looking for contacts, inching her legs towards the side of the bed as she did. But not slowly enough. The pain tore at her and she doubled over as it took all the air from her lungs. She couldn't breath, couldn't swallow. She panicked and tumbled off the bed, landing on her knees and jarring her neck, gagging as her swallow reflex fought against the pain.

Time stopped as she huddled there, unable to do anything but gasp and wheeze, tears running reflexively down her face. Suddenly, a warm hand was against her back, another pressed against her shoulder. She could hear Logan's deep voice, saying the same thing over and over but she couldn't make it out.

He reached around and pulled her back against his chest, bracing his own back against the bed with Quincy in his lap. He pulled the pillow off the bed and tucked it against her chest before crossing their arms over it, providing compression for her ribs and something stable to rest her head against.

And like before, her breathing slowly calmed, the involuntary spasms in her neck and throat easing off. They sat like that for Quincy didn't know how long. It could have been minutes or it could have been hours. But eventually Logan shifted behind her, trying to see her face.

"Better?" he asked.

Quincy checked her instinct to nod. "Yes." It was gritty and barely more than a whisper, but it would have to do.

Logan shifted slowly out from behind her, then leaned down and wrapped his arms around her like a hug.

"We're going to stand up real slow, okay?" he said.

She closed her eyes, letting her forehead rest against his chest, and allowed him to guide her to her feet. She stood, held upright by Logan, and tried to keep her breathing slow and shallow.

"What...?" she managed to get out.

How he actually heard her, she had no idea. Her voice was so mangled and weak, the sound of the tracks beneath them was enough to overwhelm it.

"Do you remember anything?" he asked.

Talking was easier than shaking her head, but not by much. "No," she whispered.

"Let's get you situated first," Logan said, "and then we can talk."

Logan stepped forward, easing her backwards until the back of her legs bumped up against the bed and then, bracing her with his arms, helped her sink slowly onto it.

"Here," he said, gathering up all the pillows in the room and stacking them against the wall for her to lean against. He pulled his chair up close, sat down, and slowly lifted her feet and sat them in his lap. "There," he said. "Comfy?"

As close as I'm going to get anyway, she thought. She started to ask again what had happened but thought better of it at the last minute. Instead, without moving her arms from where they were wrapped around the pillow, she held her hands out. It was a universal gesture and Logan didn't disappoint.

The smile disappeared from his face. "Right. Do you remember being outside on the balcony car?"

When she just looked blankly back at him, he went on, "You went out there after we...talked...about Dr. Garrison."

She remembered a fight about Dr. Garrison more than a talk but she liked his version of the story better.

"We were talking and you were cold so I handed you my jacket before going back inside?"

Quincy frowned and blinked once, trying to let him know he needed to speed up the explanation. She remembered they had argued, Logan trying to convince her that RNB wasn't so bad and her saying some terribly nasty things that she wished she didn't remember before escaping to find fresh air. But she didn't remember going outside.

"Well, I followed you and we talked a little more. And then I left you outside and went back to the room. I wanted to call Dr. Garrison and let him know our progress. He wants to drive up and meet us when we get off the train but I didn't like it. Not with the Colonel and his minion still running around somewhere. I wanted to cut that idea off before it really grabbed hold of him."

Logan's eyes were serious. "I remembered I'd left my phone in the pocket of my jacket so I went back. If I hadn't..." The thought seemed to jar him. "I don't know how he managed it but the Colonel was on the train. I don't know how he knew what we were planning or how he managed to trace us so fast. He certainly had more skills than me."

Had. Quincy picked up on the past tense. Logan must have seen it on her face, because he went on.

"He slipped out onto the balcony when you had your back turned. He cut the cord off the curtains over the door and used that to," he gestured towards her neck and she blanched.

"He got you pretty good. You were already unconscious by the time I made my way back. We fought," Logan said abruptly, "and then he fell over the railing. He was gone before I could do anything." Logan looked down at this, idly running his hands up and down her feet.

"I'm sorry," Quincy managed to squeeze out past the gravel.

"For what?" he asked, surprised. "Neither of us believed he'd be able to get that close again. And even if we did, I'm not sure if there was anything we could have done differently anyway."

"You killed him." she said with difficulty. "For me. I'm sorry."

Logan was a soldier and had seen combat, she knew, but Logan was also sweet and easy going and killing wasn't something he would ever be casual about. It would mean something to him, no matter who it was.

Logan held her eyes for another few seconds before dropping them back down. He swallowed hard, reigning himself back in, then gave her feet a squeeze before saying, "You're safe. That's all that matters."

69

Chapter 69

Q**uincy**

They stayed like that for a few minutes, soaking in the relief that this trip from hell might finally have an end in sight. Quincy didn't realize she'd closed her eyes until Logan cleared his throat. She opened them, shooting him a glare without moving her head, which was situated just perfectly to take the strain off her neck.

"That's looking pretty bad," he said, gesturing towards her neck. Or maybe her face. She didn't really know. "I'm going to grab some more ice. And maybe some ibuprofen."

She shut her eyes again and he stood, lifting her feet and setting them back down onto the chair.

"Anything else you need?"

She flicked a finger, enough to make him laugh and shoo him away without effort. It was hard to believe it was over. She could say it had been a rough couple of weeks but in truth, it had been so much longer.

It had started in that truck stop back in Boise, back when

she was Kara Scott. It seemed like a lifetime ago but that had been her first taste of the paranoia. That she remembered, of course. It seemed pretty likely someone else had come before Kara Scott.

But she had been running, first as Kara, and then as Grace Elliott, and finally as Quincy O'Connell, for so long that she didn't know what she was supposed to do now. Of course, the company was still out there but without their lead bird dog, it seemed unlikely she'd be back on their radar for awhile.

She could go wherever she wanted. Start a new life with another new identity. Settle down and make some real friends – make a real life, like Logan suggested. But the thought didn't sit well with her. One more identity wouldn't help her figure out what had happened in the past. It wouldn't help her figure out what was going on right now, in the present. If RNB was real, and at this point she couldn't very well deny it, then she needed to learn how to deal with it. She needed to know as much about it as she could and learn what she could do to manage the symptoms.

Symptoms, she thought with disdain. That was too mild a word. And she really didn't even know what all of those symptoms were. She knew she didn't sleep much. She knew her brain didn't stop. She knew she memorized weird, random things without trying. But she didn't know what it all actually meant. There was only one place she could go to deal with the disease. Only one person who could help her.

Well, *two*, she thought, as Logan pushed the door open with an elbow, the ice, a Coke, and a bottle of ibuprofen in his hands, and waltzed in like he was the Queen of England. She couldn't help but smile back, his relief and energy contagious.

"Here," he said, sitting the coke on the tiny nightstand and opening the bottle of pills. "How many do you want?"

She held up four fingers and he shook them out onto her palm. She popped them and took the can he offered. She looked at it, not sure how she was going to drink it without being able to move but he quickly produced a straw and dropped it into the can with more flourish than it deserved.

"Thanks," she managed to squeak out.

He frowned. "Would you quit trying to talk?" he scolded. "You were strangled. I think you can forego the rules of polite society for awhile."

"But how will I annoy you without my verbal wit and charm?"

The comeback lost a little something as a gravelly whisper but still, mission accomplished. He just shook his head, took the can back from her, and set the ice pack in her hand instead.

"Where...?" she asked weakly, gesturing towards the supplies.

"They come by way of our good buddy Albert." She looked at him blankly.

"Oh yeah," he said, chagrined. "You were busy dancing with the Colonel while I was making friends. Sorry," he said, falsely contrite. "Anyway," he continued at her look, "Albert is our porter. Our overly helpful, blindingly cheerful porter. He also saw me carry you back to the car, by the way. You apparently went out onto the balcony to have a drink, had a little too much, and slipped, busting a very expensive decanter and hitting your head."

So, he'd made her a lush. Swell. He was getting pretty good at reading her mind, or at least her facial expressions, because he quickly continued.

"An accident. Just someone who enjoyed a little too much

of the bubbly on her honeymoon," he assured her.

"Hmm."

"Plus, I had to think on my feet and that was the best I could do." He stretched the ice out to her, arranging it against her neck and throat. "Let's put this ice on your neck while it's still cold."

She thought about making more of a protest but decided against it. She really did hurt. The ice rested gingerly against her neck and she relaxed into it as the cold started to numb the skin around her throat. But there was still something she needed to do. She snapped her fingers and he looked up.

"You rang?" he asked drolly.

She brought her hand slowly up towards her ear, pantomiming a phone call, and then pointed back at him. He got the message.

"Sure," he said, pulling his phone out of his pocket and handing it over. "But are you sure you really want to? It's kind of horrific."

No, she didn't really want to. The ice felt so good against her neck and what she didn't know couldn't hurt her, but she unlocked his phone anyway, ignoring his mock irritation that she had used her cool new super powers to figure out his password. The camera screen popped open, already set on selfie mode, and when she peeled the ice away she could see the full scope of the damage.

Her throat was angry and raw, purple and red bruises tracing where the cord had pressed against her throat, the skin burned from the friction. As bad as it hurt, she knew it was going to look bad. And it did. But what shocked her the most were her eyes. She hadn't expected the blood, though she probably should have. As many books as she'd read, she knew strangulation caused the tiny blood vessels in the eyes to burst and fill the whites. But she had never seen it in real life before. She looked like she should be dead.

"Hey," Logan said, drawing her attention away from the gruesome image. "I have an idea. Now that we're real friends and not lying to each other about stupid things, I have some questions for you."

She frowned and tipped her head just a fraction. He knew she didn't have any answers.

"Not about your birthday or your family, maybe. But there are some things you do know." He shot her a grin. "For example, I've always wondered - is this your natural hair color?" he asked, reaching up and tucking a strand that had fallen onto her face behind her ear. "It was the first thing I noticed that day in the quad," he said absently, moving back and propping his forearms against his knees.

"I had seen the picture you were using at the school but it didn't exactly do you justice. You were blonde as Kara and brunette as Grace. I'm just curious which is real."

Instead of answering, she just pointed up at her head, surprised he'd remembered what her aliases looked like. She had gotten tired of coloring it with every move so she'd just stripped the brown out for Quincy, letting the red take back over.

Logan nodded like this didn't surprise him. "That's what I thought," he said, sounding supremely satisfied. "Then I guess green is your real eye color, too?"

"I see better without the colored contacts," she managed. "And the glasses are just for show, too."

"So, a redheaded, green-eyed master of disguise." He grinned. "And with those freckles, I bet a sunburn is never far away." She smiled.

"SPF 50 all the way baby."

"So let's see, what else?" His eyes light up. "I know! Tattoos and piercings." He looked her over appraisingly. "Anything I should know about?"

Quincy decided a change in subject was in order. "Maybe you should be the one answering questions," she winced, trying to work a swallow past the swelling. The speculative look Logan threw her said he wasn't going to give up on that topic forever, but he cut her some slack.

"Sure. Let's see, something personal...," he paused to think about it. "I think I told you I grew up along the coast of Oregon. It was this little town called Winchester Bay. Well, it's not really even a town. More of a village. The same people have lived there forever and everyone knows everyone. We do have a lighthouse you can visit and some of the highest dunes in Oregon."

Quincy smiled. "Fancy," she mouthed.

"Absolutely," Logan agreed. "What else? My dad was a crabber. He'd toss out his traps and we'd go check them every morning and evening and we'd spend some time clamming in between." She must have looked lost because he laughed.

"You know. Clamming. Wading around at low tide to see if you can find any clams burrowing down in the leftover pools. Kids love it."

"Idyllic," she managed to force out. And it really did sound it. Maybe she'd try it sometime.

Logan smiled. "It was. For awhile. My dad died in a boating accident when I was fourteen and my mom tried, but she couldn't hold it together after that. She'd always been kind of flighty but my dad was her anchor. While he was alive, she

403

could be happy having roots.

"She stuck around for a couple of months after he died but took off while I was in school one day. I haven't heard from her since."

Logan leaned back against the wall of their tiny compartment and stretched his legs out in front of him, not upset in the least, like his childhood tragedy was nothing more than a story he'd heard. It caught Quincy off-guard.

"Okay?" she finally asked. Wasn't he mad or hurt or, or *something*, when his mother left him?

"No, not at all. I was a kid who'd just lost his dad and whose mom didn't even bother to say goodbye. I was definitely not okay. I was mad and hurt and whatever other emotion you want to toss in there. But that was twenty years ago. I had to let go of the hurt eventually or it would have killed me."

He shrugged. "Plus, I do understand. She hadn't been built to settle in one place but my dad was worth the sacrifice. When he died, she was devastated. She fell back on old patterns because that's what people do when they're hurting and because she didn't know how else to survive."

He saw her look. "Oh, she tried to make it work for me. But even at fourteen or fifteen, I could see what was coming. Even when she was there, she was barely functioning. I was taking care of her instead of the other way around. I think, looking back," he said reflectively, "she ultimately left because she was trying to protect me."

Interesting angle to take. "My mom might have been gone when I came home from school that day but I wasn't alone," he went on. "My high school football coach and his wife were sitting on my couch. Mom left them a letter and they always made sure I wasn't alone."

Logan was so eternally optimistic and energetic. Quincy would have never imagined his childhood was so tragic. And to see all he'd seen overseas and lose his best friend the way he had...how was he this man after enduring all that?

"Bad things happen. And are going to keep happening. You can let them change you into something better or something worse. I chose better. It's not a big deal."

But it was. And it did explain why he felt so strongly about helping her and all of these other people out there that he didn't know. He knew what tragedy looked like. He had been rescued from his by the kindness of a high school football coach and his wife. Logan was the kind of man who could hardly do different.

Logan must have taken her silence for exhaustion because he tugged a blanket off the back of the chair her feet were propped up on and leaned over to tuck it around her legs.

"We still have a couple of hours before the train pulls into the next depot. Why don't you see if you can get some more sleep. I wouldn't mind some myself."

She looked around the compartment skeptically. Where exactly did he think he was going to find that kind of space?

He shrugged off the look she gave him with, "I've slept in worse places than this floor. I'll be fine."

"Scoot?" she offered painfully, not quite sure how she would accomplish it but willing to try. He just shook his head.

"No need. I really am fine down here." He tucked a pillow under his head and spread his coat over his chest. "Wake me up if you need anything."

He closed his eyes and dropped off to sleep almost immediately. She realized he had probably been awake the whole time she was out, keeping watch. After the fight with the

Colonel, he had to be exhausted and sore. She had noticed he seemed stiff and his shoulder looked to be hurting him some. The floor certainly wasn't going to help matters. But he did seem comfy enough.

She felt the tug of sleep against her own eyes and knew enough not to fight it, letting them close and wondering what came next.

70

Chapter 70

Logan

The train whistle blew, waking Logan up from a deeper sleep than he'd had in awhile, despite being on the floor. He reached for his phone out of habit, checking the time and making sure he hadn't missed anything.

Huh. He must have been more tired than he thought if he'd slept a full six hours. He dropped his phone onto his chest and ran both hands over his face, trying to wake up. Despite the deep sleep, he was going to feel it when he got up - the sad reality of a 35-year old man sleeping on the floor after a brutal fight, no matter what he'd said to Quincy.

Speaking of, he glanced over at her, glad to see she was still asleep. He winced at the bruising and the burns, obvious signs of his failure to keep her safe. They had to hurt more than she was letting on; she could barely move after all, but she hadn't complained. And despite the pain, she looked like she was sleeping pretty well herself.

Once she recovered from being almost strangled to death,

he knew she'd probably never sleep so soundly again. She was still propped up against the pillows where he'd left her but she had wadded the blanket up and was holding it tight against her chest like a pillow with her left arm, her right tucked up under her cheek. If he could ignore the angry red welts wrapping around her neck, he'd say she almost looked serene.

Logan closed his eyes, replaying that moment when he'd seen what was happening but had been too far away to prevent it. It was terrifying, how close he'd come to losing her. He had realized long ago that Quincy was more than just a mission to him, so it came as no surprise. He just hadn't realize how very much he cared.

She'd worked her way in deep and now she was stuck with him. He hoped she would take him up on his offer to stay with him and Dr. Garrison. Dave had a pretty sweet set-up on the outskirts of Boulder right now. He had partnered with a medical school inside the city proper and ran a clinic that serviced the homeless and underserved populations in the greater metropolitan area. The clinic was staffed by medical and nursing school students and included full imaging suites.

A general practice was a huge waste of Dr. Garrison's knowledge and expertise but if Dave thought it beneath him, he never showed it. He had thrown himself into the clinic with such enthusiasm, even Logan wouldn't have known it was only a fraction of his work if he didn't have the inside track.

The clinic was an excellent cover for the medical equipment and research facilities Dave needed in order to continue researching and finding patients with RNB. There was a fully finished basement underneath the clinic, which they used as both base of operations and home.

Dave's office doubled as a bedroom and they'd put up a couple of dividers to form a makeshift living/kitchenette area and a place where Logan had thrown a mattress and a tv. It had been easy enough to build false walls around the inside of the clinic rooms that had openings to the basement so they could come and go without being seen by the staff.

The setup was perfect for their needs and one of the reasons Logan had tried to keep Dave from coming to meet them at their next stop. They needed to keep the clinic location off the agency's radar. And they needed to keep Dave's location off the radar as well.

Logan frowned, uncomfortable with the thought that Dave was a high-priority target too. The agency wanted the patients he had identified so it would make sense that they wanted him too. He was the leading, well, only, expert on RNB and the agency would want him to continue his research so that they could...what had Quincy said? Weaponize it.

That wasn't something either of them were going to allow in their lifetimes so their base of operations was sacred.

Quincy wasn't the only one who needed a safe place. Every victim they managed to find could be treated at the clinic. Dave had been slowly stocking up on the different testing and treatment equipment he thought they would need and, combined with the fully-stocked clinic above them, they were well on their way. Now that they had Quincy and she was maybe on board, he felt confident this might actually work.

Logan exhaled loudly, trying to work up the nerve to roll over and heave his sore body off the floor. He really needed to call Dave and tell him about the Colonel. With their bloodhound gone, there was really no reason he couldn't meet the train at one of their stops.

The poor man. Logan rarely let him out of the clinic but he never complained. They had developed a strong friendship over the last four years and Dave trusted Logan as much as Logan trusted him. With the Colonel out of the way, it was probably safe for Dave to venture out. Logan knew he was worried about both of them and would only relax once he checked them over himself. It would do him good to get out.

Except for Brandon. Logan shut his eyes, mentally cursing himself. He had been so relieved to lose the Colonel that he hadn't even thought about Brandon. He couldn't believe he had forgotten about him. He'd slept for six hours with that guy still on the loose. Surely if he was on the train, he would have made a move by now.

Logan tried to relax the muscles in his back that had tensed up at the thought. With his boss dead, maybe he would just disappear. Logan felt a pang at the thought, knowing he had been responsible for the man's death, but that it couldn't have been helped. He was a threat to Quincy. Actively in the process of trying to kill her when they fought and he fell. As a soldier, Logan had become accustomed to violence but he had never quite shaken the responsibility he felt when he had to take a life, no matter how justified.

"You look troubled, Soldier."

Logan opened his eyes and found Quincy looking at him from atop her pillow mountain. "Care to share?"

"You know, you've kind of got this gravelly, sultry Greta Garbo thing going on," he remarked, hiding the relief he felt that she could talk at all.

She rolled her eyes but wasn't deterred. "Boys are so weird. So what's up?"

He sighed. "Nothing. I hope. I just realized I was so focused on shaking the Colonel that I forgot he had a lap dog."

Quincy frowned. "You mean Brandon?"

Her voice really did sound a little better, even if her neck and eyes looked even angrier than before. And it didn't seem to hurt her to speak like it did yesterday.

"I can't believe I just brushed him off," he berated himself. "I mean, he was the first to find us, after all. Could be, he found us again but the Colonel decided to take the lead and sent him on to the next stop."

"I don't think that's going to be a problem," she said after a moment's pause.

Logan turned over onto his side facing Quincy and propped his arm up under his head. "What makes you say that?" he asked curiously.

She shrugged gingerly. "I don't really remember what happened with the Colonel, but I keep getting flashes. Just bits and pieces, you know? And when you mentioned Brandon, I remembered something the Colonel said. It was kind of in the middle of all this, I think," she said dryly, motioning towards her neck, "but I'm pretty sure Brandon isn't around anymore. Like, anywhere."

"You mean...?" he slid a finger across his throat.

"He sleeps with the fishes," she agreed.

"We're joking about murder," Logan remarked.

"We are. It's a healthy and appropriate coping mechanism," she assured him

"Sure," Logan said. "Very healthy. Let's move on."

"So what's the plan, army man?"

He couldn't help but smile. "Lauren Bacall. Dynamite."

She smiled back. "Without the talent, the money, or the

411

body." He started to correct her on two of the three but she went on. "Seriously. What are we doing?"

Logan mentally shifted gears, thinking through what was coming next. "We'll get off in Green Valley this afternoon. Dave was hoping to be able to pick us up and take us home. I nixed that idea when I was afraid we might still have a tail but I guess with the Colonel and Brandon both gone, there's no reason why he couldn't."

"Will that put him in danger? I guess the agency would be after him too, wouldn't they?"

"I don't know if he's a primary target but I'm sure they wouldn't mind having him back. If they're planning to weaponize RNB, he would be key to making that happen."

"Where exactly is home?" Quincy asked.

"I guess it's probably safe enough to tell you now. We moved around a lot at first, bouncing between cheap motels and even cheaper office spaces before we settled down around Boulder."

"Why Boulder?" she asked curiously.

"Why not?" Logan answered with a shrug. "It's a big enough city to get lost in but quiet enough to lay low. The place is perfect. We just lucked into it, really. Dave runs a low-income clinic connected with one of the medical schools in the city so he has access to equipment and supplies and the building has a huge basement underneath where we set up shop."

"Your Dr. Garrison is quite the do-gooder, isn't he?" Quincy remarked offhandedly.

"Why do you say that?" Logan asked curiously.

"I don't know," she said. "Because he runs a low-income medical clinic while on the run from some super secret organization that wants to take his research and do who-knows-what with it, all after giving up a prestigious medical practice, fame, and fortune to diagnose a disease no one else even believes in." She blew out her breath. "It's a lot to take in."

"Yeah," Logan agreed. "When you put it like that, I guess it does seem like a lot." He finally heaved himself up off the floor, trying to keep the manly groans and creaks inside. "I'm going to go call Dave and maybe rustle up some breakfast. Need anything before I go?"

"I don't think so," Quincy said. "I'm going to see if I can get myself up and take a shower. Maybe once I do, I'll feel more human."

"Want a hand?" he asked.

"With what? Getting up or taking a shower?" she shot back.

Logan blushed, mortified, and tried to backpedal but Quincy just smiled. "I think I can do it. Bring back some coffee," she said, "and hold the breakfast. When I'm done, we'll hit the food compartment together. We probably need to be seen."

Logan saw the wisdom in what she said. "It wouldn't hurt Albert to see you up and about after yesterday."

"Albert?"

"Our porter. Remember? He saw me carry you back here, I told him you had had a bit too much to drink..."

He watched her as he talked but she just looked quizzically back at him. "Nothing, huh? I guess you were still pretty out of if when we talked yesterday. Let's just say it might not be a bad thing to prove you're up and about."

"Okay then," she said. "Get out so I can get going."

He snapped off a quick salute before turning for the door. "Yes ma'am."

71

Chapter 71

Quincy

The moment the door snapped shut behind Logan, the smile dropped from Quincy's face. She had been burning since she woke up, the need to escape practically clawing its way out of her. She tried to distract herself by focusing on Logan, all cramped and out of sorts on the floor, but that only made it worse. Logan already had everything all worked out, tied up in a neat little bow. They were going to skip off this train, hand in hand, and group hug all the way back to Dr. Garrison's super secret public medical clinic, where they would fight bad guys and be bestest friends forever.

But Quincy wasn't born yesterday. She actually wasn't sure when she was born, come to think of it, but she did know it wasn't yesterday. Things were never going to be that easy. Maybe for Logan, but not for her.

Logan was the kind of guy that things just happened for. Whether it was his sunny personality, his optimistic disposition, or the sheer force of his determination, things just seemed to bend to his will. She was a prime example of that.

But that wasn't her way. Things didn't happen for her. They happened to her. A life-altering head injury, eight missing years after, all the years missing before. Running, hiding, lying...pain, exhaustion, loneliness. No, settling down with a brand new, ready-made family wasn't going to be simple for her and Logan's exuberance was a little overwhelming. He was inexhaustible, hammering at her over and over until she finally caved. It's what had happened when they first met and it was going to keep happening. Because Logan didn't know how else to be.

He had said she could go anywhere she wanted, but did he really mean it? She had the feeling he would be devastated if she chose to leave. It wasn't really about her, she knew that. Logan had lost someone very close to him. Someone he had tried so hard to help and he carried that burden with him wherever he went.

Logically he knew Jones's death wasn't his fault, but knowing and believing were two different things and he was still working to convince himself. In order to correct what he saw as a past mistake, he had exchanged Quincy for Jones and the pressure was crushing her.

Quincy shoved herself up off the pillows and gasped as fire swept down her neck and chest. She balanced precariously on the edge of the bed, gripping one of the pillows to her chest to ease the pain and breathed as deeply and slowly as she could, knowing the dizziness would eventually pass.

How was she supposed to fight a battle on so many fronts? If Logan had his way, she would train with him and Dr. Garrison, learning to use her abilities to rescue others like her. It would give her a purpose, a reason to soldier on. She wanted that, right? Because who wouldn't? Who wouldn't want to hide and run and fight and lose, in a cycle that looped over and over until it claimed everyone around her? But Logan, with his big, puppy dog eyes and his earnest soul, would never stop fighting. And it was exhausting her.

Quincy finally staggered to her feet, gripping the back of the chair Logan had sat in the night before to make sure she had her balance, then lurched forward into the tiny shower stall.

At least in here, she was completely alone. He couldn't talk to her, or prod her, or turn the power of his persuasion in her direction. It was just her and the hot water. And as it ran down her face and touched the burns around her throat, she was reminded again of the price Logan's road was going to cost her.

Quincy forced herself to stay under the water, letting it hit and irritate the already angry skin around her throat in the hopes it would also ease the bruised and knotted muscles of her neck and shoulders. The steam built around her, loosening the tightness in her chest and helping her breath a little easier.

What if she just stayed right here in this shower forever? She had already decided she was going to have to live, for Logan if for no other reason. But could she actually do it? Now that she was aware of the cycle of sleeplessness and pain, she could feel the toll it was taking on her.

The thoughts she had before, about just stopping, letting go, were undoubtedly influenced by exhaustion.

Jones had taken his own life. It was completely possible

RNB played into those thoughts as well. So the question was, would she even have any control over it? Or would thoughts of ending it all continue, poking and prodding, finding her weaknesses and pushing until she finally gave in. How long could someone fight that kind of finality?

Quincy closed her eyes and sank to the floor, pulling her legs into her chest and leaning her head back against the wall, water and tears streaming down her face.

72

Chapter 72

Logan

The shower was still running when Logan got back to the room, steam billowing out from under the door. He smiled. She was so stubborn. She'd almost been killed, yet again, but God forbid she ask for help getting up.

He set Quincy's coffee on the bedside table and plopped back down in the same chair he'd been glued to the night before, relieved to be so close to home.

When he'd left Quincy in their compartment, he'd decided to call Dr. Garrison before grabbing the coffee. He knew Dave would be worried about them after what had happened last night. Logan grimaced as he took a drink of his own coffee, the action pulling against his shoulder wound. He was glad Quincy had been too out of it yesterday to realize some of the blood had been from him. He set his cup down and gingerly pulled his sleeve up so he could peel back the gauze he'd taped haphazardly in place.

The Colonel had gotten lucky with his knife, catching Logan

right below his left bicep. The wound was jagged and long, curving down his arm and wrapping inside his elbow, but it wasn't deep. He had mentioned it to Dave though, and the doctor had taken it hard.

"Yes, I have the first aid kit you packed for me," Logan had told him. "No, it doesn't need stitches." A pause. "That's just the job," Logan finally told him. "We talked about this," Logan gently prodded. "The agency isn't going to just let these people walk away. It's dangerous, but it's worth it."

Dr. Garrison had sighed and finally relented. Logan knew it was partly guilt. Dave felt responsible not only for Jones's death but for dragging Logan on this mission in the first place. After all these years, Logan still had to remind him that it wasn't just his mission anymore.

And speaking of missions, was Quincy ever planning to get out of the shower? A man needed to eat. Logan's enthusiasm dimmed slightly as he considered Quincy. Dave had told him how to take care of the immediate issues with strangulation but had warned she would have trouble swallowing liquids at first, and anything solid would be nearly impossible for awhile. So maybe Quincy wasn't as eager as he was to get to breakfast.

The one upside to this whole ordeal was now Logan felt safe enough to let Dave meet them at the train station.

Not that I could have stopped him, he thought wryly. When Logan had called and given him the all clear, Dave had nonchalantly mentioned he was already on the way. Had been driving since they'd caught the train, in fact.

Logan merely shook his head as Dave told him he'd be at the Port Mason depot at 10:00. Logan had been planning to ride as far as Denver, but this would work too. He was ready to get off this train though he had to admit, it really was nice. Small, but who knew train travel could be so luxurious? Of course, for two thousand dollars, it should be.

Logan leaned his head back against the wall and closed his eyes. He was so ready to sleep in his own bed. Not that a mattress on the floor really qualified as a bed, but the California King fit his oversized body and he longed to sprawl out and sleep for as long and as deeply as he wanted. It must be making him downright giddy, he thought suddenly, because he was starting to hear things.

He listened for a minute, trying to track where the sound was coming from. The bathroom? It was hard to hear over the sound of running water but he angled his head closer and listened. And felt his heart drop.

Quincy was crying.

73

Chapter 73

Quincy

Quincy opened the door of the shower to find Logan sacked out in the chair waiting for her. She smiled, glad she had gotten her emotions under control before venturing out.

"I didn't mean to keep you," she said. "The water just felt so good."

"Did it?" he asked. He gestured towards her, pointing out the obvious. "That looks pretty rough."

The hot water had felt good - on her shoulders and back. But the burns around her throat hadn't fared as well. They felt red and swollen so she could only assume they looked worse.

"Well, some of it felt good," she amended. "Ready for breakfast?" Hopefully the thought of food would be enough to derail any interrogation Logan felt might be necessary.

He hesitated, looking torn, before agreeing. "Yeah. I could eat."

Quincy pulled her old ball cap out of her backpack and tugged it on before sliding her sunglasses over her eyes. There were enough windows on the train to justify the glasses and they would attract less attention than her blood-filled eyes. Between that and the hoodie she'd pulled on in the bathroom, she looked practically normal. No one would be able to tell she'd been shot at, kidnapped, and murdered within the span of a week.

"You weren't murdered," Logan said dryly from behind her.

"What?" she asked, startled. Had she said that out loud?

"You said no one would be able to tell you'd been murdered. Technically, it was only attempted murder."

Apparently so. "Ah yes, my mistake," she said. "I only *feel* like I've been murdered."

"So, no appetite?"

She thought it over. No, she was definitely not hungry. Nauseated, sick to her stomach, sick of life? Yes. Hungry, not so much. But she had to play the part.

"Ice cream?" she asked, infusing as much child-like hope into the question as possible.

Logan laughed, but it was a strained and awkward thing, and he averted his eyes - a very un-Logan like thing to do. "I'm sure we can find something."

Quincy stepped back and looked at him, the question all over her face, but the guy who'd been so adept at deciphering what she was trying to say last night had either lost the skill or was simply paying it no mind this morning.

"Come on," he said, turning abruptly for the door. "Let's see what we can find."

Quincy just nodded mutely. It was the first time he'd lied

to her since Sheraton.

74

Chapter 74

" *L* *ong is the way and hard, that out of Hell leads up to light.*" *John Milton*

The soldier can't help her. The doctor can't help her. In the end, all the girl has is herself.

And me.

* * *

Quincy

Breakfast was a quiet affair, what with her damaged voice and Logan's sudden bout of muteness. They refused to bring out the ice cream until the lunch meal so Quincy settled for some oatmeal mixed with yogurt. The heat was almost soothing as she ate, once she was able to shove it past her angry gag reflex. Post-strangulation eating was tough.

"So, what's your damage?" she finally asked. Logan had been hunched over, staring into his coffee cup since they sat down. Thirty minutes of staring and brooding and she was done with it.

"What?" At least she'd finally gotten his attention.

"What's with the sullenness, Mr. Sunshine? You were way too perky when you left the room and all...this," she said, waving her hand, "when you came back. So what gives?"

She paused as a thought occurred to her. "Everything was alright with Dr. Garrison when you checked in, right?"

It was the only thing she could think of that might cause this kind of change. The Colonel was gone. They were practically home-free. Logan should be on top of the world, flashing his mega star smile and teasing her out of her depression, not the other way around.

"Are you finished?" he asked by way of answer, nodding towards her bowl, still half full of oatmeal.

"Yeah, I guess," she managed, not sure what else to say. Maybe something really had happened to Dr. Garrison?

Logan shoved his chair back and stood, tossing a couple of dollars on the table. "Let's head back then."

Quincy grabbed his hand as he turned, stopping him. "Logan..."

He sighed. "Dave is fine. We are fine. Let's just go back to the room, okay?" he said. "We can talk there."

She would assume *Dave* was Dr. Garrison and she breathed a little sigh of relief. So nothing on that front. She frowned. And Logan had said they were fine, too.

So what was the problem? Quincy trotted along behind him, struggling to keep up with his long strides and breathe at the same time. Logan reached the door to their room first and pushed it open, waiting for her to go in before following and closing the door behind them. He turned and leaned against the door, dropped his head, and sighed.

Quincy stiffened, her survival instincts reacting to what felt very much like a threat. "What are you doing?" she asked, as calmly as possible. When Logan looked up, it was clear she hadn't been calm at all.

"I can't make you want to live," he said quietly. "You can't want this for me."

Quincy blinked, taken aback. "What are you talking about?"

"I heard you," he said, "in the shower earlier." He stopped, cleared his throat, and started again. "It's bad, right? The thoughts?"

Quincy licked her lips. She could pretend she didn't know what he was talking about, but why prolong the inevitable? He wasn't going to let this go. He felt like he hadn't pushed enough with Jones so he was going to go overboard with her. She felt the pressure in her head start to build again.

"What would you consider bad?" she asked philosophically. "Wishing I could just go to sleep and never wake up? Or thinking that death has to be better than what I'm living through now? Yeah," she snapped. "It's bad."

Logan started to respond but she wasn't finished.

"But so what?" she asked. "So what if it's bad? What's it to you? As long as I keep a stiff upper lip and smile so you think I'm happy, why do you care? I mean, that's what you want isn't it? You want me to smile and go along with all your little plans to save the world and me to be fine. But I'm not fine and apparently, neither is anyone else with this stupid head injury. Apparently, we commit suicide. That's just the way it is."

It was the first time she'd ever seen Logan truly speechless, but she couldn't bring herself to enjoy it.

The words had felt so right coming out of her mouth, but so wrong at the same time. Was that how she really felt? Was this always going to end the same way, no matter how hard she fought? If so, what was the point of even trying?

As Quincy looked at Logan, breathing hard from both her tirade and the realization that she might not have a choice, and Logan looked back at her, color started to spill into his face.

She watched curiously as it spread higher and higher, the red finally reaching his hairline. A vein beside his right eye was bulging as he worked his jaw. He was angry. Really and truly angry. It was a side of him she'd never seen before.

She started to say something but he cut her off.

"It's my turn to talk," he said. "And you're going to listen."

Quincy backed into the corner of the car, as far from Logan as she could get. He wasn't going to hurt her, she knew that. But she had a feeling she wasn't going to like what he had to say.

"Do you have any idea what it's like to watch someone you care about self-destruct right in front of you? No, you don't." He looked at her for a moment, trying to find the words.

"I can tell you about RNB. Or what I know about it anyway. Dr. Garrison can run tests and help you learn to cope with your symptoms. But none of that will mean a thing if you aren't invested in it. *You* have to be invested in living. You can't decide to live for me, or for Dave, or even for the others out there that are suffering too. You have to live for *you*. We can't do it for you.

"You're a fighter Quincy," Logan said. "You have to be, to survive on the run, alone, for as long as you have. Are you going to keep fighting?"

Was she? She wanted to. She wanted...something. She just didn't know what.

"Some wounds never quite heal," she said softly. She turned, looking out their tiny window. "I hear it," she said suddenly. "The voice that tells me it would be so much easier to stop."

"I know," Logan said.

"What am I supposed to do?" she asked him. She wanted him to tell her what to do. She wanted someone else to make the decision for her. For once in her life, she wanted to not have to decide to survive.

"I can't make that decision for you," Logan responded, as she knew he would. "This isn't about me. Or Jones, or Dave, or anyone else. This is about you."

Logan stayed where he was, not making an attempt to close the distance she'd put between them.

"Dave can give you all the facts and figures he has. We can come up with a plan to deal with whatever comes our way. I can promise that you won't have to go through this alone anymore. But in the end, it's all going to come down to you. Only you."

Quincy's sigh was deep, a sad, lonely thing. "Doesn't it always?"

75

EPILOGUE

"*The hour of departure has arrived, and we go our separate ways, I to die, and you to live. Which of these two is better only God knows.*" *Socrates*

* * *

Reflexive Neurological Bias

I am what I am and attempts to define me are useless. How can you define something without definition? Humans. Constantly seeking order, control.

You try to box me in, fold me nicely and neatly and tuck me away so that no sharp edges or tears remain. But that is impossible because I am not one thing. I am different for each of you. I am neither good nor bad, yet I am both.

Do I deal in death? Yes, quite certainly. But I am also life. You can live with me, but you can also die with me. That is a choice I leave in your hands.

Nothing is ever just a gift or just a curse. Life isn't that simple. Black and white exists only on paper. I am shades of gray. The gift that comes with the curse, but also the curse that comes with the gift. And yet, that is precisely what the soldier is striving so diligently to convince the girl of.

But she knows. She understands so much more than he ever will. Because even when she didn't know me, she lived with me, and he never will.

I have been her constant companion these many years, and she mine. She understands the price I exact. She gives, but I give as well. Consequences aren't always damnable. They exist in balance. Inescapable pain after escaping death. A lost self after a life saved.

Ebbs and flows. Checks and balances. Is the price steep? Yes. But shouldn't it be, when the purchase is a life?

The train has stopped. The doctor is here, waiting. It's time to go. It's time to choose. We step off the train and the soldier looks the girl in the eye. He looks *us* in the eye. And he holds out his hand. She doesn't take it.

That hand, it speaks so clearly. *Choose life*, it begs. Pleads. But the girl, this constant companion of mine, she understands.

She understands that life and death are not the stark terms he paints, not the blacks and whites but the shades in between. She deliberates. I feel her hesitation, her despair over the choice she faces. And we understand that this choice determines what becomes of her.

I can't help her make this choice. I wouldn't if I could. The choice is hers, as it's always been.

I wait on an edge, ready to tip. The girl stares at the soldier, at the hand extended towards her, a lifeline in the middle of an ocean. And still she hesitates. Life or death isn't such an easy choice when it isn't one or the other. One or the other. One or the other. One or the other...

But finally, she chooses.

About the Author

A native of the Midwestern United States, Tara N. Hathcock spent 16 years in the healthcare field as a radiologic technologist, where the first inklings of *Shattered Highways* was born. Having since made the jump to academics, Tara now works as full-time staff for an area community college and teaches anatomy on the side while she continues to write stories that blend elements of science fiction with everyday life.

Shattered Highways is her first novel.

You can connect with me on:
- 🌐 https://books.taranhathcock.com
- 🇫 https://www.facebook.com/TNHAuthor
- 🔗 https://www.instagram.com/tnhauthor

Subscribe to my newsletter:
- ✉ https://www.taranhathcock.com

Also by Tara N. Hathcock

Burning Bridges

Caught in a tug-of-war between the monster in her head and the monster at her heels, Quincy's only options are to keep running or plant her feet and fight. Either path will cost her something, but is it a price she can afford to pay?

Burning Bridges, part II in the Shattered Highways series, coming July 2021.

The End of the Road

The explosive final chapter of the Shattered Highways series, on sale June 2022.

Want to learn more about the world of Shattered Highways?
Click Here for a free bonus chapter from Mr. and Mrs. Boatright.

Visit https://www.facebook.com/TNHAuth or for updates on *Burning Bridges*, part two in the *Shattered Highways* series.

Shattered Highways Bonus Chapter
Click Here for a look inside the mind of no one's favorite surly assassin.

www.ingramcontent.com/pod-product-compliance
Lightning Source LLC
Chambersburg PA
CBHW030849030726
47495CB00005B/1449